MOUNTAINS WILL CRUMBLE

CARISSA HARDCASTLE

HARDCASTLE PUBLISHING HOUSE

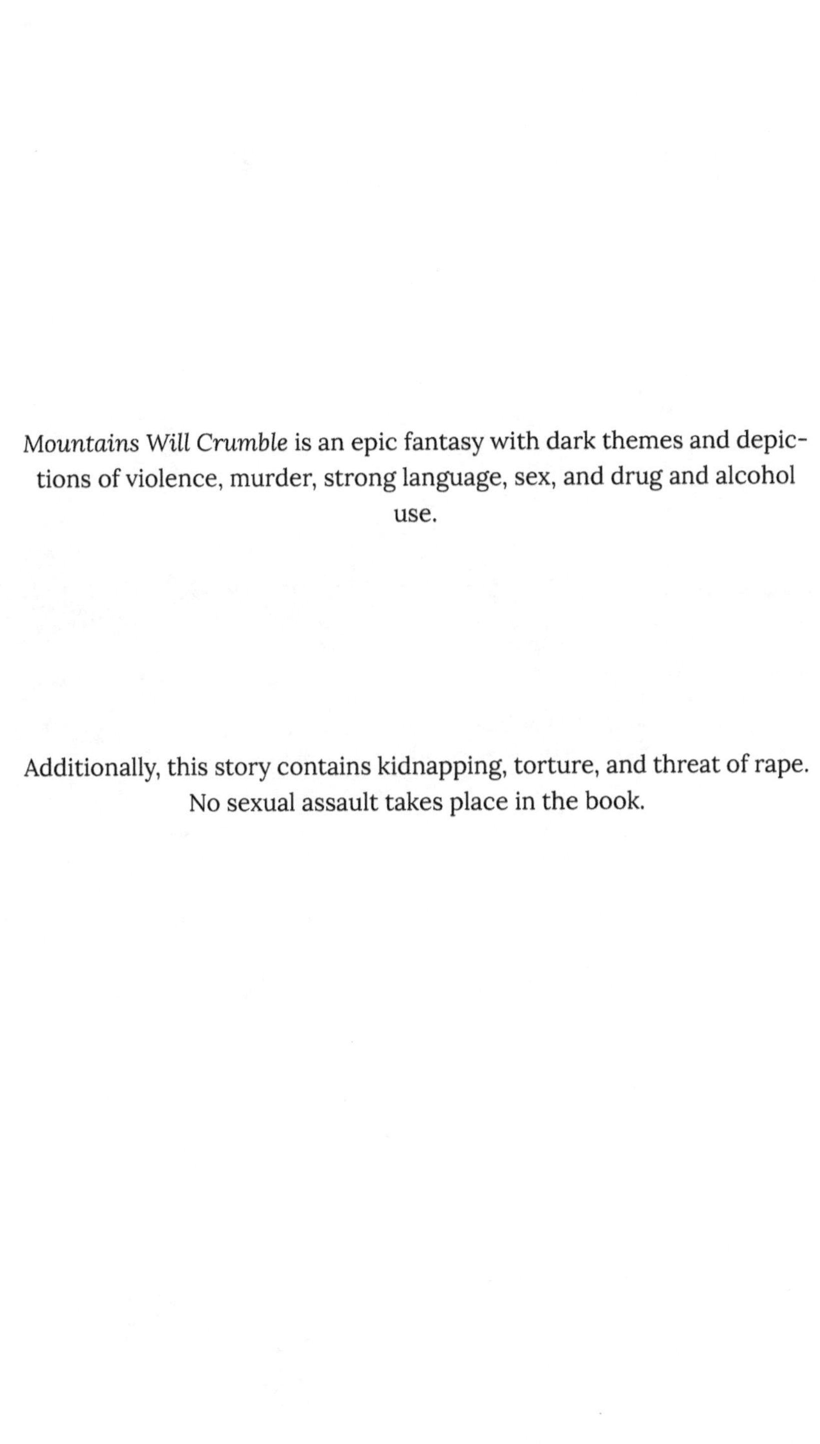

Mountains Will Crumble is an epic fantasy with dark themes and depictions of violence, murder, strong language, sex, and drug and alcohol use.

Additionally, this story contains kidnapping, torture, and threat of rape. No sexual assault takes place in the book.

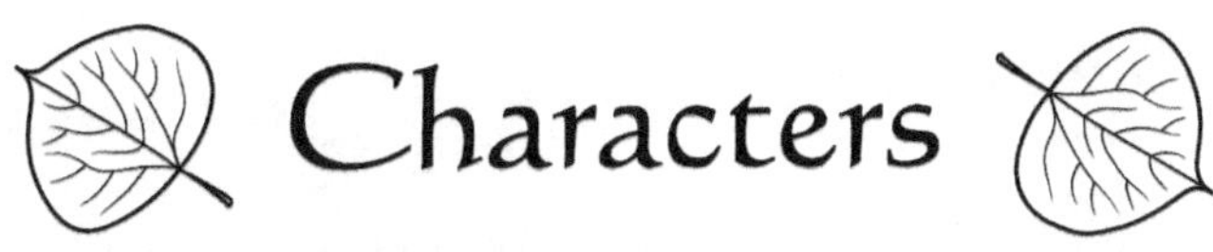 Characters

The Stonebane Line

Regenya 414 Keeper
  (reh-jehn-yuh)
Darius 371 high fae
  (dair-ee-us)
Mollian 25 Keeper
  (mahl-ee-ehn)
Ryddan 6 Keeper/half-demon
  (rihd-ehn)

The Royal Guard

Name	Age	Role	Race
Merriam (mair-ee-uhm)	25	Marshal of Sekha	human
Pos Ferrick (pahs Fair-ihck)	321	Captain of the Guard	high fae
Kottor Dio (kaht-or Dee-oh)	244	Ranger | Commander	high fae
Eskar (ehsk-ar)	128	Ranger | Commander	high fae
Rovin Arwood (rah-vihn Ar-wUd)	28	Ranger | Lieutenant	half-fae/human
Rillak (rihl-ehk)	284	Guard | Sergeant	high fae
Kodi (koh-dee)	26	Ranger	high fae
Bellamy (behl-uh-mee)	20	Ranger	high fae
Evangeline (ee-vAn-jeh-leen)	20	Ranger	high fae

The Mercenaries

Name	Age	Race	Experience
Jasper (jAs-per)	33	fair folk (fae)	14yrs a merc
Aleah (uh-lee-uh)	23	half fae/human	9yrs a merc
Leonidas (lee-oh-nI-dihs)	29	human	8yrs a merc
Campbell (kAm-behl)	25	fair folk (fae)	4yrs a merc
Calysta (kuh-lihs-tuh)	169	fair folk (nymph)	4yrs a merc

Guildmasters, Overseers, & Others

Name	Age	Role	Race
Cruspen (kruhs-pihn)	503	recordsmaster	fair folk (fae)
Graigory (greh-gor-ee)	301	roadsmaster	high fae
Portimer (por-tihm-er)	170	forestrymaster	high fae
Lydia (lih-dee-uh)	109	nursemaid	high fae
Spiro Kinbriar (spee-roh Kihn-brI-ar)	247	Overseer of Do Lech	high fae
Larna Kinbriar (lar-nuh Kihn-brI-ar)	153	Overseer of Do Lech	high fae
Chetney Kinbriar (cheht-nee Kihn-brI-ar)	42	heir to Do Lech	high fae
Shiloh (shI-loh)	24	street performer	fair folk (fae)

Demons

Dronin Djuhl (droh-nihn) (jUl)		Donova (duh-noh-vuh)	warlock | dreamwalker
Lyvin (lI-vihn)	General	Perran (pair-ehn)	lesser demon | servant
Nevra (neh-vruh)	General		

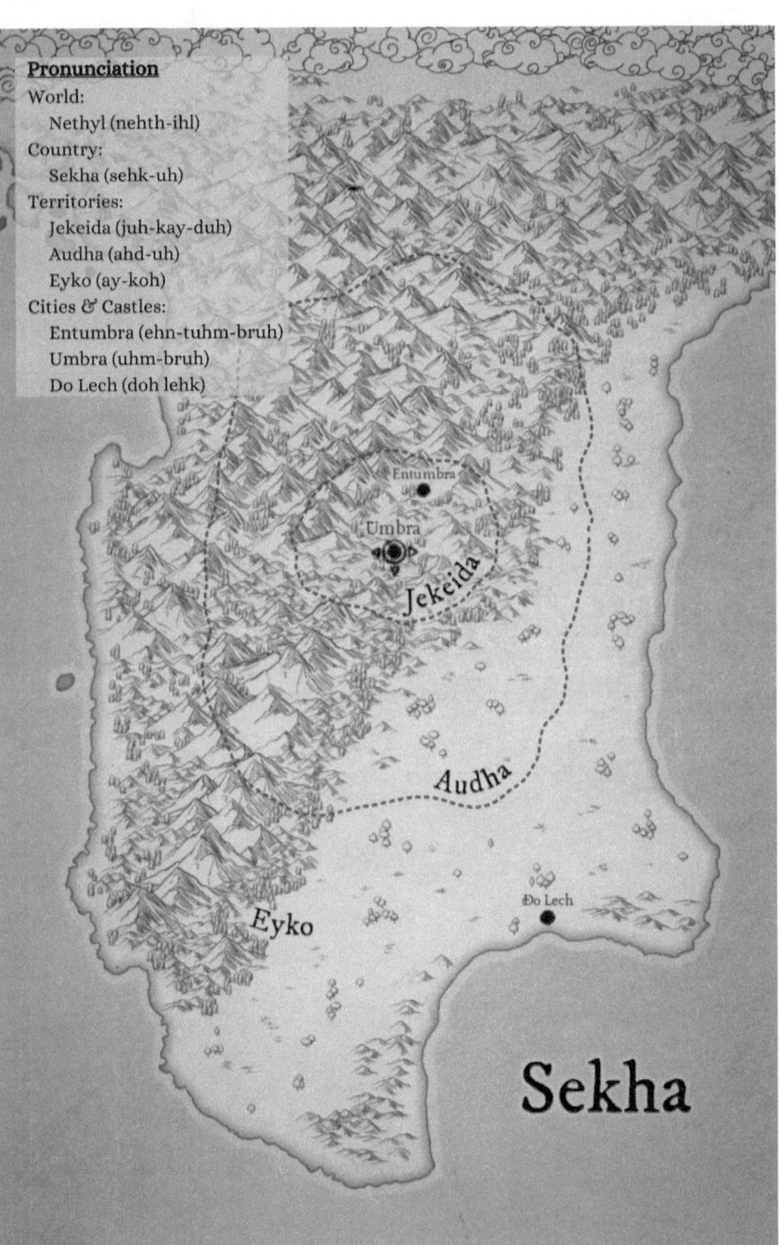

Pronunciation
World:
Nethyl (nehth-ihl)
Country:
Sekha (sehk-uh)
Territories:
Jekeida (juh-kay-duh)
Audha (ahd-uh)
Eyko (ay-koh)
Cities & Castles:
Entumbra (ehn-tuhm-bruh)
Umbra (uhm-bruh)
Do Lech (doh lehk)
Entumbra
Umbra
Jekeida
Audha
Eyko
Do Lech
Sekha

Eleven months before ...

ALMOST A MONTH HAD gone by since Gressia's family had come to Entumbra to lay her brother to rest. Almost a month since Mollian had told her that Basta killed Oren.

No, it hadn't been Basta. It was whatever lived inside of him.

Gressia knew that more than just the human's conscience resided inside of his body. She'd known since Ryddan's conception. Her pregnancy should have been impossible. The fact that she'd carried a child to term despite her tenure in the iron-laced castle of Entumbra and extended proximity to the Gate was a greater anomaly than even Mollian's third-born existence.

When she'd first looked into her son's cat-like eyes, there'd been no question that his father was not of Nethyl. His ability to shift as he grew older only further confirmed the fact. But it wasn't until Mollian recounted his abduction and the botched rescue that followed that she'd had a name for what Ryddan's father was: demon.

Finding the realm where Basta picked up the demon was almost impossible. All she had to go on was the description of possession and the parts of Ryddan that weren't fae. So she stopped obsessing over it, instead putting extra effort into keeping the wards around Entumbra and the Gate secure and strong.

Basta hadn't returned after Oren's death, but she knew he would be back eventually.

For almost a month, Gressia lived in constant fear for her child. Basta still didn't know about him, but if something were to happen to her ... Each day she woke wondering if she should take Ryddan to Umbra, but by the time she fell asleep again, she felt sure that he was safest off-world until Basta and the demon inside of him had been eradicated.

Once her mother sent word that Mollian was to come stay in Entumbra in preparation to take the crown, something in her chest eased. The normalcy of it gave her hope that they were close to capturing Basta, that the threat to Sekha was almost over. Then she would bring Ryddan to Nethyl and let her family meet the little Keeper that never should have been.

She smiled as she got ready for the day, twisting sections of long white curls to pin behind her head as thoughts of Mollian meeting Ryddan filled her mind. Her son's curious nature reminded her so much of when Mollian was young, and she could easily imagine her brother helping Ryddan get into every kind of mischief.

The warmth that had filled Gressia guttered when a scream of terror cut through the morning. She ran to the window with her heart in her throat.

The courtyard was being completely overrun with demons. Nightmarish creatures streamed from the trees, cutting through the light fog that blanketed the mountains and launching themselves toward the detachment of the Royal Guard that had been tasked to protect Entumbra. The grounds below were already a blood bath. Gressia's stomach rolled, but she was unable to turn away from the slaughter.

Basta stepped into the open, and her gaze immediately locked on him. He pushed a hand through his sandy hair as he watched the carnage around him with a wicked smile twisting his lips.

That's not Basta. The same terror that had rooted her to the spot now flooded her blood with adrenaline, and Gressia backed away just as his eyes traveled up the side of the castle.

The greater demon's eyes locked on the Keeper's window. He couldn't see her, but he knew she was there. Charn hated Entumbra. The very essence of the castle made him feel sick, like the form he kept twined with this meat suit would explode if he stayed there too long.

But it was the only way to access the Gate, and the human he'd struck a bargain with had a strange, sentimental attachment to the Keeper that Charn truly didn't understand. Whenever they visited Entumbra, Charn fled Basta's consciousness. He would coil himself tightly inside of the human's body, not returning to Basta's mind until they left.

A few times, though, he'd slipped back while Basta was in the throes of passion. He almost couldn't help it. His power sensed the Keeper's, and touching that magic, wrapping his own through it, was exhilarating.

Today was different, though. Basta knew they had reached a point of no return, but he hadn't wanted to be the one to harm the Keeper. The *guilt* he felt over attacking her made Charn sneer. So the greater demon took over, letting Basta hide away inside his own mind while Charn's army decimated Entumbra's feeble protectors.

The stench of blood and sulfur filled the air, and Charn reached out, his hand made of flesh and shadows gripping a guardsman by the neck. That hand was the only demonic part of Basta's body. The greater demon had conjured it after that human bitch had damaged the limb beyond repair. She would pay for that, of course.

The guard in Charn's grasp screamed, swinging a sword in a wild arc toward his side. Charn caught the guard's wrist with his free hand and briskly twisted it, feeling the bones snap in his grip, as a cry of agony tore itself free from the fae's throat. Charn laughed, hauling the fae closer to sink his teeth into the base of his neck and tearing loose a chunk of flesh.

He dropped the guard and stalked toward the castle. His human stomach rebelled at the blood and flesh he swallowed, but Charn grinned, red glistening in his beard and on his teeth. He would take Entumbra, and if Gressia didn't help him pull the wards around the castle down, he would find the third-born again and possess *him* to do it.

As his army slaughtered the Guard in the courtyard, Charn climbed the steps, unhurried, but irritated. He wanted to let his power roll free, but there was so much fucking *iron*, and it kept him too contained.

The sounds of death followed him into the atrium, then grew muted as he entered the stairwell. Even the damn steps and banisters were crafted from iron, and he grit his teeth, letting the discomfort fuel his rage and bloodlust.

He looked up at the same time Gressia gasped, throwing a hand over her mouth and whirling around, racing back to her room.

Charn chuckled, following at a measured pace. She had nowhere to go, not up here. She was too far above the ground to risk Traveling. "Come back, *rouiko*," he taunted in Basta's human tongue, using the man's pet name for her.

The slam of a door answered him, and he walked down the hall to her room, lightly rapping a knuckle against the door. "Let me in, Keeper," he said in the Common language of Nethyl, dropping all pretense. "This does not have to end badly for you."

Gressia clenched a knife in her hand, a blade Mollian had made her when he was still just a child. Crudely carved trees decorated its hilt, well worn from years of use. But she'd kept the blade sharp and honed. "You will never take the Gate!"

A laugh from the other side of the door. "You poor, beautiful creature. I already have. The only question left is whether or not your life will be forfeit with this castle."

Her heart thundered against her ribs, her mind working to figure a way out. She needed to get to the ground and find a way to warn Mollian he might be walking into another trap.

Basta couldn't have known her brother was going to arrive today, could he?

She flipped through possible worlds in her mind, trying to think of which ones she could Travel to that would drop her over a body of water, and, preferably, water that wasn't inhabited by flesh-hungry monsters.

Her door burst open then, Basta storming into the room.

No, *not Basta*, she reminded herself, scrambling back behind the bed and raising her knife. "I know you're not him, and I will not hesitate to kill you."

Charn strode forward, wiping blood from his chin. "You have not even given me a chance to explain what I offer," he chided. "Will you not hear me out?"

"I don't negotiate with demon scum," Gressia hissed, watching his movements.

He laughed. "It is no negotiation, Keeper. It is a choice. You either die here today, or you help me. Wield your portal magic for me, and you can live. The human whose mind I share is quite fond of you. It would be a shame to have to use his body to kill you."

"Fuck you." Gressia threw her knife as soon as Charn rounded the bed. It sailed blade over hilt, propulsion aided by her magic, and sank heavily into his shoulder, but she didn't wait around to watch. As soon as the weapon left her fingers, she'd sprung for the bed, crawling across it to get past him and to the door.

Charn roared, an entirely inhuman cry, and ripped the knife free, lunging after her. He wrapped his demonic hand around her ankle, hauling from the bed. She landed on the floor, and he flipped her onto her back, straddling her. "Why do you fight me?" he asked, holding her own blade to her throat, black blood dripping from his shoulder to soak her chest. "Your family has abandoned you here. You, who holds the Gate's power closest. You could rule entire realms by my side, beautiful creature." He searched her eyes, leaning his face close to hers. "What holds your loyalty here?"

"My purpose is to protect the Gate's power from filth like you." Gressia lifted her chin, glaring defiantly. "You may as well kill me, because I will not help you."

Charn sneered, moving the knife from her throat. "Power is wasted on people like you and your sniveling brothers. Your lack of ambition disgusts me." Then he buried the knife in her stomach.

Gressia choked on a scream, and she flung her hands out, throwing her magic against Charn and knocking him back.

He hit the wall, laughing as he watched her attempt to pull herself up. One of her hands pressed to her abdomen, the other grasping at the blankets hanging from the side of the bed. "So much fight. And for what reason?"

Gressia ignored him, blood thundering in her ears as she pushed past the pain, trying to stand, trying to find another weapon.

Charn stood, moving over to her and kicking her back to the ground.

Gressia cried out, coughing up blood.

He pulled the knife free and stabbed her again, watching her expression as she fought.

She clawed at his face, lashing out with her magic again, but it was weak and uncoordinated in her panic. "You'll never win," Gressia grit out, fire in her pale green eyes. *Make him leave make him leave make him leave.* It repeated on a loop in her head. Mollian would arrive sometime later that day, completely unprepared for a demon presence. She had no misconceptions about making it out alive, but she had to protect Mollian.

Because her brother was the only person on Nethyl who she'd ever told about Ryddan. Mollian was the only person she could count on to protect him, to watch out for him, to keep him safe. So she fought.

She fought, and she lied through her teeth.

"You can bring a whole legion of fucking demons here," she spat, venom lacing her words as she struggled, ripping her nails down his throat. Seeing black blood well in those wounds was more gratifying than she cared to admit. "Nothing you can do will beat the firepower my brother is amassing."

Charn paused, pinning her to the ground with a hand around her throat. "What?"

Gressia's eyes went wide, and she shook her head, pressing her lips together.

"What does that mean?" he growled, slamming her head into the floor.

Gressia's vision swam, but she kept her mouth closed.

Then a lightning bolt of agony ripped from her stomach, and she screamed. "I will not ask again," Charn said calmly, pulling his fingers from her knife wound and licking them free of blood.

Gressia grit her teeth, panting as tears streamed from her eyes. She hadn't known it was possible to feel that kind of pain and remain conscious. "Merriam," she panted, gripping the hand that held her throat. "The girl, she's ..." Her face twisted in the image of betrayal. "She's from Earth, where you got the fire weapon. She and ... m-my brother have been Traveling there since you killed Oren. They're stockpiling guns on the eastern border of Jekeida. They said they'd ... bring them here the next full moon. Drop off enough to arm me and the Guard, then take the rest to Umbra until they figure out where you're hiding." The very real pain that clouded her eyes hid any spark of deception her desperation might have shown.

Charn's grip tightened when she finished talking, rage simmering low in his blood. "NO!" he yelled into her face. She would have yelped if he hadn't been squeezing her neck so tightly. "That fucking low-class *bitch!*" He sat back on his heels, releasing Gressia as he wiped a hand over his mouth. He looked back down at Gressia, gauging the fear and pain on her face. "You just doomed the rest of your family. I appreciate your help,

Keeper."

Then he grabbed her head and slammed it into the floorboards. Again. And again, until her eyes fluttered closed.

The pressure against Gressia's skull was overwhelmingly intense, bright spots of light bursting in across her vision as her teeth clacked together. Then it stopped, the weight lifting from her body as Charn stood. She was fading fast, but the demons were leaving. The demons were leaving, and Mollian would be safe. Ryddan would be safe, and that was all that mattered. *My baby*, she latched onto the thought as she slipped into unconsciousness.

But Gressia didn't just think the words, she spoke them. Charn paused on his way out of the room, tipping his head to the side curiously. Those were words to consider, but later. First, he needed to take his demons east.

THE AIR WAS STATIC: deceptively calm, but pressurized. Everything was dark. Or maybe there was light, but everything was so deeply black that nothing was discernible.

Mollian stood in the center of the space, or possibly right on the edge. He breathed evenly, turning in a slow circle. Though there was no apparent source of light, the mess of white curls falling over the aspen branch tattoo that crowned his brow shone in stark contrast to the light brown of his skin.

"Hello?" he called, and his voice echoed back to him from some unseen obstacle.

He took a few tentative steps forward, one hand held out to keep from smashing his face into something.

He felt like he should be scared, or at least concerned, but he was almost void of emotion aside from a light curiosity about where he was and how he'd come to be there.

Looking down at his feet, he took a few more steps forward, and then backward. Then he sidestepped. A chuckle fell from his lips, the echo returning to him from all sides.

The ground was moving with him, like his steps weren't propelling his body, but the surface underneath him. Curiosity winning out, Mollian lunged forward, running with long strides. The ground rolled seamlessly beneath him, no matter if he slowed to a jog or launched into a full sprint.

Eventually he stopped, clasping his hands at the back of his head as he panted, trying to catch his breath.

His surroundings were still the same heavy black nothing they'd always been, but he noticed he felt lighter, less compressed, the longer he spent in this place.

My magic. The realization slammed into him. The pressure he typically felt from it pushing at the constraints of his body was no longer present.

Out of sheer curiosity, Mollian summoned his power. There was nothing in this room to reach for, so he just shot it forward.

It rushed from him like a siphon, taking his breath with it.

He tried to pull back, not having meant to unleash such a strong burst of power.

Pull. Pull. Pull, his magic seemed to whisper, refusing to settle.

Mollian held up his other hand in a futile attempt to restrain the magic that poured from him freely.

Rip. Tear.

Shred.

His magic settled, moving calmly through his blood as he dropped onto his hands and knees. He waited for a moment and was about to push himself up when he heard a ripping sound from far above him.

It was soft, but echoed in the stillness of the space, soon followed by a soft hiss. Air brushed across Mollian's skin, gently ruffling his curls as it sought escape from its confines.

He glanced up, standing slowly while his eyes stayed locked on to the source of the sound above him.

A narrow tear had appeared in the vast expanse of black, and light spilled through in a rotating prism of color.

Mollian licked his lips, realizing his mouth had gone dry.

Pull. Rip. Tear. His magic stirred, eager.

Taking a deep breath, he set his feet firmly and held out both hands, letting his magic flow through him.

Pull! Rip! Tear!

He felt his power wriggle into the open seam, momentarily stopping the rush of air seeping out. His magic squeezed into that rip, gripping it from each end, threading through the molecular makeup of the blackness.

Mollian clenched his fists and threw his arms wide, his magic following the movement and tearing the seam into a large gap.

Pull! Rip! Tear!

Thousands upon thousands of threads appeared through the hole, each one shimmering with color and light. He hardly even noticed though, too preoccupied with following the call of his power, focusing on tearing the blackness further and further back.

A guttural growl ripped from his chest, turning into a yell as he again pulled at the long tear.

Shred.

With one final cry, Mollian rent the blackness completely in two, and it dropped from around him like a curtain.

"What the ..." he panted, finally looking around. What had appeared to be thousands of threads crossing the sky turned out to be millions, interwoven and extending in every direction. They all seemed to originate from a point behind him, and he turned slowly, apprehension suddenly filling his chest. He blinked away a drop of sweat that rolled from his brow.

Mollian's eyes flew open, his magic rippling outward in a pulse that flung the blankets from his bed and sent the objects on his nightstands scattering. He panted, instinctively reaching out for Merriam with his mind before remembering she wasn't there.

"Entumbra, she's in Entumbra," he whispered to himself. He took a deep breath, reining in his magic and forcing it to settle. It stretched underneath his skin for a few moments before it finally quieted. He lay there for a while, testing to see if he could fall back asleep, but he was restless.

Mollian sat up with a groan, moonlight catching the sheen of cold sweat on his chest. He swung his legs out of bed, pulling the bedding back onto the mattress with a flick of his fingers as he made his way into his bathroom.

With another careless wave of his hand in the general direction of the shower, he turned on the tap, letting the water warm while he filled a cup from the sink and drank.

Mollian couldn't remember anything from his dream aside from the vast expanse of blackness and the blinding, colorful light. His brow furrowed, but nothing else would come to him. His power felt roiling and restless inside him, but his *mehhen* had been gone for over a week, so he didn't think much of it.

Ever since he'd been tattooed with the crown of aspen leaves, the ink mixed with finely crushed pieces of the Gate, his magic had felt more immense and harder to dampen. Merriam's presence helped with it, though. Something about the way their souls were bound allowed it more space to stretch.

Mollian stepped under the stream of water, his hair plastering to his face. He pushed it back, the water cascading over him and washing away the last unsettling remnants of the dream.

After drying off, Mollian dressed in simple pants and a cotton shirt to head down to the kitchens.

Rillak, a sergeant in the Royal Guard, was stationed outside the outer door to Mollian's chambers. The burly Guard looked down at him curiously. "Yer Majesty's up early this mornin'."

Mollian smiled, waving him off. "Guess I was just eager to start the day."

"What's on the agenda?"

Mollian stared off down the hallway. "Roads, Rillak. Roads are on the agenda," he said with a heavy sigh.

The kitchen staff rushed to prepare him breakfast, though he tried to assure them it wasn't pressing. Even after almost eleven months as king, he still wasn't used to the way everyone jumped to attend to his every want and need. It made him exceedingly uncomfortable, but as much as he tried to explain he didn't need to be waited on hand and foot, his denizens continued to rush to do things for him.

Mollian ate his breakfast in the courtyard, staying until the sky slowly began to lighten over the mountains to the east. He considered changing, knowing Ferrick would be attending the meeting, more than likely in full uniform. But he was feeling ornery, and he was king. Why should he have to dress a certain way? He had no one to impress.

Graigory would be the most important person present, and Mollian would bet good coin he could show up naked and the roadsmaster wouldn't notice as long as plans were out on the table prior to his arrival.

"Good morning, Your Majesty," a Guard greeted as he made his way back inside.

"Good morning," Mollian returned with a smile. He cringed inwardly that he hadn't even realized there'd been a shift change. Merriam would be disappointed in his lack of observation.

Almost a year had passed since she'd killed Basta, and there hadn't been any reported demon activity since, but Merriam still worried. She'd become almost obsessive with making sure the ley lines spread throughout the country stayed warded, sending birds back and forth with every outpost to make sure nothing out of the ordinary was happening without their knowledge.

Mollian understood, though. Losing Oren had almost broken her, and sometimes she still blamed herself for not doing things differently. As the second-born prince with no set destiny, Mollian had never been under the same guard as his brother and parents. Merriam knew that lack of security had led to his kidnapping, the rescue of which had led to Oren's death.

Mollian still blamed himself, too. He knew he'd had the power to pull the demon from his brother and collapse the cave, but he'd been too slow in harnessing his magic, and Merriam had been too argumentative, too questioning.

It was a thought he had never shared with anyone and would take to his grave, but even if Oren had been able to get out, Mollian never would have been able to bring down the cave with Merriam still inside. A part of him knew that he could have killed them all, but not her. He would never have been able to be the cause of her death.

Even if it wasn't intentional, he had chosen Merriam over his brother that day, and that knowledge ate away at him, the guilt adding to the perpetual feeling that he was only an impostor parading as king.

Oren never would have been so selfish.

But ... hadn't he?

Wasn't it Oren's love for Merriam that had made him angry enough to take back control from the demon possessing him and turn on Basta?

Mollian shook his head to clear it of the dismal thoughts.

It was nearing a year since his brother's death, and it was dredging up emotions and feelings more frequently than he'd dealt with in the past few months.

He missed Oren, especially on days like today, when he would be deciding things that could possibly change the course of their country, change history. Mollian often wondered if his brother would have made the same choices. If he would be proud.

The war room was empty when Mollian entered, and he slipped into the office at the back, buckling a sword around his waist. A small detail, especially considering his attire, but one that Ferrick's warrior mind would see and respect. Grabbing the plans and various agendas and budget charts from the top of his desk, he went back to the main room, piling everything neatly onto the table overlaid with a map of Sekha.

He sorted through the notes he'd written, refreshing himself for any potential arguments or questions to come.

Ferrick was the first to enter, accompanied by a few advisors and representatives from other territories. "Good morning, Your Majesty," he greeted, dipping his head respectfully, but his eyes traveled down Mollian's body, judging. His expression had cleared by the time he met Mollian's eyes again.

"Good morning, Captain." Mollian returned the nod before addressing the others. "Go ahead and take your seats. Master Graigory should be here shortly, and then we'll get started."

Polite conversation filled the room, and after a bit of deliberation, Mollian took his seat at the head of the table, forcing his legs to remain still when they wanted to bounce with nervous energy.

Mollian shouldn't have been surprised when Graigory strolled in, his arms filled with papers and research of his own and light blue eyes bright with excitement.

"Thank you for your patience, Majesty. I hope you weren't waiting on me too long. I'd forgotten one of the maps and had to run back home," the roadsmaster apologized, setting up at the end of the table opposite Mollian.

"No worries at all, Master Graigory. We've only just assembled," Mollian assured him, fighting off a grimace at the formality of his words.

Once the fae had finished organizing his papers, he looked to Mollian with a broad smile.

At least one of us is looking forward to this, he thought, before clearing his throat. "Thank you all for being here first thing in the morning and clearing your schedules. We have a lot to discuss, and I'd like to get as much of the groundwork done today as possible."

Mollian took a deep breath. He'd discussed bits and pieces of this project with everyone in some manner, but never all of it together. He'd wanted to be sure it was a viable possibility before dedicating himself to the cause, knowing that if he'd thrown the idea out without any research and it turned out not to be probable, many would think it was directly related to his age and inexperience.

The only one who knew the entirety of this proposal was Graigory. Mollian had approached him with the idea first, getting reports back with additional inquiries that he forwarded off to the appropriate people.

"As you're aware, Master Graigory and I have been collaborating on a way to advance trade throughout Sekha. Currently, it takes roughly a week to travel from Do Lech to Umbra, longer if large amounts of cargo are being transported. I believe there's a way the trip can be completed in two days or less." Mollian confidently met the eyes of each person in attendance as he spoke, keeping his voice smooth and measured.

Mollian unrolled one of his diagrams, clipping it to a stand beside him so that everyone could easily see. "This, my friends, is a train. It will be capable of moving large quantities of food, cloth, stone, people—anything imaginable, really—at high speeds using the power of steam."

"Steam?" one of the guildmasters questioned.

"Yes." Mollian picked up another stack of papers to be passed around the table. "Here's a rough idea of the contraption we'd need to build. I've talked with the head of the smithsguild in Umbra and have been assured that they're capable of creating it."

The king kept to himself that he'd tasked Merriam with hunting down old blueprints of steam engines from Earth. Though crude electricity was possible throughout Nethyl, more intricate technology was incompatible with magic and the way it moved through the world. But steam was just another form of hydropower, and Mollian was interested to see how much industrialization magic would allow. Merriam had found a few very informative books that she'd brought back for him, helping him translate some of the more intricate English into Common so he could study on his own. He kept them locked away in the desk in his room, but would eventually have them fully translated and kept in the castle library to use as reference.

Mollian gave everyone a moment to look over the simplified versions of the plans for the large steam engine and the designs for different carts it could pull before continuing. "The biggest challenge with this project will be building a rail system for the train to travel on. Master Graigory, would you like to go into the details?"

The roadsmaster stood, spreading his own map over the table. "Absolutely, Your Majesty."

Graigory explained, in great detail, how they would be able to lay steel and wood down along the side of the major roads already cut through the foothills, setting up small stations along the way that could be manned with people who could make sure the tracks stayed in safe condition.

Mollian sat in his seat, elbows propped on the table and his eyes following Graigory's hands as they moved over the map. His expression stayed attentive, but his mind wandered. He had initially been excited about the idea of implementing train travel in Sekha, but it was really just the engineering of it that piqued his interest. Once he'd worked out whether or not they would be capable of creating a steam engine and how to make it work in his world without having a drastic impact on the environment, he'd learned that getting it put into action was all politics. And if Graigory could talk all night long about simple roads, he had ten times as much to say about *railroads*.

Mollian felt guilty for it, but this part of it bored him nearly to tears. He was excited for what it meant for his country, but he'd done his part of figuring out how it would work. What was the point of having advisors and people in charge of different branches of politics if they couldn't work the rest of it out themselves?

He stifled a sigh, sliding one hand into his lap and playing with a small penknife under the table just to have something to do with his hands. At least if Merriam were here, they could make a game to play together. His magic flared slightly, as if remembering she was gone.

Soon, he promised. *She'll be home soon.*

RAIN POURED FROM THE sky in thick, cold sheets. Droplets hammered the ground, turning the courtyard outside of the stone and iron castle into a field of mud.

"Does this mean we're staying another night?" The small voice barely carried over the sound of the storm.

Merriam dropped her hand onto a head of fine white hair, brushing the straight strands to the side as she stared out of the window. "It'll be too treacherous to navigate the pass in these conditions, Rydd."

The child frowned, leaning into her touch as he watched rainwater slide down the glass. "I don't like it here. This place makes me fizzy."

"I know." Lightning cut across the sky, followed shortly by a loud crack of thunder. "You can sleep out in the stablehouse with Bellamy tonight. I'll handle your grandmother."

Ryddan was unique, born of a Keeper and a greater demon from another realm. He'd inherited the physical traits of a Keeper—snow white hair, light brown skin, green eyes—as well as the magical ability to open portals between worlds, but he'd also inherited power from his father that enabled him to shift into any creature imaginable, as well as vertically slit pupils that set him apart.

The demon blood in his veins was also much more susceptible to ill-effects from iron than his fae blood, which made prolonged stays in Entumbra taxing.

The castle of Entumbra was half-composed of cold-wrought iron in an attempt to keep the magic buried deep underneath the mountain from seeping out. The iron had minimal impact on fae and Keepers, so long as they weren't physically touching it, but even the air around the iron bothered Ryddan.

"Can I go find him?" The six-year-old tilted his head up to look at Merriam.

"Of course, just don't get your clothes too muddy running around out there or Lydia will string me up by my toes," Merriam cautioned.

"I won't!" Ryddan skipped off to the atrium doors that led to the only access from ground to the castle proper: a set of steep, stone stairs.

And stay close to the castle! she Cast as he ran through the door. The ability to send thoughts to other Keepers and, with effort, others that could wield magic, was another Keeper trait. Merriam had gained the ability when she'd Bonded herself to Mollian, taking his blood through a rune tattooed between her shoulder blades. The loop, bordered by dots and curved lines on opposite corners, was doubled on her back, the second a Bond to Oren.

Ryddan raised a small hand over his shoulder in acknowledgment before shifting into a gray wolf and bounding down the steps. Merriam watched him pause at the bottom, lifting his nose to scent the air before shaking out his fur and plodding off, mud splashing up each time he set a paw down.

"He needs to become comfortable here, Merriam. This will be his home." Regenya came to stand beside her, watching as the wolf disappeared into the trees.

Merriam took a slow breath, closing her eyes to clear them of annoyance.

Regenya had been queen of Sekha for over three hundred years, until her two eldest children had been taken from her almost a year ago.

After Gressia was murdered, the responsibility of Entumbra had fallen to Regenya, who'd stepped down and given Mollian an early throne.

"He is the firstborn of his generation. He will be the Keeper of Entumbra," Regenya said quietly.

Opening her eyes, Merriam turned to face the former queen. "He may be a Keeper, Your Highness, but he's not high fae."

"Keepers have been born of impure blood in the past, but they are always fully a Keeper." Regenya didn't meet Merriam's eyes, staring stubbornly into the woods.

"Ryddan is half demon. It doesn't matter what's happened in the past or the way Keeper blood typically works. His father also possessed powerful magic—that's the only reason he even exists. Entumbra is suffocating to his demon nature," Merriam pressed.

"Maybe if he stays here long enough, it will burn away the parts of him given by his father."

Merriam bristled, amber eyes narrowing in a glare. "That's not how that works, Regenya. You only see Ryddan as a Keeper, but he is just as much his demon bloodline. You can't just remove half of him or expect that can even be a possibility."

Regenya shook her head, folding her hands in front of her to maintain composure. "I am well aware of what my grandson is and what his parentage entails. I love him, Merriam, and I know you would never deign to imply otherwise. But the fact remains that someone will need to guard Entumbra when I die. I am already old, and both you and I know Mollian will not be producing an heir in the near future. Someone must keep the Gate and maintain the warding. That is Ryddan's birthright."

Anger flared through Merriam, and she turned her gaze back out of the window. "In case you haven't noticed, neither you nor Mollian are where your birthrights intended. Things change, even tradition. Every other firstborn has felt a strong connection to the Gate and a sense of belonging in Entumbra. It's possible that connection will grow in Ryddan as he ages, but I will die before I let him be sentenced to a life of suffocation."

Regenya's bright green eyes finally turned to Merriam, burning with disdain.

Merriam clenched her jaw, throwing her hands up placatingly before the fae had a chance to speak. She whirled on her heel, walking off across the atrium before the argument turned into a full fight.

Without really thinking, Merriam headed down a spiral staircase into the belly of the castle. The stairs ended in a room filled with arch supports, and she wove through them to a door at the back.

The wood pulled open with a creak, and the scent of damp earth wafted around her. She stepped into the cooler air of the tunnel that led deep below the mountain, following the vibrations in her blood more than the dim lighting in the staircase. Dirt steps soon turned into granite, and still Merriam continued downward.

The tunnel opened up into a large cavern, the Gate glinting at its center. Merriam paid it no heed, moving across with hardly a glance at the umbrite and orydite arch, purple stone wrapped around gold-veined black. She slipped into an opening in the cave wall so shrouded in shadow it wouldn't be noticeable to anyone who didn't know to look for it, and emerged from a short tunnel into a cavern that glowed a soft blue from the hundreds of bioluminescent moths that flitted about.

The walls of this cave were lined with notches that had been carved from the coarse stone long ago. Many of them were now open graves, the bodies lying inside wrapped in heavy cloth. Remains of every Keeper Nethyl had ever produced.

Merriam slowed her pace when she entered. Even with the movement of the moths, everything felt still here, and the air was warmer than the main cave. She made her way to one of the only two graves not yet heavily marked by time.

"Hi, O," she whispered, leaning her shoulder against the head of the grave. Her fingers came to rest just inside the lip of it, not touching the fabric-swathed body. She bit her lip, a sudden swell of emotion clogging her throat. "Legends, I wish you were here."

Taking a few settling breaths, she shook her head, pulling her long, pale blonde braid over her shoulder to toy with the end of it. "Your mother is still infuriating, in case you were wondering. It's almost worse now that she treats me as a person with my own merit. I'm no longer just Mollian's *mehhen* to her; she knows the status I hold in this country and in the lives of her family. She respects me, but somehow that has made her even more unbearable.

"She's set in her opinion that Ryddan will live here when he's older. I know he's firstborn, but I don't think he belongs here—not in perpetuity. This place grates on him. I know it wasn't always the easiest environment for your sister, either, but Gress didn't have demon blood in her veins."

Merriam sighed, crossing her arms over her chest.

"I threw in her face that she and Molli aren't where their birthrights intended for them to be, and I know I shouldn't have without tact. She still feels the loss of you and Gressia so deeply, and she's scared for Molli. She still sees him as the young prince with no destiny, running around and getting into any trouble he could find. I know he's the youngest king Sekha has ever had, but he's not *that* young. He would have taken the crown in five years, and that's nothing in your lifespan."

Merriam frowned, rolling to her back and resting her head against the stone. "I guess it's possible that Ryddan could grow used to Entumbra. This is only his third time visiting, and the Gate's effects are strange to all of us at first. In any case, we have time to figure it out, I suppose."

Her frustration ebbed, and she changed the course of the conversation. "You'd love seeing Molli in Umbra, though." A fond smile spread across her face. "He's made such a good king, even if his methods are driving Ferrick and some of the others up a wall." Merriam talked about life, her responsibilities as marshal, and her recent interactions with the mercenaries.

In the past, she'd always looked forward to visiting Entumbra because it meant seeing Oren. That was different now, but disappearing below the castle to vent about life when she brought Ryddan to visit had been essential in her grieving process. He had been one of only a few people Merriam had ever let herself open up to, and now his resting place had become somewhere she could be completely open and vulnerable.

The growl of her stomach echoed through the cave, and she laughed lightly. "As someone once told me, the living must eat. Thank you for letting me rant. I miss you, Oren." Merriam pushed away from the wall, casting one last look into the grave as her chest tightened. "I love you."

"We're having supper in the stables at the princeling's request if you want to join," Bellamy greeted when Merriam walked into the dining hall.

Merriam looked at the platter of food in the Ranger's arms. "Sure, I love the smell of horse and wet hay with my meals." She dipped into a side door next to the kitchen entry, grabbing a bottle of wine.

"I thought we were leaving early tomorrow morning?" Bellamy raised an eyebrow, stretching the scar that ran down his face.

"We'll hydrate before bed." Merriam flashed him a grin, leading the way up the stairs.

The rain had let up a bit, coming down in a light but steady drizzle. Bellamy had had the forethought to grab something to shield the food, but their boots were caked in mud, and droplets of water coated their hair by the time the two slid into the stables.

Ryddan was crouched on the floor, wiggling around a sprig of straw for a barn cat to chase. He looked up when they entered, brushing a lock of straight white hair from his eyes. "I tried to be a cat with her, but she kept hissing at me. She likes people, though!"

"Go wash up, and you can play with her more after you eat," Bellamy told him while Merriam pulled a blanket from a shelf to spread across the floor.

Ryddan stood, brushing his hands off on his pants and running over to the sink in the corner, the cat scampering off into a stall at his quick movements. "If I were a cat, I wouldn't have to wash my hands," he called over his shoulder.

"If you were a cat, you'd wash your hands by licking them, and you'd have no opposable thumbs," Bellamy pointed out, helping Merriam set out the food.

Ryddan frowned as he walked over, drying his hands on his pants.

Merriam saw, but turned her attention back to the food, knowing some things weren't worth the battle. Lydia, his nursemaid, would be appalled, but Merriam had eaten many a meal on the forest floor and knew a little dirt wouldn't hurt anything.

"Raccoons have opposable thumbs, and they don't wash their hands." Ryddan plopped down into Bellamy's lap.

Merriam tilted her head to the side. "Not always, but sometimes they do."

"You wouldn't even know," Ryddan challenged, reaching for an entire loaf of bread.

Bellamy grabbed it, ripping off a chunk to hand to him before he could take a bite out of the side.

"Actually, I would," Merriam said matter-of-factly, slathering butter onto a cob of corn and sprinkling it liberally with salt.

Ryddan's green eyes narrowed in suspicion.

"People have recorded it happening on Earth."

Ryddan tilted his head up, looking at Bellamy to see if he would confirm her claims.

"Don't look at me, buddy. She's the expert."

The three ate with companionable conversation, Ryddan challenging most of what they said. Just when his interjections reached the cusp of being annoying, he would add a comment that showed thought and maturity far past what a six year old would usually possess.

Bellamy and Merriam polished off the bottle of wine along the way.

After supper, Ryddan sought out the barn cat again, and Bellamy and Merriam climbed up to the balcony overlooking the courtyard, both with cups of water.

Moonlight glittered in the puddles below, a light breeze rippling over them. Bellamy cocked his head to the side, listening for Ryddan. When he heard the prince happily chattering away at the cat, he licked his lips, turning stormy blue eyes to Merriam.

"Are you comfortable here?" he asked. "Do you feel what Rydd feels, I mean."

Merriam took a long sip, considering how to explain. "Yes and no. I'm sure you can feel the Gate in the stillness; it's very powerful. But its magic in my blood is a constant vibration. It was a little jarring the first few times I felt it, but it's not uncomfortable. Something in its magic has always reminded me of Mollian, too, so I always felt ... safe around it. Now I only really notice it when I'm near the Gate, or when I'm very drunk, but I wouldn't call it uncomfortable." Merriam turned to face Bellamy fully. "It's different, though, for Rydd. You know how a Keeper's magic is different? Than normal fae magic, I mean."

Bellamy glanced at her curiously. "It's blood magic."

"Yes, it's the fact that that power is already embedded in blood, which contains iron, that allows them—me, even—to use the magic regardless of the metal, right?"

"Sure." He wasn't well-versed in the science of it, but the logic was sound, so Bellamy nodded.

"I don't think Rydd's blood is the same as ours, and I think that changes the way Entumbra affects him."

Bellamy set his cup down on the narrow railing to pull long curls back from his face, tying them at the nape of his neck. "I know it's not my place to speak on it, Mer, but being here isn't ... it's not good for him." He rotated the cup in his hands, brow furrowed. The responsibility he felt for Ryddan's well-being went deeper than professional obligation, even if he'd never acknowledged it outright.

"You spend more time with him than any of us, other than maybe Lydia. Plus, I'd argue that as the head of his personal guard, it's more your place than anyone's to speak up on his behalf. You sell yourself short too often, Bell." Merriam knocked her shoulder into him to lighten her words.

Bellamy gave her a soft smile, drinking more water. "He's different here. Less vibrant, if you can believe it. The iron weakens him so much when it's near."

Merriam nodded. "I see it, too. Regenya is convinced that this will be his home one day, but I'm not sold on it. Fate and birthright be damned. This would be the worst kind of prison for him."

"True, but those of royal blood have always had to learn to step into roles that they might not have wanted," Bellamy pointed out, thinking of Mollian.

Merriam read as much on his face. "There are different levels. Molli never wanted the crown, but being king was never going to kill him. Even if he's stressed, he is well-suited to regency."

"And Ryddan?" Bellamy asked quietly, searching Merriam's eyes.

Her brow furrowed in confusion.

"If Ryddan isn't meant to be in Entumbra, he's meant to rule. He's a prince of Sekha, after all. Possibly the only one we'll ever have," he said.

"Molli is so young, though. There's never been two Keepers of different generations born so close together before. By the time Molli is ready to pass on the crown, Ryddan will be decades away from doing the same," she argued.

"Do we know that?" Bellamy looked off into the courtyard, contemplating how little they truly understood of Ryddan's heritage.

"Regardless, that's a problem for the future. We have years to figure all of that out. Maybe there will be two other heirs, and he'll get to live like Molli grew up, free from the weight of future responsibility."

"Perhaps," Bellamy agreed, though he thought it highly unlikely.

Merriam finished her water before stretching deeply. "I'm going to head in. Don't let him keep you up too late."

"I'll get him into bed shortly," Bellamy promised. "Just a quick night run, then heading over to the river for a swim, and back into the kitchens to bake a cake for dessert first."

"Sounds like a light evening," Merriam laughed. "Thank you, Bell. For everything."

"You don't have to thank me. I'm just glad to do what I can, where I can." Bellamy shrugged, tucking his hands into his pockets.

"Again with the selling yourself short," Merriam teased, squeezing his arm before making her way back to the castle.

Fourteen years before...

ROVIN ARWOOD GREW UP in a small town in West Eyko with his mother and sister, and, all things considered, had an extremely happy childhood filled with warmth and love.

His mother, Loran, had married her childhood sweetheart, and the years she'd had with him were nothing short of bliss. He worked in lumber, and she in conservation, a combination that suited them well. Then they had brought Cessie into the world, and Loran couldn't have imagined being any happier than she was.

But one day, her husband had suffered a fatal wound while felling trees, leaving Loran and her four-year-old daughter alone.

Several years had passed, seventy-five, to be exact, and Loran had yet to attach herself to another male, though she had taken other lovers.

One of those lovers had been a charming human, passing through town on his way up north for trapping season. He'd never returned, but several short months later, Rovin was born.

Half-fae were much more accepted than they had been in the past, but several fae in remote areas still harbored prejudice against them. Fair folk, or lesser fae, as some still called them, couldn't cast glamors or use magic to move objects, but they all possessed an animal characteristic—wings, horns, a tail—*something* that set them apart. Halflings, however, looked exactly like the high fae, with tapered ears and elongated canines. In the past, when much of Sekha was ruled by classism, the fact that they could pass as high fae was taken as an affront to those who saw themselves as superior for the ability to use magic.

As much as Loran loved the small town she lived in, the population was mostly trappers and lumber workers, all proud, full-blooded fae. Humans had never settled there, and thus many of the citizens had easily been able to hold on to out-dated opinions and still accept outlawed practices as the norm.

Because of this, Loran never told her son what he was. Rovin was a sweet, mild-tempered child with more empathy and emotional intelligence than anyone she'd ever met. He brought so much light and life into their home, and she and Cessie were both completely enamored.

Loran wanted to hide him away from the world, not wanting the cruelness of it to touch him or mar his innocence, and, for a while, she succeeded. He was friendly and full of life, and he loved to play with the other children in town. As they grew, many of their games evolved to require the use of magic.

Magic that young Rovin didn't have.

He tried to fake it for a while, but eventually came to the realization that he was without. Loran assured him that he was just a late bloomer, still determined to hide his parentage in a misguided attempt to keep him from ever feeling inferior. The other children noticed his lack of magic, though, and started treating him as an outcast because of it.

Despite the taunts and ridicule Rovin received from some of the children, he held onto his soft, cheerful demeanor. He was able to brush off the strange looks and mean words easily, comforted always by the love and assurance of his mother and sister.

The older he got, the less he interacted with the other children, spending most of his time wandering the forest outside of his home. He craved companionship, but that was not something his peers were eager to give.

Rovin understood on some basal level that he was different, but it had never truly bothered him until one summer when he was fourteen.

He was walking down the street, a bag of loaves from the baker swinging from one hand, when another boy ran up behind him, snatching it away.

Rovin sighed, stopping and folding his arms over his chest. "Give it back, Courten."

The boy in front of him smiled cruelly, tossing it over Rovin's head to a boy behind him, arcing it high out of reach. "Take it, Arwood."

Rovin turned around, reaching out, but the bag was tossed back overhead. "Stop, it's not funny."

Courten tossed the bag to a third boy. "Feel like a game of halfling in the middle?"

The third boy tossed it back to the second when Rovin turned to look at him. His cheeks grew warm at the slur. "I'm not a halfling."

Courten scoffed, catching the bag as it was tossed back to him. "Then take it back. If you're not a halfling, pull it out of the air."

Rovin stood his ground, irritation simmering low in his blood. "You know I can't."

"Yeah, because you're a dirty, filthy *halfling*," Courten taunted, and the other boys joined in.

"Halfling, halfling, Rovin's a rotten halfling!" they chanted.

Rovin spun, his ears hot. He jumped, reaching high for the bread bag, but his fruitless attempts only fueled their efforts.

Standing in the middle of the three boys, Rovin's hands curled into fists at his sides, and as he met Courten's cruel gaze, something snapped in his chest.

For the first time in his life, Rovin was angry.

His vision narrowed on Courten, and he crouched to the ground, his fingers curling around a rock. Rovin cocked his arm back, launching the stone at Courten's face with an enraged roar.

The rock connected high on the boy's cheek, and his head rocked back with the impact, the only sound Courten's high cry as he held his face.

The other boys instantly silenced, the bag falling to the ground with a soft thump.

Courten quieted, lowering his hands as blood gushed from a gash below his eye, already swelling with bruising and the bone no doubt shattered beneath. "You fucking little cocksucker," he seethed.

Rovin, still in a crouch, froze as the righteous indignation rushed from his blood. He swallowed, throat bobbing as fear flooded the void. "Shit," he breathed.

His legs regained function a heartbeat later, and he scrambled into a sprint, racing into the forest. The other three boys chased after him, and though he may have been faster, they had magic, and he didn't.

Courten's magic wrapped around his boots, jerking him to the ground.

Rovin caught himself, hands sliding painfully in the dirt but protecting his face. He tried to stand back up, but the other boys were on him before he could get to his feet.

A foot slammed into his ribs, and Rovin curled up, his breath leaving his body.

Another attack came from the back, hitting the base of his spine, and he grit his teeth together, shielding his face and the back of his head with his arms and curling his knees up to his chest.

"Stop!" he cried out, unable to hold back any longer as bright spots of agony bloomed across his body. The three boys were unrelenting in their assault, feeding off of each other and Courten's violent energy.

"Get him on his belly," Courten ordered.

Fear and adrenaline raced through Rovin's veins in a sickening concoction, and his stomach lurched dangerously. "Nonono, please, Courten."

A fist connected with his jaw, and his head slammed into the dirt, stars exploding behind his eyes. "Shut your filthy mouth, halfling."

Rovin was strong, but he couldn't fight against the hold of the others, not when they used their magic to help anchor his legs and pin his arms to his sides.

Courten straddled him, sitting on his back.

Rovin cried out as blinding pain radiated from his ribs, broken bones pressing against each other under the pressure. Tears spilled from his eyes, tears of pain and terror and frustration and *anger*. Anger that burned deep in his gut. Anger that heated his blood and forced him to cry out again, releasing the energy that had nowhere else to go.

Courten pressed the side of Rovin's face into the dirt, pulling a small knife from his pocket and flipping it open. "You'll never be able to pretend that you're one of us again. And everyone will know that you don't belong." He grabbed the tapered point of Rovin's ear, pulling it out and sawing into it with the blade.

Rovin screamed, unable to move with his head held against the ground and the other boys holding him still. He bit his tongue to cut off the noise, clenching his fists so hard he could feel blood seeping from his palms. He seethed, breathing heavily through his nose as Courten cut through his ear, tossing the tip into the dirt in front of Rovin's face.

Warm blood dripped into his hair, down his neck, and over his cheek, into his mouth. He spat at the saltiness of it, fresh tears leaking from his eyes, but he refused to give his tormentors another sound.

"Try picking a fight again, halfling, and you'll be limping home blind." Courten stood, a strangled groan escaping from Rovin as his ribs were again jostled. The other two followed suit, and Rovin could move.

"Can we get in trouble for this, Courten?" one asked as they walked away.

"He won't tell anyone. Besides, nobody is going to protect someone as useless as him against three high fae."

Rovin, taking short, shallow breaths, pushed slowly to his feet, hearing their voices and footsteps fade away. He sat on his knees for a long moment, trying to assess his injuries.

At least a few ribs were definitely broken, that pain almost overwhelming. His back was bruised, and internal damage was highly probable. His ear still leaked blood down the side of his face, warm and uncomfortably sticky where it was drying against his neck.

Slowly, he stood and began the walk home. Each step was agonizing, jostling his ribs, his legs also bruised from the assault.

The sun had fully set behind the mountains by the time he made it home. His sister came running from the house when he approached. "Rovin, what happened?"

Rovin held out a hand to ward her off. "I'm fine, Cessie."

"Legends above, Rovi, you're covered in blood and bruised to shit." Her tone was harsh, but only to cover the worry. "Let me help you."

She tried to dip under one of Rovin's arms to help him walk, but he cried out when his arm was raised, the pain in his ribs making his vision fade momentarily.

"Momma! Momma, come help!" she called.

Their mother came running from the house, and they helped Rovin get inside, sitting him down at the kitchen table to tend to his wounds.

"What happened, Rovin?" Loran asked, her voice tight as she tried to hold back tears, washing blood from his face and neck with a wet cloth and trembling hands.

Rovin looked at his mother, tears filling his eyes. "What am I?"

"Oh, honey." Her face crumpled, and she shook her head.

With an agonized hiss, Rovin reached his hand up to his ear, now forever marked to set him apart as less-than. "No more bullshit, Ma," he said, his voice cracking.

"I never wanted you to feel different, Rovin. Who your father is makes no difference to the way Cessie and I see you."

Rovin shook his head, tears cutting tracks down the dirt still ground into his cheek. "Why did you make me think I was like them?" Anger seeped into his voice, fueled by pain.

"I wanted to protect you," Loran answered quietly.

Rovin choked back a scoff, his measured, shallow breaths already excruciating enough. But he still had his anger, and he wrapped himself in it, letting it stave off any other emotions. "Worked well," he replied flatly.

She broke down, still cleaning him up.

Cessie came over with a poultice, setting the bowl on the table. "Let's get your shirt off."

Rovin bit back against the wail that wanted to rip from his throat as he raised his arms to help his sister remove his shirt. "You knew, too, didn't you?" he asked as she slathered the poultice over his back to help reduce the bruising there.

"Does it matter now, Rovi?" Her voice was quiet, subdued.

"You lied to me." Rovin licked his lips, meeting his mother's sad eyes. "My whole life, you lied to me."

"I'm so sorry," Loran cried softly. "I love you so much. I never wanted to hurt you."

Guilt at his mother's and sister's tears battled the fury that burned in Rovin's blood. He loved them, and he knew they'd only wanted what was best for him, but they had left him weak and vulnerable and unable to protect himself. He was hurt and confused, and everything threatened to overwhelm him.

"I know, Ma," he said eventually. The carefree innocence of youth had been stripped from him, and something in his soul hardened, as did the warm depths of his brown eyes.

It took roughly a month for Rovin's ribs to heal. The injuries were nasty, but his half-fae blood did hold some accelerated healing ability. While he healed, he seethed, holding Courten's words in his heart, wrapping himself in the scorn of the other boys. He replayed the interaction over and over again, anger fueling his every heartbeat. He swore that he would never be bested again. Would never let himself be vulnerable. As soon as he was able to raise his arms without pain, he began to train.

Rovin ran, chopped wood, swam in the river, climbed trees, perfected his balance and control of his body. He knew it would be hard to find someone in the town to teach him combat, so he schooled himself in every other way he could. And two years later, when he turned sixteen, he kissed the cheeks of his mother and sister and left for Umbra to join the Royal Guard.

Rovin Arwood may have been a bastard halfling, but he didn't need magic to be stronger, faster, better than his peers, and he was going to prove to everyone that he was a force to be reckoned with.

Chapter 4

THE JOURNEY BACK TO Umbra was slow and wet. Merriam had decided to alter their route so that they could stay the night at an inn in lieu of trying to set up tents on the muddy mountainside, which lengthened the trip.

Ryddan spent the majority of the time as a mallard, sitting contentedly on the back of Bellamy's horse as water rolled from his feathers and occasionally flying ahead to splash around in puddles or waddle after a beetle or two.

I'm sleepy, he Cast to Merriam, little duck head bobbing up and down with the movement of the horse.

Merriam sighed, but motioned him over. *If you pick something smelly, I'll throw you into the trees.*

With a move somewhere between a hop and a glide, Ryddan landed in front of Merriam before shifting into a small, furry creature. He crawled beneath Merriam's cloak, long body curling around her neck inside her hood. *I could also be a snake,* he offered.

Merriam snorted, tilting her head to brush her cheek against his soft fur. "I'm a fan of the marten, actually."

I'm a stoat, Ryddan corrected, little voice grumpy with exhaustion.

"My apologies, princeling." Merriam rolled her eyes.

Ryddan's breathing evened out within moments, his animal instincts associating Merriam's rain and wildflower scent with safety and his child's mind knowing the same.

It had been dark for several hours by the time the group made it to Umbra. Clouds blotted out any light the moons and stars would have given, the buildings of the town proper dark, looming shapes around them.

"Feels a bit ominous, don't you think?" Bellamy remarked quietly, pulling his horse up next to Merriam's. "I know it's late, but the city just feels so quiet and empty."

Merriam shrugged, looking up to where light shone from the ramparts of the castle. Ryddan shifted with her movement, little claws scraping against her skin. "I think most things feel a bit foreboding when you're tired."

Bellamy's lips lifted in half a smile that pulled at the scar running down his face. "I hope you're right, Marshal."

"You're too superstitious for your own good sometimes, Bell."

"It's kept me alive this long," he replied companionably before pulling ahead again, picking up the pace to let the Guard know they were back.

Contentment stirred in Merriam's veins with recognition of Mollian's proximity, and she sighed, closing her eyes and reaching out for that sense of him in her mind.

Lydia was waiting at the stables, alert but sleep still in her eyes. She'd been woken, at her request, when the party returned. Ryddan was her charge, and it made her nervous to think of the interruption to routine the past several days had been. She hadn't been invited to Entumbra with them, and she hadn't felt it had been her place to ask. By the look Merriam had given her when she'd handed the marshal a stack of things to keep Ryddan on track with his lessons, Lydia knew there was little chance the curriculum had been followed.

She sighed. Routine was so very important for a child, but she had no doubts about who would win if she tried to argue the point with

Merriam.

The marshal slid from her horse, landing in a puddle that sent mud splashing against her boots.

Lydia cringed at the dirty droplets spotting Merriam's legs, quickly fixing her features into a smile when she met the girl's eyes.

Merriam reached into her hood, gently removing the sleeping prince from her neck. "I assume you're here for this?" she asked. The stoat's form drooped slightly between her outstretched hands, small chest rising and falling, undisturbed.

Lydia bit the inside of her cheek to hold back a comment about his form. She felt it was proper for the prince to remain a fae aside from the times when he was being instructed in magic, when a specific animal was strictly necessary, or *occasionally* during play. Her heart softened, thinking of how tired the poor child must have been, though, and she reached to take him, cradling him to her chest. She squirmed slightly when he yawned, showing small, sharp teeth, and curled against her. "A rodent was an interesting choice."

Merriam laughed. "A mustelid, actually. Same family as badgers and wolverines." Her grin widened at the startled look that came over Lydia's face. "The stuff you and Mordecai sent with him is on one of the packhorses. I'm sure the stablehands will have it sent up. I didn't check over any of it, but all the worksheets should be completed."

Lydia's jaw dropped open slightly. "Oh, yes, thank you. I'll have that sorted out."

Merriam nodded cordially, stepping away. "Good night, then."

"Good night," Lydia replied.

Merriam pulled her personal bag from the back of her horse, slinging it over her shoulder as she walked up to Bellamy. "I'm going to head up if you don't need me."

"We've got it handled," he assured her.

"Okay. I hope some of those heebie-jeebies have worn off now that you're back home." Merriam smiled, poking him in the ribs.

"You're a little shit." Bellamy pushed her shoulder before pulling her into his side. "Go get some sleep. You look exhausted."

"Right back at ya, Belly." She pulled away, walking backwards between the stalls. "Your girl's waiting outside."

Bellamy's brows pulled low over his eyes. "Don't tease, it's mean."

"Her knight in shining armor." Merriam winked, spinning around to head up to the castle.

"Nobody gets your Earth fairytale references!" he called after her, tossing his hair behind his shoulders before continuing to help unload everything.

Merriam felt every ache from the long ride with more intensity the closer her body got to her bed. She made it to a side door, fumbling with the latch as a tall Ranger rounded the corner.

"Back so soon?"

Merriam turned her attention back to the door, heat crawling up her cheeks. She didn't need to see the deep brown eyes or thick chestnut waves shrouded by the hood of his cloak to recognize the one ceaseless irritation in her life. Because of Aleah and Kodi's dalliances, she'd spent more time in his presence in the last year than she would have thought previously bearable. If she was honest with herself, though, she didn't hate it. Their time in forced proximity had evolved into a challenge to see who could get further under the other's skin, and she took great pride in winning. But she was entirely too tired for whatever game he was ready to play, and told herself the blush on her cheeks was only due to the way he'd caught her struggling. "Not soon enough," she bit out, jerking at the handle. The door moved only the smallest amount before sticking against the jamb.

Rovin walked closer, an amused smile on his lips. "It's swollen from the rain," he pointed out, reaching to help.

He was close enough for Merriam to see his face now, and she tugged her hands back as his fingers brushed hers. "Thanks for the science lesson."

Ignoring the sarcastic remark, Rovin thumbed the latch and pulled. He was barely able to restrain a grunt of effort, but the door came free. "Should talk to someone about replacing it," he offered, finally looking down at her.

Merriam met his eyes for a few heartbeats longer than necessary before turning away, forcing a huff of exasperation. "Any other maintenance requests you want me to run up the chain for you, Ranger-man?" Her shoulder brushing his chest as she squeezed past him.

"Not at all, Marshal. Enjoy your night." He dipped his head in mock deference before turning to resume his patrol.

Merriam pulled the door shut behind her, having to throw all of her weight into it to get the latch to catch. She powered up the stairs, pushing the encounter to the back of her mind with concentrated effort, and gave a sleepy wave to the guards posted outside of the door to the quarters she shared with Mollian.

They let her by with a silent nod, and she walked into the large receiving room. She dropped her bag unceremoniously on a couch before bending down to unlace her boots so she could toe them off, kicking them underneath a small table. Entering her bedroom, she peeled off her dirty clothes, still damp from the rain, and tossed them into a basket in a corner.

After brushing her teeth and splashing water over her face, she briefly contemplated her hair, but waved off her reflection in the mirror. The braid would last.

She tugged a clean shirt over her head as she walked from her room, treading across the lush carpet runner to Mollian's door. She navigated the room in the dark, clouds still blocking the light from the sky. But she moved on muscle memory, easily finding her side of the bed.

Merriam slipped underneath the blankets, her eyes sliding closed even as she slithered across the cool sheets to the warmth at the center of the bed.

A sigh escaped her when she felt him, his presence settling something restless inside her. Merriam pressed her forehead against Mollian's shoulder, some of his magic spilling from him, mingling with the magic in her Bonded blood, stretching like a contented cat before it returned, curling up again inside the king.

Merriam wouldn't have been able to explain the feeling to anyone, or how she knew what it was—it was just a part of her Bond with Mollian and a part of the way his power had grown since he'd been crowned.

Mollian shifted, pressing his body closer to her.

She sighed again, stretching out next to him and falling into an easy sleep.

Mollian's left arm was completely numb when he woke up the next morning. "Ria," he grumbled, shaking her.

She'd ended up with her back against his side, her head pillowed on his shoulder and his arm clasped in both of hers. He would have been able to feel her eyelashes flutter against his arm if he'd had any blood circulating there.

He shook her again, kicking at her feet.

An angry grumble crawled up her throat, but she rolled away—over his dead arm—to face him. Her eyes opened just long enough to shoot him a glare before slipping closed again.

I missed you, too, he Cast, sitting up and attempting to shake out his arm.

Breakfast? came her sleepy reply.

Mollian snorted. "Of course, Your Highness. I have some meetings scheduled this morning. Are you ready to jump back into things?"

Merriam sighed, forcing her eyes open. "What kind of meetings?"

Mollian shrugged, raising his arms in a stretch before flexing the tingling fingers of his left hand. "I launched the train proposal while you were away. We're going to reconvene today."

"Oh, lovely. How much will you hate me if I decide I need the morning off?"

"I could never hate you, Ria." Mollian gave her a pointed look as he dropped his legs over the side of the bed. "But I would take my soul back."

A bark of laughter escaped Merriam. "How do you know it's your soul we share and not mine?"

Mollian, his back to Merriam as he walked toward his bathroom, raised his fingers and pulled the pillow from under her head. "Everyone knows the soul belongs to the one with magic."

Merriam made it out of bed by the time Mollian had gotten dressed. "I sent down for food," she told him before moving to her bathroom to fully bathe and wash her hair. When she emerged, Mollian was already sitting at the small dining table in one corner of the room.

"I waited for you." He waved her over, starting in on his plate before she even scooted her chair in.

Merriam raised a brow as she looked at him. "How gracious of you, Lord King."

Mollian flashed her a grin, brushing a curl from his forehead with the back of a hand. "How is my mother?"

"As infuriating as ever." Merriam used a fork to scoop eggs onto a piece of toast, recounting the conversation they'd had about Ryddan between bites.

Mollian crossed his arms over his chest, leaning back in his chair. "She's not wrong. She probably only has around a hundred years left to live. It sounds like a lot in theory, but someone has to be able to take charge of Entumbra after that." He ran his tongue over his teeth.

Merriam offered a small smile, knowing he didn't want to volunteer himself as Entumbra's keeper. "We have time. Ryddan has time. Now, get me up to speed on everything going on with the railroad."

Mollian explained the qualms each individual had expressed about building a track between Do Lech and Umbra and eventually connecting other major towns, but Merriam was still unprepared for the tension and animosity heavy in the war room when everyone once again assembled to discuss the issue.

"All I'm saying is we don't know what sort of impact this would end up having on the environment long term," the forestrymaster insisted, his arms folded defensively across his chest.

"It will be built along the roads that already exist, Portimer." Graigory ran a hand over his short brown hair in exasperation.

"Plus, think of the impact this will have on commerce!" the trademaster argued in favor, leaning forward.

"Trade won't matter if our forests and rivers are poisoned with runoff," Portimer met her eyes pointedly.

"There won't be any poison, Master Portimer," Mollian attempted to appease him. "Steam will be the only element expelled from the engine, and I can assure you nobody will be dumping the ashes left from the charcoal used to boil the water anywhere other than the places outlined by procedure."

Build a railroad, you said, Mollian Cast to Merriam. *It will be fun, you said. Simple.*

And you trusted I knew what I was talking about? Merriam fought back a smile.

The different guildmasters continued to argue back and forth, most of them excited by the plan, but the few with concerns loud and adamant to be heard.

"You know I'm in favor of moving forward, Your Majesty," the coinmaster spoke up. "But where in Do Lech would you build the station? Umbra has space, but Do Lech's docks are filled. Would it be outside the city?"

"I'm already in the process of discussing these possibilities with Over-seer Kinbriar," Mollian answered. "I'll be sending delegates to Do Lech once we have things mostly sorted out here, but Spiro is aware of the proposal."

Ferrick watched the king shift uncomfortably, the young fae unused to being so deep in politics. His lip twitched as he fought back a smile, amused at Mollian's discomfort. Nothing nefarious, he assured himself; it was just fun to see him squirm every once in a while. "I can organize a party to travel south, Your Majesty," Ferrick offered. "The Guard can accompany Master Portimer and others who need better eyes on the scene before setting any plans in stone."

"I'll actually be heading the expedition, Pos." Merriam flashed him a saccharine smile to accompany the use of his first name. "But of course you can decide which of the Guard will be joining us."

Ferrick's jaw clenched, irritation flitting across his face at the informal address. He swallowed it down, smiling back and baring the points of his canines. "Of course, Marshal."

The meeting continued on for a while longer, then people started to trickle out, needing to tend to other tasks throughout the day.

Graigory was in the middle of a long-winded discussion with Portimer about where to harvest the lumber for the tracks when Merriam gently cleared her throat, pushing her chair back. "Apologies, Master Graigory, but the king has a full schedule today."

"Oh, of course, don't let me hold you up. We can continue this over supper some evening this week if you'd like, Portimer. You're welcome, too, Your Majesty, Marshal." Graigory turned to each of them in turn.

"I'll check my schedule, Master Graigory," Mollian replied, standing to help gather the papers spread across the table before following Merriam from the room.

Thanks for the save.

I know how much you love the inner workings of government.

Would be a convenient interest to have, what with being king and all. Mollian snorted, dropping his arm over her shoulder.

Merriam sighed, chewing on her lip as they made their way up to the library, where the next appointment was scheduled with the records-master. She hadn't been lying about having places to be. "Has Cruspen still been trying to talk you out of this?"

"He thinks it's a bad idea to remind everyone that I wasn't raised to rule." Mollian shoved his hands into his pockets, blowing a curl from his forehead.

Merriam tilted her head up to look at him, watching his face. "How do you feel about it?"

"He was my brother. I want to honor his memory, and even if it makes the people question my title, I want them all to know his sacrifice." Mollian paused, glancing down to meet her amber eyes. "Thank you for doing this with me."

"I would never make you go through it alone," Merriam replied simply. "I love that you're doing this for him."

Cruspen, the recordsmaster, was already waiting for them in the library. He was as ancient as his title suggested, but he clung to life like a stubborn old goat. Horns curled from his temples, pushing past long, wiry strands of gray hair. "Never wise to keep an old male waiting, Your Majesty," he greeted upon Mollian's entry.

"My apologies, Master Cruspen. I've been trying to get the rest of the guildmasters to agree on this new mode of transportation, and it's going about as smoothly as rolling a wooden crate downhill," Mollian explained as he took a seat across from the fae.

Cruspen just blinked at the king, a small, polite smile on his lips.

Mollian cleared his throat, shifting. "Well, then, where do you want to begin?"

"You have requested to turn your brother into a Legend. I am simply here to record the tale. Once the recordsguild has rewritten it appropriately, it will be sent to you for final approval before being formally published." Cruspen already had a pen and paper in hand, waiting to copy down the details.

Almost three months ago, on the day Oren would have turned thirty and taken the crown, Mollian had formally petitioned the recordsguild to acknowledge Oren as an official Legend. Cementing his brother's place in history would be his final gift. It felt like the smallest "thank you" for his sacrifice, but it was within his power to accomplish, so he'd driven forward with it.

The request had been granted, but even having it fast-tracked by Mollian's title, it had still taken several weeks for the approval, and then an appointment had to be scheduled for the formal recording.

Merriam sat next to her *mehhen,* pulling her knees up to her chest as she listened to him recount what had happened under the mountain almost a year ago to the day. Mollian had been kidnapped by a demon-possessed man named Basta, a trap to get Oren vulnerable. Basta had commanded a lesser demon to possess the crown prince and ordered him to kill Merriam. But Oren had wrested control from the demon, turning on Basta to try to take him out. He'd gotten killed in the process, but Oren's sacrifice had saved Mollian and Merriam, who later killed the demon possessing Basta.

Mollian swallowed past a lump in his throat, staring intently at the carpet beneath his feet. "Without Oren, Nethyl and the power it houses and protects would have fallen into dangerous hands."

Merriam bit her cheek, fingers brushing over the colorful aspen leaves tattooed on her arm, but she noticed that Mollian didn't mention his failed attempt to sacrifice himself to save her and his brother. His magic had been so strong, so overpowering, that her body had almost been compelled by his commands for her to leave, despite the iron chain around her neck meant to protect her from him.

That day had been the first time Mollian had ever attempted to use the full depth of his magic, but he'd been shoving it down for so long that it had taken too much time for him to wrangle it to his will.

Losing Oren had shattered her, but she'd managed to piece together the broken shards of her heart. If Mollian had sacrificed himself to kill the demons and those threads tying her soul to his snapped, she would have forever been a husk of her former self.

Merriam shook herself from her thoughts, just catching the tail end of Cruspen asking for a few clarifying details.

Both the recordsmaster and Mollian were staring at her, and she looked to Mollian in question.

Oren's eyes. Did they change before he died?

"When I was on the ground, and he stood over me ..." Merriam's voice caught, her throat closing up as memories filled her head. She cleared her throat, blinking past the sting of tears in her eyes. "They turned green again before he ran at Basta. Only for a heartbeat. I almost second-guessed what I saw, but I think that's when he slipped back into himself. It had to be," she told Cruspen.

The fae nodded, scrawling along the paper. "Well, I think I have everything I need, Your Majesty."

Mollian took a deep breath, pushing back the tightness in his chest. "Thank you for meeting with me." He bowed respectfully, standing to lead the guildmaster from the library.

PREPARATIONS FOR THE JOURNEY to Do Lech made Merriam wish she had Aleah's mind for organization and planning. Much of her time was spent running from one side of the castle to the next, trying to figure out who needed to accompany her, what sort of paperwork she needed to bring, and countless other details that popped up just when she felt she'd gotten everything under control.

Mollian was still trying to appease each of his guildmasters' and advisors' concerns, while also continuing to run a country. Matters of state didn't stop just because he was trying to implement something revolutionary. After their meeting for Oren's Legendom, the two hardly saw each other at all except in passing.

Three days after her return, Merriam finally sent a bird to the mercs, requesting Aleah's help with planning the trip. She knew her friend's sordid history in Do Lech and had held off on involving her because of it. Aleah had drafted travel and expense forms that the mercenaries used on every job, but Merriam felt uncomfortable asking to use them, considering who she would be visiting. It wasn't until she was about to pull her hair out that she finally broke.

Once the letter was sent off, Merriam wandered through the castle, her feet taking her to the library. She pulled an old favorite from one of the shelves and sank into an overstuffed armchair, but her mind wouldn't fall into the story.

She was uncharacteristically antsy, and it had nothing to do with trains or Do Lech. Merriam looked over at the large, intricate calendar pasted to one wall.

Today marked one full year since Oren's death.

She pulled her feet up onto the chair next to her, fingers drifting to her ankle. Oren had once tied a string around it, promising his love when she had been too frightened to publicly swear hers.

The string had broken a few months back, worn thin and frayed in multiple places from constant wear. She'd brought the string to Mollian, who'd woven it into a hair tie, securing it at the tail of her customary braid.

She still wore it every day, but for some reason, was scared to touch it now. Scared of what feelings that might pull forward.

Merriam had spent weeks consumed by grief after Oren's death. It had taken time to learn how to navigate that grief in a healthy way, to be able to acknowledge the loss and sadness that creeped in at unsuspecting moments and give herself permission to feel those feelings instead of shoving them all down until she could no longer bear their weight.

She knew how to handle her grief, but today she was struggling.

Oren had been her first great love, and she would be perfectly fine if he ended up being her only one. But even though she still missed him, she knew that specific wound had healed over.

Guilt is what kept her from pulling her braid over her shoulder and touching that small token of Oren's love.

Guilt because her heart didn't ache when she opened her eyes and knew he wasn't there.

Guilt because she was able to eat and drink and laugh with her friends when he would never join those circles.

Guilt because she had given her body to others, seeking pleasure regardless of whether or not her heart was in it.

The tattoo between her shoulder blades itched, bringing her back to the present. Not the rune that Bonded her to Mollian, but the one that was offset from it. The one connected to the aspen branch that trailed down her arm. The one blended with Oren's blood.

She shifted in her seat, creating friction against the ink. Being Bonded to him, even if it had taken place after his death, usually brought her comfort. She closed her eyes, holding her breath and focusing on the feel of magic in her veins. Pushing everything else from her mind, she sifted through the feel of Mollian until she sensed the parts that were neither her nor him. Until she felt Oren, underneath everything else, still with her.

Her lungs ached, and she relented, the distinct feel of Oren fleeing as her senses returned to the world around her.

She rubbed at the ache in her chest with a sigh as she reached out for Mollian, knowing he was busy, but wanting the assurance that he was near. He returned a brush against her mind, almost curious in nature, and she softly pushed him away, hoping he understood she was alright.

Merriam didn't know how long it might take for Aleah to get back to her, but she wanted to keep busy. Her initial idea had been to head down to the courtyard and run some drills, but she heard the Guard in the middle of practice and didn't want to interrupt.

As she made her way back to her rooms, she passed the door to the smaller library that doubled as a classroom for the children whose parents lived or worked in the castle.

She smiled at the guard who stood outside of the door and poked her head in, Ryddan's bright green eyes immediately meeting hers from across the room.

An old fae, sleek black hair secured smartly at the nape of his neck, stopped talking at her appearance. "Might I help you, Marshal?" he asked, raising one thin brow.

"Good morning, Mordecai. I need to borrow the prince," Merriam responded.

He blinked at her. "If it can wait, Marshal, we are in the middle of a lesson."

Merriam only blinked back, a polite smile stretching her lips.

Mordecai sighed. "Very well, then. Prince Ryddan, clean up your area before you go."

Where are we going? Ryddan Cast as he stacked his books, walking them over to shove onto a shelf.

For a different kind of lesson, Merriam replied, holding out her hand to him as he approached. "Take a break," she told his guard. "I'll have him back with his classmates for lunch."

Ryddan was so smart and quick to learn that Merriam often forgot how young he truly was. But his small hand clasping hers, filled with childlike trust and curiosity, was a staunch reminder.

Merriam briefly tightened her hold on his little hand, letting the physical touch comfort her even as a need to protect him, and a knowledge that she always would, solidified in her chest.

"What's wrong, Ria?" he asked, straight white hair falling away from his face as he looked up at her.

She smiled at him, sadness limning her amber eyes. Ryddan had picked up the nickname from Mollian, and was the only other person Merriam allowed to address her as such. "I miss Oren," she answered truthfully.

Ryddan pressed his lips together and nodded thoughtfully. "More today?"

"Than usual, yes."

Ryddan's fingers squeezed hers. "Sometimes I miss momma more, too. Are we going somewhere to forget a little bit?"

His emotional maturity hurt Merriam's heart. No child should have had to endure so much. "We are," she answered, squeezing him back. She bit her lip, knowing Lydia would tell her these problems were not meant for a child to bear.

Merriam felt guilty at that, too, not wanting to add any more darkness to what Ryddan had already seen. She would never tell him about the guilt she felt or the depth of her grief over Oren, but she couldn't lie to him, either. Yes, he was just a child, but he was still a person, and she didn't want him to ever doubt whether or not he could trust her.

Merriam and Ryddan walked out into the courtyard and over to a stone bench across from a group of Rangers warming up in a training ring. Merriam sat on the back of it, legs on the seat, and patted the space next to her.

"We're going to watch the Rangers?" Ryddan asked. He stood on the bench, leaning against the backrest. His legs were still too short to sit the way Merriam was. He waved excitedly when Bellamy looked over.

Bellamy waved back before locking eyes with Merriam. He shook his head, an amused pull to his lips. He knew Ryddan hadn't been the one to suggest ditching his classes for the morning. Merriam smiled broadly in return and shrugged in a *what can you do* way.

"There's a lot you can learn from watching how others fight," Merriam explained, brushing Ryddan's hair from his forehead as the Rangers paired up to spar.

Rovin stood to the side as Bellamy and an older Ranger went into the ring. He briefly met Merriam's gaze, cocking an eyebrow in silent invitation. She tipped her head toward Ryddan to decline, and Rovin's attention went back to the ring.

Bellamy wielded a wooden sword, the other two wooden maces with capped tips. Though the weapons were not designed to mortally wound, they could still easily injure.

The two opponents circled each other, the Ranger with the maces swinging first.

Bellamy attempted to block the blow with his sword, leaping back as the other came in for his side. After watching them parry for several moments, Merriam glanced at Ryddan, who watched the duel with a serious expression. "What differences do you see in the way they fight?"

Ryddan's head cocked to the side, eyes never leaving the spar. "The older one is ... you can tell he knows more." Ryddan moved his hands around as he searched for the right word. "Or like he thinks he knows more about what he's doing?"

"He's confident," Merriam offered.

Ryddan nodded. "He's more confident in what he does. He doesn't pause much before he moves. Belly is paying more attention. He watches more closely and is trying to guess what the other will do and how best to react to it."

"You couldn't be more accurate," Merriam said proudly, watching as Bellamy almost got a leg up on the older Ranger before being knocked to his back.

The other Ranger kicked his sword from his hand and lowered a mace to Bellamy's throat.

Rovin called the match, and the Ranger helped Bellamy to his feet, clapping him on the back.

Sweat dripped from Bellamy's face, soaking the neckline of his shirt. His hair had been pulled back into a low ponytail, but stray curls escaped, sticking to his cheeks.

Rovin handed them both a cup of water, debriefing the fight and giving pointers to both fae, loud enough for the rest of the Guard watching to hear.

Merriam and Ryddan watched a few more rounds, Merriam asking questions and pointing out smaller details to the prince, who observed studiously.

Rovin eventually stepped into the ring to spar, twirling a short sword in his fingers as he set his feet for the fight. He let his opponent attack first, countering easily.

"Will Rovin tire himself out faster with how much more he has to move? His weapon is so much smaller than the broadsword." Ryddan had perched up on the seat back next to Merriam, kicking his feet as he watched the spar.

Merriam shook her head, eyes trained on the ring. "Rovin's weapon of choice has always been a short sword. Yes, it limits his reach, but watch." She gestured with her chin to the lieutenant, muscles flexing under the exposed skin of his arms as he stepped in close, swinging his practice sword up in a would-be-deadly arc.

The other Ranger jumped back, the wooden tip of the sword still raking across his side hard enough to break skin. He doubled down on his efforts against Rovin, pushing back with a volley of blows that Rovin smoothly blocked.

"He uses a short sword because it allows him to get in closer to his opponent. Once he has a grasp of their strengths and weaknesses, he can maneuver inside their reach to better exploit them."

"Is that awe in your voice, Ria?" Mollian's voice, filled with amusement, washed over her.

"Only appreciation for the craft," Merriam insisted, even as her cheeks flushed. "Don't you have royal business to attend to, Lord King?"

Mollian stepped up to her side, draping an arm across her shoulders. "Isn't checking up on the training of my Rangers royal business?"

Merriam continued to watch the practice ring as Rovin knocked the weapon from the other's hand and pinned him on his back in one fluid motion. "It is, but hovering around to make sure I'm not about to fall apart isn't."

I feel weird being away from you today, like my skin is too tight. Mollian sighed.

I know. I feel it, too. And antsy, like I'm waiting for something to happen.

Mollian Cast back a slight grunt of agreement, dropping his arm as the Rangers in the clearing slowly started to notice his presence.

Rovin, who'd just finished helping up the bested Ranger, stood at attention and saluted. "Your Majesty, I wasn't expecting you," he called.

"I apologize for dropping in unannounced. I had a few moments to spare and wanted to check in on my nephew." Mollian waved for Rovin and the others to continue.

Ryddan glanced up at Mollian with a suspicious expression, opening his mouth to speak before turning his eyes to Merriam. She gave him a slight shake of her head, a smile pulling at her lips, and he turned his eyes back to the ring. "Ria was explaining to me about the fighting and why the weapons matter," he told Mollian.

"Well, that seems an appropriate lesson for a six-year-old," Mollian joked.

Ryddan again flicked his eyes to Merriam cautiously, but her lips were pressed together, fighting back a smile. Ryddan shrugged, tipping his head back to look at Mollian. "Belly doesn't think I should be watching fighting so much, but Ria says the more comfortable I am with it, the easier it will be for me to learn when I'm older. Because combat is a skill required of a prince."

"And where are your assigned tutors for this morning?" Mollian asked as Rovin stepped from the ring, two more Rangers taking positions to fight.

"Mordecai has other children to focus on," Merriam answered for the boy, turning to face Mollian. "I thought a little time outdoors would be good for him, plus he could learn something a little more exciting than arithmetic."

"I like arithmetic," Ryddan mumbled as he watched the sparring Rangers.

I needed something to keep my mind occupied. He's enough of a handful that I don't have much time for introspection.

I think I'm going to clear off my schedule for the rest of the day. I can't concentrate, anyway.

Merriam nodded. "Rydd's classmates should be ready for lunch by the time the Rangers are finished. I'll find you then."

Mollian raised his hand, and Merriam pressed her palm to his, feeling his magic stir in her veins. "I'll arrange for dinner to be sent up for us tonight. Have you reached out to Jasper today?"

Merriam shook her head meekly. "No, I haven't yet. I'll send him a message. I haven't seen any of them since I've been back, actually. I'll probably visit them tomorrow."

"At the merc house? Can I come, too?" Ryddan asked eagerly.

"Maybe for a bit. We'll have to convince Lydia it's a good idea, though," Merriam answered.

Ryddan's eyes, pupils vertically slit, shone conspiratorially. "Have Belly come with us! She won't say no if he comes to take me away." Merriam covered her mouth with her hand to stifle her laughter. Ryddan smiled at the reaction, spurred on. "She makes eyes at him all the time."

Mollian ruffled his nephew's hair. "Don't tease her, it's mean."

"She doesn't know I know. She thinks I'm just a child." Ryddan slapped Mollian's hand away, grinning.

"You *are* just a child, buddy, and that doesn't excuse you from being nice to those who care about you." Mollian gave him a stern look before raising his cracked green eyes to Merriam. "Don't egg him on," he warned, pointing a finger at her.

Merriam gave him an appalled look. "Your lack of faith in my morals wounds."

"I'm sure it does." Mollian grinned at her before walking away.

Ten years before …

Droplets of blood spattered against the floor, gleaming brightly in the sunlight that poured through the open window.

The young prince casually slid a foot to the side to cover the evidence, clenching his fist in his lap in an effort to stop the flow of blood. He held a pencil in his other hand, lightly tapping the end against his chin as he studied the paper in front of him.

A fae with sleek black hair tied back smartly at the nape of his neck walked into the room. "How are we doing in here?"

Mollian made a final mark before glancing up with a bright smile. "Just finished!"

"Prince Mollian, what is in your lap?"

Hoping the cut on his palm had had enough time to start to clot, Mollian placed his hand on the desk, still curled into a loose fist. White curls spilled into his eyes when he tilted his head to the side in question, giving a clear view of the aspen branch tattooed on his temple.

Pinching the bridge of his nose in exasperation, the scholar used magic to raise the items from Mollian's lap, letting them fall to the desktop with a soft clatter. "Now is not the time for creative arts, Your Highness," he said with a sigh. His lips pressed into a thin line as he eyed the tools now spread in front of the prince: thin blades and chisels used for carving and a large hunting knife.

Mollian shrugged, examining his palm which had, indeed, stopped bleeding freely. "I finished early." And cut himself on the exceptionally sharp blade scooping everything into his lap when he'd heard his instructor's footsteps in the hall.

Mordecai sighed again. "I thought we had agreed you would let me know when you were done so we could move on to the next assignment. Maybe find something that would present more of a challenge, if you need it?"

"I know, but I wanted to work on this while the idea was fresh," Mollian offered, pale green eyes, one shot through with brown, shining innocently.

"A time and a place, Prince." Mordecai shook his head. "Why have you been so distracted these past few weeks? You have always loved science."

"I'm not," he answered, intending to elaborate until he heard a familiar gait coming down the hall. *Help me!* he Cast.

His brother came up to the door, leaning casually against the frame. One side of his head was shaved, but thick, white waves fell freely down the other, brushing his shoulder. "How much longer do you need him, Mordecai?"

The scholar turned around at Oren's voice, inclining his head respectfully. "We still have a couple of hours scheduled, but of course I can fit those lessons into tomorrow's plan if need be."

Oren smiled pleasantly. "Only if it's not too much of a hassle."

"Of course not, Your Highness."

"Pack up your shit, little brother. We've got places to be," Oren said, pushing off the doorframe.

Mollian smiled, shooting Mordecai an apologetic glance paired with a shrug. He pulled the small case for his tools and a sheath for the knife from a shelf across the room with a flick of his fingers. Attaching both to his belt, he stood and followed Oren down the hall.

"You owe me, princeling." Oren mussed a hand through Mollian's curls before dropping an arm over his shoulders.

Mollian ducked free with a laugh. "I'd say this one makes us even, if anything."

The difference between the two princes was always evident. Even as they walked down the hall, Oren was acknowledged by every person they passed, whether it be verbally or with a simple nod of the head, and he received it all with a quiet grace.

Mollian could never handle that level of attention nor receive it with such dignity.

He was treated with the utmost respect, but he was also able to wander the castle without much notice, and, when Oren was around, almost blended into the background. Being the heir apparent threw Oren into a spotlight that he thrived in, a spotlight Mollian was exceedingly thankful he never had to perform under.

"I think I found something that can get you out of the castle for at least a few weeks," Oren said, leading Mollian up to his chambers.

Mollian perked up, magic rolling through him in response to the hope that flared in his chest. He swallowed, pushing the magic down with concentrated effort.

Once in his chambers, Oren grabbed a map from his desk and brought it over to the couch where he'd gestured for Mollian to sit. Unrolling it on the table before them, he placed a paperweight at each end and ran a finger down the lines drawn across the map of Sekha. "One of the ley lines in West Eyko is leaching. It's only a trickle, but the warding could use some patching up."

"Do you think I can make it out to the coast?" Mollian asked, eyes scanning the map before flicking up to meet Oren's.

"As your future king, I'd say it would be irresponsible not to run the whole track just to be safe." Oren smiled, sitting back.

Mollian looked back down to the map, committing the ley line to memory so he could cross-reference it with the map he kept in his chambers, slowly marking off every area he'd already looked for her.

His *mehhen.*

Not that he was sure of it, not yet, but he was confident enough that he'd bet his ability to Travel on it.

Five years had gone by since the last time he'd seen the human girl. Five years of finding every excuse to visit Earth, the reality parallel to the one in which he lived. Five years of feeling the threads of his soul that were bound to hers, shared with her, pulled taut and aching with her absence. Five years of his magic pushing, restless inside of him as it grew without an outlet.

Oren saw the hope shining in his brother's eyes, and his heart ached. He remembered clearly the day a young Mollian had bounded into his rooms, excitedly chattering about the girl he'd met in the woods.

He'd been annoyed at first. Time and time again, he had told Mollian not to Travel alone. It was dangerous; he didn't understand the power of the Gate yet—neither of them did. Not only that, but Mollian had glamored her, when she didn't even know enough to understand that she needed protection against magic and the sort of control Mollian was capable of having over her.

As Keepers, the only beings in their universe capable of wielding the power held by the Gate that connected every reality, the Stonebanes were capable of stronger magic than most high fae. Even so, Oren sometimes suspected his brother's abilities were outside that realm of explanation. Mollian had learned to suppress it at a young age, but Oren was perceptive and had spent enough time with him to know the younger prince had to put forth a more concentrated effort to corral his magic than anyone else in their family.

Because of this, knowing Mollian was sneaking off to Earth and using magic around unsuspecting, uneducated humans had scared him. Mollian was a sweet kid and mild-tempered, but it was hard to tell if he understood the depth of his power or how to use it without unleashing its full strength.

But Oren had also known better than to order him not to return or to take the rings Mollian used to Travel, stolen from Entumbra when they'd gone to visit their sister. Mollian would find a way regardless, and if he was doing something potentially dangerous, Oren would rather Mollian feel comfortable telling him.

Oren's fears were for naught, though. Mollian had Traveled to meet with the girl almost every day that entire summer, and it grew more and more clear from his tales of their adventures that Mollian was very aware of his ability to hurt her and would do everything in his power to keep her from harm.

If those old fears had ever crept back up, they were completely dispelled when Mollian had come to him at ten years old, asking him for help commissioning a piece of jewelry much more delicate than the weapons he was always decorating. A simple iron aspen leaf—the symbol of Sekha, but also the symbol of the Stonebanes, Mollian's own way of claiming the girl as family—on an iron chain. A gift that would protect her from any of the mind tricks Mollian's magic would be able to play on her.

Oren knew, then, that Mollian understood the depth of his power to some extent, and he also knew that if his brother had been born anyone else—anyone but pure, enthusiastic Mollian—every world would have been in grave danger.

The bond between the fae prince and the human girl was also undeniable. Even five years after last seeing her, Mollian constantly searched for her. Oren helped where he could. If there was a chance this girl was his brother's *mehhen*, he would need her. Now that their souls knew each other, it was too late to go back. Her proximity would act as a reserve for the magic he tried so desperately to shove down and help him keep a hold on it without it overpowering him.

"Have you told our parents? Am I allowed to go?" Mollian looked up, cracked green eyes bright with excitement.

"Not yet. I was actually on my way to talk to them about it when you called. I wanted to clear it with them first before I told you, just in case, but I can't see why they would deny it."

Mollian nodded, his fingers digging into the cushion on either side of him, making the cut on his palm sting. It had been well over half a year since he'd been able to leave Umbra for an extended period of time, and he was antsy to continue searching. "When do you think we'll go?"

"It's possible we'll be able to leave tomorrow." Oren rolled the map up, slapping it in his palm a couple times before standing. "I'd have you tag along while I talk to Mother, but she might question why you're done with your lessons so early."

"That's okay, I can start packing. And I should probably deal with this." Mollian raised his hand to show Oren the wound. "Accidentally nicked myself with a hunting knife."

Oren rolled his eyes, reaching over to muss Mollian's curls. "Weapons aren't toys, brother."

Mollian swatted his hand away, grinning up at the crown prince. "Not toys, Oren. Art."

Oren laughed. "Art and destruction."

Mollian followed Oren from the room, parting ways to hurry down the steps, throwing open the door to his chambers and heading into his bathroom. He rifled around under the sink for ointment and a bandage, supplies he pilfered from the medics due to his weapon-modification hobby. After cleaning and wrapping the cut on his hand, he moved to the spare room on the other side of his chambers. One entire wall was taken up by maps: one labeled "Sekha" and one labeled, in a human language, "The United States of America."

The majority of Jekeida, the inner territory of Sekha, was shaded in along with parts of North and East Audha and North and East Eyko. Similarly, the entire square of Colorado had little x's drawn over every city. Most of the middle was covered, cities and towns crossed off as far north as Minnesota and as far east as Kentucky, with other marks sporadically stretching out all the way to North Carolina on the east coast and up through Idaho and Montana to the west. The marks on the southern half of either country were few and far between, as well as the marks on either country's west coast.

Mollian pursed his lips in frustration as he surveyed how much area he hadn't been able to search yet. Traveling wasn't teleportation. He couldn't open a portal to any place he wanted and hop through, he could only move through realms. Whatever spot he was in on Nethyl would be the same spot he landed in on Earth or any other world he visited. With his blood, he could choose any reality imaginable to Travel to, but he couldn't choose *where* in that reality to go.

But lamenting the limitations of his magic wouldn't help anything, so Mollian pushed the thoughts aside.

Picturing the map of the ley lines, Mollian ran his finger over the map of Sekha, tracing the path he remembered through the mountains of his country. Then he stepped over, tracing the same path through the western side of America. The leak was in the area parallel to southern Nevada, but the lines ran all the way to the coast. He looked at the names of the cities near to the path or close enough to detour to. All new, none that he'd been able to search before.

He brushed an errant curl from his forehead, pressing his uninjured palm to the map. His soul ached, stretched taut but unable to lead him directly to her, only able to tell him that she was nowhere near.

"I'm coming, Ria. I'll find you," he promised.

AFTER EATING DINNER ON the floor of their common room, Merriam and Mollian got drunk on sparkling wine. After each sip, they shared with each other the things they held in their hearts. Though they both knew how the other felt, sensed it in the way their souls were tied together, they spoke the words aloud, setting them free into the universe.

They voiced their regrets first.

Merriam took a long swig, wiping the back of her hand across her mouth when she had finished. "I wish I had let myself love him more loudly."

Mollian took the bottle from her and tipped it back. "I wish I had gone to see him more when he was in Entumbra."

"I wish I had told him I would marry him." Merriam finally pulled the end of her braid over her shoulder, tracing over the tie that held Oren's token of love.

The two continued like that until most of the bottle had been consumed. But once their regrets and guilts were spoken, they moved on to happier memories, neither willing to let the other dwell in the darkness of the past.

Merriam popped open another bottle, sipping from it as Mollian told a story from their childhood. "You should have seen the look on Mordecai's face. There were frogs hopping around the castle for weeks after that. Oren hadn't meant for them to get loose. I'm not sure how he even managed to gather them all, because he was absolutely horrible at wrangling them back up."

Merriam passed the wine to him, bursting out into laughter as Mollian Cast her an image from his memory: a young Oren chasing frogs around, trying to use his magic to pluck them up or keep them still long enough to grab them. The ability to share images along with words was unique to the two of them and something she didn't take for granted in times like this.

Merriam told her own stories of the times she visited Oren in Entumbra, when the depth of their friendship truly grew. As she talked, she Cast her memories to Mollian. Oren's eyes lit with excitement as he shared with her a new discovery of one of the worlds he'd visited most often. Oren sitting on the mountainside, drinking a Shirley Temple for the first time after Merriam convinced him to Travel to Earth with her for one of her favorite childhood treats. Oren teasing her and listening to her troubles and offering to train with her.

They finished the second bottle, and Mollian reached to open a third.

"Wait." Merriam put her hand over his, searching his face.

Concern flitted across Mollian's face at her serious expression before he caught the mischievous gleam in her amber eyes.

"Do you want to do something fun?" she asked, her tongue flicking out to wet her lips.

Mollian tilted his head to the side, a white curl falling over his brow. "Why do I get the feeling that whatever you're about to suggest is potentially reckless?"

A slow smile spread across Merriam's face, and she leaned back with a shrug. "Aren't all the best adventures a little reckless?"

"What do you have in mind?"

Merriam pushed to her feet, reaching with both hands to pull Mollian up after her. "Bring the wine," she ordered with a grin, letting go of one of his hands to drag him by the other out the door.

The guards posted outside exchanged a concerned glance, unsure of whether to follow or stay at their post.

On drunken instinct and feeling like he was sneaking out, Mollian hid the wine behind his back, flashing a reassuring smile. The points of his canines dimpled into his bottom lip.

"Your presence won't be necessary," Merriam said, holding Mollian's hand behind her back as if to hide him on that same inebriated instinct. "We won't be leaving the castle."

The guards looked to Mollian, who saluted them with two fingers, the neck of the bottle held by his ring finger, pinky, and thumb. One shrugged as the *mehhen* walked off, Merriam pulling Mollian along excitedly.

"Is this the kind of activity the captain wanted in our reports?" the younger of the two asked when the king and his marshal had disappeared down the hallway.

The older pursed his lips in contemplation. "I suppose it's better to be safe than sorry," he finally decided.

The guards needn't have worried about whether or not to report Mollian's sudden departure to Captain Ferrick, because, as luck would have it, he was walking through the courtyard.

Eskar, one of his Rangers, had been promoted to commander a few months back and promptly left on her first mission. She'd been sent to one of the major ports in East Eyko to conduct a routine inspection on the Guard there as well as a few outposts along the way and had just returned earlier that week. Ferrick had finally found the time to meet with her for a debrief earlier that evening.

He'd planned his schedule to only allow for an evening brief on purpose. Eskar, like all of his commanders, was a stickler for procedure and following protocol. But she was also intelligent, motivated, and ambitious. Above all, she was attracted to power, which was something

Ferrick had no shortage of.

The captain was well aware that it was mostly his political stance that held appeal to her. There were no feelings involved between them other than what one could do for the other, and he appreciated that.

He also appreciated her tight cunt and the way she worked him with her mouth. Ferrick had missed their trysts while she was gone and had been perhaps a little more ... enthusiastic than usual after their official meeting. His lips quirked in a smile as he pictured the bruises his hands had left on her body, and his own arms burned slightly where she'd scratched him when he'd gotten too rough. The fire in her eyes had been intoxicating, and he'd made her lick the blood from his arms before he'd let her come. Power was a renewable resource, meant to be wielded at every opportunity; that was his motto.

The captain now made his way back to his private quarters behind the Rangers' barracks. He preferred living on the castle grounds because it made it easier for him to stay privy to everything that was happening and ensured he could more easily keep his hand in most decisions.

A soft giggle reached his ears, and he stopped, tilting his head slightly to one side to better gauge where the noise had come from.

There was a "Shhh!" followed by another, louder giggle from above, and Ferrick quietly moved further from the castle, his gaze traveling up the side of the structure. He stood far enough back that he could see the sloped roof of one of the lower spires.

Merriam and Mollian lay on their backs, knees bent and feet planted against the flat shingles of the roof. Merriam held a bottle in one hand, the other pointing up into the cloudless sky. Mollian followed the pattern she traced through the air, his arms tucked underneath his head. He turned to whisper something with a grin before reaching to take the bottle from her and sitting up slightly to drink.

Merriam's hand dropped to cover her mouth, her body shaking with laughter.

Ferrick's eyes narrowed as he watched them. The moonlight shone brightly off Mollian's white hair, the dark lines of his crown distinct against the light brown of his skin, but the shape indiscernible from this distance. He watched Merriam's face grow serious as she turned to the king, whispering indistinctly.

Mollian nodded, his gaze on the stars as he listened.

Up on the rooftop, oblivious to the captain watching below, the wine buzzing in Merriam's veins encouraged her to share her fears. "I've been thinking about the trip to Do Lech, and I'm nervous about the potential perception. I know that most people here accept me, have watched me prove myself to the kingdom, but stories and their truths only travel so far, Molli. I know you have things to take care of here, but how will the overseers of Do Lech take having to receive instructions and conduct negotiations with a twenty-five-year-old human?"

Mollian looked at the person who held half of his soul, emotion rolling through his chest as he reached for her hand. "You are the only person in all of the worlds who I can trust to speak for me. They'll know we're *mehhen*, and they'll have to trust in your reputation. The Guard that goes with you will be people who have fought alongside you, and they'll spread those stories until everyone knows how much you've done for Sekha."

"I don't want them to think you're weak and impressionable. You are king in your own right."

Mollian smiled. "A king who doubted his position wouldn't have the balls to send a human to revolutionize his country, would he?"

Ferrick's hands curled into fists, his eyes darting from one to the other and his teeth bared in a silent snarl. He couldn't hear the conversation, but he didn't have to. The human girl had unlimited access to the king, and Ferrick felt with every fiber of his being that it was dangerous.

Most people had to schedule meetings, wait days or even weeks to bring their ideas to the ruler of Sekha. But that human could sidle up to his side in the dead of night, wake him from sleep, and feed him whatever ideas were in that conniving little head of hers. She'd slowly worked her way into Oren's good graces, and Ferrick wouldn't have been surprised if it came out that she'd had a hand in his death, knowing she would always have more influence over Mollian than his brother.

Merriam had found access to a bottomless well of political power, and he knew she'd also taken some of the king's magic for herself as well, harnessing the ability to Travel between realms and realities. Ferrick could almost admire her for how high she'd managed to climb if it wasn't for the fact that she usurped him at every opportunity.

Every bit of control he tried to wield, she did her best to steal from him. She'd managed some level of manipulation over *his* Rangers last year when they were preparing to fight the demons, tricking those in the lower ranks into thinking she was their friend and comrade-in-arms. She'd created a new title for herself, giving her the ability to create taskings for those in the Guard and speak on behalf of the king in matters of state. She'd brought in a *halfling*, parading him around as a prince. Sure, the child's Keeper lineage was undeniable, but he wasn't *fae*.

Most recently, she had named herself head of the expedition to Do Lech to introduce this new mode of transport. Ferrick saw the advantage of such a contraption, but seethed at how little his input and opinion on the matter seemed to be taken into account.

And now Merriam had the king on the roof of the castle, of all places, whispering Legends-only-knew-what in his ear.

Ferrick scoffed, reaching out with his magic. She was far away, but he just might be able to reach her, loosen a few of the shingles beneath her. Magic didn't like to grab onto the living, and even he was able to admit that he'd never be able to coerce it into holding her from such a distance.

Mollian slipped his hand into hers, his brow knit together, and Ferrick pulled back. He wanted to be rid of her, but he knew he would have to be smart about it. For months, he'd been scheming, trying to fool-proof a plan that wouldn't be able to be traced back to him.

The captain continued walking toward his quarters, the wheels of his mind turning. If ... *If* Merriam were to be ripped from the picture, there was an angle for it to happen in a way that would raise Ferrick up in the eyes of the king. If there was ever an extra morsel of power to be had, it was worth the effort to try to attain it.

Ferrick smiled, moonlight glinting off his blue eyes as he slipped indoors.

Chapter 8

MERRIAM SLEPT IN THE next morning. She and Mollian had ended the night with a water-only drinking game, and that, coupled with solid rest, had alleviated whatever hangover might have been brewing.

She stretched, rolling over and letting her legs drop to the floor. The sound of running water filtered through her open doorway, and a light search of her consciousness confirmed that Mollian was close by. She dressed in old training clothes, brushing through her hair and braiding it back.

She threw a change of clothes into a sack before moving into the common room and dropping onto the couch. One of the staff had already brought in a tray of breakfast foods, and Merriam happily dug in.

"Morning, sunshine," Mollian greeted, his curls still damp.

"Good morning. How are you feeling?"

Mollian sat across from her, bracing his feet against the table as he tipped his head back. "I am not looking forward to having to play catch-up from ditching all my responsibilities yesterday."

He pulled a biscuit to his hand with a quick curl of his fingers, taking a bite. "But physically I'm fine. You?"

"Never better." Merriam flashed him a smile. "But that'll probably change in a couple of hours."

"You gonna train with the mercs today?"

Merriam nodded. "We'll more than likely end up going out after, as well. Would you want to join?"

Mollian finished the biscuit, wiping his hand across his pants. "How upset will you be with me if I say no?"

"The heat of my anger would be marginally less than the fiery wrath of a thousand suns," she answered.

Mollian scraped his teeth over his lower lip in thought. "But will you still go to Do Lech to work out all of this train business for me?"

Merriam shrugged noncommittally. "I suppose a commitment is a commitment, plus I still need a job, since you convinced me to quit the mercenary lifestyle and all."

"Very good point. Do you want your old rooms back? I'd hate to make you have to deal with my presence every day."

"That's very thoughtful of you, Lord King. I appreciate it."

Mollian's gaze returned to the ceiling, and he waved a hand indifferently. "Don't mention it. But also don't expect any of my staff to help you relocate your things, either, which I'll want done by the end of the day."

Merriam tossed a grape at his face, and it smacked against his cheek before falling to the floor. Mollian leaned forward to grab a sandwich of meat and eggs before standing and taking a bite. "Thanks for the invite. I'll let you know if I change my mind." He held his free hand out to her.

She pressed her palm to his.

Mollian opened the door, and, without looking at him, Merriam Cast, *Don't forget your sword.*

He paused, raising a hand in thanks before holding the sandwich in his mouth and pulling his weapons belt to him from where it rested against the coffee table. He buckled it around his waist as he walked, the door closing behind him.

When she'd finished with breakfast, Merriam quickly laced up her boots and slung her axes over her hips. She gave the guards posted outside a friendly smile and made her way through Umbra to the mercenary house.

She stopped at a bakery stall along the way, selecting a loaf of sunflower and garlic bread along with a box of assorted muffins. Carefully balancing her goods in one hand, she slipped a key from a pocket on her belt and let herself in the back door.

"You look like trouble," Leonidas greeted when she came down the hall, crossing his brightly tattooed arms over his chest.

Merriam rolled her eyes, pushing past his imposing frame and into the kitchen. "Well, I'll take my treats and leave, then."

Panic greeted her with a screech from his perch.

"Hello, handsome boy!" she cooed, depositing the breads on the counter and dropping her bag to the floor so she could hold her arm out to the falcon.

"What treats?" Leonidas questioned, walking behind her to unwrap the loaf.

Merriam winced involuntarily as Panic lighted on her forearm, the tips of his talons pricking her skin as he figured out his balance. "Jasper's favorite, along with some sweets for the rest of you so Aleah doesn't gut me in my sleep," she answered, stroking Panic's chest with the backs of her fingers.

"Why am I gutting people?" Aleah asked, hopping down from the third step. She bounced back up onto her tiptoes when she landed and craned her neck to peer over Merriam's shoulder to the counter. Her hazel eyes focused on Merriam, and she grinned, skipping over to wrap her in a hug. "You are too good to me, Mer."

Panic let out a short, disgruntled scream at the commotion, slapping the back of Aleah's head with a wing as he went back to his perch.

Aleah pulled away from Merriam before her flame-red hair had even settled, moving to the counter. She pulled back the wrapped loaf, gently shoving it to the side when she saw the sunflower seeds dotting the surface, and opened the box of muffins. "Oh, yes, please." She pulled out a muffin iced with a sweet orange glaze, hopping up to sit on the edge of the counter while she ate.

"So easily appeased," Leonidas teased, poking her in the ribs as he looked over his options.

"Is Jasper around?" Merriam asked.

"Up in the office," Aleah answered through a mouthful.

Merriam headed up the stairs, rapping her knuckles against the door at the top before nudging it open.

"Good morning, Marshal. To what do I owe the pleasure?" Jasper glanced up from his paperwork, waving Merriam into the room.

She walked over to the window, leaning against the sill while Jasper finished reviewing whatever needed his attention. When he was done, he stretched dark, muscular arms over his head, feathered wings flaring.

"I'm sorry I didn't come see you yesterday."

Jasper turned to look at her, pain flashing in his silver eyes along with memories. "I kept purposefully busy, and it was more important for you to spend the day with Mollian."

Merriam shook her head. "You were his brother, too, Jaz. Molli and I aren't the only ones who lost more than just a future king."

Jasper's mind went back to training with the Royal Guard, he and Oren barely more than children. But even then, both of them had dreams of making a difference in Sekha. They'd grown close and had managed to hold on to that friendship despite Jasper's decision to leave the Guard. Oren had never judged him for feeling he needed to do things in his own way; there had only ever been support.

The sting of tears in his eyes brought him back to the present, and he blinked, clearing his throat of emotion before speaking. "Did you talk to the recordsmaster?"

"A few days ago. Oren will be a Legend in his own right before the year's end."

A small smile stretched Jasper's lips. "I'm glad to hear it."

"We can celebrate later with a drink, my treat." Merriam hooked her thumbs through her belt.

"Apology accepted, then." Jasper stood. "I'm assuming by your attire you're planning to use the training room."

"Wouldn't want to lose the edge of all those skills you spent five years helping me hone." Merriam pushed from the windowsill with a smile.

He eyed the well-oiled axes at her hips. "Those are certainly pretty enough to be a decoration."

"If you're jealous of my finery, I can ask the king to spruce up your lance," she said coyly, brushing past him. "Oh, I brought you some sunflower loaf. It's in the kitchen."

"Has anyone told you you're a suck up?" Jasper asked as he followed her down the stairs.

"Not recently," Merriam replied, heading for the training room.

After several rounds of hand-to-hand combat, knife and axe throwing, and scaling up and across the climbing wall, Merriam was tired and drenched in sweat. She'd peeled her shirt off shortly after starting, the material sticking to her back and belly uncomfortably, the fabric of her bra damp from pressing against her skin.

"I both love it and hate it when you come around," Aleah panted, sprawled on the floor and dribbling water over her flushed face. "I swear Jasper runs us harder with you here."

"It just feels that way because Mer always brings sweets, and you don't have the impulse control to wait until later in the day to indulge." Jasper was wiping down the mats underneath the climbing wall and paused to toss a towel at Aleah.

It landed across her face, and she pulled it down with a glare. "I have plenty of impulse control, thank you."

Leonidas snorted, choking on the water he'd been drinking.

Merriam smiled, letting their familiar banter warm her as she hydrated. "I miss you fuckers."

Aleah rolled onto her belly, stretching a freckled arm across the floor in Merriam's direction. "Likewise."

Leonidas, having finished coughing, reached down to ruffle her hair.

Merriam shoved against his leg with a laugh before standing. She grabbed her bag from the floor of the mushroom and dashed upstairs to shower, dressing in her old room and wrapping her hair in a towel before heading downstairs.

The smell of spices and cooking meat hit her as soon as she opened the bedroom door, her mouth instantly watering.

A male with antlers jutting from a head of short, dark curls was in the kitchen, washing off a cutting board.

"Whatever you're doing in here smells like heaven." Merriam leaned against the counter.

"It's just chicken," Campbell replied, but smiled at the compliment. "I heard we're drinking tonight, so I have potatoes baking on the side as well as butter noodles."

"You're a gem, Cam, and don't ever let anyone tell you otherwise."

Calysta, the green-skinned wood nymph, joined them just before supper was ready, having worked a job on the outskirts of town. Though it wasn't often the six of them got to spend an evening together anymore, they very easily fell back into their normal routine and dynamic when it happened. Not only were there years of history among them, but also an undying sense of trust and support, the kind that had been proven in the past and would never fade from the simple passage of time.

True to her word, Merriam bought not just Jasper, but all of the mercenaries their first round of drinks, dedicating it to Oren's memory. Without him, she never would have met these people who'd become her family over the years, and it crossed her mind that she hadn't thanked him enough for that initial push.

Sensing where her thoughts had gone, Jasper reached over to squeeze her knee before clinking his glass to hers.

It only took two rounds for the group to slip into old habits. Leonidas and Jasper remained the ever watchful, responsible ones, while Calysta goaded Merriam, Aleah, and Campbell. The younger three were easily influenced and not to be outdone, which the wood nymph absolutely used for her own amusement.

Merriam tossed back a shot, shaking her head at the burn in her throat so quickly her teeth rattled together. She watched Aleah do the same, even though she'd won that round of their current game of guessing the next action random patrons would take.

Merriam flipped her braid over her shoulder, leaning into the redhead.

"If you're going to Do Lech, I'll go with you," Aleah said out of the blue, eyes landing on a dark-haired fae across the room. "That guy is going to order mead."

Merriam narrowed her eyes. "Nah, he's going for ale. You want to go south?" Concern flitted through her. Aleah never took any jobs in South Eyko, much less went anywhere near her former hometown.

"You're both wrong. A shot and a water to chase it with," Campbell interjected from Aleah's other side.

The three waited as the male walked up to the bar.

Merriam and Aleah groaned when the bartender slid over a shot, followed by a cup of water. The two clinked their own shots together before tipping them back. "You're too good at reading people, Cam." Merriam glared at the antlered male.

Campbell shrugged. "I'll go grab another round. Or three. You two might need it."

"Pace yourselves," Jasper warned from where he sat playing cards with Leonidas, the corner of his mouth quirking up in a smile.

"Always." Campbell winked before walking away.

Leonidas watched him, blue eyes gleaming with equal parts endearment and exasperation.

"I have a job close by," Aleah said quietly, spinning an empty shot glass around on the worn wooden tabletop.

"You took a job in South Eyko?" Merriam almost coughed, she was so shocked.

"And she's been getting slowly but surely more unhinged since." Leonidas placed a card on the table.

Aleah stuck her tongue out at him.

"Why did you take the job?" Merriam asked.

"I don't know, it just sort of happened. But I've got to face my past eventually, right? May as well do it when I'm getting paid to be there. Jasper's going, too. Apparently, I can't be trusted to take care of myself even though I still have a higher death toll than any of you." Aleah spun the glass against the table again, watching it twirl.

Jasper snorted, picking up the card Leonidas had set down. "If you can name the city while you're sober or mention the overseers by name, I'll stay behind."

Aleah wrinkled her nose and flipped him off before flicking her hazel eyes up to meet Merriam's. "But if you're going south on official business, I can travel with you! We can make it an adventure, and I won't have time to worry about any of my family."

Merriam blinked, looking to Jasper for help. "Aleah, you understand who I'm going to be meeting with, right?"

Calysta showed up with a platter of snack foods then, setting it down in the middle of the table and wrapping an olive-green arm around Merriam's waist. "Shhh, don't go talking sense to her Mer, you'll pop her fantasy."

Aleah snorted, picking a delicate cookie from the tray. "Yeah, don't treat me like I'm fragile or anything."

Calysta blinked large, entirely black eyes at the redhead. "You're not."

"I won't be staying there, obviously. And as far as my dear grandparents know, I'm dead, anyway."

Before Merriam could reply, the door to the bar burst open, and in strolled a group of Rangers, already loud and rowdy with drink.

Leonidas rolled his eyes. "There goes a pleasant evening."

"Hey, I've made my peace with most of them," Merriam grumbled over the rim of her cup, taking a long drink of ale.

"For once, your proclivity for riling them up isn't my concern." Leonidas grabbed her now-empty cup as well as his own and stood, heading over to the bar.

"Well, hello there, pretty thing. Come here often?" A male with a short mohawk of curly hair and a dangerous gleam ever-present in his bi-colored eyes slid into the seat next to Aleah, draping his arm over her shoulder.

Aleah turned her head to look at him, amusement glittering in her eyes. "No, but if I'd known it was a watering hole for Rangers, I would have stayed away."

Kodi slapped a dramatic hand to his chest. "You wound me, maiden." He leaned in and whispered, "If you'd rather leave, I would happily escort you home if you promise to wrap your legs around my head while I make you forget everything but my name."

Aleah's cheeks flushed red, and she folded her lips inward against a smile. Shrugging his arm from her shoulders, she turned her concentration to the drink in front of her. "Awfully presumptuous of you, killer."

Kodi grinned. "I'll be back, but if you need me, you know where to find me." He twirled a lock of her flame-red hair around his finger before rising from his seat to join the other Rangers across the bar.

Merriam raised an eyebrow. "Care to share what's got you all flustered?"

Aleah's canines dimpled her bottom lip as she smiled. "Nope." She and

Kodi had been seeing each other for the past year. They made a wild pair, completely enamored with one another in a way that could only be described as violently passionate.

Leonidas came back then with Campbell, setting drinks down around the table.

They continued their games for a while, then Aleah sauntered over to where the Rangers sat.

"And you were worried about me causing trouble," Merriam joked to Leonidas.

"Kodi can handle the kind of trouble she's looking for," he shot back. "*Your* trouble, on the other hand ... " His ice-blue eyes tracked movement across the bar.

Merriam's brow furrowed, and she swiveled in her seat a bit too eagerly to follow Leonidas' gaze.

Rovin approached the table of Rangers, chestnut waves brushing against his broad shoulders, deep brown eyes lit with merriment as he greeted his comrades.

Merriam turned back around with a scoff and folded her arms over chest. "He's not *my* anything."

"Uh-huh." Leonidas grinned.

She glared at the blonde.

"Leo, I'm not going to step in when she tries to gut-punch you later," Campbell warned. "Don't start fights you don't want to finish."

Leonidas turned his gaze to the male beside him, sliding a hand into the hair at the base of Campbell's antlers. "I'll finish something tonight, buck." His words dripped with carnal promise.

Jasper and Calysta finished their card game. "Do you guys want to move somewhere else? A tavern down the street was starting to brew a seasonal cider." Calysta ran claw-tipped fingers through the lengths of her petal pink hair, smoothing out nonexistent knots.

"Absolutely always down for a new cider," Campbell answered, pushing his chair back to stand.

Jasper glanced over to where Aleah sat with the Rangers, perched on Kodi's lap with an arm slung over his shoulder while she goaded another.

Merriam followed his gaze, catching the worried gleam in his silver eyes. "I'll hang back with her. We'll catch up."

Jasper nodded, squeezing her shoulder in thanks as he passed, black wings tucked tight against his back to prevent from knocking into anyone.

When Aleah saw Merriam approach, she nudged her foot against the leg of the Ranger sitting next to her. "Move over!"

The Ranger aimed a saccharine smile at her. "If Kodi's lap is uncomfortable, you're more than welcome to use mine."

Kodi's gaze slid to the male over Aleah's shoulder, the corner of his mouth lifting in a smirk. "Be careful what you ask for, Percy. She bites." His fingers curled around Aleah's hip as she flashed her teeth at the Ranger.

"Not asking for me, anyway." Aleah tilted her head in Merriam's direction.

Percy turned to look where the half-fae indicated, promptly standing from his seat. "Marshal," he greeted, respect replacing the flirtation in his voice. He'd fought with her in the cave.

"Hello, demonslayer," Kodi said as she passed behind him, taking the offered seat.

"Thank you," she smiled at Percy, who moved further down the table, saluting her with a mug of ale. "You didn't have to make him move," she told Aleah.

"Percy's a twat," Kodi answered, and Aleah giggled.

"He seems nice enough," Merriam defended.

"Because he wants in your pants, Mer." Kodi reached around Aleah for his drink.

"Kodi." Rovin shot him a warning look.

Merriam watched him, her alcohol-muddied mind wanting to pick apart his defense.

"What? Half of the Rangers do!" Kodi defended, flicking his gaze back to Merriam with a wink. "It's something about a woman in power, especially if you know she could cut your cock off and feed it to you in your sleep."

Merriam laughed loudly at that, but Rovin rolled his eyes. "Not everyone is a masochist, Ko."

Kodi's teeth sank into his lower lip, raising a brow at his friend in silent challenge.

"To the cutting of cocks!" Aleah raised her glass to Merriam, who clinked hers against it before they both drank. "Let's play a game: me and Mer against Rov and Kodi." Aleah slid from Kodi's lap, gesturing for him to sit across from her.

"One game, little merc. I have to work in the morning." Kodi settled into his new seat. "So pick your poison."

Aleah peeked over at Merriam, grinning as she pulled a copper from her belt and flipped it to the blonde. "Slaps."

Merriam caught the coin, bringing her hand down flat onto the table, covering it. "Let's add in an extra layer. If the slap is guessed correctly, the holder of the coin still drinks. But whoever guessed has to pick crown or pile. If they get it right, the slapper drinks again. If they get it wrong, they drink."

The two Rangers nodded their agreement, and Merriam and Aleah put their hands under the table, passing the coin. When they were ready, they both slapped their palms against the table, the coin nestled underneath Aleah's right hand sounding a muffled *clack* against the wood.

Rovin searched their faces, pointing to the hand covering the coin. Merriam and Aleah lifted up their other hands, Aleah taking a sip of her drink. "Pile," Rovin guessed, and Aleah revealed the coin, a disgruntled noise falling from her lips as she took another drink.

The game continued on that way, the four of them becoming louder and more teasing as more alcohol was consumed. Almost finished with their second round of drinks for this game and definitely feeling the open giddiness that came with being drunk, Merriam took the coin from Aleah under the table, pressing the warm metal against her palm and running her thumb over the back side of it. She felt the many lines and grooves that made up the mountain range stamped onto the backside of the coin.

"Slap!" Aleah called, and they slammed their hands against the table.

It was Rovin's turn to guess again, and Merriam felt her cheeks flush involuntarily as those deep brown eyes met hers. He ran a hand through his hair, pulling the chestnut waves from his face as he watched her curl her lips into her mouth.

"That's not very nonchalant, Marshal."

Merriam shrugged. "It's all part of the mind game."

Rovin pointed to the hand that held the coin, and she scoffed, taking a long pull from her cup. "I take it mind games aren't your strong suit, then."

Merriam propped her elbow on the table, leaning her chin in her hand while the other stayed flat, hiding the coin underneath her palm. She met

Rovin's gaze evenly, lips playing in a smile that matched the challenge lighting her eyes. "What would you be willing to stake on that claim, Rovi? Crown or pile?" Her lashes fluttered, hiding the surprise that rolled her stomach with how easily the nickname had slipped from her tongue, but she never dropped the eye contact.

Rovin folded his arms on the table, leaning forward to search her face. "You know what it is." Her cheeks were flushed from laughter and liquor, and Rovin let himself acknowledge the spark of happiness he felt in his chest seeing her this way. Over time, the lost, haunted look had faded from her eyes, and the past several months, he'd watched from the sidelines as she grew into her new title and role in the kingdom.

Not that she still wasn't a royal pain in his ass. Though they were no longer at each other's throats, she still rose to every occasion to get under his skin, and he'd be lying if he said he didn't also goad her on purpose. Hel, he could even admit to himself that annoying her had become a halfway enjoyable pastime. But a mutual respect had grown between them just the same, and he wasn't too prideful to admit that he was glad she was allowing herself to relax and enjoy life.

Merriam's amber eyes hadn't left his, mischief bright within them. "Maybe. Maybe not." Merriam bit her lip, and Rovin's gaze dropped to her mouth. Hunger curled at the base of his spine, and he dragged a hand over the short scruff of his beard, returning her stare and hoping she couldn't read the lust in his eyes.

Annoyance rolled through him at how badly he wanted to pull her across the table and taste that lip for himself.

"I'll make it easy for you, Lieutenant." She blinked sweetly. "It's crown."

Rovin narrowed his eyes suspiciously as she bit back another smile. "Pile."

Merriam raised her hand with a smirk, sitting back smugly. "Drink." She and Aleah high-fived.

Rovin's second cup was now empty, along with Kodi's.

"Look at us, reigning slap champions." Aleah beamed.

Kodi cocked an eyebrow at her. "You're still drunker than us, though."

Aleah shot him a withering look. "One, we've been here longer than you. Two, in case you haven't noticed, I'm about half your size. And three, bet I can still wield a blade better than you."

Kodi grinned, leaning forward and running his tongue over his teeth. "Is that a threat or a promise?"

"You'll have to ask Percy tomorrow morning," Aleah purred, standing to head to the bathroom.

Kodi caught her wrist as she passed, pulling her down so that her face was even with his. "Try me, little merc," he said lowly.

Aleah angled her head to brush her nose against his. "I intend to," she promised, licking the tip of his nose before slipping free of his grip and scampering off.

Kodi's fingers curled into fists, his jaw flexing as his eyes followed her retreat.

Merriam watched him, worried at the tense set of his shoulders.

But when he turned around, he slumped over the table dramatically, chin resting on his arms. "I'm going to marry that fucking female one day."

Merriam shook her head with a laugh, standing to follow her friend. "You know she's never going to get any more compliant."

A dreamy smile stretched Kodi's lips. "Trust me, Mer, I'm very well aware."

When the two came back, Aleah was ready to meet back up with the mercs, dragging Kodi and Rovin along while also convincing some of the other Rangers to relocate with them. Alcohol ran freely through the redhead's system. The more people, the better, because it allowed for more distraction and less opportunity to worry about the impending trip to her homeland.

Merriam and Aleah skipped arm-in-arm down the street, giggling as they went. "Kodi, I bet you—" As Aleah turned her head to call to him, she tripped over a loose stone in the road, stumbling to the ground and pulling Merriam with her.

"You're a mess, little merc." Kodi walked up and pulled her to her feet before helping Merriam.

"And you're obsessed with it." Aleah grinned, wiping her palms against her pants. "Where would you be without me to make things exciting?"

"Back in the barracks, asleep." Kodi hooked a finger under her chin.

Merriam groaned, pushing a hand into her hair. "Legends. I just remembered Molli scheduled that final meeting about all this train stuff tomorrow morning."

"Are you sure that wouldn't be more fun if you stayed out all night and showed up drunk?" Aleah asked.

"Sounds like a great way for me to end up fighting Ferrick in the war room," Merriam laughed.

"Just throw little battle markers at his head whenever he makes a dumb comment." Aleah giggled.

Merriam clutched her belly in laughter. "I don't think we have enough markers for that."

Aleah and Merriam realized at the same time Ferrick's affiliation to their current company, and laughed harder, collapsing together.

"I should quit before I get myself into trouble," Merriam stage-whispered.

"A little late for that, demonslayer." Kodi rolled his eyes, holding a hand out to Aleah. "If you need to call it a night, I'll make sure Aleah makes it back to the rest of the mercs in one piece."

Aleah jokingly pretended to dart away, but Kodi, much less inebriated, lunged after her, picking her up and crouching down to set her on his shoulders. She clapped a hand over her mouth to muffle a surprised shriek, the other hand fisting into the curls of his mohawk for balance.

With a salute to Rovin and Merriam, Kodi walked off.

"Come on, Marshal, I'll escort you home," Rovin offered.

Merriam sighed, wiping her fingers under an eye to clear the tears there. "Okay," she agreed, but winced when she put her foot to the ground. "Fucking Hel," she hissed, grasping onto Rovin's arm to keep from falling again, her balance uneven as she took the pressure off of her ankle.

"You're rather clumsy for someone with a reputation of being sure on their feet," Rovin teased. He tried to appear carefree, but his posture was stiff, unsure of if he should have moved to support her or not. There was a time not too long ago she would have probably slammed a hand into his throat if he were to try.

"Only around you," Merriam accused, but the bite in her words was entirely playful.

The moons reflected in her amber eyes, still slightly wet from her tears of laughter. Realizing he was staring, Rovin looked up the street toward the castle, clearing his throat.

At the same time, it dawned on Merriam that she was still gripping the firm muscle of his arm, and she quickly let go, balancing on her good foot for half a second before reaching out to him again. "Legends, why did I drink so much?"

"If I recall correctly, there was something between you and Aleah about not backing down from a challenge followed by what some might call complete idiocy," Rovin offered.

Merriam glowered. "Some like you?" She was acutely aware of her heartbeat as she watched him, and her stomach churned with unexpected nervousness.

Rovin's head tilted to the side as he met her gaze. His mouth had gone dry under her scrutiny, and he wet his lips, not missing the way her eyes dropped down to his mouth as he did so. "No," he finally answered. "I was very impressed, actually."

Merriam searched his eyes, finally rolling hers and pushing him. "You're being a dick."

Rovin laughed, flinching at her assault. "Would you be offended if I offered to carry you back to the castle? I'm sure there's a part of you that would rather crawl than accept the help, but I once again find myself responsible for your safe return to the male who is now my king, and I'd like to get back before the sun comes up."

"I'm not *that* stubborn," Merriam defended, moving to cross her arms before remembering at the last second that her drunken self was dependent on him for balance. "Piggyback?"

"What?" Rovin raised a brow.

"You offered to carry me. I was clarifying the method. On your back?"

Rovin laughed again, and Merriam's first instinct was irritated defensiveness. "What are you laughing at? You're the one who offered."

"Why in this Legends-blessed world would you call a pack carry a piggyback?"

Some of the fight left her, and she put a hand to her face, shaking her head with a laugh. "Oh, wow. Yeah, I'm not sure how drunk Mer pulled that one out. It's what I grew up calling it."

"Was that like ... a familial term?" he asked, turning his back to her and slowly lowering to a knee.

Merriam grabbed his shoulders, lifting her legs where he waited to grab them. "No, it was absolutely a widespread thing. Worldwide, I think. At least in all the English-speaking countries."

"English. Is that your version of Common?" Rovin asked, standing. He'd only learned that Merriam wasn't born on Nethyl just over a year ago, and at the time they'd been on less than friendly terms. He knew next to nothing about the world she'd been raised in.

She giggled, letting her arms wrap around his shoulders to help hold her weight. "Most Americans would like to think so, but no. Just a language a few countries speak."

Rovin let the conversation die out as he made his way up the hill toward the castle. His quads would be on fire in the morning, and he made a mental note to stretch them out before bed to help alleviate some of the inevitable soreness.

Merriam's head dropped to his shoulder as he walked. She could feel the heat from his back all along her front, his muscles shifting with each movement. His scent surrounded her: fallen leaves and apples. Warmth bloomed through her, and in her drunken state, she imagined what it might be like to thread her fingers through his thick chestnut hair, to feel his hands on her and his body fit against hers ...

This is wrong. Her mind screamed it at her, snapping her out of her thoughts. *This is wrong. This is wrong.* It looped in her head, guilt flooding her system.

She'd slept with others since Oren's death, but they were mostly strangers. Rovin was ...

Merriam bit her tongue. Rovin had been her tormentor for seven long years, and she'd done her fair share to make life harder for him as well. Her mouth pulled into a frown at how comfortable she'd been. Her stomach churned again that she'd even briefly considered fucking him.

Wrong, she repeated. Her chest tightened as she looked up at the stars, forcing back the sudden urge to cry. Pine and plum and the night sky—Oren's smell that used to make her melt against him, entirely content. The prickle of short hair against her palms as she gripped the back of his head—that's the feeling she should have craved. None of that was what Rovin was. Rovin was *wrong.*

But she was drunk, and it was late, so she again let her head fall to his shoulder.

Rovin shifted her weight, repositioning his hold on her legs in the process. His thumb brushed over the side of her knee, his grip tightening momentarily.

Merriam could have screamed at the way everything in her abdomen rolled at the touch. "I still don't like you," she mumbled before she could stop herself.

"Don't worry, pet. I still don't like you, either," he replied, his voice light.

DJUHL DRONIN STOOD AT his balcony, tapping the three long, sharp claws of his hand against the rough stone. Fury burned through his blood, a low growl pulling from his broad, bare chest. His large, leathery wings snapped open, the webbing connecting from his shoulders down to the small of his back. The wind pulled at them, and he angled them back. Lightning flashed across the indigo sky, glinting off his claws.

"Tell me you have found a warlock capable of creating a simple fucking portal." His voice was deep, rolling across the stone balcony with a menacing rumble.

"There is one, Your Eminence, who claims she can wield such magic." The lesser demon shifted uncomfortably.

Dronin turned, his dark red eyes focusing on the messenger. He tilted his head to the side, long dark hair falling over his shoulder and the three sharp horns jutting from his forehead catching the light from another flash of lightning. "You have brought her to me, I presume?"

The lesser demon lowered his gaze from the Djuhl's stare, squaring his shoulders. Though he was smaller than Dronin, his body was still composed of strong, powerful muscles. "She is waiting in the throne room, Your Eminence."

Dronin nodded, turning back to the balcony. "Tell her I will be there shortly." He drew his claws down the dark charcoal skin of his chest, tilting his head up to the sky as the thick smell of sulfur from the sea below him filled the air. "And Perran?"

"My Djuhl." The lesser demon halted his retreat.

"Find Lyvin and Nevra, send them to the throne room as well."

"Yes, Your Eminence." Perran turned, leaving the Djuhl on the balcony.

In one smooth leap, Dronin stood on the railing, the three curved claws of his feet curling around the stone as the wind buffeted him. He again let his wings flare open, feeling the pull of the air trying to rip him free.

It had been a full season since his brother had been slain by a human female. Now the large, hollow mountains in the southern half of his land were bubbling with magma, the molten rock slowly starting to seep from their peaks.

It angered him that his brother had been so insolent as to let himself be bested by a creature so fragile. It angered him that his brother had been the one to make a pact with the human from another reality. It angered him that he himself had failed to learn the secret behind portal magic. And it angered him that his brother had left a spawn somewhere in this other world.

Dronin didn't care so much that it was an heir to the realm. But this spawn was capable of portal magic. Dronin's claws curled into a fist, pricking the skin of his palm as he imagined the breed of demon that this djuhlin could be capable of producing. Unlimited power at their fingertips. Worlds unimaginable, ready to fall under their rule.

That promise of an empire greater than anything known in history sang in Dronin's blood, consuming his every thought.

But getting to this world, this realm where the djuhlin was being kept, had proved to be a difficult task. Not for the first time that day, Dronin cursed his brother's patience and stupidity.

Stretching out his wings as another bolt of lightning flashed through dark indigo clouds, Dronin uncurled the claws of his feet, letting the wind take him, pulling him up into the sky.

Electricity swam around him, pulling the strands of his hair higher and arcing from his horns. Tucking his wings, he fell back down to the balcony off his throne room, throwing the doors open and walking straight to the dark, lusterless throne carved from the same stone as the rest of his castle.

He sat, crossing one ankle over the other and lifting his gaze to the warlock who stood before him.

Her skin was alabaster white, her eyes a glowing gold that met his with an amused glint before she dutifully lowered her head, her body sinking in a low bow. Her hair, blacker than night, was pulled to the top of her head and fell over her shoulder when she bent. Her ears were long, the thin, pointed tips of them ending above her head.

"I'm told you are capable of portal magic," Dronin spoke, foregoing formalities.

The warlock stood, once again raising her eyes to meet his. "Yes, Your Eminence, I believe it to be achievable."

Dronin narrowed his eyes, his vertically slit pupils growing thinner. "You believe?"

The warlock shrugged, tossing her hair back over her shoulder, small rings of gold knotted into the strands clinking together softly.

"If you waste my time, warlock, it will mean your life," Dronin threatened, his growl reverberating through the hall.

The warlock laughed, tipping her head back and flashing sharp, pointed teeth. "I assure you, Your Eminence, that I would not have traveled all the way across the realm if I weren't confident in my abilities." She blinked at him, taking a step forward towards his throne.

"The season of riverock is well upon us. Why has it taken you so long to answer my call?" Dronin raised a hand to his chin, tapping his claws against his cheek.

The warlock moved closer, her gaze drifting out to the balcony, the doors still open. "I am a dreamwalker, My Djuhl. There are many worlds, many realities that exist. Some are very far from ours, and reaching them is almost impossible. Indeed, I heard your summons for a warlock capable of jumping through realms when you first demanded, but I wanted to be sure the request was even feasible before I offered my services." She turned her eyes back to him, a cruel smile playing at her lips. "You have killed many of my kind in your search. Forgive me if I was hesitant to join their numbers."

A low chuckle escaped Dronin despite himself. "Very well, but now you are here. What has made you think you can enter the world where the djuhlin resides?"

"I have dreamed of it," she answered simply. "It is a world not too far separated from ours, and there are places where the barrier thins, where it would be easier to tear through."

Approval rumbled from Dronin's chest. "How long would it take you to create a spell capable of doing so?"

"It is hard to say. That kind of magic is highly unpredictable, and the spells complicated. I would need to prepare, collect knowledge and ingredients."

Dronin nodded, raising a hand and summoning another demon to him. It rolled in as an inky, liquid-black cloud before materializing in the form of a lizard-like cat. He whispered to it, and it ran off. "The meat-suit my brother inhabited when he moved between realms possessed two pieces of stone. They stink of heavy magic, though it does not seem a demon is able to wield it."

The warlock's eyes seemed to glow a brighter gold in intrigue. "Would it be possible for me to examine these stones, Your Eminence?"

Dronin cocked an eyebrow. "I have already sent one to fetch them."

The doors at the back of the throne room burst open, two greater demons walking into the room.

"You called, My Djuhl?" the male spoke, his deep red eyes gleaming wickedly. A long, heavy sword was strapped to his back. His feet and hands ended in three claws, much like Dronin's and his female companion's, and a ridge of spikes poked through the long silver hair on his head.

Dronin smiled, showing the long, pointed fangs in both his upper and lower jaws. "Lyvin, Nevra, this warlock believes herself capable of portal magic. If her claim proves true, she will be working alongside you as we plan our attack."

Lyvin and Nevra were Dronin's most trusted generals, damnably cruel and fiercely loyal.

"Donova," the warlock introduced herself, turning to look at the newcomers.

Nevra looked from Dronin to the warlock, mauve eyes trailing from the warlock's feet up to the tips of her ears. A forked tongue flicked out to wet her lips, and she smiled. "Well, Donova, I hope your confidence in your abilities is well-placed. We have gone far too long without bloodshed, and I'm itching to steal away a djuhlin."

Before Donova could answer, the lesser demon came back, holding a pouch between its teeth that it dropped into Dronin's waiting hand before scampering away again.

Donova's attention went immediately to what the djuhl now held in his palm. It stirred the magic in her blood, and she walked up to him not quite of her own volition, golden eyes wide.

Her hands stretched out, and Dronin emptied the pouch into them, watching her face as she studied the two rings with something like worship in her expression.

Each ring had a band of silver. One was a dark purple stone, the other black shot through with small veins of gold.

Donova held them up, letting them catch the light from the lightning that arced through the sky. "Do you know what these are?" she whispered.

Dronin raised a brow, looking from his generals back to the warlock.

"These are pieces of that which connects everything." Donova raised her eyes to meet Dronin's stare, reverence lacing her words.

Chapter 10

Solid play

MERRIAM LET ROVIN CARRY her through the castle gates before tapping him on the shoulder, and he dropped her gently to the ground. "I can take it from here," she said as he turned to face her. "Thank you for the assistance, Lieutenant."

Rovin's chest tightened as she smiled up at him. Eight years he'd known her, and for over seven of them she had never once looked at him with any expression even remotely resembling friendship. *Wasted years.* The thought filtered through him, and he shook it off, running a hand through his hair. "I do what I can, Marshal. Just don't make a habit of needing me."

Merriam rolled her eyes. "Cocky bastard," she shot the insult over her shoulder as she slowly walked off, favoring her strained ankle.

Rovin didn't fight the smile that stretched his lips as he made his way to the barracks and the third floor where the officers slept. Out of habit, he glanced at the taskings posted to the wall of the common room as he passed, pausing when he noticed his name crossed off of the next morning's shift.

"You've been reassigned."

Rovin jumped, turning to see Eskar sprawled across a couch, cleaning her nails with a knife. "Reassigned?"

Eskar smirked, rolling her head against the arm of the couch to look at him. "We're going on a trip, Rov."

Rovin leaned against the wall, crossing his arms over his chest and cocking an eyebrow.

"Merriam will be leading her little expedition down south in only a few days, and Captain Ferrick wants us to accompany her. I've picked the rest of the Rangers and Guard who will be going as well. You can hand out those taskings tomorrow." Eskar tucked her knife back into her belt and stood. "I'm calling it a night. There's a final meeting about the train project in the morning that I'll be attending. It'll be up to you to let everyone else know."

"Yes, Commander," Rovin replied as she left the room.

He pushed a hand through his hair again as he walked to his quarters, feeling the phantom heat of Merriam at his back. He shrugged the sensation off with a scowl, annoyed that his initial response to being forced to spend so much time around her had been so eager.

Merriam was going to be in charge of this expedition, and if history had taught him anything, that responsibility would go right to her head, especially once she realized she could use her presumed authority to annoy Eskar. And him.

Pulling his shirt over his head and kicking off his boots, Rovin sank down onto his bed, running a hand over the scruff on his jaw as he tried to sift through the emotions warring inside him.

Despite reminding himself of all the ways Merriam could be an insufferable headache, by the time Rovin had gotten ready for bed and nestled under his blankets, the last thought that crossed his mind was an image of her, blonde braid tousled and moonlight shining in her amber eyes as she smiled up at him. An irritated frown pulled at his lips as sleep took him.

Mollian had been asleep by the time Merriam came in, and she'd gone to her own bed, not wanting to stumble around and wake him in her impaired state.

She woke slightly when his weight settled next to her. "Up and at 'em, sleepy-willow." He tugged at the long strands of her hair that fanned out over her pillow.

"Molli, stop." She scowled, tucking her face underneath the blanket.

"You can't be in charge of negotiations if you don't show up to the final planning and preparations." Mollian drummed his fingers lightly against the top of her head.

Merriam ripped the covers free, rolling over to glare at him. Pillow lines crossed one freckled cheek, undermining the ferocity in her eyes. "Are you trying to lose your fingers?"

Mollian grinned, pushing up from the bed. "Not wise to threaten a king, Ria. Hurry up and get dressed. Breakfast is already waiting."

Merriam pulled the back of her hand across an eye, blinking in the light already streaming through her window. "Legends, how did it get so late?" she grumbled, swinging her legs out of bed. She gingerly rotated her foot, feeling only a slight soreness from the ligaments, before stumbling into her bathroom for a quick shower.

When she'd dressed, she joined Mollian in the common room, plopping down and grabbing a sweet roll.

"How was your night?"

Merriam glanced up suspiciously, then questioned why she felt defensive. "It was fun. I hate how much time I let pass between my visits with the mercs. I miss them."

"Marshal business isn't keeping you too busy, is it?" Mollian asked, feeling guilty for pulling her from the life she'd previously chosen.

Merriam shook her head. "Nothing I can't handle, just poor time management on my part," she assured him. After finishing the sweet roll, she forced herself to tell him about the end of the night. If it meant nothing, then there was no point in hiding it, after all. "I twisted my ankle skipping with Aleah. Not bad, I can walk fine this morning, but Rovin pack carried me back to the castle."

Mollian's brows shot up, a coy smile spreading across his face. "One more and that's a pattern, Ria."

"He was just there hanging out with Kodi and happened to be ready to head back at the same time." Merriam grabbed a small bunch of grapes.

"I'm glad some of that animosity has died down," Mollian said. "Sometimes I get nervous about ..." he trailed off, shaking his head.

Merriam tilted her head to the side, munching on the grapes. *About what?*

Mollian's fingers ran across the aspen leaves tattooed on his forehead, not meeting her eyes. *Nobody is allowed to say anything about my position, but I sometimes worry that I put a target on your back. I couldn't do any of this without you, but I don't want anyone to hate you because of your connection to me.*

Merriam snorted, tossing a grape at her *mehhen*. *I hate to break it to you, Molli, but people have always hated me because of my connection to you.*

He turned his eyes to her, sadness pooled in the pale green depths. *Yes, but now that connection holds weight.*

Merriam shrugged, offering an assuring smile. "I can hold my own, Lord King. Don't worry about me."

"Either way, it makes me feel better knowing your circle of friends at court is growing."

She scoffed, standing and securing her axes around her waist. "Rovin is not my friend."

"Just a male who carries you home every once in a while, got it." Mollian stood to follow her down to the war room.

The meeting took the entire morning, but all of the final details were ironed out to a point that everyone could agree on. Graigory would be going to Do Lech as well as Portimer, and Merriam was delighted to learn that Ferrick would be staying behind and immediately disappointed to hear Eskar would be heading the detachment of the Guard that would be accompanying them.

But she had a lot to prepare for in the two days before they'd be leaving, her only saving grace Aleah's index and account templates to help keep track of everything.

Merriam was working on filling them out in the office at the back of the war room when Aleah poked her head in. "Got room for a couple more?"

Merriam motioned for her to sit. "We should talk about that. I'm assuming whatever job you booked down there is less than savory?"

Aleah sank into a chair on the opposite side of the desk. "You'd be correct." She grinned, the kind of smile that made strangers worry she might try to eat them.

Merriam nodded, sliding the aspen charm at her throat across its chain as she filled in a few more numbers. "I'm going to hire you and Jaz to scope out the locations that have been chosen to build stations. After-hours sort of deal. If you're going to be seen traveling with us, it'll give the Crown plausible deniability and you an alibi should you need it."

"Oh, official work!" Aleah clapped her hands in mock delight as Merriam dug through her papers to slide over a contract for the mercenaries to look over along with the expense sheet to let Aleah double-check her math.

"Does Kodi know?"

"That I'm going south? Of course." Aleah's eyes stayed glued to the papers in front of her.

"Don't play dumb," Merriam said evenly.

Aleah pressed her lips together as she scanned the numbers, finally pushing the list back toward Merriam and shaking her head. "I've tried to tell him, I just … I can't talk about it. The words get stuck in my throat." She folded her arms over the desk, resting her chin on them. Her past wasn't something she ever talked about freely. Kodi didn't know where she was from, much less who her family had been. "He's going, though, so I guess I'll either figure out how to tell him on the way there, or he'll think I'm more and more insane the closer we get. If it's the latter, I'll just find a way to make it up to him when we get back to Umbra and make sure to never venture south again." She sighed heavily.

Merriam's brows raised. "Kodi is going?"

"Yeah, Rovin gave him the assignment this morning," Aleah answered, tucking a lock of flame-red hair behind her clipped ear.

"Rovin?" She sat back abruptly.

Aleah grinned. "Oh, you didn't know."

Merriam frowned, pulling all of her lists together and standing. "No, I didn't. I only found out this morning that Eskar would be the commanding officer."

"It can't be that bad. You guys seemed to be getting along pretty well last night." Aleah leaned back in her chair. "You were practically fucking him with that eye contact."

Merriam's cheeks heated. "I was just playing the game," she insisted. "But that's different, anyway. It wasn't work, and he wasn't around the others."

Aleah gave Merriam an incredulous look. "I won't argue the point that Ko was there, but unless I was entirely more drunk than I remember being, weren't we at a table with an entire group of Rangers?"

"Not his superiors." Merriam huffed, hugging the papers to her chest as she exited the office. "It's one thing for him to relax and let loose in a tavern with his peers, but he's not going to be insubordinate or cut out of line when he's on the job. He's already one of the youngest Rangers to earn lieutenant, which has put him under a lot of scrutiny. He's not going to give Eskar or any other commander any reason to question his competency."

Aleah followed Merriam, tucking her lips between her teeth to ward off a smile.

Merriam, suspicious of her silence, peered at the mercenary over her shoulder. "Do you have a comment, Aleah?"

"So you definitely haven't put any thought into the situation or his motives, then. Don't care enough to spare him even a moment's consideration. Got it."

"That's not what I—"

Aleah brushed past Merriam, cutting her off with a wink. "Don't protest too much, there, Mer, or I might think you *do* care. I've got to head out before Jasper starts to worry. I never went home last night. I'll meet you bright and early for the trip down south." Aleah blew her a kiss before turning and scurrying off, contract in hand.

Merriam scowled at her feet as she walked through the castle toward the stables to drop off an inventory list of everything the stablehands would need to pack. She looked up right before slamming into a wall of muscle.

"In a hurry, pet?" Rovin watched in amusement as she shuffled back a couple of steps.

Merriam glared at him. "Yes, actually."

The smile playing at the corners of his lips dropped, and he stepped aside. "Anything I can do to help?"

Merriam tore her eyes away from his face, knowing her irritation was only heightened because of her conversation with Aleah. The fact that part of her wanted to accept his offer of assistance added to her annoyance. She worked her jaw, fighting the urge to snap at him. "I've got it. Just running lists and orders so everyone will be prepared to leave."

Rovin let her pass, watching her stalk purposefully toward the stables. "Mer," he called.

She stopped, not turning to look at him.

He ran a hand through his hair, confused by the nervous tension that squeezed his chest. "We're doing special skills training tonight. For scouting. If you're not busy."

Merriam slowly turned around, amber eyes narrowed. "Are you insinuating that I need the extra instruction?"

Rovin broke into laughter at the fire in her eyes, some of the pressure in him easing as she forced the interaction back into their old routine. "You said it, not me. Enjoy your errands, Marshal." He flashed her a winning smile and walked off.

Merriam's mouth popped open. Had he just used her own irritation tactic against her? "Solid play, Ranger-man," she whispered as she continued on her way. He was getting better at the sort of games she usually played, and she was begrudgingly impressed.

TWO DAYS LATER, THE caravan headed out on the week-long journey south. Calysta had decided to accompany Jasper and Aleah, claiming she had nymph business to take care of and joking about not wanting to be alone with Leonidas and Campbell for the better part of a month. Though Leonidas had been interested in tagging along, he didn't feel comfortable leaving his birds for that long, and Campbell was more than willing to stay behind with him.

Being head of an official envoy accompanied by a full detachment of the Guard meant Merriam wasn't expected to scout or pull watch, which left her feeling antsy and unsure of what to do with herself. Most of the presentation for the railroad would be given by Graigory, and after the first night of listening to him and Portimer continue to talk through the points they'd been arguing all week, Merriam excused herself and didn't volunteer to sit in on any of their other meetings.

After supper on the second night, she walked up to the circle of Rangers, who were finishing up their meal.

"Merriam, to what do we owe the pleasure?" Eskar asked, a thinly veiled sneer pulling at her lip.

"Commander." Merriam dipped her head respectfully. *Keep the peace. Keep the peace.* She repeated the mantra in her head, determined to keep up the best of appearances, if only because she traveled under Mollian's name. "If you'd like another body, I don't mind being added to the watch rotation."

Disdain filled Eskar's brown eyes, narrowed into a thin glare. "I can assure you, *Marshal*, that we have it under control."

Merriam bit the inside of her cheek, fighting the warmth that wanted to spread over her face at the dismissal. Her eyes locked onto Rovin's, and her embarrassment quickly heated to irritation. "Great, enjoy the sleep deprivation." She turned back to Eskar with a tight smile, amber eyes cold.

Eskar snorted, watching Merriam retreat to where the mercenaries had set up camp for the night. "Fucking merc needs to mind her business."

"She's not a merc; she's our marshal." Rovin's voice carried strong, and he met Eskar's gaze evenly.

The commander crossed her arms, feeling the eyes of the other Guard focus on them as casual conversation died down. "What was that, Lieutenant?" The challenge in her voice was clear. She was giving him a chance to rethink his rebuttal.

Rovin was a little surprised he'd spoken, but as he met Eskar's cool glare, the light from the fire shining off her short, dark hair, he realized he was right. Regardless of whatever prejudice Eskar had against Merriam in the past, she was now a servant of the Crown and had offered to help when she'd been under no obligation. So Rovin lifted his chin, repeating, "She's our marshal."

Eskar's lip curled, baring pointed canines. "A position given to her because she is the king's *mehhen*."

Rovin understood that arguing with her, especially in front of the other Guard, was stupid, but he was unable to hold his tongue. "You fought next to her against those demons, Eskar. You've seen more than most how much she has sacrificed for this country. She and King Mollian may be connected, but that shouldn't discredit what we've all witnessed to be true."

"And what is that?" Eskar asked, a dangerous gleam in her eyes.

Rovin pulled his gaze away, looking into the fire. "She's sworn to this country just like the rest of us—has even marked herself with aspen leaves. She does take her appointment as marshal seriously, and that title demands a certain level of respect."

A low sound like a snarl pulled from Eskar's throat, and Rovin flicked his gaze back up to her. "She only swore herself to the Crown when it was convenient for her. A blatant play for power deserves no respect, Ranger. You'd do well to remember that."

Taking a deep breath through his nose, Rovin stood, seeing this conversation would go nowhere and uncomfortable with the attention from the other guardsmen. "Yes, Commander."

He walked away from the fire, irritation prickling his skin. He wanted to be surprised by his need to stand up for Merriam, pretend he didn't understand it, but he couldn't. Rovin knew it was his leadership that had caused Merriam so much pain when she first came to Umbra. While she never failed to get under his skin and find countless ways to annoy him and push his temper, after the events of the past year, he could no longer deny that she had more than earned her place in the kingdom. She may be a brat, but she also took pride in her title and did the job to the best of her ability. Acting as marshal was a lot of responsibility for being only twenty-five, and she handled it with an unexpected level of grace.

Rovin rolled his shoulders, trying to shake off the bad taste the confrontation with Eskar had left in his mouth as well as his need to protect Merriam's image in front of the others.

He ended up at the far edge of camp, where Kodi was currently on watch. Rovin smoothly pulled himself into the tree, settling on a branch near his oldest friend, one leg propped up in front of him, resting over his knee as he tilted his head back against the trunk.

Kodi leaned forward, draping his arms over a branch at his chest. "You look like you have a story to téll, but I'm on watch, and my lieutenant will have my ass if he finds out I let myself be distracted by personal matters."

Rovin smiled, pulling a leaf from a branch near his head and ripping it into thin strips. "Your lieutenant just picked a fight with Eskar in front of the rest of the Guard."

Kodi's brows shot up. "No shit? And of course I missed the one time Rovin Arwood was insubordinate."

Rovin let the remains of the leaf drop to the forest floor, tucking an arm behind his head. "Mer offered to help out with the watch. Eskar sent her away, of course, but she called her a merc, and I, uh … corrected her."

Kodi listened with a devious grin while Rovin recounted his conversation with their commander. "Harboring a little soft spot for your old nemesis, then?" he teased.

Rovin rolled his eyes, but his brow pulled low in a frown. "I don't know what I feel for her, Ko. It's so confusing." He trailed off, shaking his head. For over five years, every second in her presence had made his blood boil, and now … "She still gets under my skin. She annoys the ever-loving shit out of me, but I still find myself taking every excuse to be around her."

"You need to get it out of your system. I've heard a good hate fuck works wonders for mental clarity," Kodi offered.

Rovin glared at him. "I don't need to fuck her. I need to not care about her. I don't even *like* her, which is what makes this so damn frustrating."

"Do you remember back in the beginning when Ferrick first told us she wanted to be a Ranger?" Kodi waited for Rovin to nod. "You admired her gumption and her drive. You told me as much, even after Ferrick tried to pound it through your pretty little head that she was just an entitled bitch. You've been fighting her ever since, but you've also been fighting yourself. Every time she bested one of us or found a way around the hurdles we put in her way, you wanted to be proud of her for it. But you were so far up Ferrick's ass that you fought those feelings before you'd even had a chance to acknowledge them, turning them into resentment. It's probably so much a habit for you now that it's fucking with your head that you *want* to admit you admire her."

"When did you get so insightful?" Rovin laughed softly, ripping up another leaf.

Kodi kicked at him, knocking Rovin's leg from the branch. "I'm a prick, rarely follow the rules, and can't hold my tongue for shit, but there's a reason I'm a Ranger." He tapped a finger against a temple with a cocky smile. "I am and always have been very attentive. You've been harboring feelings for much longer than you probably want to admit, brother."

Rovin wanted to argue that he most certainly hadn't, but could already see the knowing gleam in Kodi's blue and green eyes if he tried to defend himself, so he changed the topic. "What about your little merc? She seemed to be testing you a bit more than usual the other night."

Kodi sighed, brushing his fingers through the wide strip of hair that ran over his head, causing the curls to stick up every which way. "Something is bugging her, but she won't tell me what. I think it's got something to do with Do Lech. She shrinks into herself every time someone mentions it and can hardly say the name herself."

"She have history there?" Rovin asked.

"That's my assumption. I don't know what it is, but it's gotta be bad to knock her this far off of her game." Kodi licked his lips, picturing the scars that marred her torso. "Something bad happened to her, but she won't tell me what. If it happened in Do Lech … if whoever hurt her still walks free …" Kodi gripped the branch he hung over, protective possession flaring in his blood. Somewhere overhead, a branch snapped, plummeting to the forest floor below as Kodi reined in his magic.

Rovin bit his tongue, knowing it would be pointless to remind Kodi that they were on official business, that despite what he might feel for Aleah, he was still a Ranger first. That meant he was held to a higher standard and a much more stringent code of conduct. Punitive when broken. "Be careful, brother."

Kodi met his gaze, nodding even as anger ticked in his jaw.

Merriam was exceedingly thankful for her friends' presence during the days on the road. The familiar dynamic she had with them remained unchanged despite her title, and being with them set her at ease and bolstered her confidence. Even after the less than pleasant experience with Eskar, she was able to find a comfortable stride between the guildsfolk and Guard while they traveled, and was half-surprised by how relaxed she truly felt in their midst, even if she did spend most of her free time with the mercenaries.

Aleah shrunk a little further into herself with each day that passed, and Merriam's heart hurt for the child she'd been: alone and abused for simply existing. Jasper hardly left Aleah's side, providing a constant comfort when marshal duties pulled Merriam away. Kodi had watched most of it from a distance, unwilling to push Aleah and just thankful that she had someone to rely on.

The night before they would reach Do Lech, Aleah beckoned him over. She sat huddled between Jasper and Merriam, Calysta off in the forest somewhere. Her hazel eyes glimmered with sorrow in the firelight, and Kodi's chest tightened at her pain.

He stood, tucking his hands into his pockets as he walked over to them. Jasper scooted over as he approached, making room for him on the ground next to Aleah.

She smiled at him, reaching up a hand to guide him down and resting her head against his shoulder, emotion clogging her throat.

Kodi felt the shift in her, her hand tightening around his. "If you're about to apologize for being distant, I'm going to leave," he said.

Aleah huffed, turning her head to bite his shoulder. "Don't be an ass or I'll sic Jasper on you."

"You're on your own, red. I'm still not convinced your Ranger isn't rabid," Jasper joked.

Kodi ignored the warmth that spread through him at the term of possession, knowing if he called attention to it, Aleah would deny it on principle. But he buried his nose in her hair, breathing in her sweet smell of strawberries and not bothering to hide his smile as she continued to cling to him.

"Remember when you asked me what my surname was?" Aleah's voice was soft and quiet.

"If I remember correctly, both you and Mer claimed not to have one. 'Wildlings of the world' is what you called yourselves for the rest of the night," he answered.

A small smile tugged at Aleah's lips with the memory. "Yeah, no family ties, just us and the wind at our heels."

"But you do have family out there, don't you?" Kodi prompted gently.

"I'm ... I *was* ... a Kinbriar." Kinbriar, the family who had sat as overseers of Do Lech for almost as long as the Stonebanes held the throne, and the people Merriam had been sent south to meet with.

Kodi stiffened, looking down at the mercenary as she stared into the fire, and his mouth went dry.

Aleah ignored him, glancing at Merriam and Jasper instead. "I'll be fine," she told them.

They stood, Merriam dropping a hand to scratch Aleah's head before they walked from the fire. Aleah rarely talked about her past. It made her feel too vulnerable, and Jasper and Merriam understood she'd want privacy.

Aleah's mother and uncle had been twins, and one of the few known *mehhen* who also shared blood. When Aleah's mother died in childbirth, losing that connection had destroyed her uncle. He'd used his grief as an excuse to feed into his prejudices, killing Aleah's human father and clipping her ear despite the practice being illegal. For years, he had hurt her, her presence a constant reminder that his *mehhen* was gone. He'd never marked her where someone might accidentally see, but her entire torso was littered with scars. Kodi had seen them, of course, but never pushed when Aleah refused to talk about them.

Jasper leaned back against a tree and stretched his wings. "I'm going to stick close."

Merriam gave him a look. "She's not going to like you babying her."

"Who says I'm here for her?" He smirked, tipping his chin back to where Aleah sat with the Ranger. "This is going to be a lot for him to take in, especially so close to your arrival at the Kinbriar estate. He'll need guidance, tools to work through his anger so that he doesn't do anything brash."

Merriam swallowed, worrying her bottom lip between her teeth. "Should I have pushed for him to stay in Umbra?"

"I won't speak to problems he might potentially cause for you, but Kodi's presence here is good for Aleah. Especially now that she's opening up to him, he grounds her in a way that none of us ever have."

"I think she loves him," Merriam said. "Though of course I'd never let her hear me say it."

Jasper chuckled at that, knocking the toe of his boot into Merriam's shin. "Because you're so much more open with your emotions."

Merriam hopped back out of his reach. "I'm learning, okay?" She briefly looked back to the couple by the fire. "I think I'll go for a little walk. Clear my head in preparation for tomorrow."

"Enjoy," he told her as she slipped into the trees.

Soon after Merriam entered a denser part of the forest, she looked up to see the aspens waving softly above her, despite the stillness of the air.

She walked toward them, and the trees a little further along caught the movement as the ones next to her settled. She smiled, following them until she reached where Calysta sat on a felled trunk next to a small creek, the green of her skin almost blending into the forest around her in the moonlight. She'd manipulated the plants to lead Merriam to her.

"They like you, the trees," the nymph told her, glancing up.

Merriam laughed, taking a seat next to her. Calysta couldn't really talk to plants, but her magic enabled her to feel and interpret their vibrations and the way different flora communicated with each other. The aspens shared a root system, letting Calysta and other wood nymphs get a feel for anything unusual happening in the forest. "Glad to know my presence is welcome."

"How's Aleah?"

"Finally talking to Kodi." Merriam rested her head against the nymph's shoulder, taking a lock of pink hair and twisting it between her fingers. "That's a big step for her and what he means to her."

Calysta hummed her agreement. "Hopefully Rovin is smart enough to keep him in check, though. Kodi doesn't strike me as the kind to let bygones be bygones, regardless of whether or not Aleah Kinbriar is a ghost."

Merriam bit her lip, sliding her thumb over the smooth strands. "This could definitely end badly. Kodi has less self control than I do, as well as less official connection to the Crown, as weird a fact as that is. But there's every possibility her uncle won't even be around. It's her grandparents that run Do Lech."

Calysta spread her fingers, blades of glass slithering around her feet and Merriam's boots. "They run most of South Eyko," she said quietly. "Spiro Kinbriar may be the overseer of Do Lech, but he holds almost as much political power as Mollian."

Merriam sat up, turning to face the nymph. "You're from South Eyko, right?"

Calysta nodded. "I grew up near here. An old friend asked me to come back. There's an overseer who runs a small fishing town west of Do Lech. She's close with the Kinbriars and has forced a lot of legislation to put boundaries on nymphs and our practices, and the folk have grown tired of being governed by anything other than Nethyl."

Merriam frowned. "Is there anything Mollian can do to help?"

"No, the laws aren't worded to be discriminatory. We're mostly so solitary that it doesn't affect us much. But every decade, we used to gather and push our magic back into Nethyl, feeding the ley lines and letting them feed us, a way to thank the planet for the life it gives us. It's these ceremonies that Illiziana didn't like. Aside from being solitary, we're also not very welcoming to outsiders, especially not on those occasions when we do band together. People tend to fear things they don't understand, and the fact that nymphs have magic—and blood magic, at that—when we aren't high fae has always made us a target."

"Sprites have blood magic, too."

Calysta's musical laughter filled the night. "Yes, but they don't possess the intelligence to plot and create mischief any more than a herd of common goats, do they?" She quieted, watching the plants she manipulated. "We're closer to Nethyl's magic here because the ley lines run the same level across the world regardless of altitude. The Gate is so far beneath the mountains, and the magic that comes from it even deeper. But here … it's so much easier to touch. Can you feel it?"

Merriam set her palms against the bark on either side of her, concentrating on the magic in her blood. Her eyes fluttered closed, and she pushed past the feel of Mollian, searching for the slight hum she associated with the Gate. In the stillness, that faint, familiar brush of Oren's magic washed over her, and she held her breath, terrified of losing it. Underneath even that, though, she could sense the immense power that ran beneath her, and her whole body stilled in trepidation.

"Breathe, Mer." Calysta ran her fingers down Merriam's spine, eliciting a shiver that broke Merriam free from her focus.

She blinked, sinking back into her body with a deep breath. "We're right on top of it."

Calysta nodded, letting the grass go back to its natural state. "It'll start to curve away from the main road as we get closer to Do Lech."

"Does being so far above the magic back home bug you?" Merriam asked.

The nymph hummed in amusement. "Yes, and no. I see the way you have to focus in order to feel the magic, but it's not like that for me. Connecting to Nethyl is like breathing, and it's as easy to acclimate to being so far above the magic as it is to breathing the thinner air of the mountains. Regardless, being with all of you makes Umbra more comfortable than anywhere else could be."

Merriam smiled, pressing her shoulder against Calysta's. "I fully agree with that."

Chapter 12

Demonslayer

THE CARAVAN REACHED THE outskirts of Do Lech just before midday, the mercenaries splitting off once the sparse settlements around the city grew closer together.

"I booked an inn not too far to the west," Aleah said, her eyes locked on the huge buildings looming on the horizon.

Kodi, who had been watching the rear of the group, slid from his horse when he pulled up next to them. He placed his hand on Aleah's thigh, looking up at her with concern. "I'll come when I can, but if you need me ..." he trailed off, turning his gaze to Jasper. "Find me."

Aleah forced a laugh, squeezing Kodi's fingers. "I'll be okay."

Kodi's eyes stayed locked with Jasper's until Jasper nodded in silent promise, then he turned back to Aleah. "I know. You're a fighter, that's—" he broke off, swallowing past the emotion lumped in his throat. "You're a fighter."

Aleah nodded, releasing his hand. "Don't go soft on me, killer," she whispered, pulling her foot from the stirrup and tapping the center of his chest.

Kodi grabbed her boot and bit the side of her shin, pulling a hiss from her as she jerked her leg back. They smiled at each other, and Merriam averted her eyes, feeling like she was watching something entirely intimate.

"Good luck in there," Aleah called to her.

"Same to you." Merriam waved as Aleah, Jasper, and Calysta headed off.

Kodi watched them leave for a moment before climbing back onto his horse with a grunt that was more frustration than effort. "I don't know if I can do it, Mer."

Merriam laughed darkly, pushing her horse forward. Even with the time she'd had to sit with the knowledge, the fact that she would be politicking in the same residence Aleah's abuser likely resided hadn't gotten any easier to stomach. She'd asked once if Aleah wanted to come forward, speak out against her uncle, and bring him to justice. But Aleah Kinbriar was long dead as far as anyone knew, and the mercenary preferred to keep it that way. "You don't have to sit in meetings with any of them and look them in the eyes. Just be thankful for that."

"How do you do it? Live with so much self-restraint?"

Merriam shrugged. "I had to learn to keep my responses and reactions in check early on in life. Masks become second-nature when you wear one for so long." With that, she urged her horse into a gallop, pushing her way back to the front of the caravan.

The streets of Do Lech were unlike anything else in Sekha. The buildings were made of light-colored stone, built high and fortified against the wind and rain that blew in off the coast. The smell of the sea was heavy in the air, humidity curling the hairs that had escaped from Merriam's braid.

She stopped outside the gate of the overseer's estate, dropping gracefully from her mount. The guards, who'd been expecting them, waved her through, and she walked her horse into the vast courtyard, the rest of the party following.

Stablehands were there to greet them, taking horses as the stablemaster who'd ridden with them helped track inventory and what needed to go to which room. Merriam fought the urge to curl her hands into the folds of her riding cloak, instead squaring her shoulders and letting her gaze scan the courtyard with purpose, even if she was chewing on the inside of her cheek.

Master Graigory met her gaze, smiling in encouragement and eagerness. Merriam returned his grin, but movement from the grand building in her peripheral pulled her away before she could speak. A tall fae with short, flame-red hair and a beard to match descend the white stone steps with an elegantly dressed female by his side, her strawberry-gold hair forced into curls that defied the heavy humidity in the air.

The resemblance to Aleah was unmistakable, and something bitter churned in Merriam's gut.

She swallowed it down as she stepped up to greet them, proffering her hand. "Overseer Kinbriar, I presume? I'm Merriam, Marshal of Sekha and advisor to His Majesty the King."

The male shook her hand, his eyes traveling over her in an obvious once-over. "Spiro Kinbriar, at His Majesty's service and, thus, yours. This is my wife, Larna."

Merriam reached out to shake Larna's hand, and the female smiled, something like confusion in her soft blue eyes. "We'd heard to expect you, Marshal, but I apologize, none of the correspondence contained a surname. Nor the fact that you're ..."

Merriam's cheeks heated. *Of course, they never would have assumed I'm human.* But she forced back the embarrassment, opening her mouth to respond.

"She's Merriam Demonslayer, Lady Kinbriar." Merriam stiffened as Kodi came up behind her. "I'm sure you've heard the stories of grandeur, badassery, and her prowess with those axes. I can confirm they're all true." Kodi touched his hand to his chest sincerely, dipping his head in respect to Spiro and Larna. Though Merriam was thankful for his rescue, she could sense the tension in him and guessed that he was merely waiting for an excuse to shed blood.

Larna's face flushed at both his crass words and his boldness, and she flicked her eyes subserviently to her husband, unsure how to respond.

"Spiro, Larna! It's been ages." Graigory walked up with his arms spread wide, saving them.

Merriam looked at Kodi, who shoved his hands into his pockets with a wink before spinning on his heel to join the rest of the Guard. Rovin stood at the edge of their circle, watching the two of them. Merriam met his gaze, forcing a small smile before she turned back to the politicians.

Rovin tilted his head, eyes drifting from her to Kodi. "Tell me you're not causing trouble already," he said quietly.

"Preventing trouble," Kodi clarified. "You can thank me later."

Letting Rovin take charge of the Guard, Eskar joined the small group gathered by the steps, introducing herself smoothly and without hesitation.

Merriam's fingers brushed over the hilts of her axes, feeling the flowering vines carved there and letting the familiarity settle her. *It doesn't matter if all these bastards are a hundred years older. You are the only one who speaks with the authority of the king.* She couldn't tell if it was her voice or Mollian's in her head, but she relaxed, watching as Portimer pushed between Graigory and Eskar, completing the circle of political power.

"We don't have any train business on the schedule until tomorrow," Spiro explained, leading them inside. "We figured you'd appreciate a night to relax after so many days of traveling."

"We encourage you to explore the city while you're here." Larna's voice was soft and as elegant as her attire. "Do Lech has much to offer, and we can provide guides if you wish."

Graigory struck up a conversation about the layout of their streets, and Merriam let her mind wander as he talked. Larna seemed to be all soft edges. It was hard to imagine she was capable of condoning any level of violence. Spiro, on the other hand, was much more gruff, but clearly coddled. His hand had been soft when she'd shaken it, and even though the muscles in his shoulders filled out the sleeves of his jacket, Merriam would guess he hadn't wielded a weapon within her lifetime, if he'd even held one. His position, much like Mollian's, had been a birthright, and peace had thrived throughout Sekha for the majority of his life.

"Ah, Chetney!" Spiro called, cutting off his reply to Graigory about the updated road composition.

A male the spitting image of Spiro altered his course to meet the group, a diplomatic smile stretching his lips.

"This is my eldest son and one of Do Lech's leading officials, Lord Chetney Kinbriar," Spiro introduced when the fae grew close.

Merriam fought back a snort at his title that wasn't a title, disdain curling in her gut as her gaze tracked from his boots up to his face. His hazel eyes, identical to Aleah's, took in the group with mild interest, but just underneath the friendly glimmer was something that made unease and disgust curl tight in Merriam's gut.

I know what you are, she Cast to him, knowing he wouldn't be able to hear the words but hoping that some of the venom laced into them would manage to seep into his head.

"These are our guests from Umbra," Spiro told Chetney. "Commander Eskar of the Royal Guard, Master Graigory of the roadsguild, Master Portimer of the forestryguild, and Merriam, the king's marshal."

Chetney greeted them each in turn, his gaze drifting over Merriam's ears, her braid doing nothing to hide the human roundness of them, before he met her eyes. Merriam smiled with her teeth, ensuring he could see her short, dull canines, not removing her eyes from his. *Give me a reason, I beg you.* She silently threw the challenge at him, the tattoos between her shoulder blades itching.

He saw the challenge in her eyes, completely misinterpreting it. A smirk played at the corner of Chetney's mouth, and he wiped it away with a hand. "I hope you all enjoy your stay in our city. It's an honor to host you."

The visitors from Umbra were given instructions on where and when meals would be served throughout the day before being shown to their rooms.

Merriam unclasped her cloak, tossing it to the bench at the foot of her bed, and pushed her fingers into her hair, massaging her scalp as she walked out onto the small balcony. The city teemed with people, and beyond the streets, the harbor was just as busy. Merriam's fingers drifted to the iron aspen leaf hanging at her neck, sliding it slowly across its chain as she observed the dense activity below.

As the discomfort and frustration she'd felt in Chetney's presence subsided, Merriam was struck by an overwhelming feeling of loneliness, missing her friends. Missing Mollian. The interwoven threads of their souls were stretched with the distance, but strong. It was more his magic in her blood that made his absence loud and unforgettable. She sighed, turning to the luggage that had been brought to her room. Might as well unpack and settle in for a long week of politics.

The Guard had been given lodging at an inn right outside the gates of the overseer's residence. As Ferrick's representative, Eskar would be staying in the main house, which left Rovin as commanding officer of their unit and in charge of keeping everything under control.

He could already feel a headache forming behind one temple. Trying to keep accountability of a detachment of soldiers in a city known for its gambling dens, theaters, and brothels was a tall order. The young lieutenant had never felt his lack of experience so strongly.

He'd worked out a schedule for the Guard, keeping some of them at the ready at all times. He'd been provided with a rough itinerary of the week's events so that they would be prepared to escort the delegates around the city if needed.

"Let's go stay out of trouble." Kodi leaned against Rovin's doorframe, the need to move and distance himself from the Kinbriar estate an incessant buzz in his veins.

Rovin raised an eyebrow, giving his notes a final glance.

"Work doesn't start until tomorrow. Set it down."

"There's a reason I have rank and you don't, you know." Rovin tossed the papers onto his desk.

"Because I don't have a stick up my ass." Kodi grinned. "Now come on before I leave you behind."

Rovin growled playfully, bending low as he ran for Kodi, who let himself be tossed over Rovin's shoulder, springing from his hands to land dramatically on his back before bouncing to his feet.

"There he is." Kodi threw a jaunty punch into Rovin's ribs and slung his arm over Rovin's shoulder, directing him out the door. "Food first."

"I think the inn was going to provide us with—"

"We're in Do Lech, Rov. We're not eating at the inn when there are gambling dens that will let you eat all you can for a single silver coin." Kodi dropped his arm, taking the steps two at a time.

They melted into the crowd along the street, Rovin keeping a hand on the hilt of his short sword out of habit.

Kodi bought two flagons of ale from the first cart they passed, shoving one into Rovin's hand and clinking the cups together. "To a week of no leadership!"

Rovin smiled, chugging the cool ale. "*I'm* leadership, fucker," he said as he wiped his hand over his mouth.

"And thank the Legends I'm not." Kodi led them inside of a tall building, and Rovin's jaw dropped open.

The ceiling was high above them, painted to look like the sky, and a stream cut through the center of the structure, winding along past countless tables of various card and dice games. "This is unreal," he whispered.

"No, *that's* unreal," Kodi replied, elbowing him in the side.

Rovin followed Kodi's gaze to where tables lined an entire wall, stacked with platter upon platter of food.

Kodi practically skipped over to the buffet, exchanging a silver coin for a red paper wristband that would allow them access to the food throughout the night. He piled a plate high with several different kinds of meat, waiting for Rovin to pass through the line before finding a table to sit at.

More ale appeared next to their plates, the waitress setting them down with a wink. "First round is free for servants of the Crown." She glanced purposefully at the aspen leaves tattooed over their wrists and forearms. Her gaze lingered over them for a moment longer before she turned, walking away with a seductive sway to her hips.

"Any interest, brother?" Kodi asked, cocking an eyebrow.

Rovin shook his head in disinterest. "Food, drink, and a little irresponsibility with my coin. That's tonight's agenda."

"My kind of night." Kodi raised his glass, chugging down the ale.

A few hours and several drinks later, Rovin and Kodi stumbled back onto the street, their bellies full and their coin purses only marginally lighter than when they'd first arrived. Rovin had found a proclivity for a game of chance involving dice, and had done well, some of the other Guard showing up and betting alongside him.

A small crowd was gathering at a corner across the street, and they wandered over, curious.

"Show it to some friends, commit it to memory." The voice carried easily over the crowd, pleasant and holding a conspiratory edge. "Now, just slide it in there—don't be shy. Oh, not a phrase you're used to hearing, then."

Laughter spilled through the crowd, along with a couple of whoops.

"Settle, settle. I'm sure his partner is entirely satisfied."

More laughter, and the two reached the edge of the group just as the speaker hopped up onto the lip of a large stone planter, using it as a makeshift stage. A set of four slim, iridescent wings fluttered behind them as they found their balance, dropping to hang down their back once the fae was settled.

Their pale skin shone in the light of the streetlamps, a shock of dark hair falling over their face from the top of their head, the sides trimmed short. They wore a slim black vest, their arms covered in fine lines of black ink. Silver rings adorned their fingers, their nose, and their ears, the metal catching the light as they moved theatrically, addressing the crowd.

"What we're going to do first is throw out all of the kings." Their fingers worked quickly through the deck, dropping four cards to the ground. "You seem like a nice enough male, sir, but let's not have delusions of grandeur."

Laughter again rippled through the crowd, the male who'd presumably picked the original card throwing his hands up in acquiescence.

The performer discarded several more cards, each one with a joke or anecdote aimed at the one who picked the card, the city, the weather, or even the crowd.

"You're his friend, right?" The performer pointed out a male who'd been hollering the loudest at every dig aimed at the card-chooser. "If you had to take a guess, how long would you say he lasts in bed? Just between us."

"Three minutes!" his friend yelled enthusiastically.

"Three minutes?" the performer repeated, their wings fluttering in disbelief. "Harsh, my friend, harsh," they laughed. "I'm going to give him the benefit of the doubt and go with six." Their deft fingers skimmed through the cards, dropping all but three.

The performer's brow furrowed, and they licked their lips as they regarded the cards they held in confusion. "Well, this is ..." They dropped to the ground, making a show of picking up the fallen cards and quickly flipping through them. Tossing the cards onto the planter, they hopped back up, holding only the three sixes in their hand. They ran their fingers through their hair, giving their head a confused scratch before tossing the sixes over their shoulder. Placing a hand on their hip, they narrowed their eyes. "Now, sir, when I asked you to put your card back into the deck, did you keep it?"

The male in question shook his head.

The performer narrowed their eyes, beckoning him forward with a curl of their finger.

The male stepped up, and the performer leaned down, reaching behind his head. With a dramatic flourish of their hand, a card appeared from behind his ear, and the performer stood, showing the card to the crowd and then to the male. "Is this your card?"

The male nodded, a wide smile on his face as he clapped, and the fae gave a little bow, placing a hand against their chest and mouthing a "thank you" to the male for his participation and good spirit before turning back to the group, already rolling into a new trick.

On the other end of the crowd, Merriam stood on the edge of her own planter, one hand wrapped around a branch of the tree it surrounded as she leaned, watching the show. Kodi spied her first, knocking an elbow into Rovin to get his attention and gesturing with his head before working his way through the crowd to reach her.

He hopped up next to her, draping an arm over her shoulder cordially. "Fancy finding you here, demonslayer."

Rovin watched them, feeling jealousy knot uncomfortably in his chest. Kodi's touch was entirely platonic and comfortable—Merriam didn't even tense at the weight of his arm. Rovin would never be able to touch her like that, without a second thought of his actions or wondering how she would respond. He'd always been too aware of her, and this forced reminder of that awareness annoyed him. He leaned against the edge of the planter at Kodi's feet, trying to focus on the show.

"You know who would absolutely eat this up?" Merriam asked, an easy smile on her lips. "Aleah and Bellamy."

Rovin scratched the stubble on his cheek, another flare of jealousy rising in his chest, followed immediately by more annoyance at his reaction. Why should he care that she was thinking of anyone?

Merriam sat, crossing her legs and bracing her hands on either side of her. "We have magicians like this where I'm from," she explained, glancing at Rovin almost shyly. "It's not real magic, just sleight of hand, but even knowing that I'm still awestruck by some of the tricks. There's so much talent involved."

Rovin turned to look at her, one of her hands idly pulling the aspen leaf across the chain of her necklace as she watched the show.

"Do I have something on my face, Lieutenant?" She flicked her eyes back to Rovin, a blush crawling up her cheeks.

Rovin tore his gaze from her, and Kodi laughed, dropping between them. "He's had quite a bit to drink tonight and is probably trying to figure out if he can get you to carry *him* home this time. I'd offer, except that I don't want to."

They watched the rest of the performance, and, when it was finished, Merriam hopped to the ground. "I'm going to go tip them. I'll be right back."

"Mer," Kodi called, tossing her an extra silver when she turned, then she wound her way through the crowd. Kodi leveled his gaze at Rovin, an amused gleam in his eyes.

"Don't." Rovin scowled, looking away.

"I've got five gold coins that say you'll start a fight with her before the end of this trip so you can have a reason to be around her, even if it is just to glare and hurl insults."

"I'm not indulging whatever fantasy you've built up about this." Rovin crossed his arms over his chest, then realized the gesture was defensive, and rested his hands against the lip of stone on either side of him.

"You need to be indulging whatever fantasy *you've* built up before you make a fool of yourself." Kodi kicked his feet happily against the planter.

Rovin frowned at the carefree cadence of Kodi's legs. He knew his irritation was mostly due to the fact that Kodi was right—he would rather have Merriam's indignation than her indifference. He *wanted* to be a part of her life, even if the only role she would give him was as a nemesis. Acknowledging how much he admired her was terrifying enough on its own, without the added thought of admitting it to her.

Kodi stilled, every muscle in his body slowly going rigid.

The lack of movement pulled Rovin from his thoughts, and he looked up, following Kodi's line of sight to a giant board built into the side of one of the gambling dens. Lights lined the top, illuminating the advertisement for what appeared to be a new fleet of ships being built to enhance trade with other countries. Next to it, larger than life, was painted the likeness of a fae with freckled skin, fire-red hair, and hazel eyes.

Even though the pictured fae was male, the resemblance to Aleah was uncanny.

Kodi stared at the portrait of Chetney with unmasked hatred, rage boiling in his blood.

Rovin made a mental note to double-check the itinerary he was given and make sure that Kodi wasn't scheduled to work an activity where the heir would be present. Kodi had only shared the barest of details with him about Aleah's past, but it was enough for Rovin to know without a doubt that no number of laws or threats of retribution would save Chetney Kinbriar if Kodi got close enough to touch him.

Eight years before ...

ROVIN HAD JUST FINISHED showering and wanted nothing more than to fall into bed and sleep for an entire day. His last shift rotation had been brutal.

"The captain wants us all in the common room. Informal brief." One of his comrades poked his head into the room before Rovin had even had a chance to pull back his blanket.

He stifled a groan, grabbing a shirt from his wall locker and pulling it over his head as he walked down the hall.

Captain Ferrick leaned against a table at the head of the room, hands resting on either side of him and one ankle crossed in front of the other. Rovin watched him curiously as he made his way across the room. He'd seen the captain with casual posture on very rare occasions, but something about this felt forced, like this brief was more important than he wanted to let on.

Rovin stood against a wall to the side of the room, looking around as he waited. Only the newer Rangers were there, along with a couple of lieutenants who'd accompanied Ferrick. Kodi sidled up next to him, dropping to sit on the floor with his legs stretched out.

When everyone had settled, the captain cleared his throat, crossing his arms over his burly chest before he began. "As most of you are aware, the younger prince has brought a human girl to live with him. She's gotten it into her little head that she wants to join the Guard."

Everyone kept silent, unsure of the expected response.

Ferrick continued, dropping his gaze to the floor in what he hoped was a thoughtful expression. "Moreso, she has her sights set on becoming a Ranger, and has asked to train with us."

The gasps of shock and indignation Ferrick had been hoping for finally came.

Rovin tilted his head to the side, trying to sort through the information and the way it was being delivered.

"She thinks because the prince is enamored by her, she gets a free pass to whatever life she pleases. That's never been the way of the Guard, and even less so for us Rangers," the captain told them.

Several around the room nodded in agreement.

Rovin watched the male he damn near idolized with slight confusion. He'd been on shift that afternoon and had missed Mollian bringing the girl with him to training, but he'd been told about the debacle afterwards. She hadn't finished the run, which was admittedly embarrassing, but apparently her pride wasn't too bruised for her to want to come back and try again.

Ferrick's eyes turned to him, hardening with disdain at the softness in Rovin's face. "No one gets the easy route. Every single one of us has earned our place here."

Pride swelled in Rovin's chest as the captain's blue eyes bore into him. Ranger training had been the longest, most brutal three years of his life. Even as a half-fae, he was held to the same physical standards as his comrades and had fought tooth and nail not just to graduate, but to do so at the top of his class. Every grueling moment had been worth it for the aspen leaves he wore on his arms. He was one of the elite. The best of the best. And everyone would know just by seeing the tattoos that so few were awarded: he had earned his title.

Ferrick nodded, seeing the pride light the young Ranger's brown eyes. From the beginning, Rovin had shown signs of leadership. He had a knack for getting those around him to listen and follow his ideas and suggestions, which is something the captain had seen so rarely in lesser fae and never in a halfling. He also had a way of making the others feel heard, and thus easier to corral. If the younger Rangers were going to push the girl out, he would need Rovin on board.

"The girl is obviously welcome to earn her place among you, but I just wanted to make it clear that I don't expect her to be treated any differently just because of her station. She may be living with Prince Mollian, but that doesn't entitle her to special treatment." Ferrick knew he couldn't order them to exclude her, but he could push them along the path that would freeze her out. He had clawed for every scrap of power he'd earned. The queen trusted him implicitly, and his political standing in Sekha had been second only to hers for many years.

But the heir apparent didn't seem to be as easy to win over, which made Ferrick uneasy. Anyone who was being given a seat of power or prestige was automatically a threat. His reasoning behind it didn't matter, only the fact that his hold was still strong enough to cut down any potential opponents.

And that's exactly what he did.

Rovin, a newly minted Ranger, was more than familiar with the sort of … mostly harmless hazing that took place with recruits. And when he walked into the training room the next morning to see an unfamiliar head of pale golden hair, braided back with no attempt to hide the human curve of her ears, any thought he may have had about holding back on this girl who was determined to prove herself in a place where parentage held so much weight completely vanished.

Merriam wasn't just trying to *join* the Guard, she was actually training with them—with people who already earned the tattoos on their wrists—instead of slipping in with the other recruits.

"Prince's pet," Rovin spat at her, irritation at her privilege heating his blood. The look of indignation that had earned him fueled something deep in his chest. She had fire, and he was strangely looking forward to seeing how far he could push her.

At the end of that training session, she confronted him. He was almost proud of her for standing up for herself so readily, but then her gaze flicked over the clipped tip of his ear, and a cruel smile stretched her lips.

"*Halfling*," she'd cooed at him with a challenge, tilting her head and blinking sweetly.

Any thought of respect or admiration turned to acid inside of Rovin. Anger, bitter and cultivated through years of taunts and discrimination, heated his blood. Merriam was not his ally. She was not his comrade. She was a spoiled girl who clearly thought she was better than others because the second prince thought she was special.

The taint of hatred spread through his blood with that slur and the stupid, self-assured look on her face that accompanied it.

After that first encounter, Rovin was already poisoned against her, but Ferrick still took every instance available to point out the ways in which Merriam was spoiled by her relationship with Mollian.

It didn't help that Merriam rose to every occasion to prove her arrogance. She had a hot temper and met each and every push back with one of her own.

A week was all it took for Rovin to be endlessly annoyed by her, convinced she was an entitled thing given an unfair run of his playground. Without further prompting from his captain, he took every opportunity to make the girl's life among them miserable. Just as Ferrick expected, once Rovin grew to dislike her, the others soon followed his lead.

Chapter 14

MOLLIAN WAS ONCE AGAIN in the black place, and even though he had no recollection of it while awake, he remembered it vividly now that he was back.

His magic remembered, too, stirring in his blood.

Rip. Tear. Pull.

He breathed deeply, trying to shake off the plea of his power begging to pull free. But he looked around, seeing nothing, and closed his eyes, letting it rip from his skin and fly above him. It hit that solid blackness and sank into it, searching for a hold. It found purchase, tearing through whatever was above him.

Shred.

Opening his eyes, Mollian raised his hands, feeling his magic seep into the very fabric of the blackness and rip it down and away like it was a sheet.

The color almost blinded him.

Ropes of sparkling, swirling color crossed and wound around each other in an almost indecipherable tangle. Dark purples and blues wove into greens and pinks, all in various hues and vibrant in a way that hurt his mind to try to decipher.

The light reflected in his eyes, drowning out the pale green in a kaleidoscope of other colors. The shot of brown through his left eye was like a dark patch in the midst of it. His hair, too, shone with the colors surrounding him, the bright white of his curls reflecting everything without hindrance.

Mollian closed his eyes, the pattern of light playing across his eyelids as he took a settling breath. When he opened them again, he focused on a bright purple strand, following its path overhead.

He lost sight of its path where it wove through others, and he couldn't tell if the strand he picked up on the other side was the same one or not. Out of sheer curiosity—or possibly some level of instinct—Mollian reached out with his magic, letting it wrap loosely around the rope of cosmic, neon starlight and slide along its surface.

It was strangely soft, like if he really wanted to, he could manipulate its place, coil it another direction, or pinch it off.

He blinked, wetting his lips as he slowly tightened his magic around the tether he held, feeling initial give, but then resistance below. He squeezed tighter, then abruptly let go, stumbling backwards with a sharp intake of breath.

"What the—"

Mollian swallowed, rubbing the heel of his hand over the aspen leaf crown tattooed on his brow. A ghost of a tingle still ran through the ink in his skin, and he dropped his hand, peering back up.

When he'd applied pressure to the tether, he'd felt movement. A fast, heavy stream of power ran through that strand of celestial light, and his magic had leapt for it in a way that scared him.

Rip. Pull.

Magic sang in his blood, building in intensity as it coursed through him.

Mollian shook his head, crossing his arms over his stomach and leaning forward as he attempted to rein it in, shove it down, quiet it. He closed his eyes, sinking to his knees as he grit his teeth. *Stop stop stop,* he pleaded with it, struggling to keep it from reaching back out into the cosmos.

"*Stop!*"

Mollian's eyes flew open, and he was barely able to contain the wave of magic that tried to ripple from him. He sat up in bed, panting, white curls slicked to his forehead with sweat. His magic swirled under his skin in a way that made him squirm, and he forced his erratic breathing to slow into calm, measured breaths.

Throwing off the covers, he walked to the window, pushing the shutter open and looking out. Clouds blocked the moons and the stars, but the horizon was dark, mountains blending into the sky almost seamlessly.

Morning was still a ways off.

He sighed, pushing his hair off of his forehead and stumbling into the bathroom. He splashed water on his face, trying to remember what he'd been dreaming about that had him so unsettled. The harder he tried to pull pieces of it together, the less detail he could remember.

He knew he'd gone back to a place he'd been before. He knew he'd seen something, something no living being should have access to, and he knew he wanted to touch it. His *magic* wanted to touch it.

Pull. The echo of it stirred in his blood, and he shook his head roughly, throwing himself back into bed.

He pulled the blankets over his head, stretching out on his belly with one leg bent and his arms folded under the pillow. The ache of Merriam's absence stirred in his soul, and he wished that she were here, that he'd never sent her away. The feeling that he needed her in a way that she could never need him rose high in his chest. It had flooded him sporadically throughout the past year and made him uncomfortable to examine too closely.

An unbidden ache filled him, tears clogging his throat as he wished Oren were there to take the weight of his responsibility. As he wished for Gressia and her prickly humor but endless knowledge of the power their family possessed. Mollian squeezed his eyes shut, feeling alone and adrift.

"Stop," he whispered, not quite sure why or what he was talking to. His eyes closed, and he slipped back into sleep.

The day had been long and full of entirely too many matters of state, but that evening, Bellamy and Mollian sat in the king's chambers with a deck of cards spread on the small table between them along with an array of colorful plastic bags and wrappers. Craving a little bit of mischief, Mollian had taken Bellamy to Earth for a quick gas station run. One was conveniently located just on the other side of reality from the castle gates and contained snacks of every conceivable type and thin, shiny booklets filled with pictures of machines and buildings.

Merriam had gone with the two males on multiple occasions, and never failed to laugh when they stood in front of the magazine rack, excitedly picking out editions of cars, military news, or architecture and design without even looking at the stacks off to the side, tastefully concealed but obviously filled with naked people.

Mollian's head was leaned against the back of the couch, staring up at the ceiling. "You're my friend, right?"

Bellamy looked up at him from where he'd been studying an article on trains, of all things. The writing on it was so similar to the human tongue of Nethyl, but just different enough to make his head swim as he looked at it. Merriam was the one who typically read to them and tried to better explain the nuances of her home world's dialect. "Whenever I'm not on shift, if you're talking about formalities," he answered.

"I miss her."

Bellamy agreed, glancing back down at the magazine, almost equally as frustrating as it was interesting without Merriam there to interpret. But he knew that the way Mollian felt her absence was vastly different and unrelated to literature. "You haven't been sleeping well." He said it as an observation rather than a question.

A grim smile spread Mollian's lips. "I need her, Bell. I mean, I always have, it's part of being *mehhen*, but since I was crowned, it's different. It's like ... like my magic needs her. There's too much of it in me to contain on my own."

Bellamy remembered those first few days of Mollian's rule. Merriam hadn't left his side for more than a few moments at a time, uneasy whenever she'd been pulled away. Not from fear of something happening to Mollian, but like the lack of proximity made her physically uncomfortable.

Mollian sat forward and rested his elbows on his knees. "I've been having these dreams, but I can't remember what they're about. All I can remember is blackness and then flashes of color, but I think when I'm dreaming I can remember everything else. And the dreams … they rattle my hold on my magic, like it has a mind of its own or something."

Bellamy straightened, watching Mollian with concern. "Are the dreams bad?"

Mollian frowned, a crease forming in the center of his aspen crown. "I don't think so. It doesn't feel ominous at all, more like I'm in a place that nobody is supposed to be. Like, it shouldn't be possible to be there or have access to whatever I'm seeing and whatever knowledge that gives me."

"And you forget everything else as soon as you wake up?"

Mollian ran his hands through his hair. "I forget, but my magic remembers, I think. Does that even make sense?"

Bellamy shrugged. "I guess it can, especially if your magic isn't just yours."

Mollian cocked his head to the side.

"You're not a normal high fae, right? Sure, you have our power to manipulate things with your mind, but your magic also comes from Nethyl, from the Gate and the pieces of it that are in your blood and in your crown. Maybe whatever place you're going to in your dreams is a place your magic knows."

Mollian wiped his hands down his face. "Why is that somehow even *more* unsettling?"

Bellamy didn't have an answer for that, so he offered something else. "Mer settles your magic?"

Mollian nodded.

"Then, as your friend, I suggest you not send her away again for a while, at least until you figure out what any of this means."

"Wise council." Mollian laughed mirthlessly. "Whose dumb idea was it to ask her to go halfway across the country, anyway?"

"Especially so soon after she got back from Entumbra," Bellamy pointed out. "I'm surprised either of your codependent asses were okay with it."

Mollian truly laughed then, stealing the magazine from Bellamy's lap with a flick of his fingers. "Watch it, kid, or no more Earth secrets for you."

Bellamy raised an eyebrow, stretching the scar that cut down his face, and snatched the magazine back with his own magic. "Think twice about who's had more extensive combat training before you go around calling people kid."

"You forget that, as king, I can call in a champion to fight for me," Mollian shot back.

"Yes, and it seems your champion is a week's ride south." Bellamy opened the magazine, averting his attention for dramatic effect. "But I'll try to hold on to my intimidation until she's able to return."

Chapter 15

I'm scared of you

PROGRESS WITH PLANNING THE railroad was going well in Do Lech. Graigory led most of the meetings, always prepared with plans, charts, and notes that were refreshed after each session. Though Merriam was aware of her *mehhen's* inherent annoyance with the roadsmaster—more a grievance of forced proximity than any real issue with the male himself—she was entirely grateful for his presence in the port city.

Not only was Graigory highly knowledgeable when it came to planning and construction, but he was also a good critical thinker, sorting through problems that were brought up in ways that were both logical and creative.

Portimer had even become less combative, bringing up potential environmental issues as problems to be solved rather than arguments against the construction as a whole.

Spiro Kinbriar was very eager to please, helping work through where the stations should be located within Do Lech and how to deviate resources to allow for a swift and successful build. While he was friendly, his underlying motives were selfish. He knew Do Lech was already the most important port in Sekha and his family one of the most powerful. He also knew that adding in this revolutionary mode of transportation would only further solidify the city's importance and add to their political power.

Merriam didn't trust him.

His reach for more power left a bad taste in her mouth, but more than that, she was sickened by his pride in his son. Every time Chetney would enter a room, Spiro would wave him over or stop to include him in whatever was going on, treating the ground he walked on like it was blessed by the Legends.

When Merriam saw Chetney's face, her mind filled with images of Aleah's scarred skin. Not the wounds of fights and battles won that peppered her arms and legs, but the web of old scars across her abdomen and back. Wounds given to her because of what she was and how she came to be.

Each time he spoke, she remembered Aleah's soft recollection of him tossing her to the ground at her human father's feet. *"You created this abomination, and it killed my sister."* Merriam could now hear the words in Chetney's voice, the unctuous tones he used around the visitors turned cold and harsh with disgust.

Spiro and Chetney's interactions made her think of young Aleah watching as her uncle slaughtered her father and left her covered in blood for Spiro and Larna to find. She thought of Aleah's clipped ear, how her grandparents must have known who mutilated her.

All of those vile acts, all of that trauma inflicted on a helpless child, and Spiro had let it happen. Even if he didn't outright condone Chetney's actions, he did nothing to stop them. Did nothing to show his disdain for his son's despicable acts.

And that, to Merriam, made him just as guilty as Chetney.

She also didn't fail to notice that out of the small detachment of Guard present in Do Lech, Kodi was never scheduled to work any of the events outside of guarding the doors of the meetings. No lunches, suppers, or tours of the town included the wild-willed Ranger.

One day, when the group was on break from planning, Merriam rested against the wall next to where Kodi stood, using a knife to pick at his nails. She propped one foot up, crossing her arms over her chest in a relaxed manner.

"How can I help you, demonslayer? Or do you just miss the joy of my company?"

Merriam rolled her eyes, resisting the urge to throw an elbow at him. "Have you seen Aleah since we've been here?"

Kodi nodded, gliding the blade underneath a fingernail. "I made it out last night."

"How is she?"

"Could be worse. She's focused on her job, and I think that's helping with the proximity. She's not giving herself time or energy to dwell on it," Kodi replied.

Merriam studied the careful composure of his expression. "Rovin keeps you away from the Kinbriars."

"Is that a question, or do you want congratulations on your observational skills, ex-merc?" Kodi, head tilted toward his hands, looked up at her through thick lashes.

Merriam's lips twitched at one corner, and she shrugged.

"If he so much as looks at me, I'll snap. I'm wound so fucking tight, Mer." Kodi's voice was strained. "Have you seen the way Spiro looks at him?"

"Like he's the Legends' gift to Sekha," Merriam huffed, shaking her head.

"Do you think any of them ever even think about her? Ever wonder what happened to her?" Kodi's knife slipped, cutting into the side of his finger, and he hissed, bringing it to his mouth. "How can they be so unconcerned? How can she matter so little in their eyes? It makes my blood fucking boil."

Portimer popped his head out of the door before Merriam could reply. "We're ready to resume, Marshal."

She squeezed Kodi's elbow in silent solidarity as she passed, heading back into the conference room.

When they were done for the day, Merriam went up to her room, but she was restless. Changing into clothes more comfortable for walking the warm, humid streets, she headed out into the city.

Spiro and Larna had arranged an elegant supper for the following evening at one of the high-end entertainment centers right on the harbor. It was an all-inclusive establishment with gambling, an arena for shows, multiple shops and bars and dining facilities, and a few floors that operated as a pleasure house.

She hadn't had the forethought to bring anything fancy enough for such a meal, so she slipped into a boutique off the strip, browsing the elegant gowns. It didn't take her long to find something suitable, and the salesperson offered to have it delivered directly to the Kinbriar estate. "Is this being charged to the Kinbriar account as well?"

A wicked smile spread Merriam's lips, and she nodded graciously. "Yes, thank you."

With time to kill and no real destination in mind, Merriam wandered through the crowds. When the sun grew uncomfortably warm against her skin and the humidity became too stifling, she slipped into one of the buildings, letting the cool air brush her skin.

She wondered how they managed air conditioning here, imagining it was some sort of contraption that ran the air over water to cool it, but she didn't know enough about the physics behind it to be sure. *Mollian would have so much fun trying to figure it out*, she thought with a smile. A pang of homesickness filled her, his absence singing clearly in her blood. Only a few more days, and then they would be on the road back home.

A banner of Chetney promoting some restaurant or another was plastered to the wall, and she wrinkled her nose, averting her gaze and walking past. Home could not come soon enough.

Merriam was looking around at the various tables and machines when she noticed a vaguely familiar fae sitting alone at a table. Dark hair hung over their face, but was shorter on the back and sides. Four narrow, translucent wings hung down their back, and a cigarette was pinched between their fingers.

If the game wasn't roulette, it was at the very least similar enough that Merriam figured she could grasp it easily, so she walked over, sliding onto the stool next to the street performer.

"I saw your show the other day," she said conversationally, pulling out a few silvers to exchange for painted brass chips. "You're really good."

The fae smiled, inhaling deeply before blowing a stream of smoke up into the air above them.

Merriam recognized the heady smell. Not tobacco, cannabis.

"Wait, I think I remember you. Visiting from Umbra, yeah?" they asked, dark eyes rimmed with red.

Merriam smiled, placing some chips onto the felt table as the attendant started a small white ball spinning over a numbered wheel. "Yes, that's right."

The performer regarded the table for a moment before placing their own chips. "Shiloh," they said, offering their hand.

"Merriam." She shook it.

After a couple rounds in comfortable silence, Merriam asked, "Where did you learn sleight of hand? I've seriously never seen it done so well."

Shiloh laughed, tossing their head to move the hair from their face. "Thanks. I grew up here, watching various street shows. Saw a traveling performer do some card tricks one day and decided to learn them for myself. Never looked back after that."

They both placed a new round of chips.

"You didn't call it magic."

Merriam glanced over at Shiloh, missing which number the ball landed on. "What?"

"My tricks. You didn't even second-guess that it was all just fancy movement and deception. Even high fae who know damn well I don't possess any magic start to doubt themselves on that fact."

Merriam collected the chips she'd won, setting new ones on the field. "I saw a few shows like that where I grew up," she said carefully, then smiled, sliding a sideways glance to Shiloh. "I actually know a couple of card tricks myself, though nothing anywhere near your level."

"No shit!" Shiloh doused the end of the joint in an ashtray, dropping it into a pocket of their vest, and folded their arms, leaning back. "Let me buy you a drink and you can show me what you've got."

They cashed their chips back in for coin and relocated to a bar inside the building. Once their drinks were ordered, Shiloh slapped a deck of cards onto the bartop. "Let's see it."

Merriam shuffled, making a show of getting a feel for the cards. It was a simple trick where she forced Shiloh to pick a predetermined card, but made "finding" it after the fact an overly complicated process. In the end, she held up Shiloh's card sandwiched between two others, grinning.

"Not half bad," Shiloh complimented, raising their glass in a salute.

They sat and drank for a while, ordering some food and exchanging random stories and anecdotes, and Merriam knew how relaxed she felt didn't have anything to do with the alcohol, but with the ease of Shiloh's company.

Shiloh leaned back in the barstool, looking up to the skylights. "Legends, it got late. I've gotta run. But it was nice to meet you, Mer. I mean it."

Merriam slid from her stool, leaving a few coins on the bar to cover their tab. "This was the best time I've had here, so thank you."

Shiloh draped their arm over Merriam's shoulder, directing her toward the door. "That doesn't bode well for my poor city if a few drinks in a gambling den has been the highlight of your trip."

"Well, it's been for work, if that makes you feel better. It's not Do Lech's fault that politics are stupidly stressful," Merriam assured them.

Shiloh laughed, dropping their arm. "Tell ya what, I'm around most nights. Find me before you leave, and I'll make sure to show you a good time. The best Do Lech has to offer." Shiloh's gaze slid past Merriam to an advertisement behind her, and they scoffed, smile dropping.

Merriam turned to look at what caused the reaction, apprehension coiling in her gut when she saw Chetney's face on the wall. "Not a fan of the Kinbriar heir?"

Shiloh pressed their lips together, looking away uncomfortably. "Live in a place long enough and you learn a lot of unsavory things. I won't say I put a lot of weight behind every bit of gossip I hear, but something about him just makes me uneasy. It's in his eyes, like he's hiding behind a mask. Gross stuff." Shiloh shuddered, wings trembling with the movement.

Merriam nodded grimly. "I've heard stories of my own," she said quietly. "How is it no one has called him on his shit? Or tried to hold him accountable?"

Shiloh ran their teeth over their lip as the two stepped out into the night. "He's untouchable, Merriam. The Stonebanes may rule Sekha, but we are far from the eyes of the king down here."

Merriam looked toward the overseer's estate. "Then I guess it's a good thing the king sent his eyes south. No one is untouchable."

Shiloh tilted their head to the side, tucking their hands into their pockets. "Be careful in there, okay? Humans aren't ... there's a story floating around that a human caused the death of Chetney's *mehhen*. He pretends not to have a prejudice, but ..." Shiloh trailed off.

Merriam smiled grimly. "Don't worry. I'll take care of myself."

With a parting nod, Shiloh walked off down the street, in the opposite direction of the grand estate.

Merriam's dress was pale lavender silk, draping over one shoulder at the top and falling from her hips in a single piece. Soft, intricate lace replaced the silk around her midsection, and the same fabric created a sleeve that hugged the length of her arm.

The other was left free, her aspen branch tattoo on full display, reds fading into yellows fading into greens in vibrant shades that clashed with the color of her dress.

Unwilling to manipulate the lengths of her hair in the humid environment, she undid her braid, brushing through the pale blonde waves with her fingers and pinning back small sections on either side of her face.

She looked longingly to where her axes hung on a bedpost, craving the comfort of their weight at her hips. Instead, she opted for a more dainty belt, soft tan leather and simple flats she'd bought to accompany it. The scabbard hanging from the belt was cut from the same leather, but the dagger sheathed inside was one of Merriam's favorite creations—second to her axes.

Mollian had wrapped the grip in strips of white silk braided with sparkling silver thread, the pommel and cross-guard dotted with silver stones that glinted in the light. While the hilt was more decorative than practical, the blade was sharp and well-maintained, with a deep groove near the top to allow for blood-letting. With the weapon on her waist, Merriam left her room to meet up with the others in the courtyard, where they would be taking a couple of carriages to the harbor.

A feeling of unfamiliarity, and with it, discomfort, flooded Merriam as she stood outside. It wasn't inferiority or a lack of confidence, but an overall awareness that she was different from the rest of the group. She didn't want to sit around a table and discuss politics and create relationships that could possibly add to her power. She just wanted to eat good food and enjoy the night, maybe dance a bit, let loose some of the stress from the week.

Taking a deep breath, Merriam stepped forward to join the group of politicians while they waited to depart.

The carriage ride to the pier was comfortably quiet, everyone taking in the sights of Do Lech's nightlife. When they reached their destination, they were ushered onto a lift operated by two of the resort staff that took them up to the top floor.

Merriam's jaw dropped when they walked into the grand room. A giant crystal chandelier hung from the tall ceiling, strings of sparkling stone and airy white gauze draped around it, secured in the uppermost corner of the wall and hanging down to the floor. Prisms of light sparkled around the entire room. Large tables with bright white tablecloths lined the space, though all were empty aside from centerpieces of various white flowers.

Merriam toyed with the aspen leaf at her throat while she took it all in, completely mesmerized.

"Check out the harbor."

Merriam jumped, Rovin's sleeve brushing her arm as he stepped beside her. "What are you doing here?" she asked without thinking, taking half a step back.

"Security," he said, as though it should be obvious.

"Right." Merriam bit her lip, looking out the open windows to the water. The harbor was filled with ships of various sizes. Their lights twinkled off the water, dark with the reflection of the sky. "I didn't see you. At the estate." She hadn't expected him to be here, and it set her on edge for reasons she couldn't fully name.

"Did you look?" Rovin asked without glancing at her.

Merriam scoffed before she could stop herself. "Why would I have?"

His gaze moved to her, eyes narrowing for a moment. "Enjoy your dinner, pet."

Merriam glared at his back as he walked away, taking a position against the far wall with a few of the other Guard.

Like Rovin, Eskar was clad in the deep green dress jacket of the Rangers. The golden aspen leaf of a commander was sewn to each bicep, matching Ranger badge shining on her chest, and the hilt of the sword strapped to her side.

Merriam, ripe with inexplicable irritation, slid into the open seat next to her. "Missed some lint on your jacket there, Commander."

Eskar scoffed, raising a goblet of deep golden wine to her lips. "Jealous that your official rank bears no symbolism, Marshal?"

Merriam leaned back as a waiter came up, pouring wine into the goblet in front of her. She smiled her thanks at him before replying. "I'm not so insecure in my position that I need people to be aware of it the moment they look at me." She made a show of lightly swirling the wine in her glass, watching the legs sink slowly down the sides before taking a sip.

The wine was a faerie vintage, with bright, intense flavors that coated Merriam's tongue and seemed to rush right to her head when she swallowed. *Pace yourself.*

"Yet you continue to wear the king's collar around your neck." Eskar smirked, turning and striking up a conversation with Chetney, who sat a little further down the table.

Merriam's face heated, and she bit the inside of her cheek, fisting her hands in her lap to keep from toying with her necklace.

The meal began soon enough, Spiro standing to give a toast before servers brought in the first course. Merriam exchanged brief lines with the servers whenever they came by, joking with them about the food, the ambient noise from the harbor, or other aspects of Do Lech.

The first waiter came by halfway through the second course with a slim flute, setting it in front of Merriam and filling it with sparkling wine. "Figured you'd like something easier to sip on if you have to be in this company all night," he told her quietly.

They shared a conspiratory smile, and he smoothly cleared away the other goblet while collecting finished plates, winking at Merriam before he left.

With the familiarity of a human wine in hand, something her tolerance was much better suited for, Merriam tuned back to the conversation around her, adding comments and remarks and answering questions about things happening behind the scenes in Umbra. Throughout the meal, she felt Rovin's eyes on her from across the room. Her skin burned under the weight of his gaze. Underneath her instinctive annoyance, she liked that he was glued to her, and she didn't want to examine what that meant.

After the final course, Merriam sagged with relief, hoping it was time to leave, but a cocktail hour followed.

The dining hall opened up to other high-level fae from the city, and the incessant mingling continued. Merriam's gaze met that of the waiter who'd brought her the wine, and she widened her eyes, lips pressed together in a dramatic expression of exasperation. He laughed, pointing to her flute—now on its second fill—and gave a questioning thumbs-up.

Merriam returned it with a smile, signaling she was all good, and let him disappear into the crowd.

She looked around, telling herself her search of the crowd had nothing to do with Rovin's sudden absence, and spied a set of double doors near the back of the room. Merriam walked over, slipping through and onto a balcony that overlooked the sea. Leaning against the railing, she looked up at the sky and frowned.

So few stars were visible here, even though neither of the moons were full.

"The light from the city is too bright."

For the second time that night, Merriam jumped, whirling around.

Rovin leaned against the wall, arms crossed over his chest. Silver lieutenant stripes shone on the sleeves of his jacket. A smirk played on his lips, a mixture of amusement and disappointment in his deep brown eyes.

"You scared me," Merriam said, needing to fill the suddenly uncomfortable silence.

Rovin pushed from the wall to stand at the balcony next to her, hands tucked into his pockets as he looked from her face to the water below. "There was a time not too long ago when you immediately noticed my presence. Even just my proximity was enough to tense your shoulders and warrant a death glare."

Merriam bit her lip, taking a half step away because her focus had narrowed to the minimal space between them. "To be fair, you used to be a complete and total prick. I had to be aware of you so I could stay on the defensive."

"And now?" Rovin asked, turning his head to look at her.

Merriam shrugged. "We're on the same side, right? We're in a truce."

Rovin snorted. "Is that what you call this?"

"I don't know." Merriam crossed her arms defensively. Heat spread across her skin as his eyes met hers, and her mouth went dry. She blinked, forcing up the irritation she would have already been filled with a year ago. When he continued to watch her, his eyes traveling over her hair, across her face, back to her eyes, the emotion finally came to her rescue. "Why are you looking at me like that?"

Rovin tilted his head to the side. "Like what?"

Merriam glared, but there was no fire behind it. Her breathing slowed, nerves churning in her stomach as she forced the words out. "Like you wish you were looking at anything else, but can't force yourself to look away."

He did look away at that. They both knew there was truth in her words.

Rovin ran a hand over his mouth, staring out across the harbor. Wind blew off the sea, lifting his hair from his shoulders and stinging his cheeks with the bite of salty air. "I'm scared of you."

Merriam's fingers lifted to the aspen leaf at her throat, one arm curling around her middle. She wanted to make a retort, but every sharp word stilled on her tongue, the weight of his words heavy in her chest.

"I'm scared of how much you never needed any of this, of how determined you were to forge a place for yourself regardless and never let anything we said deter you. I'm scared of how much you've always known who you are and where you needed to be. You don't need me or anyone else, and I'm scared of how much I *want* you to need me and how much I admire you even when you're digging under my skin and annoying the shit out of me and testing me in every way." Rovin gripped the balcony, turning his eyes up to the sky and taking a deep breath before he finally looked at Merriam again.

His gaze drifted over her face, her lips, the tendrils of flaxen hair tugged across her freckled cheeks by the wind, her wide amber eyes watching him with something disconcertingly similar to denial and perhaps a bit of hope.

Reaching out, Rovin brushed the hair from her face, tucking it behind her ear. She didn't lean into his touch, but she didn't pull away. Her eyes closed for a few moments longer than what a blink should be, and her lips parted slightly.

She looked at him again, and Rovin dropped his hand. "I'm scared of how much I want to be around you and how much it bothers me that you've found friends among the Rangers while I've remained your enemy. I'm scared of—of ..." Rovin trailed off, looking away from her in frustration.

"Rov," she said quietly, gripping her necklace like it was a lifeline. Her heart slammed against her ribcage, and she couldn't quite catch her breath as she waited for him to finish, terrified by the depth of her hope that his words were an admission of something more.

Rovin met her gaze again, torment shining in his deep brown eyes.

"Legends." He ran his hands through his hair. "This isn't your burden. I shouldn't have … shit." He spun, stalking back inside.

That budding sense of expectation was buried under a blanket of rejection as he walked away. "Rovin!" Merriam called, the heat of anger in her voice hiding the disappointment that coursed through her. Rovin stilled, his body rigid. "Look at me." Her throat was tight with emotion.

He turned his head marginally, keeping his back to her.

"You know what? *Fuck you.*" Merriam walked up and shoved her hands into his back so that he stumbled forward, catching himself on the door frame. "You don't get to come out here after fucking staring at me all night and then dump all of *your* feelings and turn around and leave like you're some noble asshole saving me from having to process that or figure out what the fuck it even means!"

Rovin laughed, resting a forearm on the door frame and burying his face in the crook of his elbow as his chest shook.

Merriam clenched her hands into fists, tears of anger and confusion lining her eyes. "What is *wrong* with you?"

Kodi's words played through his head. "*I've got five gold coins that say you'll start a fight with her before the end of this.*" Unintentional as it might have been, he'd definitely just started something. "It's nothing."

Merriam threw her hands up in exasperation. "What am I supposed to do with the knowledge that I scare you?"

Rovin shook his head, finally meeting her eyes again, but his were guarded, every wall thrown back up as he shrugged, dragging a hand across his jaw. "What do you want to do with it, pet?" His voice was laced with challenge.

"You're a fucking *asshole,*" she spat, pushing past him. She stormed down the hall, down the stairs, and onto the street, tripping on her dress as she went. Resting her hand against the side of the building, she took a second, panting as she swallowed down her feelings, clearing her vision.

"Stupid fucking dress," she muttered, reaching down to grab the hem and ripping a slit up the center. Then she wove her way through the crowds and back to the overseer's estate.

BELLAMY WOKE AT DAWN, pushing wild, golden brown curls from his face and yawning. He was on a full day of princeling duty, as they'd taken to calling it. Ryddan had lessons with Mordecai and the other children half the day, and Lydia was around for most of the rest, so it wasn't particularly exciting or adventurous work, but Bellamy always looked forward to these shifts. Something about watching Ryddan grow and take in the world around him was refreshing, especially compared to the bitter and jaded outlook of some of the Royal Guard.

Bellamy dressed, tying back the top half of his hair and strapping his sword to his belt. He grabbed a couple of honey biscuits and as many links of sausage as he could fit in a hand before walking out of the barracks, heading up to the castle as he ate.

As he climbed up to Ryddan's room, muffled sounds of commotion reached his ears. He paused, biscuit hanging from his lips while he listened.

"NO! You're not in charge of me!"

"Ah, Hel," Bellamy muttered around the food, shoving the rest into his mouth as he finished the climb. He threw open the door, almost choking trying to hold in laughter at the scene before him.

Lydia stood to one side of the room, hands on her hips and face flushed with irritation.

Ryddan had tucked himself into a corner by the desk, only a patch of light brown skin and a flash of white hair visible through a few gaps in the wall of furniture he'd managed to build around him.

The couch, heavier than the chairs and side tables that Ryddan had already moved to shield himself, was slowly sliding across the carpet as he tried to reinforce his barrier.

"Ryddan Stonebane, stop your nonsense this instant! Legends help me if you make me pull you out of there," Lydia threatened, stamping one foot noiselessly on the carpet.

"Go away!" Ryddan yelled, and the couch lurched a little bit closer.

Bellamy stepped forward and placed a hand on one arm of the couch, effectively stopping its slide. "Rydd, can you tell me what's wrong?" he asked calmly, struggling to keep the smile from his face.

Lydia turned, registering his presence for the first time, and her whole face and neck grew to the color of a tomato. She dropped her arms, but Bellamy held a hand up to keep her from talking, waiting for Ryddan to reply.

"Lydia's being *mean* and *controlling* and *hateful*," Ryddan half-wailed in that way that young children do when a minor inconvenience has uprooted their lives.

Bellamy looked to Lydia, offering her a placating smile as he addressed the prince. "What a horrible morning." He reached out with his magic, giving a tentative tug against the wall of furniture, but resistance told him Ryddan was still holding tight. He could easily overpower the child, but knew that the rest of the morning would go a lot smoother if he got Ryddan to concede on his own. "How about you tell me about it over breakfast? We'll have to put the table back, though."

Ryddan was quiet for a moment, then, in a much less whiny tone than before, "Do I have to put on itchy clothes?"

"Of course not. Why would you have to put on itchy clothes?" Bellamy asked, giving another pull against the furniture. One of the chairs gave out easier, so he pulled it away, sliding it back across the room.

"They're not itchy clothes, Ryddan, they're the same clothes you wear every day." Lydia threw her hands up, exasperated.

Bellamy shot her a look. "Come eat, Rydd. No itchy clothes, I promise."

Ryddan pushed some of the furniture away and crawled out, wearing only a pair of flannel pants printed with black bears and moose that Merriam had given him. He walked over to the couch, climbing up and looking at Bellamy expectantly.

"You moved the table, buddy."

Ryddan looked over to the pile of furniture in the corner, turning back to Bellamy with wide green eyes. "Can you help me?"

"Come on, use your hands." Bellamy walked over and grabbed one end of the small table. Ryddan hoisted the other, grunting dramatically with the effort even though Bellamy used his magic to take most of the weight from Ryddan's side. They set it down in front of the couch, and Lydia brought over a breakfast tray that had been left outside.

As Ryddan ate, Lydia pulled Bellamy aside, speaking quietly. "You can't coddle him. He needs to learn how to behave in society."

Bellamy sighed, folding his arms over his chest and completely missing the way Lydia's gaze focused on the exposed muscle as he did so. "Pick your battles, Lydia. I know you're the expert here, but the first five years of his life were entirely different from any of the other children you've been nursemaid to."

As far as children went, Ryddan was generally well-behaved. The outbursts he did have seemed reasonable when taking into account that he was an orphan. Not that he didn't have people who loved him. Merriam played the part of fun aunt well and took joy in it. Mollian took a softer, more teaching role, sharing his vast wealth of knowledge readily with his nephew. And there were his grandparents, of course, but he'd only seen them a few times.

Lydia loved him in a way, but she was also employed to raise him, and she felt she had a duty to her country to raise him as a prince, not as a child.

Even though Bellamy had no personal obligation to the kid, he had always tried to be an anchor for Ryddan, a safe person that he would know he could always come to no matter what. It wouldn't always be possible for Mollian or Merriam to be there at a moment's notice, not when they were running a country, but Bellamy could be. And at some point over the past year, he had grown to love Ryddan in an unconditional way that made him want nothing more than for the prince to be safe, healthy, and generally happy, regardless of what his future may hold.

"He has to wear clothing to his classes, Bellamy," Lydia reiterated.

Bellamy placed a hand on her arm. For someone so observant, the effect he had on her was so often missed. "I know. Just let me talk to him."

Bellamy sat next to Ryddan, and the little prince tucked himself comfortably into Bellamy's side as he munched on an apple, holding it in both hands. Any irritation left in the Ranger melted away at the simple act, and he brushed his hand over Ryddan's fine white hair for a moment. "What happened this morning?"

Ryddan regarded the core of his apple, his hands sticky with the juice. Bellamy looked from the child's hands to Lydia, and she disappeared for a wet cloth.

"Well," Ryddan sighed, digging a seed from the apple and placing it on his knee. "Lydia was trying to help me get ready this morning, but none of my clothes fit right. They hurt my skin, and I said I didn't want to wear them, but she said I had to, and she said if I didn't put them on, she'd put them on for me. So I hid in the fort." Ryddan glanced over to the pile of furniture.

Lydia came back in, cloth in hand. Bellamy grabbed it from her, gently taking the apple from Ryddan and setting it, along with the seed, on the table. "Would you try again? Maybe now that your belly is full and you're more awake, your clothes will feel better." Bellamy wiped Ryddan's hands thoroughly, then his face for good measure, and tossed the cloth to the table.

"Why can't I just wear the pants Ria got me?" Ryddan asked plaintively.

"These are special pants, Rydd. Your friends don't have pants like this, and that could make them sad."

"Because only Ria and Molli can get them?" Ryddan looked up at Bellamy.

"Exactly."

Ryddan nodded thoughtfully. "I'll try again."

"Thanks, buddy." Bellamy smoothed Ryddan's hair to the side. "Do you want to put the furniture back before clothes or after?"

The prince looked back at his fort with a dramatic sigh. "Before."

They made quick work of reorganizing the room, Lydia pitching in to help. Ryddan eventually settled on clothes, Lydia forcing down her squeak of disapproval at his choice of lightweight cotton shorts and a silky vest.

"I'll take him down to Mordecai," Bellamy offered while Ryddan was brushing his teeth.

"Thank you." Lydia blushed, looking up at him through her lashes.

"Of course," Bellamy smiled, but the way she was watching him made him feel awkward.

Ryddan shifted into a cat when they left his room, weaving through Bellamy's feet as they walked.

"Are you trying to get me in trouble with Lydia?" he asked, knowing how much she disapproved of the prince walking around as an animal.

Ryddan meowed in response, the effort of Casting to a fae with no Keeper blood still a bit too intense for him, and jumped into Bellamy's arms, planting his front paws on his chest and stretching up to rub his head against Bellamy's chin before leaping back down to the ground. He shifted back to a fae when they reached the doors of Mordecai's domain, and Ryddan waved before slipping into the room.

This was the part that grated on Bellamy. He needed to be readily available in case of emergency, so he couldn't go for a run or slip off into the courtyard for combat training. If he wasn't concerned about someone walking by and wondering where it came from, he'd peruse one of Earth's magazines. Instead, he paced the hallway, sat at the window, practiced his footwork, and did simple sword exercises.

When lunch rolled around, Lydia came for the children, taking them out into the courtyard to eat and expel some energy. Bellamy sat to the side, relaxing on a wide stone banister and leaning back against a tree growing close behind.

"Hey, Bell! Have you eaten yet?" Evangeline, a fellow Ranger and one of his oldest friends, sat beside him, unfolding a cloth-wrapped lunch.

"I'll grab something later," Bellamy said.

Evangeline held out half of a sandwich, taking a bite of the other as she watched Lydia with the children.

Bellamy took it, knocking his shoulder into hers in thanks.

Lydia turned then, a scowl flitting over her face before she whirled back around.

Evangeline laughed, covering her mouth with one hand. "Sorry to get you in trouble."

"You can't get me in trouble. She's Rydd's nursemaid, not mine," Bellamy grumbled, peeling off a piece of crust to toss to a chipmunk.

"She should know her jealousy is misplaced, anyway. You're not my type." Evangeline flashed him a smile before returning to her food, happily swinging her feet in front of her.

Bellamy laughed, half at her statement and half at how much she'd grown into herself since the fight under the mountain. They'd been such newly minted Rangers then, and she'd been wide-eyed and fearful of everything. She still clammed up around leadership and in intense situations, but she was an entirely different, relaxed person around her peers. "And what is your type, Evie?"

Evangeline wrinkled up her nose, watching the children in a game of tag. "Someone without so many feelings. I've got too much going on to worry about another fully grown person always wanting to hang out or talk about their day." She rolled her eyes, pulling a lock of dark hair back from her face and wrapping it into the bun at the top of her head.

"Isn't that pretty standard in most relationships?"

She grinned, finishing her half of the sandwich. "I prefer to dabble." She stood, wiping her hands on her pants. "I've gotta get back to work, but give the princeling my love. Will you be joining us for card games tomorrow night?"

"Yeah, I'll see you then," Bellamy promised.

As Evangeline walked off, he couldn't help but think about how different of a path he'd started on than his peers. He was still a Ranger, but none of his day-to-day duties reflected that. His gaze flicked to Ryddan, and he couldn't deny the warmth in his chest as he watched the child running carefree with his friends. Even if the option was offered, Bellamy would never go back.

He closed his eyes, feeling the sun against his skin, hearing the sounds of small voices raised in play. Behind that, though, he heard something else.

A twig snapped somewhere behind him and off to the right. It was sudden, with no other sounds of movement or scuffling before or after. Bellamy kept his posture relaxed, listening intently.

Someone was hiding in the trees, someone with enough skill to remain almost entirely undetected.

A pinprick of fear needled its way through him, and he slowly blinked open his eyes, keeping them half-lidded and lazy, but watching where

Ryddan played with the others. Safe. He was safe in the confines of the castle.

Mollian was taken from the castle.

Bellamy forced the thought away. That was different. Demons hadn't been sighted in Nethyl since Merriam had killed Basta and the demon that possessed him. But unease still swam through Bellamy's veins. Why would someone be spying on Ryddan?

You're being paranoid, he told himself, even though he knew what he'd heard.

He stood, stretching, and rolled from the stone banister with a grunt, walking off into the woods like he needed to relieve himself. When he knew he was concealed, he altered his steps, moving through the trees with a practiced stealth, blending into the shadows. He made a wide arc around to where the sound had come from, stopping a ways back and peering into the trees.

Bellamy watched only for movement and color, rather than trying to pick out the shape of a person. It took several passes, but he saw a Ranger up in the trees. A glint of light against the steel-tipped scabbard strapped to her thigh had given her away. Bellamy recognized the lieutenant, his brow furrowing as he followed her line of sight to Ryddan.

Confusion twined with the unease in his blood in an unpleasant cocktail. Bellamy wasn't sure what was happening, but he was confident he didn't like it and that it meant nothing good.

Bellamy was distracted the rest of the day, trying to figure out why a Ranger would be spying on the prince and wondering who had even assigned them the task. He'd handpicked the team that made up the prince's personal guard. Their rotation covered every moment of the day, so why was someone else keeping watch?

When his relief came, he said a quick goodnight to Ryddan, then went straight up to Mollian's chambers.

"Bellamy's here for ya, Majesty." Rillak poked his head into the room and waved Bellamy through shortly after.

"To what do—"

"Someone is having Ryddan watched," Bellamy interrupted, sinking down onto the couch across from Mollian before immediately standing back up to pace. He gathered his hair in his hands, lifting it from his neck.

Mollian blinked, watching his friend's agitated movements. "What?"

"Madalen—she's a lieutenant—was watching him from the copse of trees in the courtyard earlier today. Like, she was hiding, and she didn't want to be seen." Bellamy dropped his hair, planting his hands on his hips.

"You're sure she was a Ranger?"

Bellamy stopped his pacing long enough to shoot Mollian a withering look. "Yes, I'm sure." He resumed his steps. "I would have confronted her, but she was very clearly trying to stay hidden. And it was Ryddan she was focused on, not any of the other children."

Mollian nodded, resting his forehead in his hands. "This is bad, Bell."

Bellamy, who'd barely caught the quiet words over the scuffle of his feet against the carpet, turned, dropping again into the open couch, his knee bouncing.

Mollian felt sick, and, more than anything, he wanted Merriam, just to feel her next to him and know that everything was going to be okay. He needed to talk through everything, speculate freely. He twisted the rings around his fingers, attempting to collect his thoughts and sort through it all. "Do you trust your team?"

Bellamy considered the question thoroughly, tried to think back to any time he'd heard complaints about the prince or a tone of voice that felt overly disgruntled. "Yes," he answered finally. "None of them would do anything to endanger Rydd."

Mollian nodded, sliding his hands over his face. "I don't think details should be shared outside of this room. Don't tell them what you saw, okay? I don't want to plant seeds of strife and distrust among the Guard. Keep an eye out and see if you can find anything else that points to other Rangers being tasked to watch him, or who Madalen's closest allies might be. Until then, Ryddan's not to be left alone with anyone other than you, me, or Ria. At least two people at all times, including when he's with Lydia and Mordecai. I don't trust that they'd be able to protect him if the worst happened."

Bellamy nodded. "Consider it done." He watched his king for a moment, registering the fear in his cracked, pale green eyes. It was a fear that ran deeper than surface level, and it pulled at Bellamy's heart. The Keeper was not much older than he was, and held the weight of more than just an entire country on his shoulders. "There's something else, isn't there?"

Mollian clasped his hands between his knees, meeting Bellamy's gaze. "I don't trust Ferrick, and he holds so much power."

"Do you really think he would do something to hurt Rydd?" But even as the words left Bellamy's lips, he knew it was his own belief as well.

"He started collecting more pawns, building stronger connections, even while Oren was in Entumbra. He knew he didn't have the sway with Oren that he did with my mother, and he wanted a failsafe. He knows he has even less sway with me. I feel paranoid sometimes with how much I think he's plotting against me. He's nothing but cordial to my face. I just ..." Mollian shook his head, pushing his fingers into his hair. "If he hurts Ryddan, I'll fucking kill him."

"He won't have the chance," Bellamy swore.

Mollian nodded, a knot loosening in his chest. He knew there was no point in telling Bellamy that he and Merriam would take care of it. Ryddan may be a Stonebane prince, but Bellamy was more his guardian than Mollian or Merriam could ever be, and not just in title.

WHEN MERRIAM GOT BACK to her room at the estate, she stripped off her dress, leaving it pooled on the floor and stepping into the bathroom. She turned on the tap of the shower, letting it heat up while she pulled the pins from her hair.

Merriam stepped under the flow, relishing the burn against her skin. She sank to the floor, resting her head against her knees and letting the water pelt her back. Her hair slid down on either side of her head, completely caging her in.

Her mind went blessedly blank, the muscles of her shoulders fully relaxed for the first time all week. There was only the pressure of the water on her skin, the sound of it against her skull, and the warmth cascading down her body. A sachet of dried leaves and flowers hung beneath the showerhead, and the steam soon filled the area with the fresh, calming smell of basil, citrus, and roses.

She sat like that for a while, just breathing, eyes closed and focusing on the sensations around her.

When the temperature of the water dropped from burning to comfortably warm, she straightened up, scooting back against the tile and letting her head rest against it. Sliding the aspen leaf across its chain, she slowly started allowing the events of the night to play back so she could process everything.

Rovin was an ass. First, foremost, and forevermore. But he'd been different the past year. She wouldn't quite call him her friend, but she hadn't felt the compulsion to slam his face into a wall for several months, and that felt like progress. He was still annoying, but she respected his position in the Guard and how he'd come to earn it, just as he did her title of marshal. And there were those times they interacted outside of their duty to the Crown, when she wanted to poke at him if only so that his attention stayed on her ...

Then he'd gone and thrown all that shit at her after supper. That was the most open and vulnerable Merriam had ever seen him, but before she had even had a chance to process it, he'd closed back up and fled.

Your signature move, she thought ironically.

Merriam stood, her seat on the tile growing uncomfortable, and turned off the water. "What the fuck do you mean, I *scare* you?" she grumbled, grabbing a towel and scrunching the water from her hair. "And why is it not my problem?"

Tossing the towel to the floor, she brushed her teeth and climbed into bed, pulling the blankets tight under her chin with a scowl. She didn't want to decipher Rovin and his dumb moods and his cryptic words or the way they'd made her breath catch in her throat as she waited for more, staring at his stupid, beautiful face like an idiot.

She wanted to be home and out of this city that never stopped moving where the air was wet and the people who ruled it were unctuous and evil.

But mostly, after what had been a long several days and a confusing night, she just wanted her *mehhen.* The tethers of their souls were stretched, but strong. There. Unmistakable.

She focused on that bond as she closed her eyes and fell asleep.

Merriam took her breakfast in the courtyard the next morning, knowing she should be present for any possible rail-related discussions in the dining hall, but absolutely exhausted at the thought of having to spend even one more moment than necessary talking through the schematics. Today would be their final meeting and then back to Umbra tomorrow.

Finally.

She was also planning to find Shiloh again that evening and take them up on their offer to show her around and have some fun.

Merriam heard the purposeful shuffle of feet behind her and glanced over her shoulder to see Kodi, the shirt of his uniform slightly rumpled and his bi-colored eyes still bleary as he stifled a yawn. He mussed up the brown curls of his mohawk with one hand, coming to stand next to her.

Merriam held out her plate to offer him some food.

Kodi took a sausage link, smiling his thanks. "You had Rov pretty fucked up last night."

She scoffed, coughing on a piece of fruit that lodged in her throat. "And why are you assigning *me* that blame?"

"Setting aside my unmatched observational skills, I know him. We may not be *mehhen*, but he's still my soul-brother." He shrugged. "Listen, he may be a stubborn ass"—Merriam made a face in agreement—"but so are you."

Merriam scowled, and Kodi smiled.

"I don't know what happened at that banquet, but I have the feeling that the two of you could circle each other for years on end with nobody committing to the first move. Go talk to him. I know it's not my place to butt in, but you're Aleah's best friend, which means you matter to me."

She was unable to hold in a snort of laughter. "Thanks, Ko. I'm glad I made the cut."

Kodi bumped his shoulder into hers. "You should be. It's a position few ever ascend to."

Merriam rolled her eyes, eating the final bit of fruit from her plate. "I should get to the meeting," she said with a resigned sigh.

"Of course. Don't let me keep you from your politics, Marshal."

"Gag me," she joked, then looked back up at him for a moment, searching his face. "Thanks for the company, Kodi."

"Anytime." Kodi saluted, watching as she walked away. He still wasn't sure whether inserting himself into the middle of whatever this thing was between her and Rovin was the right move, but his chest felt a little lighter.

"Must be weird having a human as your superior."

Kodi would have jumped at the voice if his recognition of it didn't freeze every muscle in his body, his heartbeat even seeming to slow as every predator sense in him went on high alert.

Chetney stopped beside Kodi and watched Merriam slip inside his family's estate. "Although I must say, as far as humans go, you could do a lot worse. That discussion looked pretty tense. Couldn't help but overhear the mention of a gag. Are you fucking her?"

Slowly, Kodi turned his head. Rage simmered in his eyes as he stared at the heir to Do Lech, and it took every single smidgen of self-control that Kodi possessed to keep from drawing his sword and slamming it through Chetney's middle.

Chetney looked over, completely misunderstanding the murderous look on the Ranger's face, and laughed—he *laughed*—and it was a wonder Kodi didn't wrap his jaws around Chetney's throat and rip out his windpipe. "Ay, don't worry, I'll keep my hands to myself, brother. But, damn, I'll bet she's a feisty one, huh?" Having no instinct for self-preservation, Chetney slapped Kodi on the back a couple of times before heading up the wide staircase after Merriam.

The second Chetney had touched him, Kodi's hand went to the hilt of his sword, the dangerous gleam in his eyes slipping past any point of regaining control. He turned to the right, the heel of one foot spinning out as he stepped off in a move that was precise and militaristic. He stalked through the gates of the estate, gaze fixed straight ahead, jaw set.

"Hey, Kodi, are you on the—Kodi?" One of the Guard tried to get his attention, but he passed by without acknowledgement. The Guard blinked in confusion, running after him. "Wait!" He reached for him.

Kodi glanced at the hand on his arm and growled from deep in his chest. The Guard let go, his eyes wide, and Kodi continued down the street.

He went directly to a messaging service, scrawling out a quick, simple note and sliding it across the counter along with a couple coppers. "Get that to a fae named Jasper. Black-feathered wings. He's staying at the Westside Inn." When the courier repeated the instruction, Kodi left, walking through town with only one thought in his head.

He was going to kill Chetney Kinbriar.

Merriam spent the whole morning struggling to pay attention. She deferred most things to Graigory or Portimer, sometimes agreeing without even hearing the full question.

No matter how hard she tried to focus, her mind kept slipping back to her conversation with Kodi, knowing he was right. Merriam bit her lip, twirling a pen in her fingers as she pictured Rovin's face. The warm brown of his eyes, so open, hiding nothing.

It had scared her to look into them, if she was truthful with herself, and she almost laughed at the irony. It scared her, but she also hadn't been able to look away. Something had stirred in her chest, waiting for him to say more, to keep spilling his secrets to her. She had wanted so badly to pull up a thread of annoyance or spite or teasing—anything to mask the emotion that had planted itself right in the center of her being.

The emotion itself wasn't the problem. Emotions could be ignored, could be buried. She was basically an expert in the art.

What scared her was that the emotion that was growing little roots in her psyche had been reflected back at her in his stupidly beautiful eyes.

Merriam had no clue what she was supposed to do with that. Her first instinct was to rebel against it, and she'd happily acted on it, but after talking to Kodi …

Merriam sighed, running a hand over her braid.

"I agree with Merriam. It's not the best circumstance, but it may very well be our only option." Graigory leaned forward, resting his chin on a fist as he looked back over the various lists in front of him.

Merriam felt her cheeks warm, frustration flooding her veins along with embarrassment that she'd let herself drift so far off in the middle of the meeting. The frustration felt good, familiar, and she attached it back to Rovin and turned her attention to the meeting.

Everything with the railroad finished up around midday, so Merriam changed into more comfortable clothing and headed out into Do Lech. She found Shiloh a few blocks down the street, just starting a show. She caught their eye as she hopped up onto a planter to sit and watch, and they winked at her without losing stride.

After the set, Merriam waited for most of the crowd to dissipate before walking up.

"Hey, you're back!" Shiloh greeted.

"Yeah, I hope I wasn't taking you too literally when you offered to show me around."

Shiloh collected their things, tossing their head to move the hair out of their eyes. "Absolutely not. Let's drop this stuff off and then see what trouble we can get into."

Merriam followed Shiloh into one of the gambling halls, where they passed their bag across a reception table, the worker clearly knowing them and familiar with this routine. "I'll be back this evening, so tell Lane to expect me."

"Sure thing, Shiloh," the receptionist promised.

Shiloh took Merriam down to a boardwalk lined with booths of games, food, kitschy prizes, and souvenirs. "Now, the main streets of Do Lech are lavish and wild and sometimes vile in that safe and exciting way that people crave," Shiloh said, pulling a cannabis cigarette from a pocket of their vest. They procured a match, seemingly from thin air, and struck it against their thumbnail to light it, taking a deep drag. "But this"—they gestured to the boardwalk, blowing the smoke above them before looking to Merriam with a grin—"this is the good stuff." They held the joint out to her, shaking out the match.

Merriam took it, breathing in and holding the smoke in her lungs for a moment. She coughed as she handed it back, but instantly felt a head rush and her body loosen up. "Legends, Shiloh."

They grinned, taking it back for another hit. "Good shit, right?"

The two shared the joint as they walked along the pier, Shiloh smoking most of it, and played almost every game they passed. Merriam got nowhere even close to winning any of them with how high she was. Though she was typically very competitive, she was too inebriated to be upset about her lack of skill, collapsing into laughter against Shiloh.

"Fucking Legends." Merriam stopped outside of a shop window, grabbing Shiloh's hand to halt them.

"What is it?" Shiloh asked, peering inside.

Merriam smiled mischievously, absolutely giddy as she darted inside, Shiloh following, a curious smile on their lips.

Merriam headed straight for the item that had caught her eye: a horribly cheesy banner, the size of a regular sheet of paper, that was printed with a cartoon rendering of the city. "I survived the streets of Do Lech!" was written in a flashy scrawl over the top of the picture.

Shiloh cocked an eyebrow. "Mer, that's hideous."

Merriam nodded enthusiastically. "For Molli."

"What?" Shiloh laughed, following Merriam to pay for the item.

"He'll hate it." Merriam bounced on her toes, giddy. "We don't like roads."

Shiloh led Merriam back out onto the street, steering her toward food. "I'm hanging out with a girl from Umbra, Marshal of Sekha, whose best friend is the motherfucking *king*. And she buys him the dumbest souvenir I've ever seen. What is life?"

Merriam laughed, biting her lip to keep from spilling other facts about herself that would blow the fae's mind even more.

They bought more food than was strictly necessary for two people, sitting at a table near the edge of the boardwalk to eat. "This was the most fun I've had in a while," Merriam said truthfully.

"Better appreciation for my dear city?" Shiloh asked, taking a bite out of a strip of fried potato.

"Much," Merriam assured them. "I have a friend back in Umbra. He's a Ranger on special assignment or I would have had him join us, but he would absolutely love all of this. Molli would, too, of course, but Bell ... Legends he would be eating all of this up. Especially your magic."

"A friend?" Shiloh raised a brow teasingly.

Merriam rolled her eyes. "Yes, a friend." She pulled a strip of smoked turkey from a leg bone, her mind turning once again to Rovin's confession and the open vulnerability in his eyes when he'd laid himself bare. *I might like to see him laid bare,* she thought with a giggle. Then her eyes went wide, cheeks heating as she forced her attention back to the present and asked Shiloh more about their life in Do Lech to change the subject.

They finished the food, bellies uncomfortably full, and walked back down the boardwalk, conversing like old friends. As the sun started to dip closer to the horizon, they headed back toward the main street.

"Thank you for today," Merriam said, stopping outside of the gambling den where Shiloh had left their bag. She'd sobered up by then, only a slight bit of cottonmouth remaining from her high.

"I'm glad you came out. If you're ever in the area again, find me," Shiloh smiled, opening their arms.

Merriam hugged them, careful of the delicate wings draped down their slender back. "If you're ever in Umbra, you have a place with me."

"Thank you," Shiloh said sincerely, stepping back and melting into the crowd.

Still full from the boardwalk, Merriam decided to skip dinner and head to bed early. As she showered, brushed her teeth, and climbed beneath the blankets, a knot of nerves bloomed in her belly, which she attributed to the anticipation of being back home. She missed Mollian so much, and the erratic difference in emotions she'd experienced this week had been exhausting.

But as Merriam lay in bed and tried to sleep, that feeling kept nagging at her, and she knew the nerves weren't about going home.

She sat up with a groan, shoving her legs into pants and tugging a shirt over her head.

Rovin was insufferable. Infuriating.

She pulled at the laces of her boots, letting out a low growl of frustration when she struggled with the knots, her fingers shaking.

"This is stupid. This is so fucking stupid," she mumbled to herself as she left her room, heading for the inn outside of the overseer's estate.

But as she walked, hope started to fill her chest. If those things Rovin had told her on the balcony had been some fucked up confession of feelings ... If that emotion she'd seen shining in his eyes truly matched that seed that had lodged within her ...

Merriam swallowed, biting her lip. She'd waited so long with Oren, and she'd promised herself that she'd never again deny herself an opportunity for happiness.

So, despite being terrified, she walked into the inn.

"What room is Lieutenant Arwood in? I have official information from the Crown," she explained to the innkeeper.

"Twelve."

Merriam climbed the stairs, swallowing down her nerves.

Without giving herself the chance to change her mind, Merriam flung open the door to Rovin's room, taking one step inside before freezing in place.

Rovin sat on the edge of his bed, shirtless. But the light playing across the solid cords of muscle coiled beneath his skin wasn't what caused Merriam's mouth to dry up.

It was the half-naked girl standing before him, her arms crossed to cover her breasts.

"Oh," Merriam breathed, her cheeks heating. "*Oh*." Her eyes widened, and she hastily backed out of the room, slamming her shoulder into the doorjamb.

"Mer, wait." Rovin stood, his arm brushing against the girl's chest as she stumbled back a step, looking from Rovin to Merriam in confusion.

Pain lit Merriam's shoulder, and she cradled her arm. "Fuck. I didn't mean—shit, sorry." She turned and fled.

Rovin hastily grabbed his shirt from where he'd discarded it on the floor earlier, yanking it over his head as he chased after her. "Mer!" he called, running down the stairs in bare feet.

Merriam crossed her arms over her chest, head ducked low as she slipped from the inn, heading back toward the gates of the estate.

Rovin caught up to her, grabbing her arm. "Legends, will you stop?"

Merriam halted, not turning around. Not wanting to admit how much it had hurt to see a female in his room, even to herself. "It's okay," she said quietly.

"Look at me, Mer." Rovin dropped his hold on her.

"I shouldn't have barged in. I'm sorry."

"Merriam." Her name was a plea.

She took a deep breath, blinking to clear the hurt from her eyes before turning to face him. "What?"

"You came to my room," he said dumbly.

"Yes, almost in time to watch you get fucked," Merriam snapped, then cursed herself, turning her eyes up to the sky and pushing her fingers into her hair.

He shook his head, taking a step closer to her. "No, she came to *me*. I was telling her to leave," he tried to explain.

Merriam dropped her head back, throwing her arms out dramatically. "It doesn't matter who came to whom. You don't owe me anything, Rovin. It's fine! You're not on duty. It's your last night in Do Lech. She's there. Why shouldn't you fuck her? Do what you want. It's *fine.*" Merriam bit her lip, realizing she was repeating herself and cursing how desperate it made her sound.

Rovin watched her, his breaths growing shallow and measured like he was hunting a wild animal and worried he'd spook it. "Is that what you really want, pet? For me to do what I want?"

She lifted her chin, meeting his gaze evenly. "Yes."

Rovin advanced, grabbing her face in both hands and dropping his lips to hers. He sucked her lower lip into his mouth, running his tongue over it as his canines gently scraped her flesh.

Merriam's hands flew to his shoulders on instinct, seeking support as her knees threatened to buckle. Hunger lit low in her core, and she dug her fingers into him. A whimper escaped her, his tongue sweeping into her mouth when it opened.

Rovin moved one hand to her waist, sliding around to the small of her back to press her up against him.

Merriam felt the hardened length of him against her belly, and that spark of hunger ignited her entire body, erasing every rational thought from her mind other than *need.* Her fingers still digging into his shoulders for support, she dragged her leg up his, and he reached down to help her hook it over his hip, running his palm down her thigh to her ass.

"*Mer.*" It came out as a growl against her mouth.

A feeling spread through Merriam at the desperation in his voice, at the obvious need that matched her own. It was a want to give herself fully over that she hadn't felt since ... She deepened the kiss, grinding against him, anticipation flooding her veins and melting her core. This wasn't just lust, it would *mean* something, and it had been so long since sex had meant anything.

Merriam bit his lip, sliding one hand up into his hair. Her fingers curled into the thick waves at the back of his head, tangling in the lengths of his hair. It felt sinful between her fingers, soft and smooth and so fucking *pullable—*

This is wrong. The thought pricked at her mind. Pullable was wrong. Shouldn't his hair be short? *This is wrong. This is wrong.*

Merriam stilled, the feel of the hair at the nape of Rovin's neck jarring her back to reality. Guilt slammed into her hard enough to take her breath away. She wanted him. Not just with her body, but with whatever Legends-damned part of her *felt* things. A wave of nausea knocked against her.

Rovin let her go as she suddenly pushed away, his lips swollen from her kiss and his deep brown eyes dark with lust.

Merriam scrambled backward a few steps, dragging the back of her hand across her mouth and panting softly. "You're ... I can't ... I'm sorry." For the second time that night, she spun around and ran for the estate, leaving Rovin standing in the middle of the street, dazed and confused.

Chapter 18

FERRICK SAT IN HIS office down the hall at the front of the barracks, going over schedules and training regimens designed by his commanders, though his mind was elsewhere. Madalen, one of his trusted lieutenants, had come by earlier to deliver a report, and he was looking forward to assigning action to all of the information he was gathering. A light rap sounded on his door, and he set the papers to the side. "Open."

Dio came in, and Ferrick waved for him to sit. "Thank you for stopping by, Commander."

"Of course." Dio sat, back straight. "What can I do for you?"

"I wanted to check in, make sure everything was going well. You've taken over so many of Eskar's duties since she's been gone so often."

Dio's brow furrowed. "Yes, everything's fine. Was there something missed with any of the scheduling?"

"No, not at all. Your work is exemplary, as usual. I only meant that I hoped the extra responsibility isn't taxing for your personal life. I know you have two young ones. They're taught lessons here at the castle, aren't they?" Ferrick asked, keeping his tone casual.

Dio, though relieved that nothing was wrong with his work, was even more suspicious at the mention of his daughters. "Yes, they are."

"How old again?" Ferrick flicked his eyes over a sheet, as though he were only asking as a common courtesy and not because he cared.

"Six and nine, sir."

"Oh?" Ferrick responded, already well aware of their ages. "So close in age to our prince."

"Yes, they play together almost every day. He may be a strange child, but my daughters have never seemed to pick up on those nuances."

Ferrick leaned his forearms against his desk, keeping his gaze thoughtful but unassuming. "Strange." He laughed a little. "I guess that's fair, considering the child is a demon."

Dio stifled the urge to fidget. He'd learned composure of his body long ago, but this conversation made him increasingly uncomfortable. "Half-demon. And according to Legend, isn't Keeper blood always pure? His father may not have been fae, but there is no denying the boy's maternal parentage."

"A Keeper has never been able to shift before. Is the child's true form even fae?" Ferrick wondered aloud.

"Respectfully, Captain, will this line of speculation lead anywhere productive?" Dio asked.

Ferrick waved his hand dismissively, as though bored with the conversation. "Of course, we have much more important things to worry about. Just my mind wandering. Thank you, Dio."

"Have a good night, Captain," Dio offered, standing.

"Good night, Commander. Send your wife my best," Ferrick replied, returning to his papers.

Dio nodded, not bothering to correct him that he had a husband because he knew Ferrick didn't care either way. Something about the conversation didn't sit right in his gut, but he pushed it off, ready to be home with his family.

Ferrick let his mask slide as soon as the door to his office shut. With a flick of his fingers, he slid the lock into place. For several eerily quiet moments, the captain sat back in his chair, running the backs of his fingers across his beard. Then his face collapsed into a furious scowl, and he slammed his fist against the top of his desk. Again. Again. Until the side of his hand was red and hot from the pressure, his bones sore with the beginnings of bruising.

Dio was a good Ranger and, much like Ferrick always had been, a stickler for protocol and procedure. But he was too loyal to the Crown.

Ferrick was loyal to the Crown, first and foremost, but he was not blinded by that loyalty. He could see the hazard of raising a demon spawn in their court, the error of allowing a former assassin to hold a title of prestige and speak with the king's voice, and the weakness of having a king who'd never studied as those before him did, who didn't have a full understanding of his power.

What Ferrick needed were members of the Guard who trusted *him* above all and would obey him without question. He'd hoped to get Dio on his side, but he didn't think he could trust the Commander to see past his morals.

Ferrick sighed, flexing the fingers of his bruised hand and relishing in the pain it caused.

Balance would be restored. He had a plan, and he had the patience to set everything up for a flawless execution. Though Dio's cooperation would have made everything so much easier, it wasn't necessary. He had Eskar and a handful of other officers deep enough in his pocket.

His cock twitched at the thought of Eskar, and he let his mind follow that trail of thought to the last time he'd fucked her mouth, pushing so far down her throat that tears ran from her eyes as she'd looked up at him, fingers digging into his thighs to try to steady herself. She was such a power-hungry one, and fuck if her willingness to—sometimes quite literally—ride him to a higher standing didn't inflate his ego.

Ferrick adjusted his pants, semi-hard from thoughts of his ever-willing, feisty commander, and rose from his desk, grabbing his golden captain's cloak from a peg on the wall. He was in a mood now, so he may as well go into town and find someone to fuck.

On his way out, he heard voices from the courtyard, one soft and high, childish in a way that had his face pulling into a sneer on instinct. Few things were more pressing than a warm cunt, but he was curious what the little prince was doing out so late, and crept quietly into the trees to watch.

Ryddan was stretched out across a blanket, arms tossed over his head as he watched the sky. One of the moons was new, the other just on its way to half full, so their light was minimal and perfect for stargazing.

Bellamy lay next to Ryddan, hands folded across his stomach as he let the child point out all the different stars and constellations he'd learned from Mordecai.

Ferrick grit his teeth. One of *his* Rangers sitting out there with a halfling demon spawn. It was sickening.

He'd offered to take Bellamy off of the task of prince guard when he'd first been assigned the position, but the young Ranger had politely declined, saying he was more than happy to serve the Crown in this way.

Almost a year later, and now Bellamy had been deeply seduced. Maybe he saw the potential in having the child trust him so wholly. Maybe he thought it would win him better favor and a higher standing with Mollian or even perhaps with Ryddan, should his future be in Umbra.

Not on my fucking watch, Ferrick thought angrily.

The pale scar that marred one side of Bellamy's face stood out starkly in the moonlight, a scar given to him by the creatures Ryddan's father had ruled. Many of the Guard had lost their lives defending Nethyl from those demons. Their future *king* had been slain trying to defeat them.

And now Bellamy lay on a fucking blanket, ankles crossed and a smile stretching his lips as his gaze drifted from the child beside him up to the stars.

"Molli knows a lot about the stars, too," Ryddan was telling Bellamy, his hand falling to his side.

"Molli knows a lot about most things," Bellamy agreed.

Ryddan fidgeted with the hem of his shirt, his head tilting thoughtfully as he regarded the sky. "Sometimes Ria shows me her stars. She says there's hundreds of thousands of bajillions of stars across soooo many different skies, and I can see them all one day if I want to. But I need rings first, like she and Molli have."

Merriam always told Bellamy when she planned to take Ryddan off world, but the prince didn't know that, and Bellamy was more than happy to let him believe their covert excursions were a secret little rebellion. "Rings or the Gate," he agreed. Bellamy had learned long ago that these conversations were more monologues than anything, just a child wanting to share his experience and interpretation of the world.

Ferrick watched, catching bits and pieces of the innocent conversation, but disgust churned in his gut, regardless. He was about to continue toward the gates when Ryddan sat up, looking straight at him with those eerie, catlike eyes.

Bellamy shot up, hand instantly around his sword, partially unsheathing the blade. When he recognized the deep golden cloak and the male wearing it, he dropped the weapon back into its scabbard, snapping to attention with a salute. "I'm sorry, Captain, I didn't see you there."

Ferrick returned the gesture, his gaze drifting down to the prince. The way those deep green eyes watched him made the hair on the back of his neck stand. "No worries, Ranger. I was just heading into town. A bit late to have the young prince out, is it not?"

"We were just stargazing, sir. Getting a little use out of all the information Mordecai's been teaching him." Bellamy placed his hand on Ryddan's shoulder, and the child tilted his head up to study Bellamy's face curiously.

Ferrick's pupils widened at the touch, and he kept his face straight only through years of practiced masking in court. "Have a good night, Bellamy. Your Highness." He dipped his head, only slightly, to Ryddan before turning.

He seethed as he walked.

The fucking audacity.

That touch had been protective. Shielding.

Ferrick flexed his hands, filled with energy that would only be appeased by fighting or fucking. Perhaps both.

Rage boiled in his blood. A Ranger—one of *his fucking Rangers*—had mustered the gall to defy him, to label something as outside of his reach and untouchable. Ferrick stalked down the streets, ends of his cloak billowing behind him.

He would be shown the complete and utter deference he was owed as Captain of the Guard. *Nothing* was untouchable to him.

Patience, he reminded himself as he pushed his way into a tavern. *Patience, and everything you want will be yours.*

Chapter 19

Cleanup

THE HALLS OF THE estate had been blessedly empty as Merriam hurried through them, and she managed to slip into her room and close the door firmly behind her before she let out a shuddering breath, releasing the sob that had lodged in her throat. Without fully understanding why, she leaned back against the wall, buried her face in her hands, and cried.

She slowly sank to the floor, shoulders heaving as she fully gave over to the swell of emotion inside of her. Merriam sobbed because her heart had been broken, and it wasn't fair that she'd had to learn to navigate that kind of pain. She wanted to find love again, wanted not just sex, but the emotional connection that she knew could come with it. She was alone, and sorting through her feelings was exhausting and stressful and had never been something she was good at.

So she cried, letting herself be momentarily consumed by the pain of grief. When she'd tired herself, wiping her palms to clear the tears from her cheeks with a deep, calming breath, she felt worlds lighter. She pulled her braid over her shoulder, running her thumb back and forth over the string he'd given her. Most of the immediate guilt she had felt was now gone. Some sadness lingered, but the heavy ache in her chest had subsided.

Her eyes unfocused as she slid the tie from the end of her braid and began unraveling her hair. As her fingers worked methodically through the lengths, she let herself acknowledge the hunger that had fueled her with Rovin's touch. His kiss had lit a fire in her, warming a place in the core of her being that had been cold for so long. "He's the bane of your existence," she whispered, but even as she said the words, she knew there was no truth to them.

Merriam pushed herself up with a sigh, shoving thoughts of emotion and feeling to the back of her mind as she moved to the bathroom to wash her face. She was too tired to contemplate anything heavy. Whatever deluge of emotion had crashed through her had taken every-thing out of her, and she barely kicked off her boots and pants before collapsing into bed.

It felt like only moments later that Merriam's eyes flew open, and she sat up, the sheets tangled around her legs. Her hand shot to the dagger on her bedside table when she saw the silhouette of a person standing on the other side of her glass balcony doors.

Another soft knock, the same tempo as the one that had woken her. Merriam untangled herself, dropping silently to the floor and walking towards the door, knife in hand.

"Mer? Are you awake?"

Relief flooded her at the familiar voice, and she opened the door. "Legends, Jasper, you scared the shit out of me. What are you doing here?" She tossed the knife to the bed.

"We need your help moving something off world," he said without preamble.

Merriam watched him suspiciously. "To Earth?"

"From the stories you've told me about how adept they are at scouring the scene of a crime, probably not there."

"Oh, fuck." Merriam rubbed her hands down her face. "Do I want to ask questions?"

Jasper smiled grimly. "Probably not."

"Let me get some clothes on, then."

A few moments later, Merriam stepped out onto the balcony, still blinking sleep from her eyes and with her hair loosely and hastily braided. Jasper scooped her up, flying them over the ever-bustling streets of inner Do Lech out to the west. They landed on the roof of an abandoned building and swung into an open window on the top floor.

Soft voices came from downstairs, and Merriam descended to find Aleah and Kodi in the kitchen, adjusting their clothing. "Mer!" Aleah smoothed her hands over her hair. "What are you doing here?"

Merriam looked between the two, the flush on Aleah's cheeks matching the light in her eyes. She looked bright, that weightless wildness that had become her standard state of being in Umbra back in place. Aleah reached up, swiping her thumb over what looked like a still-bleeding bite mark at the base of Kodi's neck and popping it into her mouth, giving Merriam a halfway-sheepish shrug.

The Ranger, for his part, had looked abashed. His clothes were blood-soaked, and he'd been trying to straighten the laces on his pants until Aleah had touched him. Then his attention had narrowed to her, a love-drunk grin pulling at his lips as he trailed a hand down her spine.

"Cleanup," Jasper answered for Merriam, and understanding clicked into place. There was only one reason Aleah would have come so far into Do Lech, much less be so unbothered by it.

Chetney was dead.

Kodi blushed, inching toward the stairs to the basement and holding up his hands. "Shit, Mer, give me a second to, uh, put him back together."

Merriam blinked as Kodi slipped away. "Do I want to know what that means?"

"Do you?" Aleah asked, mischief lighting her eyes.

"Probably not," Jasper repeated his earlier sentiment.

But if there was one thing Merriam had never lacked, it was morbid curiosity. She looked back at Aleah, raising an eyebrow.

"It's not everyone's love language, but damn if he's not a creative little bastard." Aleah leaned back against the counter, biting her lip.

Merriam followed Kodi downstairs, her stomach turning at the thick stench of blood. She paused on the bottom step, her hand flying to her mouth. "Kodi, what the fuck?"

He paused what he was doing, looking over his shoulder. "Okay, I can explain."

"Holy shit," she breathed, stepping further into the room.

There was no denying the body Kodi had strung up used to be Chetney Kinbriar, but that shock of flame-red hair was the only part of him that had been untouched. The heir's shirt had been discarded and now stuck to the floor with vast quantities of congealing blood. Both of his ears had been clipped, the pointed tips that marked him as fae lost in the puddle of gore and bile underneath him. The pale, freckled skin of his torso was covered in cuts—some long and shallow, some short and deep, but Merriam recognized them all as replicas of the scars on Aleah's body.

What had stopped Merriam in her tracks at the foot of the stairs, though, was the way Kodi had pulled Chetney apart. Kodi had split his back down the middle, neatly skinning him before cutting through his ribs and breaking them open. Chetney's lungs had been pulled from his chest, strung up behind his open ribcage using lengths of intestine wrapped around his wrists.

Those wings were the most brutal, gruesome things Merriam had ever seen. But even as her stomach flipped with recognition of the sheer amount of agony Chetney's final moments had been filled with, she had to admit the precision it had taken was admirable.

"Aleah already told me I'm insane," Kodi offered, finally freeing one of Chetney's hands from the ropes after shoving most of his organs back into his chest cavity. "I hadn't meant to be this extravagant with it," he explained as he continued releasing the body. "I just wanted to do to him what he did to her, but he wouldn't keep his fucking mouth shut. It's like he didn't even understand he'd done anything wrong. He had no remorse, and I needed him to hurt at least half as much as she had. He doesn't get to get away with what he did."

Chetney fell to the floor with a heavy thud, a couple of his ribs breaking free with the impact. Kodi winced, picking them up and awkwardly pushing them back into the body before grabbing a drop-cloth to wrap around it.

"You're lucky you guys have magic instead of technology," Merriam told Kodi, leaning down to help him roll up the body. "This would be a forensic nightmare."

"I'm sure I'd agree with you if I understood the statement," he replied with a sheepish grin.

Merriam squatted, trying her best not to let anything but her shoes touch the gore-covered ground, and looked up at Kodi. "You got a clean knife handy?" He passed one to her, and she cut a shallow line on the side of her arm, wiping the umbrite ring on her right hand through the blood. Wrapping her arms around the body, she closed her eyes, picturing a dry, desolate place, imagining the heat of the sun against her skin and the taste of dirt in her mouth, and swiped the stones of her rings across each other.

Her stomach lurched as she flipped to a world close to what she'd requested of the stones and the magic in her blood. After she dropped the body, she wiped her hands across her pants as she stood, clearing the feel of Chetney's dead weight from her skin. She took only enough time to register the setting sun and the complete absence of buildings before brushing her ring back across her wound for good measure and sending herself back home. She crouched in the bloody basement, breathing past the head rush that came with such a heavy use of magic and opening her eyes to find Kodi watching her with wonder in his.

"That's it, then?" he asked.

Merriam stood, rolling her shoulders against the itch from her Bonding runes, and handed the knife back to him. "No, it's not. It won't be long before his absence is noticed, and people are going to be looking for him. Powerful people. While they'll never find a body, they'll question anyone who ever looked at him sideways, you and myself included."

Kodi swallowed, nodding. "He was vile, Mer. Absolutely, unapologetically vile. I know this will probably cause a lot of headache, but I couldn't let Aleah live in fear of him anymore." He clenched his fist around the knife hilt, knuckles white with the pressure.

Merriam shook her head, lips pressed together. He'd been impulsive and brash, but, as stupid as his actions may have been, she couldn't guilt him for it. Taking a step closer, Merriam threw her arms around him, feeling his shocked hesitation before he returned the embrace. "Thank you," she whispered. "Headache or not, I'm glad she has you."

Kodi squeezed her before letting her go. "She does. Forever."

Chapter 20

Donova dreamed.

The demon warlock walked through a world filled with life that was dying. Greens faded to brilliant yellows and reds, littering the ground beneath her feet. The plants here grew taller than any demon she had ever seen, and her lip curled back in distaste. She made her way through the forest, her feet not touching the ground because she wasn't truly there.

She could tell from the way the scene shimmered around her that she was walking through an echo, a memory from this world of an event that had happened in years past.

Donova walked into a clearing where several creatures were gathered, and she tilted her head, her glowing golden eyes blinking curiously.

These creatures had skin in varying shades of blue and green, a very small number of them red. Regardless of skin color, they all had talon-tipped fingers and sharp, pointed teeth, and their eyes were blacker than the darkest night.

The once-demons, as she thought of them, were dumping magic into the ground where a thick river of it swam beneath the surface. Donova, seeing only what this world remembered, could feel the enormity of this power exchange, the image in front of her vortexing where the magic was present.

She watched, reaching out a hand to run through the places where magic was being exchanged, and her consciousness was pulled in, surrounded by the magic as it blasted past her, buffeting her skin like a sharp, powerful wind.

Donova's eyes flew open, a light sheen of sweat over her alabaster skin. She knew that magic. She stood from where she'd been sitting in the center of a circle drawn in ash. Candles made with muted gray wax burned on either side of her, just inside of the circle, and black blood, now dried, was dribbled across her forehead, droplets flaking from her eyelashes and lips.

Not bothering to blow out the candles, Donova stepped from the circle and hurried down the hall, looking for the small yet powerfully built frame of the Djuhl's personal servant.

"Perran!" she called to him, grabbing him by both shoulders and looking at him with wild golden eyes. "Where is the Djuhl? I must speak with him at once."

Perran brushed her hands away, stepping down the hall to the throne room. He left her outside as he entered. "Your Eminence, Donova is here to see you." Perran approached the table where Djuhl Dronin sat.

The greater demon was ripping the heads from large prawn-like insects harvested from the coast, sucking the insides out before discarding them to the floor for his beasts to devour later. A large bowl of the insects was in front of him, the sound of their legs and claws skittering against the smooth ceramic and each other's hard-shelled bodies filling the room.

"Send her in." Dronin tossed an emptied shell to the ground.

Perran walked back to the door, opening it for the warlock.

"Your Eminence," she greeted with a deep curtsey, waiting for him to acknowledge her before stepping closer to the table. "I have had a dream."

Dronin snorted, snapping the head from an insect. "I, too, have dreams, sorceress, yet no one pays me to talk of them."

Donova glared, lifting her chin. "With all due respect, My Djuhl, whatever visions of fucking and foolery fuel your fantasies will not win you another realm."

Dronin's eyes gleamed at the challenge in her voice as he slurped from the body of the insect, tossing the shell and licking his lips. "And if my fantasies include you?"

"I would think you have more important things to worry about," Donova answered coolly.

Dronin pushed the bowl to the side with a dark chuckle, motioning for Donova to sit. "Tell me."

Dried flakes of blood fell from Donova's lashes as she blinked, settling into a chair next to him. "I've been learning more about the world at the center, where your djuhlin resides. A rite has been performed in the past, a powerful culmination of magic from creatures connected to the world by the magic that runs in their blood. Such an exchange of power makes the layers between our worlds grow ... thinner."

The djuhl waited, dragging a claw across his mouth in consideration.

"If we situate ourselves opposite one of these rites, I am confident I can reach through to the other side."

"How long can you keep a portal open?"

Donova shook her head, the rings in her dark hair tinkling. "That magic is tricky and difficult to contain. I can send something through, I'm sure of that, but I cannot promise how long I can keep the portal open to allow it back."

Dronin folded his arms across the wide expanse of his chest, a flash of lightning from outside glinting from his great black horns. "You have been studying the maps my brother left?"

"Yes, but the place he talks about most, the place where our world is connected to the center, is inaccessible to us. They have it locked down and heavily warded from the other side. From what I can sense, and from the notes left by Djuhl Charn, it will require much effort to take them down. Once that has happened, though, we should be able to move freely between the realms."

Dronin waved a hand in dismissal. "The Gate is a second priority. We must find the djuhlin. He is the most important piece of this. The magic that runs in his blood is the key. You said a rite will thin the barrier between our worlds. Where and when will this take place?"

"I will try to pinpoint a location, but the rite will happen soon. I can feel it."

"And you're certain of this?" Dronin's eyes narrowed, the red darkening as his mind filled with images of blood and battle and the subsequent conquests that would all be *his* if only he could find his brother's damned spawn.

Donova stood, meeting his gaze with her own, golden embers flaring in confidence that comes only with immense experience. "My dreams have never lied to me, Your Eminence, nor has my magic ever failed me."

Dronin also stood, towering over the sorceress. She lifted her chin to hold his gaze, and he dragged a claw down the line of her jaw. "My fantasies do include you."

Donova cocked an eyebrow. "Me? Or my power?"

Dronin leaned down, and Donova tilted her head, exposing her neck on instinct as desire curled low in her belly. Dronin hovered just over her skin, breathing in deeply. "Your magic runs so thick in your veins I can smell it from across the room. You *are* your power, sorceress. Just as I am mine." He could also sense her arousal, the need rolling from her almost palpably. His cock hardened against the seam of his leathers, and the desire to lay her across the table and fuck her senseless was almost all-consuming.

But she was a being of magic, almost equal in power to his, though in different ways. That, at least, deserved respect. So he straightened, brushing past her. "Find where the djuhlin is kept and come to my bed. I do not care the order."

Donova's jaw clenched, her claws pricking against the skin of her palm as her hands curled into fists. "You do not own me," she ground out, despite the heat pooling in her core.

Dronin paused only briefly, great wings flaring out as he glanced over his shoulder. "No, but you would like me to."

"I cannot perform my rituals if you insist on agitating me."

"Then I suggest you come to my bed first." And then Dronin was gone, slipping from the room.

DESPITE THE LATE AND exhausting night, Merriam was up early the next morning with her things packed up and set just inside the door to be collected. She felt the tense atmosphere of the estate as soon as she stepped from her room. Pulling her braid over one shoulder to twist the end through her fingers, she walked down to the dining room for breakfast.

Her stomach was in knots, but she dropped her hands as she entered the room, not wanting anyone to think she seemed nervous at all. She hadn't expected Chetney's disappearance to be noticed so quickly, and she'd hoped to be well on the way back to Umbra before foul play was suspected.

Merriam stepped up to the buffet already spread against one wall, filled a plate, and made her way out the doors and into the garden where she'd eaten yesterday. She sat on the steps, picking at her food and praying to the Legends that they wouldn't be held back for questioning.

"Did you hear the news?" Portimer came up behind her.

Merriam furrowed her brow in what she hoped was a curious confusion. "No."

Portimer sat down next to her, stretching his legs out in front of him. "Illiziana Fielder was murdered."

Merriam choked on a bite of toast. "What?" The relief at hearing a name other than Chetney's was so heavy it buzzed in her teeth, and she set her plate down, folding her hands between her legs to keep her fingers from shaking with the rush of adrenaline.

"In her sleep." Portimer nodded seriously.

"Legends," Merriam breathed. A cold flash of guilt followed the heady relief. Someone had died, someone who was probably loved. "Did we know her? The name sounds vaguely familiar."

The forestrymaster shrugged. "I've only met her once or twice. She was an overseer in one of the fishing towns close by, Red Marsh."

Merriam's brows pulled together in a frown. Something was scratching at her brain, but she couldn't quite conjure it. "Does anyone know what happened?"

"Someone broke into her home and slit her throat, but that's all I know for sure. Nothing was taken, so the commander of the city guard is making a list of anyone who would've had a reason to want her gone."

"Wow," Merriam picked her plate back up and took another careful bite of fruit. "Did she have a lot of people who hated her?"

"I'm not sure about who hated her, but I know she was very close with the Kinbriars. She and Spiro were childhood friends."

"I'm sure it's a difficult time for all of them," Merriam said somberly. Any trace of guilt at her relief disappeared. Even if Illiziana hadn't known what was happening to Aleah, Spiro enabled that abuse, and anything that caused him pain was worth it in Merriam's mind. He deserved to suffer.

After breakfast, Merriam found Kodi helping some stable hands pack.

"Good morning, demonslayer," he greeted.

"Can I steal you for a moment?"

"I am a servant of the Crown and thus a servant of you." He bowed exaggeratedly.

Merriam scowled. "Don't say things like that in public—it's weird and makes it sound like I'm abusing my position," she told him as they stepped aside and out of earshot of the others.

"Weird and insinuating is the only language I speak." Kodi grinned, leaning his forearm against the stone wall that surrounded the estate. "You heard, I take it?"

Merriam nodded. "I was so nervous that they somehow already knew, but this distraction couldn't have come at a better time."

"Our girl did good, didn't she?" Kodi sighed dreamily.

Merriam blinked, looking up at him. "What?"

"She didn't tell you?"

Merriam threw her arms out, gesturing vaguely at the tattoo on her arm. "Plausible deniability, Ko. I'm the Crown's now, remember?"

"Fuck, I thought you knew. Why else would she have even come down here?"

"I knew she had a job, but no specifics." Merriam ran a hand over her braid, trying to calm down. "You haven't talked about her on the grounds, have you? None of the Guard have?"

"I told some of the guys when I was going to see her earlier in the week, but that was at the inn. They'd have no reason to mention her around the Kinbriars' staff."

Merriam chewed her lip, fingers flitting up to the aspen leaf at her throat. "That's two political figures removed while we were down here. If any questions come up, if they're connected and—"

"Hey, settle, Mer." Kodi rested his hands against her arms, searching her face. "According to Spiro and Larna, Aleah Kinbriar drowned nine years ago. This can't be traced back to her. It can't be traced back to us. This is no different than any other job you or the others have been hired for in the past. And you know damn well she's a professional."

"Okay." Merriam dropped her hand, choosing to let his words comfort her. "Sorry, I just feel so unsettled this morning. I think ..." she trailed off, a prickling awareness raising the hair on the back of her neck. She looked over to see Rovin watching them. When her eyes met his, he started walking over.

"I'm going to thank our hosts for their hospitality and make sure everything is good to go," she told Kodi, slipping off toward the house.

Kodi tilted his head in confusion, then caught sight of Rovin and rolled his eyes, scrubbing a hand down his face. "You two have *got* to work your shit out," he said as Rovin approached.

The lieutenant sagged against the wall next to Kodi, not even bothering to deny anything as he watched Merriam depart. "I kissed her last night."

Kodi's brows shot up. "Oh?"

"And now I don't know if I'll ever be able to get her out from under my fucking skin." Rovin shoved a hand into his hair, pushing the chestnut waves away from his face. "I already went on a run this morning, and I still feel wired."

"Can't say that'll get any better, brother." Kodi clapped him on the back and returned to helping get everything prepared to depart.

The mercenaries met back up with the group just north of Do Lech, falling into the back of the caravan.

"Tell me, Marshal, why was the presence of your friends necessary?" Eskar asked haughtily, bringing her horse up next to Merriam's.

"I'm sorry, did I miss the change where I report to you, Commander?" Merriam made a show of inspecting her wrists for Ranger tattoos.

"I'm only pointing out that the coincidence is ... interesting."

"If you're trying to insinuate something, speak plainly," Merriam bit out.

Eskar smirked, enjoying Merriam's irritation. "The mercenaries traveled with us to Do Lech, but no one saw hide nor hair of them inside the city. The morning we leave, the assassination of the neighboring town's overseer is reported. I'm only saying that it seems a bit too coordinated for mere happenstance."

Merriam reigned in her annoyance, letting her shoulders drop. "Ever heard of a concept called 'cover your ass,' Eskar?" she asked, tossing the fae a condescending look. "They were hired to scope out the areas where we will be setting up construction and, later, storage houses and stations. Are you telling me you expect the Kinbriars to be completely open and honest about everything that happens in their city? You think that they didn't polish everything up and show it all to us in the best light?"

Eskar huffed. "That's the first I've heard of any such job."

"Like I said, I don't report to Ferrick, and I sure as Hel don't report to you. But if you're that concerned about the Crown's knowledge of the operation, you can view the contract once we're back in Umbra," Merriam offered, flashing one of her most brilliant saccharine smiles.

"Entitled brat," Eskar muttered, barely loud enough for Merriam to hear, before pulling away.

"It's cute when you throw a fit!" Merriam called after her with a grin. She almost felt bad for the way her voice carried, knowing others could hear, but she'd put up with enough shit from Eskar over the years to justify the retort.

The rest of the day went by uneventfully, and Merriam made camp with the mercenaries that night. Calysta had wandered off already, looking preoccupied but assuring the others that she was fine, just needed some space from all of the people. After supper, in the middle of a game of cards, Aleah caught movement over Merriam's shoulder.

"Hey, Jasper, take a walk with me?" She hopped to her feet, reaching to pull Jasper up behind her.

Merriam looked at them in confusion before glancing behind her. Her heart rate sped up with recognition of the Ranger walking toward their small circle. "Wait, Aleah!" But the redhead was fast, and she and Jasper were already several paces away and heading further into the forest.

"Mind if I sit?" Rovin stood by the fire, hands tucked into his pockets.

Merriam, stomach knotted, shrugged, looking at him for only a moment before averting her gaze.

"You can say no," he said quietly.

A small flicker of irritation lit in her chest, and she latched onto it, tipping her head back to meet his eyes. "Thanks for letting me know I have a choice in the matter, Lieutenant. Now, would you like to sit or not?"

A smile played at the corners of Rovin's lips as he sat beside her. He tried his best to hold it back, but her annoyance with him filled him with some level of warmth, settling the nerves curled tight in his own chest. "Do you think we'll ever be able to have a conversation where one of us isn't making the other's blood boil?"

Merriam snorted. "I hope not." Her face flushed, eyes going wide. That was not what she had meant to say.

Rovin shifted, angling to better face her. His leg pressed against hers, and she closed her eyes at the wave of awareness that almost knocked her over. Awareness of him and how much she wanted him to be near her.

And then frustration, because she didn't want to feel whatever this softness was toward him. She glared at the place where their legs pressed together.

He pushed a hand into his hair, letting out a slow breath. "I would rather you look at me like you want to disembowel me than to have you not even register my presence." His eyes shone in the firelight, deep and brown and entirely open, vulnerable to her.

Merriam's heart dropped into her stomach before picking up speed, returning to its proper place in her chest to thump against her ribcage. She wanted more than anything to tell him to fuck off. That would be the easiest thing. Their dynamic didn't have to change.

Rovin leaned in, studying her with vague amusement. "You're just as fucking affected by me as I am by you."

"No," Merriam breathed, undeniably aware that they were sharing the same air.

Rovin tilted his head closer, and her mouth opened slightly of its own accord. Her body remembered what that kiss had been like. That kiss that had lit the whole of her being until she remembered it should feel entirely wrong.

Merriam leaned away slightly and tipped her chin up defiantly. When Rovin laughed, she could feel his breath brush across her lips, and she forgot to breathe.

Touch me. The thought filled her head with a clamor, and she met his gaze. Their faces were so close she could only focus on one eye at a time.

His eyelids fluttered closed, and he rested his forehead against hers. "Don't look at me like that, pet."

"Why?" Heat coiled in her core, pounding in her blood as the scent of fallen leaves and crisp apple surrounded her.

"Because I only have a finite amount of self-control, and we are in the middle of the Legends-damned camp." Rovin's nose brushed against hers, and she was so sure he was going to kiss her.

She didn't want that, though. Did she? Guilt over how heavily her body had responded to him pricked at her conscience, but desire overpowered it, heating every part of her. *It doesn't have to mean anything.* "I can take us out of the camp." Her thumb brushed against the band of the orydite ring on her finger, rotating the stone.

But then he pulled away, his eyes meeting hers for a moment that was filled with more heat and want than she knew how to process before he turned to the fire.

His fucking leg was still touching hers, though.

Merriam curled her fingers against her knees, watching him.

When Rovin turned to look at her, his gaze lingered on her mouth before he met her eyes. From the moment they'd met, there had been so much emotion between them. Annoyance and animosity may have slowly turned into admiration at times, but nothing that happened between the two of them would ever have the possibility of being neutral. Of that, he was sure. "Find me when you're ready to let yourself admit that it would mean something." He stood, and Merriam barely stopped herself from reaching out to pull him back.

The knowledge that she wanted him that badly slammed into her, and she desperately wanted to hate him for it. "You think pretty highly of yourself, Ranger-man," she spat with a glare.

Rovin smiled, reaching down to rest a finger under her chin, his thumb brushing against her cheek. "Like I said, stay angry if you have to."

Merriam jerked her head back, swatting his hand away. "Next time you touch me, I'm going to rip that smug smile off your face with my teeth."

"Atta girl," he purred, stepping away and heading back across the camp.

Merriam leapt to her feet, hands curled into fists at her sides. There it was, that familiar urge to grab a fistful of his hair and slam his face into the ground.

But at the thought of her fingers in his hair, the urge to hold his face somewhere else entirely chewed through her irritation, and she wondered what the scruff of his beard would feel like against her thighs.

A fresh surge of anger washed through her when she registered where her thoughts had gone. In one smooth, practiced movement, Merriam unhooked the clasp on one of her axes, pulled it free, and tossed it into the air. Her fingers wrapped low on the handle when she caught it, her arm angling back over her shoulder before she swung it forward, releasing the axe with a grunt of restrained frustration.

It cut through the air with a whistle, sinking into the trunk of a nearby tree with a solid thud. Merriam stalked over, ripping it free, and repeated the process until her arms were sore and she'd burned through the larger part of her volatile emotions.

The trip back to Umbra felt torturously slow. Merriam spent half her time avoiding Rovin and the other half watching him from across the camp or feeling him watching her. Kodi and Aleah teased them both about it endlessly, one or the other always slipping off to join the other's place in the caravan. Eskar watched, too, blind to the interactions between Kodi and Aleah, with her focus on every glance from her lieutenant to the marshal, a mixture of disdain and unease curling hard and sour in her gut.

Rovin had once been someone Eskar thought she could trust implicitly, but now she questioned where his true loyalties lay. He'd had so much potential, it would be a shame for it all to go to waste. Something had to be done about the girl, and soon. Merriam was gaining too much power. Her hold over the king was dangerous, as was her standing with the younger Guard. And that was without accounting for the amount of knowledge she possessed about Nethyl and the magic it contained.

How anyone could trust a conniving little human—not even from their world—to make decisions for the whole country was beyond Eskar's comprehension, and she yearned to put Merriam back in her place.

The group arrived home in Umbra early in the evening.

Eskar had just dismounted, unstrapping her bag from the saddle, when a small form blew past her, almost knocking into her legs.

"RIA!" Ryddan ran through the courtyard, barely giving Merriam enough time to turn and drop her pack before he launched himself into her arms.

Merriam hugged the child to her chest, his arms looping around her neck. "I missed you, princeling!"

Eskar rolled her eyes, hooking her bag over her shoulder. She brushed past Bellamy, not registering who he was, only the Ranger badge on his chest. "Watch it," she growled, annoyed he'd been in her way. She had much to report to the captain, and she stalked importantly through the crowd gathered in the courtyard, people parting to let her pass.

Bellamy's brow furrowed, pulling at his scar as he briefly watched Eskar's retreat before following his charge up to Merriam. The joy on the little prince's face as he looked up at her, excitedly spouting off a list of all the things he had to tell her from their time apart, warmed Bellamy's chest.

Merriam ran her fingers through Ryddan's hair, pushing the fine white strands back from his forehead. "I cannot wait to hear all about it, Rydd." She smiled at Bellamy as he approached, setting the child down. "Maybe we can talk Bellamy into stealing you from your classes tomorrow. We can go up into the mountains for a picnic."

"Molli, too?" Ryddan asked.

Merriam felt the tension in her soul relax, those tethers singing with relief and filling her with contentment. "Molli, too," she promised, looking up and meeting a pair of pale green eyes, one shot through with brown. The sun gleamed against the snow-white curls that partially covered the aspen branch tattoo across his brow, and he pushed them back with a smile.

Merriam's heart clenched at the dark circles below his eyes, worry heavy in her gut, but she threw her arms around the king much the same way Ryddan had thrown his around her. *Legends, I missed you.*

You have no idea, he Cast, releasing her. "Barely back in Umbra and already taking control of my schedule, Marshal?"

"We're going to go on a picnic tomorrow," Ryddan told him before Merriam could reply.

"I suppose I can't refuse that." His hand found Merriam's, fingers threading through hers in an almost childlike gesture of self-comfort.

What's wrong? she Cast, squeezing his hand.

Later. Mollian met her worried glance with a tired smile. *I'm fine, promise. Just glad you're home.*

"I can grab your bags for you if you need," Bellamy offered, looking from Merriam to Mollian, his features tight.

Merriam narrowed her eyes suspiciously, but Bellamy gave her the smallest shake of his head, glancing down at Ryddan. "I appreciate the help. Thank you."

It wasn't until after supper that Merriam and Mollian were finally left alone, Bellamy walking Ryddan back down to his quarters with promises to come up once his guards for the night were in place.

"Since when does Rydd need an escort to his room at night?" Merriam asked, tucking her knees up on the couch in front of her.

"I think Ferrick is having him watched." Mollian dragged his hands over his face.

Merriam's eyes widened. "What?" Her voice came out squeakier than intended.

"Bellamy saw a Ranger spying on him. I don't have any other proof, but you know Ferrick. You know the sides of him that he never allowed my parents or my brother to see. Tell me you don't think he's capable of viewing Ryddan only as his demon blood, not as a prince or even as a child."

Merriam wrapped her arms around her legs, resting her chin on her knees. "Do you think he'd have the gall to hurt him within the castle?" Fear chilled her to the bone, that she even had to ask the question ...

"I think there's no point in taking the risk," Mollian answered quietly. "He's only to be left alone with you, me, or Bell. Always two others outside of that."

An ache flooded Merriam's chest at how unfair it was to Ryddan to be kept under constant watch, never able to run around and explore on his own, even within his home. Alongside that ache was the heat of anger, and she flexed her jaw to keep her teeth from clenching too tightly. "Something has got to be done about Ferrick."

"He's too powerful, Ria. He has the whole of the Guard behind him, as well as countless politicians and guildmasters. I can't remove him without just cause." Mollian worried his lip between his teeth, the tattoo on his brow creasing with distress.

Merriam reached out, gently pulling his lip free with a thumb before dropping her hand. "That's my move, Lord King," she teased softly, trying to lighten the mood. "He'll slip up eventually, and we'll be ready to take him down." She met his gaze evenly, letting him see the promise there.

The steady confidence in those familiar amber eyes filled Mollian with assurance, and the depth of his exhaustion truly hit him now that he didn't have to hold everything alone. "You're not allowed to leave again for at least a year. That's an order."

"Talk to the king; he's the one who keeps sending me on assignments. If I didn't know any better, I'd think he didn't like me." Merriam gave a wry smile.

"Can't stand you, I've heard," Mollian agreed solemnly.

Merriam stretched her legs out, draping them over his lap as she rested against the arm of the couch, staring up at the ceiling. "Rovin kissed me," she said, her stomach flipping with the admittance.

Mollian watched her refuse to look at him before turning his attention to her legs, plucking stray pieces of lint and horse hair from her shins. "Well, how did that go?"

Merriam's stomach dipped again, and she covered her face with her hands.

A smile tugged at Mollian's lips, and he poked her knees. "You like him."

Merriam draped her arms over her eyes. "I ran away from him. Twice. Then threatened to bite his face off."

"Kinky."

"Molli." Merriam lifted her arms to glare at him. "This is serious." Her mouth dropped open, hands moving to cover it as her eyes widened.

Mollian cocked a brow.

"Shit." Merriam dropped her hands, pulling her legs back to sit up straight. "That just ... it *is* serious. Why is it serious? *Shit.*" Nerves tumbled through her, exploding like butterflies in her belly.

Mollian laughed at the horrified expression on her face, but she was still too stunned at her own realization to retaliate. "What an altogether shocking turn of events." A strange mixture of pain and pride filled him. It had taken her so long to admit her feelings for Oren, both to herself and to him. She'd grown so much since then.

The click of a door closing made Merriam jump, which sent Mollian into another fit of laughter.

"What's a shocking turn of events?" Bellamy asked, stepping further into the room.

"You scared me." Merriam turned to glare at Bellamy, irritable at her own revelations.

"Ria and Rovin, sittin' in a tree," Mollian sang, and Merriam turned her glare to him, regretting ever having taught him the song.

Bellamy plopped onto the couch across from them, amusement sparkling in his stormy blue eyes. "I leave you alone for a few moments and the two of you devolve into utter nonsense. Should I fear for the future of Sekha?" he joked.

"We should all fear for the future of Sekha," Mollian answered. "My *mehhen* has lost her sanity, and it is only a matter of time before the disease leaks from her soul into my own. Mad King Mollian, that will be my legacy."

Merriam snorted, lightly kicking his side. "That's dramatic."

Mollian caught her foot, holding it to protect himself from another attack, still addressing Bellamy. "My dear Ria has a *thing* for Rovin, and it's serious."

Bellamy's eyes widened, and he moved to the edge of the couch. "Should I fetch a medic? Can we even mend that sort of illness?"

"Oh, fuck off." Merriam pulled a pillow from behind her and tossed it at Bellamy.

He easily deflected it, grinning like a fool as he reclined back. "Seriously, though, I'm happy for you, Mer."

Mollian guffawed in a distinctly unkingly manner, earning another glare from Merriam. "You can't honestly think it's going to be that easy, Bell." Mollian wiped a tear from his eye. "Ria and feelings notoriously don't get along. She'll fight this sort of attachment until she's bloodied and bruised."

Merriam folded her arms across her chest. "I'm not that bad," she grumbled half-heartedly.

"That's true," Mollian acquiesced, reaching over to pat her leg. "You have already admitted the attachment exists. That's a big step for you."

"Say one more patronizing thing, Molli. I dare you." Merriam leveled him with her gaze.

Mollian raised his hands in surrender.

You're lucky I probably couldn't survive without you, Merriam Cast.

Oh, I'm well aware.

"Anyway," Merriam continued out loud, turning to Bellamy. "Thank you, and Molli's wrong."

Mollian's brows shot up, a teasing gleam still in his pale green eyes. "So you're going to go talk to him, then?"

"Yes," Merriam replied without looking.

"Tomorrow?" Mollian pressed.

Merriam's teeth sunk into her bottom lip. "Well, we just got back. We've got briefings to attend and routines to pick back up, and—"

"Ah, I see the avoidance you're talking about," Bellamy interrupted.

Mollian said nothing, but raised his eyebrows in a way that clearly communicated *I told you so.*

"You're both insufferable." Merriam pushed up from the couch. They were right, though. She didn't have a good reason for not seeking out

Rovin, especially when he'd made his feelings clear the last time they'd talked. "I'll talk to him when I talk to him, okay? But it sure as Hel isn't going to happen tonight. I'm exhausted." She paused, looking at Bellamy. "I know you two probably have everything sorted, but let's make time tomorrow for you to give me a full brief of whatever is happening with Ryddan. Even if it's not Ferrick that's planning something, we need to get to the bottom of this as soon as possible."

"Absolutely. Good night, Mer," Bellamy said.

"G'night, Bell." Merriam turned to head toward the bedroom.

"Ria, your bed is the other way," Mollian called.

She flipped him off without turning around, slipping into his room and closing the door behind her.

Merriam was asleep by the time Mollian joined her, curled into a ball at the center of his bed. He lay down beside her, and she nuzzled into his arm with a sigh that Mollian felt reflected in his own being. "Let yourself have this, Ria," he whispered against the top of her head. "If you have another chance at a great love, chase it. Choose all the happiness despite the potential heartbreak."

Closing his eyes, Mollian let his magic slip free and into Merriam, mixing with what he'd given her with the Bonding all those years ago. An immense pressure left his chest, and as he relaxed, her familiar smell of rain and wildflowers surrounding him, he realized he hadn't told her about his dreams.

But he knew, somehow, with her beside him settling whatever restlessness had been in his soul, that he would stay grounded tonight, not slipping into that other place. *What a strange way to think of it,* he thought before drifting off.

DEBRIEFING THE ENTIRE WEEK of meetings they'd had in Do Lech was a much less painful process than Merriam had expected. Portimer and Graigory had taken very organized notes and were able to smoothly communicate all plans that had been pushed forward with minimal input from Merriam. Now it was on to actually drafting plans to build and acquire materials, break ground, and then, before long, Nethyl would have its first train.

Merriam smiled, glancing at Mollian as he listened. His rule would be revolutionary in Sekha, his name recorded in history throughout Nethyl. Pride swelled in her chest at all the great things he would do, whether he thought himself capable of them yet or not. And she would get to be by his side for all of it.

What are you smiling at, creeper? he Cast without looking at her.

Can a servant of the Crown not admire her king?

You're not the only one feeling admiration this morning. The thought was closely followed by an image: a furtive glance in Merriam's direction, deep brown eyes shining with something that could have equally been longing or disgust, a scruff-lined jaw, set carefully neutral, face framed by brown waves that hung soft and silky to strong shoulders.

Merriam barely caught herself from whipping her head to peer down the table at Rovin. *You made that up,* she accused, but, no, now that she was no longer lost in her own thoughts, she could feel the prickle of his gaze against her cheek.

She felt her skin warm, a blush fighting its way up her neck. Slowly, she turned her head, flicking her eyes to Rovin's.

When her gaze met his, one corner of his mouth pulled up, and he blinked. Thick lashes fanned against his cheeks for a heartbeat, and when he opened his eyes, they burned with undiluted desire. And a challenge.

Merriam's stomach plummeted, her breath catching in her chest.

That stupid smirk on the corner of his lips grew, and he blinked again, clearing his gaze of emotion and looking away.

Irritation raced through Merriam's veins, and she glared daggers at the side of Rovin's face.

Rein it in before you start a fire, Mollian teased.

Merriam immediately dropped her eyes to the table, clearing her features and taking a breath to settle herself. *Did you see him? He challenged me!*

Would you have reacted to him if he hadn't?

Merriam bit the inside of her cheek.

Looks like you're playing along well, then. For better or worse, he knows you, Ria.

Merriam focused on the table in front of her, fighting back a frown. Mollian was right. Rovin wanted a reaction from her. He'd told her as much on the road back from Do Lech, and she was letting him play her like a game of shears. Without a doubt, he knew how to irritate her, and thus how to keep himself on the forefront of her mind.

Curling her fingers into her thigh with a suppressed sigh, Merriam relaxed her posture. She'd already admitted that she felt something for him, not even just to herself, but to Mollian *and* Bellamy. That made it real. So why was it so hard for her to act on it?

She remembered being terrified of going public with her feelings for

Oren. The entire duration of their relationship, she'd worried about what other people would think, what outside opinions the two of them would face.

It was her greatest regret.

Never again, she'd promised herself.

On instinct, Merriam reached out for Mollian with her mind, letting his proximity give her comfort and courage. Anxiety swam cold in her blood, and her heart pounded in her chest, but, sitting in the war room among some of Sekha's most important political players, Merriam decided that she would pull Rovin aside as soon as this meeting was called to an end.

She looked over at him, twirling the end of her braid around a finger. When his eyes met hers, she smiled softly, and a look of surprised confusion crossed his face before he smiled dumbly back. Merriam bit back a laugh at his expression and returned her attention to Portimer, who was pointing out areas where extra precautions should be made for specific wildlife.

Mollian recognized her mood shift, but didn't provoke her, letting her figure this out on her own until she needed him. But warmth filled his chest at the thought of her happy in that way again.

He'd never felt inclined to find a romantic partner. Everything about it felt like extra work for an outcome that wasn't any more enjoyable than the life he already had. He loved his friends and his family, and he was perfectly content in those relationships. But he understood that his *mehhen* wasn't like that. He sometimes thought that every romantic and sexual desire he was missing had accidentally been given to her. Even if her initial response was to push it away, being loved was something she craved, and he wanted her to have everything she desired. It never once upset him that she needed someone else in a way that he never would. Her happiness, her fulfillment, was the same as his own. Their bond ran deeper than petty jealousies and possessiveness.

While Mollian was contemplating the deeper meanings of life and his desire to live it happily, Ferrick was stroking his beard, appearing outwardly thoughtful and attentive, but inwardly raging at the nonverbal interactions he'd witnessed between Rovin and Merriam.

Eskar had told him that something had definitely changed in the lieutenant's perspective, but Ferrick had been hesitant to make any brash decisions. Rovin was one of his finest Rangers. Even without magic, he could easily have become a great commander one day. But it was clear that his loyalties had been compromised, and that was dangerous.

Merriam was dangerous. The hold she had on the king seemed to grow tighter every day, and Ferrick was now at the point where he was ready to be rid of her. Planning her downfall had been tedious, what with how close she was to Mollian and how often they were together, but a unique opportunity had just presented itself—in the war room, of all places—and he wasn't going to wait for it to happen again.

He was a male of action.

As soon as the meeting concluded, Ferrick caught Eskar's eyes, gesturing for her to follow him with a jerk of his chin.

Mollian stood, his hand brushing across Merriam's back in comfort before he turned toward his office. Ferrick pushed his chair back and was up and moving toward Rovin before Merriam had a chance to get around the table. "Come with me, Lieutenant. I need to speak with you for a moment."

Rovin's jaw ticked underneath the short scruff of his beard, barely perceptible, but he didn't let his gaze flick to Merriam even though every cell in his body was screaming to go to her. "Yes, sir." He inclined his head respectfully, following the captain from the room as Eskar came up to walk at his side.

Merriam watched them leave, that determination and confidence that had sparked in her chest guttering. She bit her cheek, fingers playing over the handles of the axes at her hips. *This is fine*, she assured herself. There was still an entire day ahead, and Ferrick couldn't talk to him forever. She *would* find Rovin before the day's end, and she would tell him that she felt something for him.

But finding Rovin wasn't as simple as she'd expected.

After a pleasant trip into the mountains to have lunch with Ryddan as she'd promised, she resumed her hunt for the Ranger. She trained with the Guard that afternoon, but Rovin hadn't shown up. She'd asked after him, but no one could say with certainty where he'd been assigned.

She took an extra long shower, hoping the hot water and repetitive motions of washing her hair would soothe some of her irritation, but it hadn't helped.

Merriam's hair hung in damp waves down her back as she stomped into the common room she shared with Mollian, dropping ungracefully onto the couch with a heavy sigh. "I swear on every Legend I was going to talk to him," she told Mollian, who was sitting across from her, legs folded on the cushion in front of him as he carefully pressed gold leaf into the hilt of a dagger. "I looked for him *all day*. This is a sign. It's a sign that nothing good can come from sleeping with the enemy, and—"

Mollian, tongue tucked into the corner of his mouth, tossed a folded piece of paper to her without looking up, the aid of his magic making it land lightly in her lap.

"What is this?" Merriam sat up, beginning to unfold the page.

"The Guards gave it to me when I came in tonight, but unless we've been misreading things on an embarrassing level, I'm assuming it's for you."

Merriam's heart thudded against her ribcage, that swarm of butterflies that had taken residence in her stomach immediately bursting into activity. She opened the page and had to read the words three times before her mind quit jumping around long enough to comprehend them: *Sent on a last-minute tasking, but will be back by supper. Outer door is open, first room on the left. Come see me. Please.* Merriam swallowed and glanced up at Mollian, needing to gauge his reaction against her own nervousness.

He kept his eyes on his work, but was fighting a smile.

Merriam chewed on her lip, rereading the note. "Did you already call down for food tonight?" she asked casually, trying to figure out a plan of action and entirely sure that whatever rhythm her heart was beating couldn't be healthy.

Mollian finally raised his eyes to her, curls falling over his brow. "With all the love in my heart, Ria, if you don't leave by the time I'm finished with this hilt, I'll ban you from these quarters and not allow you back until you've sorted this out."

Merriam glared, but it held no fire. "Awfully pushy, aren't we?"

Mollian returned to his project.

"Fine, fine, I'm going!" Merriam groaned, pushing up and moving back into her room to change out of sleep clothes and tie up her hair.

Mollian watched her go, looking over his shoulder with a grin.

The familiar weight of her axes at her hips was calming as Merriam walked across the courtyard, and she ran her fingers over their carved handles to further steady herself. She'd briefly debated leaving them, but something about going to Rovin with her heart on her sleeve made her feel oddly naked.

"No going back now," she whispered, taking the steps on the outside of the Ranger barracks to the third story, where the lieutenants had their rooms. Nervous tension wound its way through every muscle, making it difficult for Merriam to catch her breath as she reached the top of the stairs.

The door locked from the inside, but had been propped open with a rock. Merriam pulled it open, stepping into the hallway and letting the door close softly behind her, and took a finally settling breath as she walked up to Rovin's door. She wasn't sure whether to knock or let herself in.

The last time she'd barged into his room, a girl had been there. *Don't be stupid. He asked you to come.* She shook her head, clenching her hands into fists and forcing down her irritation at her nervousness. The urge to run back to her own quarters was almost overwhelming. "Fucking scaredy-toad," she muttered, raising a fist and knocking twice. "Rov?" she called out, testing the door handle.

It wasn't locked, so she pushed it open, not stepping past the threshold. "Rovin?"

The room was dark and empty.

Merriam glanced down the hall, biting her lip before stepping in and closing the door. Maybe he'd gone to grab food, or had to double check the next day's schedule. She'd made it this far, so she could wait.

She stood in the center of the room, squinting in the dim light as she looked for a lamp. Raising a hand to play with the aspen leaf at her throat, Merriam started a slow circle. A vague recognition that something was wrong lit in her brain, but as she dropped her hands to her axes, her head rocked violently to the side, accompanied by a bright flash of pain from her temple.

And then there was nothing.

Rovin was exhausted, and frustration churned in his stomach. All day, he'd been replaying the way Merriam had looked at him. Something in her expression had been different, softer. She had looked at him many, many times throughout the years he'd known her. The majority of those looks had been filled with contempt, irritation, or a promise of violence.

But sometimes ... sometimes those looks would be impressed, amused, even borderline respectful.

Never once, though, had she ever looked at him with any measure of vulnerability, like she wanted to be near him, to take comfort in his presence.

And that one look had been enough to throw all sense of self-preservation out the window. There was nothing he wouldn't do just to have her look at him like that again.

Rovin wanted so badly to go to her, to talk to her before she gave herself a chance to close back up, but Captain Ferrick sent him out into town to hunt down information in Umbra, a task that had taken *all fucking day* because nobody seemed to have any knowledge of what the captain was looking for, or to even recall that they were supposed to have been aware of it.

And now it was late, Rovin was tired, and he was struggling to compose himself as he walked to Ferrick's office. He pushed a hand through his hair, the last outward sign of irritation he'd allow himself, and knocked.

"Open."

Rovin stepped in front of the desk, the door open behind him. "I was unable to find any information, Captain, but everyone is aware to keep a lookout for anything pertinent."

Ferrick's brow pulled low over his eyes as he sighed. "How unfortunate. Thank you for checking. Why don't you get some sleep? I need you to cover the first training shift in the morning."

Rovin clenched his teeth, swallowing down a complaint. "Not a problem, sir. Am I still running the second as well?"

"Yes, both, if you can manage."

"Of course." Rovin nodded, even as annoyance simmered in his blood.

Ferrick smiled. "Thank you, Lieutenant. I knew I could count on you." He turned back to whatever was on his desk in clear dismissal.

Rovin exited, making a conscious effort not to slam the door behind him. How he had ever idolized that prick and put him on a pedestal was confounding. Almost nothing made Rovin angrier than being played for a fool, and he couldn't shake the feeling that Ferrick had done just that.

Food was almost always spread across one table in the main common room, since the Rangers worked odd shifts and all hours of the day. Rovin swiped a couple of hand pies from a basket, unsure what they were and not quite caring, and ran up the three flights of stairs to his room.

He needed to work off some of the frustrated energy buzzing in his veins. He needed food. He needed sleep.

He needed to see Merriam.

Walking down the end of the hall to his room, he fished a key from his belt, fitting it into the lock and pushing the door open. He hadn't felt the lock turn, and looked at it curiously for a moment before shaking it off and walking inside.

He set one of the pies on the desk, biting onto an end of the other as he unstrapped his weapons belt and tossed it onto the bed. He alternated eating and undressing, moving into the bathroom he shared with another lieutenant to shower.

After, he sat down on the edge of his bed, towel around his waist and hair dripping water onto his shoulders. He pushed the strands back from his face, his finger tracing absently over the marred tip of his clipped ear. Most of his irritation had worn off with food and a hot shower. He had a responsibility to the Guard, had made a commitment, and even if he was no longer Ferrick's biggest fan, his dedication to his job and the Crown was still the same.

But he was antsy having not seen Merriam. Part of him worried that she would think he was purposefully avoiding her. But, no, she'd seen Ferrick ask him to leave, right?

Rovin sighed, falling back on his bed to figure things out. But as soon as his body hit the familiar mattress, exhaustion won over. There was no way he was getting dressed and trudging to the castle.

Sleep first. She'll be there tomorrow, he thought, forcing himself up only long enough to pull off his towel and slide underneath the blankets.

Two years before …

FERRICK SAT AT HIS desk with his feet propped up in front of him, tossing a small ring of keys from one hand to the other. They jingled softly when they hit his calloused palms. Eskar sat across from him, along with a few of his other trusted officers.

"Prince Oren will be back in a year's time. I'm unsure how his outlook or feelings have changed since his absence, but I want to present a strong front when he returns. Regenya trusts me implicitly, and we need her heir to feel the same way."

Eskar cleared her throat, sitting up straighter. "If I may, Captain."

Ferrick nodded at her.

"Rovin Arwood. He's just hit his five-year mark and is eligible for promotion. He's also loyal and obedient."

Ferrick's eyes narrowed in thought. "The halfling does know how to command a room, and he's proven himself a formidable fighter and scout, even without magic."

"And he idolizes you, Captain," Eskar pointed out.

Ferrick scratched his beard to hide the smug smile that spread across his face. *He does.* "Young Arwood gets a promotion, then. This will further solidify his loyalty and the loyalty of those who will follow him. When's the next new moon?"

"The lower moon is new in five days," one of the commanders answered.

"He can hold his vigil then. Eskar, when we're done here, find him and send him to me."

"Yes, Captain." Eskar left, checking the posted schedule before heading to the training room. He was in the middle of a spar, and she stopped at the edge of the ring, watching him fight for a moment before interrupting. "Arwood, go see the captain."

Rovin turned at Eskar's voice, dropping his practice sword. "Yes, Lieutenant." A sharp burst of pain ran up his shin, and he whirled with a hiss. "What the fuck, Ko?"

Kodi laughed, hopping back, weapon held forward. "Can't drop your guard in the middle of a fight."

"He's right. A true opponent isn't going to care who's addressing you." Eskar smirked before walking away.

Rovin grit his teeth, a trickle of sweat slipping down his forehead as he lunged for Kodi, who blocked the attack. The two Rangers stood face to face, weapons pressed between them. "That was a dirty move, brother," Rovin said lowly, challenge gleaming in his eyes.

Kodi grinned. "You know how much I love being told I'm filthy."

Rovin slid the smooth wooden blade across Kodi's, pushing back and driving forward with a thrust that Kodi barely blocked.

"*Now,* Arwood," Eskar called from across the room.

Rovin kept his eyes on Kodi's, lifting a brow in both question and provocation.

Kodi raised his arms, sword dangling loosely in his grip, free hand open in surrender. "Go on before you get yourself in trouble."

Rovin twirled his sword in his hand, tossing it into the air and catching the point, holding the hilt toward Kodi. "We'll finish this later."

"You can count on it." Kodi took the sword, wiping sweat from his temple against his shoulder.

Rovin gave him a sloppy salute before turning and jogging from the training hall. Once he rounded the side of the castle, he slowed to a walk, wiping the hem of his shirt over his forehead and straightening his clothes. He ran a hand over his hair, the top half tied up, secured in a bun at the back of his head. A wave of self-consciousness that he hadn't been able to shake, even after so many years proving his merit, washed over him, and he pulled his hair free, shaking it out to cover his clipped ear.

He felt dumb for it as soon as he did. *Captain Ferrick doesn't see you as a halfling. You've proven yourself long ago*, he thought, but the brush of hair against the side of his face still calmed him and gave him a renewed sense of confidence.

Rovin stepped into the Ranger barracks, moving down the hall to Ferrick's office. He knocked, waiting to be told to enter. "Captain," Rovin greeted with a salute, holding it until Ferrick returned it. "Lieutenant Eskar told me to come see you."

Ferrick stood, clasping his hands behind his back. "Yes, thank you, Rovin. I wanted to informally tell you that you've been selected for promotion. We'll hold your ceremony and your first night's vigil with the next new moon."

Rovin's heart slammed against his chest, and he blinked. He opened and closed his mouth a couple times, at a loss for words. He shook his head to clear it, straightening his shoulders. "Thank you, sir, I—I'm honored."

"You've worked hard. I'm impressed with your skill and dedication. You've earned this." Ferrick smiled, and pride swelled through Rovin's chest. "The next new moon is in five days. Have a set of your formal wear updated before then."

"Yes, sir." Rovin kept his composure until he made it to the room he shared with Kodi and another Ranger on the second floor of the barracks, closing the door behind him and punching his fists into the air before falling onto his bed.

"What's got you so excited?" Kodi leaned against the door leading from the bathroom. A towel was slung low on his hips, steam billowing from the small room behind him.

Rovin sat up, not bothering to wipe the goofy grin from his face. "I'm getting promoted."

"What?" Kodi's brows shot up, a smile pulling at his lips.

"Lieutenant, in five days."

Kodi launched across the room, tackling Rovin back to the bed and pummeling his chest playfully. "Look at you! Climbing the ranks and taking names! We need to celebrate!"

Rovin laughed, blocking his punches. "We've got first shift in the morning, psycho."

"It's routine patrol—we can be hungover for that. Come on, we have to live it up while we're still roommates!"

"Two drinks," Rovin offered.

"Three," Kodi countered.

"Two."

"Three, if I can keep you pinned." Kodi's bi-colored eyes glinted confidently.

Rovin reached for his wrists, bucking his hips at the same time he yanked Kodi closer to him, using the momentum to throw him off and roll on top of him, straddling him and pinning his arms by his head. "Two."

"Two," Kodi agreed, and Rovin stood, letting him up. "Hurry and wash up. You stink."

"So demanding." Rovin rolled his eyes, heading toward the bathroom. "Someone's gotta keep you in check."

Five nights later, Rovin stood on the parapets of the castle walls, keeping watch over Umbra and the gates below under the light of only a single half moon and what seemed like double the amount of stars usually seen in the sky because of the absence of the second.

Earlier that evening, as the sun's light faded behind the mountains west of Umbra, his lieutenant badge had been pinned on, each of the officers of the Guard present at his ceremony tacking the badge to his chest with their fist. He knew he'd have a bruise, but it was just another symbol of his earning this rank, this position. He would keep watch over the castle through the night, not retiring or even so much as sitting down until the sun peeked over the mountains.

It was tradition, not for every promotion, but for the first rank earned in the Ranger corps, no matter the weather. Rovin counted himself lucky that the late spring night was warm and the soft breeze mild, sometimes dying down to nothing.

Movement to the east caught his eye, and he stepped to the edge of the rampart, peering over to see Merriam walking toward the gates. Even if the pale braid hanging down her back wasn't unmistakable, the unbothered, confident stride with which she approached was a dead giveaway.

Rovin leaned over the edge, annoyance flaring through him as Merriam gave the guards her signature saccharine smile, breezing through and heading toward the castle and the rooms she shared with the younger prince.

She was a mercenary, yet she walked the castle grounds like she owned them.

The way she showed absolutely no respect for tradition or customs disgusted Rovin. She'd quit training with the Guard after only a year, joining the local mercenaries whose standards and morals were much looser, their conduct less regulated.

Rovin had been intrigued by her in the beginning. Just a no-name girl from the south who'd showed up one day with Prince Mollian. There had been a part of him that had respected her ambition to join the Guard and become a Ranger. If she also cared about Mollian, it made sense that she would want to join the Royal Guard and pledge herself to protecting the royal family and the realm.

He would even have been able to forgive her unconventional entry, which he knew was a big part of what irritated Captain Ferrick. The Guard had been entrusted to him, and the procedure for acceptance and new recruits was strict and regulated for a reason. Favor with the royal family, or with anyone of political power, shouldn't have any sway in someone being accepted into the ranks. So, when Mollian had come to Ferrick, explaining he wanted this girl—his *pet*—to train not just with the Guard, but with the Rangers, the captain was understandably angry.

Rovin could admit that they'd been hard on her in the beginning, that *he'd* been hard on her, but training was hard on everyone. It was designed that way to weed out the weak and the unworthy. Rangers were the elite. Everyone had to prove their mettle before they were accepted.

But Merriam had quit. She hadn't wanted to put in the work and had chosen an easier path. Yet still, for the past four years, she'd walked around the castle grounds like she had every right to be there. *Entitled bitch.*

Merriam stopped halfway through the courtyard, turning to look at him. The intensity of his glare had made the hair on the back of her neck stand, aware of being watched. She scoffed, folding her arms across her chest as her face tipped up to him. "Late shift tonight, Ranger-man?" she called.

Ignore her. She's not worth it. He knew it. He knew nothing would come from letting her dig further underneath his skin, but something to the arrogant gleam in her eyes set him on edge, all control and logic evaporating. "It's called a vigil, *pet*."

"A vigil?" She cocked an eyebrow, head falling to the side. Understanding spread across her face, and Rovin couldn't help the sense of satisfaction that filled him when her face tightened in annoyance. "*You?* You're kidding. The Rangers must really be hurting."

"Such strong opinions for someone who's never beaten me in a fight." A smirk pulled up one corner of Rovin's mouth, and he leaned his elbows against the rough stone barrier.

Merriam shook her head, and it was the first time he could ever remember her refusing to be goaded into an argument. "You call me pet, Rovin, but what do you think you are to Ferrick?" she asked instead.

The smirk fell from Rovin's face, eyes narrowing as his lips curled into a snarl.

The mercenary spun before he could reply, walking back toward the castle with a bounce in her step. His hands tightened into fists, and he pushed away from the edge, walking back to look out over the city. He forced the anger down, burying it as he stared at the stars. Her words meant nothing.

She meant nothing.

MERRIAM'S FACE THROBBED PAINFULLY. She was moving, her body rocking slightly, which was confusing. A whimper clawed its way up her throat, and she reached out for Mollian.

Nothing.

Panic flared in her chest. She licked her lips, forcing her eye open.

One, she discovered, was swollen almost completely shut, which explained the fierce throbbing at her temple. The night sky moved overhead, and as she listened, trying to focus on everything around her, she realized she was in a small horse-drawn cart.

Slowly, she raised a hand to the side of her face, the flesh swollen and hot and extremely tender to the touch. There was a blinding pain in her head, the ache so bad it took massive amounts of effort to think. Biting her lip to distract from the ache in her skull and around her eye, she watched the twinkle of the stars and smelled the earthy, slightly damp air of the forest mixed with the warm musk of the horse. And she forced herself to think, to remember.

Rovin left me a note, she thought, her stomach flipping and her heart fluttering as she recalled going to his room. But he hadn't been there, and something ... *What happened?*

The cart moved over the rough dirt road, and Merriam's head bounced against the wooden planks, sending a fresh wave of dizzying pain through her entire skull and down her back. And that's when it fully sunk in that she'd been attacked. She'd been taken.

A nauseating mixture of fear and panic and anger flooded her veins, and she forced herself to take deep, even breaths. *Panicking will only make this worse. Think.*

Whoever had taken her had been stupid enough to leave her un-bound, which was fortunate for Merriam. Without another thought, she dragged the backs of her hands across each other.

Nothing but skin on skin. "No no no," she cried quietly, looking at her hands. Her rings had been taken. With that realization, her hands flew to her hips, confirming her axes were also gone.

She licked her lips, quickly regrouping. The horse was moving at a brisk canter, but Merriam was confident enough in her muscle memory to know that she could land a roll if she jumped from the cart. Her head worried her, because it pounded relentlessly and lightning bolts of pain would shoot through her every time the cart was jostled. She was definitely concussed, and her eye socket was probably broken where she'd been hit.

I need to get back to Molli. The thought rang clear even through the fog in her brain. Jump from the cart, protect her head, move into the forest where she could hide. That was all she needed to do. Then she could rest and regroup.

Bracing her palms against the wooden planks, Merriam pushed herself upright. Immediately, a wave of nausea pulled at her stomach, and her vision went blurry as blood rushed from her head. She gagged, clapping a hand over her mouth and falling back to the floorboards.

The fresh jostling of her body made her gag again, and she was unable to hold back as the contents of her stomach forced their way up her throat. She did manage to turn, getting most of the vomit on the other side of the cart and pushing herself away from the putrid puddle.

Wiping her hand across her mouth, she whimpered, her eyes falling closed. *No, don't sleep!* She tried to force her good eye back open, but the lid barely even fluttered. Fatigue had fallen over her like a heavy blanket, and she could barely even make her fingers twitch as she slipped back into unconsciousness.

Merriam next woke to her hands being bound in front of her. Her good eye flew open, a scream rising in her throat. As soon as she opened her mouth, a rag was shoved into it, muffling her cry. Another strip of fabric was wrapped around her head, holding the gag in place.

She kicked out, but strong hands pulled her from the cart, and her vision went blurry as she was forced upright. *Don't puke don't puke don't puke.* All of her limited energy went to forcing her stomach to remain calm. If she threw up again, it would have nowhere to go.

Her feet dragged against the dirt as she was forced along a path and up into a cabin. She tried to get her legs under her to help alleviate the weight of her body against her arms, every jarring step by her captors sending a fresh wave of agony from her temple.

The effort of walking completely drained her. She couldn't even focus on her surroundings or look at who was handling her. Her skin felt cold and clammy, and if it weren't for the sheer terror running through her veins, she would have passed out again. But every time that curtain started to fall, a fresh dose of adrenaline would empty into her blood, forcing her back to consciousness.

She was dragged into the cabin and brought to a room, her hands lifted above her head and secured to the wall. A fog was still lying heavy in her mind, facts and memories and comprehension muddled and exhausting to decipher, but as Merriam forced herself to focus, she came to the slow realization that these were faces she'd seen before. She didn't know their names, but they were unmistakably males that she'd seen multiple times a week over the past eight years.

Her gaze dropped to their arms, and the terror that had kept her conscious grew colder, her entire body freezing as her vision tunneled onto one of the male's wrists. Her heart thudded against her ribcage, impossibly slow and heavy, a tremor traveling from the base of her neck down her entire body and repeating.

An aspen branch wrapped around his wrist, the ink a worn, dull black with age.

As if coming through a tunnel, Merriam's awareness snapped back into place, and she pulled against her bonds despite the pounding in her skull. Words couldn't be formulated around the rag in her mouth, so she screamed. She screamed, and she glared with her good eye as tears blurred her vision. *I'll kill you. I'll fucking kill you.*

The two males looked at each other, one rolling his eyes with a snort before they both left, closing the door and bolting it behind them.

Merriam continued to scream, though the sound was muffled and did nothing other than tear apart her throat. The screaming turned into great, heaving sobs, hot tears sliding down her cheeks as fear and anger consumed her. *Molli, help me.* The Cast was weak, pitiful even in her own mind. But Merriam couldn't help it. Rangers had kidnapped her. *Rangers.*

Breathing became a struggle, her nose runny with her tears, and Merriam fought to rein in her emotions and think everything through.

She stood in the dark room, head pounding and heart rate slowing. Shivers from adrenaline and emotion racked her body, but the sobs had stopped. The cloth was wet against her cheeks where her tears had soaked into it, quickly growing cold and uncomfortable.

How had this happened? Her mind kept looping between the question and a deep, undefinable longing for her *mehhen*. How had she let herself become vulnerable to attack?

Merriam blinked, tilting her head back gently in an effort not to cause her brain any extra trauma. She was confused and disoriented, and the vibrancy of the pain in her skull was too worrisome to think about, even if the agony was all-consuming. *Why would you ever walk into a dark room without checking it first for threats?* Chastising herself was useless, but the self-deprecation was easier on her body than brain-jarring sobs had been, so at least there was a plus.

Her stomach growled, and a pang of hunger added to her discomfort. When had she last eaten?

Merriam shifted her weight on her feet as she tried to play back the day's events. After the picnic, she'd gone looking for Rovin, but he'd been nowhere. She was going to eat with Mollian, but he'd given her Rovin's note, and—

Her head snapped up, the motion both painful and dizzying. Her insides knotted together uncomfortably. *Rovin,* she thought. *I'd gone to see Rovin.* She inhaled, deep and shuddering, as her mind slowly turned over the implication.

Rovin left me a note to see him. But he wasn't there.

Was he?

Merriam closed her eyes, trying to remember the room, anything she'd sensed. She'd noticed his dead leaf and crisp apple scent, but only faintly, in the way that a person's room typically carried their smell.

Right?

Merriam swallowed. What if the smell had been him?

Even if it hadn't, he'd still lured her there, alone.

Sick fucking bastard.

He'd worn her down, gotten her to drop her guard. And she'd been so fucking stupid for falling for it.

Flashes of memory crossed her mind of all of his small cruelties throughout the years, but all it had taken was a few cunning glances, some well-crafted words, and one fucking kiss, and she'd dropped every defense, ready to trust him. Rely on him. Need him.

No, she thought. No, *it couldn't have been him.*

Fresher memories bloomed in her mind's eye. The respect between them had been growing long before that kiss.

Don't lose your fucking head. Merriam took in a deep breath through her nose, letting her eyes close as she forced herself to settle, feeling her heartbeat even out to a normal rhythm. *You* will *get through this.*

She repeated it, solidifying it as fact in her mind before fatigue finally won out and pulled her under.

Something brushed against the back of Merriam's throat, and she gagged, jolting herself awake. She tried to cough, but the lack of that ability made the panic rising in her chest triple, and she thrashed against the bonds that held her.

After a few seconds of fruitless effort, her mind snapped back into place, the instinct to survive drowning out everything else.

Merriam stilled, forcing breaths through her nose as she used her tongue to shove the gag to the front of her mouth. One of her eyes throbbed, half-swollen shut where the socket around it had been broken. But that seemed to be her only real injury thus far, so she counted herself lucky.

Her wrists were tied together above her head. She knew that because her head had been resting against her arm, but she could feel nothing, both arms completely numb. She couldn't even flex her fingers. She shook out her legs, one at a time, then stretched up onto her tiptoes, trying to give her arms some relief from holding her weight.

From the light coming in through the window, Merriam could tell it was almost midday. *That's good,* she assured herself. *Molli's noticed you're gone by now.*

The only other thing in the room was a chair against the far wall.

Pins and needles filled her hands and forearms as blood slowly started to return to them, and a low moan pulled from her throat at the discomfort. Tears pricked the corners of her eyes, the gravity of the situation fully sinking in. She'd been kidnapped. She'd been kidnapped, and nobody knew where she was. Mollian had probably thought she'd spent the night with Rovin, and—

A heavy knot twisted into her gut, her chest tightening.

She'd been so fucking giddy and nervous. And she'd been played like a Legends-damned fiddle. There was a reason she never made a habit of letting her emotions show so plainly.

Merriam choked on a sob, squeezing her eyes shut as tears slipped free and soaked into the cloth tied around her head. Cold, bitter anger seeped from her heart, chilling her blood, and she screamed through the gag, jerking again at her wrists.

The door across the room opened, and Eskar walked in, a sneer on her face. "Glad to see you're up, Marshal, though I'd refrain from any more screaming if you want this to go better for you."

Merriam glared, making her black eye throb, but she couldn't stop. *I'm going to fucking end you,* she Cast, wishing the commander would be able to hear it.

"I gave Captain Ferrick my word that I would keep you alive until he's able to make it out here. You're his kill, after all." Eskar pulled the chair closer to Merriam, flipping it around and straddling it as she regarded her prisoner. "Which gives us quite a bit of alone time, doesn't it?"

Merriam, focusing her efforts because her hands were still half-asleep, raised one middle finger.

"Oh, honey," Eskar laughed. "There's no pretty little prince to protect you anymore." With a tilt of her head, she raised her hand and reached out with her magic, snapping Merriam's finger just above the first knuckle.

The pain was bright and hot and immediate, racing down Merriam's arm and into her chest with a lightning bolt of agony. Unable to help herself, she screamed, the sound ripping from her throat as her head fell back. Her stomach rolled as adrenaline rushed into her blood in response to the pain. She choked off the scream, tilting her head forward and blinking furiously, white-hot tremors still running through her.

"You wanted to play with the big dogs, little human? Well, bite back." Eskar lifted her arms out tauntingly.

Merriam's chest heaved up and down, her jaw clenching around the cloth in her mouth. She met Eskar's eyes evenly, rage simmering in molten amber.

"So much emotion in those eyes," Eskar hummed. "Funny things, emotions. So easy to manipulate."

Merriam watched her, refusing to let her tears fall.

"He was irate when given the tasking at first." Eskar sighed, tilting her head. "The first and only time I've ever seen him argue with Ferrick, believe it or not."

The room seemed to grow infinitely cold, Merriam's breath catching in her throat as Eskar's words sunk in.

"It was risky—assuming you'd grow out of your hatred of him, but Rovin is a cunning creature. There was no doubt in my mind that he would get you to drop your guard."

Merriam shook her head, pain tightening in her chest with the refusal to believe.

"That little cat and mouse game in Do Lech was cute to watch."

Fuck you, Merriam thought, and growled from low in her throat.

Eskar stood, kicking the chair to the side and walking up to Merriam. Her hand shot out, grasping a handful of Merriam's hair at the top of her head.

Despite herself, Merriam flinched, her head jerking to the side.

Knotting her fingers into Merriam's braid, Eskar forced the girl's head back with a laugh. "Scared?" she asked, narrowing her eyes as she took her free hand and traced a finger across Merriam's cheek, running it up over the dark, swollen bruise around Merriam's eye and pressing it into the soft flesh.

A moan rose from Merriam at the pressure against the broken bone, a fresh wave of pain making her vision blur at the edges and her stomach roll.

Eskar's dark eyes lit with delight. "You will be." She abruptly stepped away, leaving the room.

The conversation played on a loop in Merriam's mind, a knot of betrayal forming heavy in her gut even as she told herself it was all a lie. It had to be a lie.

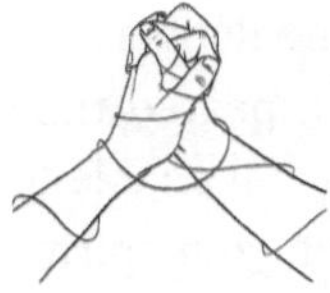

Merriam woke again, sunlight filtering through the window. The brightness hurt, her arms once again numb from holding her weight. She couldn't feel it, but she was positive her wrists were raw from the rough fibers of the rope digging into them for so long.

She shifted on her feet, trying to alleviate the pressure on her arms. One blessing of her numb limbs was that she was unable to feel the pain from her broken finger. *At least I've got that going my way, so it could be worse,* she thought, choking back something between a giggle and a sob.

Her bladder was uncomfortably full, and she shifted again, pressing her thighs together. She contemplated trying to make a racket, bring in one of the Rangers, but she'd seen the cold look in Eskar's eyes. If she was destined for death, they wouldn't give her the decency of a bathroom break. She whimpered, closing her eyes and tipping her head back against the wall. *Where are you, Molli?* she wondered, and instantly felt selfish.

She's the one who'd run off to meet a male, too absorbed in her own feelings to check her surroundings.

That seed of doubt Eskar planted had only grown. Rovin had always been her enemy, from the first time she'd met him. How much could really change in a year? She couldn't deny that he knew her well enough to know what kind of games to play to weasel himself past her defenses.

The sting of that possible betrayal stuck in her throat, tears pricking her eyes.

The door burst open, Eskar stepping through with a plate of warm meat and some sort of noodle. The heavy smell of garlic and herbs filled the air, and Merriam's mouth instantly watered.

It was so difficult to swallow around the cloth in her mouth, now uncomfortably damp with her spit. Merriam's stomach let out a loud rumble, empty for far too long and none too happy about it.

Eskar laughed, dropping into the chair and taking a large, sloppy bite out of what appeared to be chicken.

Merriam wanted to glare, wanted to yank at her bonds, but she knew Eskar was trying to goad her. So she took a deep breath, letting her gaze unfocus to stare blankly at the Ranger's feet.

I'm going to kill you. She repeated the words, Casting them toward Eskar regardless of the fae being unable to hear.

"Oh, Marshal, have I broken your spirit already?" Eskar tsked, tossing a bone at Merriam. It smacked into her stomach, leaving a small grease stain before dropping to the floor at her feet. "I expected more."

Merriam clenched her jaw, refusing to acknowledge or respond. She blinked slowly, trying to play off boredom as best she could with her hands strung up and a gag around her mouth.

"I hope you're not expecting Mollian to show up soon. Rovin told him this morning that you'd be spending all day with the mercenaries and probably all night, too." The Ranger twirled noodles around a fork, chewing thoughtfully before swallowing. "He may be cruel, but nobody can deny that he is loyal to a fault. Without him, this whole operation would have been almost impossible. Stealing you right out from under Mollian's nose ... Now he won't even think to look for you until long after you're dead."

Merriam ached. She was exhausted and hungry, and every part of her body hurt. As much as she tried to ignore Eskar's words, they seeped into her brain, spreading roots until she could no longer deny them. Hot tears of disgust and fury dripped slowly down her cheeks, soaking into the band around her face. She would not let herself be hurt by this, by him. Already, she was forcing down the dejection and confusion and disappointment, forcing her heart to stay whole and beating through sheer force of will.

Will driven by anger and a promise of retribution.

Molli will find me. Molli will find me, she consoled herself. She would get free, and she would slay Rovin Arwood where he stood. She vowed it silently, closing her eyes and tipping her head back as she swallowed past her tears. She just had to hold on long enough for Mollian to come. Because he would, despite any efforts to keep him away. He had to.

"You know, it's polite to look at people when they talk to you. Especially people who have power over you," Eskar said, anger dripping from her voice.

You're angry, are you? Tough fucking nuts. Merriam silently seethed, keeping her eyes on the floor.

Eskar stood, plate clattering on the ground. "You're lucky Ferrick has already claimed you. If I were allowed to toy with you the way I want ..." She stepped over to Merriam, grabbing the aspen leaf charm that still dangled at her throat and twisting it, tightening the chain around Merriam's neck.

The necklace dug into her skin, pinching uncomfortably. Eskar twisted again, and sharp pricks of pain dotted Merriam's neck as her skin split between a few of the links. Blood, warm and wet, welled to the surface in little droplets.

Her head grew dizzy with the diminished blood flow, and she instinctively kicked out, striking Eskar in the side of the knee.

"Fucking bitch," she hissed, releasing the chain and hopping back and out of Merriam's reach.

Merriam did meet Eskar's eyes then, small beads of blood trickling down her neck as she let her gaze shine with every ounce of hatred burning through her.

The Ranger threw her hand out, and Merriam's leg twisted to the side, slamming into the wall behind her.

She yelped into the gag and struggled against the grip of Eskar's magic.

The fae's hold tightened, and she curled her fingers with the effort of holding onto flesh. The magic kept trying to slip off, reluctant to find purchase. But Eskar fought, and Merriam's shin slowly twisted, putting immense pressure against her knee.

Bile surged up Merriam's throat, the pain darkening the edges of her vision and terror winding through her core and squeezing her lungs. She could feel her tendons stretching in a way they should never be stretched, the joint of her knee resisting the motion and about to lose that fight. Her leg kept turning, and a scream tore from her throat.

Her bladder, full to bursting, let loose.

The agonizing tension on her knee dropped, and her head fell forward as she sobbed with equal parts relief at the ability to breathe again and dehumanizing embarrassment at the stream of warm liquid soaking the legs of her pants and pooling on the floor beneath her.

Eskar tilted her head to the side, a cruel grin splitting her face. "You're disgusting, little human. It's fitting you sit in your own filth for the last pathetic moments of your life."

Merriam was left alone. And, for a moment, she completely unraveled. The hot stench of urine combined with the garlic from Eskar's dropped food, making Merriam's stomach clench in revolt. Her shoulders ached, contorted from holding her weight for so long. Feeling had seeped back into her hands and arms, and her wrists burned. Her broken finger throbbed, each beat sending a wave of agony down the center of her arm. And her head still pounded, her swollen eye hot and unbelievably tender, even to movement.

Merriam's teeth chattered against the cloth in her mouth as she came undone, sagging one second before pushing her feet back underneath her when her wrists and shoulders screamed in protest. She shifted uncomfortably, yanking at her binds as a huge sob wracked her body.

She never should have trusted someone who had made it very clear that he despised her.

Merriam clenched her teeth against the rag in her mouth, reminding herself that she would not cry over that piece of shit. She would learn from her mistakes, she would get out of this mess, and she would make him pay for ever having played her a fool.

That line of purpose kept her sane and somewhat level-headed, even though tears still spilled down her cheeks. She had nothing but desperation, and that desperation was linked to a need for vengeance that sang so loudly in her blood it was impossible to ignore.

For how much she'd slept, she was still tired. That fatigue was faintly troubling in the back of her mind as she acknowledged her concussion. She was hungry. Her whole body was sore. She was alone. And she was scared.

For the first time since Mollian had brought her to Nethyl, she truly thought she might die. Acknowledging that possibility shocked her out of her tears.

I don't want to die.

She ground her teeth against the gag in her mouth, forcing all of her panic and terror down. The pain she couldn't ignore, so she leaned into it, let it fan the flames of survival that burned inside of her. And her anger helped fuel it.

She adjusted, her boots squelching. Heat flooded her cheeks, but she shoved the embarrassment down. Pissing herself was more than likely the only reason her knee was still intact. *I will not die here.*

That promise settled in with the never-ending loop of promises to kill, and she once again gave herself over to anger.

Merriam leaned forward, wincing at the strain against her shoulders. A window was set in the wall next to her. Even if there was no latch, she could use the chair to break it open.

What if they hear? What if they chase me?

Merriam had had magic used against her in training before, people reaching out to trip her, or halt a hand. Fae magic was strong, but it wasn't gargantuan in its reach or ability. It was really only good for small movements, especially when it came to living things. Magic that affected the mind was one matter, but magic that touched physical things was, as Mollian always described it, fickle. It didn't like to touch the living, required more concentration and greater effort to touch something bright with the energy of life.

So Eskar wouldn't be able to haul her alone, but she didn't know how many of the Rangers were here. One could grab a leg, another an arm ... if they worked together, they could wrench her back.

And if they got her back, they'd probably try a lot harder to make sure she couldn't escape again. There was no way Eskar would let herself look incompetent in front of Ferrick.

Merriam looked at the chair, considering it. It was old, wooden, and possibly within her power to break it if she used the right leverage. The clatter might draw attention, but she could ambush them, especially if they came one at a time. The leg of the chair could easily be wielded as a club. All she had to do was buy herself some time.

She tilted her head up and to the side, craning her neck to try to figure out how her hands were bound above her. The strain hurt, and the angle made her dizzy, so she turned her head forward, blinking back fatigue. She just wanted to sleep.

No, she commanded herself, clenching her jaw and lifting up on her toes, trying to shake awake without aggravating her head. If she went to sleep, there was no telling when she would wake up, and she had to escape before Ferrick arrived.

But her eyelids were so, so heavy, her head swimming with fog.

No.

Her eyes slipped closed, and she sagged against her restraints.

Just before she slid away, she felt her fingers twitch, finally woken up from before. She curled the fingers of her right hand around her left, squeezing.

White hot pain jolted from Merriam's broken middle finger, running down her arm and into her side. Her eyes flew open, a cry ripping from her chest as tears sprang to her eyes. Adrenaline flooded her veins, and she set her weight back on her feet, breathing as evenly as she could, given the gag around her mouth and a nose runny from crying.

She twisted her right wrist around, trying to get a feel for how much give the rope had. The raw skin beneath the binds burned with every motion, but the pain helped ground her and keep her awake, even as her teeth worried against the cloth in her mouth.

No matter how she moved her hands, a fresh ripple of agony sliding down her arm each time her broken finger was jostled, there wasn't enough space for her to pull a hand free, the rope getting caught against the base of her thumb.

Merriam took a deep, shuddering breath, clamping her teeth down on the gag. She wrapped her fingers as tightly as she could manage around her thumb. Burrowing deep into herself, she squeezed her eyes shut, black eye throbbing from the pressure, and pulled, fast and hard.

A soft, wet *pop* came from her thumb as the joint slipped from its socket, which Merriam barely registered over the immediate, blinding wave of pain that rolled through her entire body. She panted, short, fast breaths from her nose, a low moan the only sound she was capable of.

Her heart thundered in her chest, but the pain was more than her psyche could handle, and everything faded to black.

MERRIAM WAS NOWHERE TO be found when Mollian woke up. Though it was impossible to tell for sure if her bed had been slept in, given the fact that it was rarely—if ever—made, Mollian was confident that she hadn't come back in the night.

He smiled, shaking his head as he closed the door to her room. This was a good thing. It had been over a year, and even though he knew she still grieved as he did, would likely always grieve, the fact that she was finally allowing herself to truly move on made him more happy than he knew how to express.

In an uncharacteristic move, he decided to eat breakfast in the main dining hall where everyone else in the castle took their meals.

Captain Ferrick, who usually ate with the Guard in their quarters, was seated at a table with a few of the guildmasters. Mollian didn't have the stomach for politics so early in the morning, so he changed course to eat with a few of the heads of house, the members of staff who were in charge of running specific areas of the castle. He realized with a shock of guilt that he didn't show enough face around them. His life was lived around their hard work, and he made a mental note to make sure he didn't allow them to feel taken for granted.

After breakfast, his schedule was completely full of meetings. He'd tried to give himself a break after lunch, but Ferrick had requested to talk about Royal Guard business, so he wouldn't have any free time until supper.

So lovely to be king, he thought sarcastically.

The day dragged. Mollian had periodically reached out for Merriam, eager to either tease her or listen to her rant depending on her mood, but he hadn't been able to feel her.

This wasn't initially concerning, as there was every possibility she'd decided to spend the day with the mercenaries. They hadn't talked much about everything that had happened in Do Lech on that end, but he knew that being there wouldn't have been easy on Aleah. So Mollian tried not to worry.

But later that evening, after playing a distracted round of cards with Bellamy, he stood, unable to ignore the anxiety knotting in his stomach anymore. "She wouldn't have been gone this long without talking to me," he said, pushing his hair back from his face with both hands.

"You didn't see her at all this morning?" Bellamy asked, tucking the cards into a neat pile.

Mollian shook his head, magic rolling beneath his skin as it fed off of his agitation. "Did you see her at the barracks or the training grounds?"

"No, I haven't seen her all day."

"Something is wrong," Mollian whispered, not wanting to give in to the wave of fear that crashed over him as he stalked toward the door.

Bellamy was already moving to follow the king, unease churning through him.

"Send a bird to the mercs. If she's not there, tell them to come here." Mollian's voice was all cold command, so much of his concentration focused on trying to control the power that surged inside him, sensing his distress and begging to act on it. *She's fine*, he tried to assure himself, feeling the tethers stretched between their souls.

"Where are you going?" Bellamy asked warily, keeping up with Mollian's purposeful strides.

"Have you seen our dear friend Rovin at all today?" And Mollian's control frayed to a dangerous level as he spoke the words aloud.

Bellamy's steps faltered. He hadn't, but Mollian couldn't actually think that—

They rounded a corner, nearly bumping into the Ranger in question.

Rovin stepped back, but before he could so much as incline his head in respect, Mollian was advancing. "Where is Ria?"

Rovin blinked, taking another half step back. "I'm actually looking for her."

"She spent the night with you."

Rovin frowned, shaking his head. "What? Why would you think—"

Something volatile rolled through Mollian as he interrupted. "Choose your next words carefully, Lieutenant." He threw out his awareness again, feeling for some blip from Merriam. Nothing. "You asked her to come. She went to see you. And no one has seen her since."

"No, I was out all night. Ferrick tasked me—"

Mollian was on him before he finished, his hand bracketing Rovin's throat as he threw him back into a wall. "Where. Is. Merriam?" he asked, his magic swirling dangerously through him, wrapping around him. He didn't even have the wherewithal to attempt to pull it in.

"I don't know!" Rovin forced out, pulling at Mollian's hand.

Mollian pushed him further into the wall, his magic sliding down his arms and dripping around Rovin. "I will not ask again," he snarled, teeth bared as he leaned in close to Rovin's face. His magic seeped down his arms, wrapping around Rovin and pressing into him until Mollian could feel the strong, rapid beat of Rovin's heart in every pulse point.

Rovin's eyes were wide and panicked as he tried harder to peel Mollian's hand from his throat. His airway was completely cut off, his lungs burning. He couldn't reply even if he had an answer.

"Molli, stop." Bellamy put his hand on Mollian's shoulder.

Mollian whirled around, still pinning Rovin, and raised his other hand to throw Bellamy off of him.

Bellamy caught Mollian's forearm, using his own magic to bolster the hold. "Mollian, look at me."

Mollian panted, the muscle in his arm twitching with indecision, wanting to rip free from Bellamy's hold, but the intensity of the male's gaze freezing him in place.

"You're going to kill him," Bellamy said evenly.

A tremor ran through Mollian's body, something in his chest cracking, his magic rippling out. "Where's Ria?" he whispered, pale green eyes wild.

"He can't tell you if he's dead," Bellamy said, holding Mollian's gaze.

A hot streak of pain broke through the fog in Mollian's mind, and he realized that his magic was digging into Rovin in a similar way that his hand tightened around the male's throat.

Rovin's fingers scratched the back of Mollian's hand again, and Mollian dropped him, reeling in his magic. Rovin collapsed to his knees, coughing and bringing a hand up to massage his neck.

Bellamy released Mollian's arm, stepping back.

Mollian dug his fingers into his hair, concentrating on keeping his magic pulled close, tucked in. "Jasper," he rasped. "Go send the bird, now."

Bellamy cast one worried look toward Rovin before slipping past them.

Mollian swallowed against the lump in his throat, tears flooding his eyes. He braced his hands against the wall and tipped his head back, blinking against the tears and taking a deep breath. He could have killed Rovin. It would have been so easy to apply just a little more pressure, to crush his windpipe or snap his neck.

What shook him was the fact that he wouldn't even care. If something had happened to Merriam ...

The tethers between their souls were still intact. Stretched, but whole. He turned back to Rovin, who was on his feet, one hand still rubbing his throat.

"You didn't leave the note," Mollian said quietly.

Rovin coughed. "I was down in Umbra from the time I left the war room until well after sundown. I ... I was going to come for her this morning, but I had assignments all day. I'm supposed to be on duty now, actually, but I asked Kodi to cover for me."

Nausea churned in Mollian's stomach, and he ran the back of his hand across his mouth. "Someone took her."

Rovin dragged a hand down his face. "Ferrick," he breathed. He pushed his hair back, turning around and slamming the flat of his hand against the wall with a feral cry.

Mollian straightened, barely keeping a grip on the power that wanted to flare from him. "What?"

"Ferrick made sure I was out of the castle all day yesterday. Today, he kept me busy and out of your sight." Rovin's hands trembled, and he curled his fingers into fists, anger coursing through him. "He's always been wary of the power she holds over you."

"No, I saw Ferrick almost all day today." Mollian shook his head, closing his eyes and concentrating on the places he could feel Merriam tied to him. She was alive. He clung to that knowledge.

"He needed to make sure when she turned up missing that he couldn't be implicated."

"He didn't think I'd question why she was left a note that was made to sound like it came from you? That's clearly a set-up."

Rovin's hand drifted up to his throat. "If I'd stayed on shift like I was supposed to, if you found out she was gone before I had a chance to come looking for her … he probably expected you to kill me before giving me a chance to talk."

"If Bellamy hadn't been here, I would have." Mollian ran a hand through his hair, his chest tightening. Without a word, he started walking.

"Where are you going?" Rovin moved to follow.

"To save my *mehhen*," Mollian ground out. "And to remove that motherfucker from the face of this planet."

"Wait," Rovin reached for Mollian's arm.

Mollian whirled around, a dangerous light in his eyes that made Rovin pull back. "It's been an entire fucking day." His voice wavered, forced through clenched teeth. "She's been out there for *an entire day*. Wondering when I'm going to come for her. And I didn't even know—" he stopped, voice breaking. "If she's been hurt … while I've been in fucking banal meetings all day?" Mollian shook his head, a tear slipping down the dark skin of his cheek.

Rovin followed him out, apprehension coiling in his gut as they walked through the castle at a brisk pace. In a way he couldn't explain, he could feel the king's magic—how unstable it was, how loose of a hold he had on it. The depth of it was stronger than anything he'd ever known. When it had pressed around him, Rovin had almost been afraid that it would sink inside of him and dig into the core of his being.

The Ranger shook off the thoughts, following the king across the courtyard to the barracks. Mollian stopped so abruptly that Rovin slammed into his back. He spun, his hands gripping Rovin's shoulders, eyes searching Rovin's face. "Tell me you would never hurt her."

Rovin met his gaze evenly. "I swear to you, Mollian, if it is at all within my power, I would never let her come to harm."

Mollian held his eyes for a heartbeat longer, assuring himself that Rovin hadn't had a part in this. "Who can I trust?" He cut straight to the point. "Aside from Bell, who else can you say with utmost certainty is not under Ferrick's influence?"

"Kodi," Rovin answered without hesitation. "Several of the lower-ranking Rangers who grew respect for her before Ferrick had a chance to fully sink his claws into them."

"Watch my back." Mollian turned, barreling into the barracks. He strode straight for Ferrick's office, ignoring the Rangers that scrambled to attention with his entrance. He threw open the door, magic swirling from him before he was able to pull it back in.

Rovin felt it brush over him, shivering involuntarily at the pressure of it against his skin. He still hadn't fully recovered from the attack that very well could have killed him.

The office was empty. Mollian whirled around, pushing past Rovin and walking into the common room. "Where is the captain?" It wasn't quite a shout, but close.

The Rangers standing around were stunned into silence. None of them had ever seen the king angry, and all of them hesitated to answer, unsure of how he would respond.

"He left for the evening, Your Majesty. Said he had business to take care of out of town." Evangeline, who had fought with Merriam last summer, spoke up. "He didn't say where," she offered before he could ask, clearly reading the fury in his pale green eyes.

Mollian's hands clenched into fists at his sides, and he nodded, not even recognizing her through the blinding emotions clouding his mind, and stepped back out into the night.

Rovin followed, unease tightening his chest. *This is bad.*

Bellamy found them outside, on his way back from the aviary.

Tremors worked their way up and down Mollian's spine as he struggled to maintain control.

Rovin caught Bellamy's eyes. They needed to get Mollian back inside. They couldn't risk the wrong people seeing him so unhinged. But Rovin's throat still ached, and he was hesitant to be the one to direct the king.

"Let's go back upstairs," Bellamy suggested, sensing Rovin's hesitation.

"He has her, Bell," Mollian whispered, another tremor working through him.

Bellamy stepped forward, wrapping his arms tightly around Mollian, one hand cupping the back of his head. "I know."

"We need a game plan," Rovin spoke up. Every vile rumor he'd heard of Ferrick came to the forefront of his mind along with every horrible thing he'd heard directly from the captain himself. The extent of the male's grasp for power and hatred for what Merriam had become was undeniable, but Rovin refused to let the fear freeze him. Refused to let disgust for himself at his former idolization of Ferrick overcome him. If Ferrick had Merriam, Rovin could outsmart him. He knew the male well enough for that. "Too much time has already passed."

Mollian nodded, stepping away. He squeezed Bellamy's shoulder before stepping past, leaving instructions with the guards outside to send the mercenaries to him when they showed and heading to the war room.

As soon as the doors were locked behind them, Mollian let a tendril of magic whip from him, curling an outstretched hand into a fist as the magic wrapped around a wooden chair, chewing into the seams in the wood grain. Mollian's lip curled into a snarl as he pushed it harder, feeling wisps of his magic meeting in the middle of the chair and splaying his fingers wide, his power pulling the chair apart with a loud rip, followed by a clatter as the two halves flew to opposite sides of the room.

Mollian stood, panting, as a bead of sweat dripped over one of the aspen leaves on his brow.

Bellamy cast a nervous glance at Rovin, both unsure of what their king might be capable of if something happened to Merriam, but equally positive they didn't want to find out.

Swallowing against the dryness in his mouth, Rovin walked to the table, scanning the map of Sekha laid into the top. The need to move, to act, was undeniable. He didn't want to step on Mollian's toes, but the thought of Merriam being held somewhere out there—the thought that she had been taken by people he'd considered comrades, brothers-in-arms—was too much to fully process. He needed to save her. "They can't have taken her far," he said, scanning the mountains that surrounded Umbra. "There's no way they would have made it out of Jekeida, even if they kept moving."

Bellamy joined him, curls falling over his shoulders as he leaned forward to scan the map. "What are the odds they kept moving?"

Scratching the scruff on his chin, Rovin blew out a breath. "I wouldn't bet on it. Think about it, what would kidnapping Mer accomplish?"

"If Ferrick wanted Molli unhinged, that wish is granted," Bellamy said quietly.

"No, he needs Mollian as a figurehead. But with Merriam around, Mollian would never rely on him the way Ferrick wants." Rovin crossed his arms over his chest, eyes still scanning the mountains surrounding Umbra. Something scratched in his brain, a detail he was having trouble grasping.

Mollian chuckled, a dark, hysterical sound that made the hair on Rovin's arms stand. "The logic here confounds me."

Bellamy frowned. "Ferrick clearly tried to make it look like Rovin set her up. He probably planned for you to fly into a blind rage. Kill him, kill whoever else you found responsible. But Ferrick was around all day today. Once you realized Mer was missing, he could have offered support or formed a search party, something to gain your trust."

"And when I find her? And she tells me it was Ferrick's men—*my fucking men*—who took her?" Mollian joined them at the table, placing his palms flat against the surface to keep his hands from shaking.

Rovin lifted his gaze to meet the king's. "I don't think she's meant to be found alive."

Every bit of emotion faded from Mollian's eyes, the green going hard and cold as his jaw clenched. "That is not an outcome that will end well for anyone."

A knock sounded on the door, and Rovin and Bellamy jumped. Mollian raised a hand, unengaging the latch with a twist of his fingers.

The mercenaries came in, and as soon as Rovin saw Aleah, that unknown detail scratched harder against his mind. "Get Kodi, I need him," he called to her.

Aleah's face drained completely of blood, freckles standing out starkly on her skin. Her hazel eyes were huge with fear. She gave a small shake of her head, unwilling to bring Kodi into this. Aleah was there for Merriam, she had to be, but she'd seen the way someone reacted when faced with the loss of their *mehhen*. The thought of Kodi being in the way if Mollian were to lose control was unbearable.

Rovin read the fear in her face, and though he didn't understand the depth of it, he empathized. "Please," he said. "I wouldn't ask if it wasn't vital."

Aleah bit her lip, glancing to Mollian's unnaturally still form before finally nodding and slipping away.

Jasper walked up to Mollian, resting a hand on his shoulder.

Mollian met Jasper's cool silver gaze, trying to let the quiet calm of this male his brother had called kin sink into him.

It didn't work, but he was glad to have someone here with a more level head than his. He turned to Rovin. "Do you know where Ferrick may have taken her?"

Rovin ran a hand through his hair. "Possibly, but Kodi has a better memory for these things than I do. I don't want to give false hope."

Mollian nodded, trying to push back the rage and fear that buzzed in his veins. The Rangers were adept at scouting. If anyone would be able to find Ferrick, it would be them. And the people in this room with him ... he let himself feel some small measure of comfort knowing they, too, would kill without hesitation to keep Merriam safe.

Mollian jerked his head up with a start, looking at Bellamy. "Stay with Ryddan. It's unlikely Ferrick would try something so close to taking Merriam, but he found the fucking gall for that. Now that he's stepped out, we need to figure out who he has under his thumb, whose loyalties are tied to him instead of the Crown. Ryddan isn't safe while Ferrick's loyalists are free."

Bellamy was gone with barely a word of acknowledgment, but even in his state of unrest, Mollian was thankful Ryddan had Bellamy. There was no one who cared more for the Stonebane heir than the young Ranger.

Aleah returned with Kodi, who immediately strode forward to the table. "What do you need?"

"We were practicing scouting, back when we'd first earned our Ranger marks. There was a building in the mountains, hidden in a ravine. Do you remember? We camped there with a couple of others."

Kodi tilted his head, tongue poking out of the side of his mouth as he scanned the map. "Wait, off to the east, right? We followed a game trail from the road."

Rovin felt hope flare in his chest. "Yes! Do you think you'd be able to find it again?"

Aleah stiffened, peeking between their shoulders.

"Do you think you could point out any of the landmarks? So I can lead the others?" Rovin amended.

Kodi slid an arm around Aleah's waist, pulling her close. He leaned down to press his lips into her hair. "I appreciate your concern, little merc, but she's my friend and my marshal. There's no sense in risking time wasted if Rov gets you all lost."

Aleah shuddered, sinking into him.

Rovin looked to Mollian. "If he sent her somewhere to be kept short-term, this is a safe bet. It was an old Ranger safe house at one point, but hasn't been in use for many years."

Mollian nodded. "How many people do you think he has with him?"

"If his plan is to kill her, he wouldn't want a lot of witnesses. Maybe just one or two to pin the blame on if necessary," Rovin said.

"Eskar was gone all day. I'll bet she's the one who kidnapped Mer," Kodi offered. "I haven't noticed any others missing, though that's not saying much. Ferrick isn't stupid. There's a reason he's grown so powerful. He wouldn't have let that many people know if he was planning to attack her. She's the marshal. That's treason. Only a couple of very dumb, very loyal people would have been chosen."

Mollian turned to Jasper and the rest of the mercenaries. "Two of you stay here. Help Bellamy guard Ryddan. The rest of you come with. Make a perimeter around the back of the house. Surround it. Nobody runs free. Capture them, kill them, I don't fucking care." He turned back to the Rangers, Aleah still tucked into Kodi's side. "You two are with me. We'll go in from the front."

Without waiting for questions, he left the room, and all of them followed. With a brief glance, Jasper sent Leonidas and Campbell as back up for Bellamy. Calysta's holistic plant knowledge could prove useful, and Aleah wasn't going to be leaving Kodi alone while Mollian was untethered.

Rovin stuck close to Mollian out of instinct. If anyone understood the depth of Mollian and Merriam's connection, it was the mercenaries, but Rovin had been trained for years to protect the Crown, and the thought of letting an outsider close to his king when he was in a place this vulnerable, this volatile, felt wrong.

Kodi, after muttering a few reassurances to Aleah, lengthened his stride to catch up, unstrapping a shortsword from his belt and handing it over. "I didn't have time to grab yours from your room, but here's a random from the armory."

Rovin took it, glancing down at his waist in surprise. He'd removed his weapon before showering and going to look for Merriam. With everything that had happened since then, he hadn't even realized he was unarmed. "Thanks." He strapped it around his waist.

Kodi's bi-colored eyes were bright with amusement. "You were about to run off to save your girl with no weapon and no magic. Planning to knock Ferrick down with your fists?"

"Ferrick is mine," Mollian interjected cooly, hands curling at his sides.

"Of course, Your Majesty." Kodi inclined his head, noticing that Mollian's hips were also bare. "Um, sir?"

Another shiver ran up Mollian's spine, and, with a cold confidence he couldn't quite place the origin of, he cut off Kodi's question. "As long as the two of you are capable fighters, I won't need it. Just cover me."

Kodi nodded, glancing at Rovin with a curious apprehension.

The group grabbed horses from the stables, Kodi leading the way out of Umbra and into the mountains.

Kodi was arrogant enough to call himself the best scout in the Rangers, and it wasn't a baseless claim. His natural inclination for navigation and finding his way through a forest was close to unmatched, which was the only reason he was given so much leeway for his antics.

As they thundered through the mountains, Rovin kept pace with the king, stealing himself for the confrontation ahead of them. The echo of magic still prickled his skin, but the knowledge that he could have died was insignificant compared to everything else. Even the shock of the captain's treason barely registered over his worry for Merriam. She would be okay; he refused to entertain any other possibility, but an old, deep-seated rage flared to life inside of him as he followed Kodi into the forest. Just because she could handle herself didn't mean she should have to, and energy flowed through him with the need to protect and the almost insatiable desire to exact vengeance. Rovin spared a sideways glance toward Mollian, locking down some of the possessiveness that seared his nerves.

Regardless of how charged he was, the Ranger knew better than to get in the way of the king.

Mollian threw out his awareness for Merriam, that mental connection given to them through the Bonding rune on her back had a further reach than Casting did, but it still couldn't span more than a klick, maybe two.

Kodi turned, leading them into a ravine, and Mollian's fists tightened around the reins. Cold and heat warred through him, fear and anger mixing in his blood in an all-consuming way that pushed out critical thought. If she wasn't here, if he'd wasted all this time for nothing …

Mollian knew there was no way Ferrick planned to keep her alive. He would kill her, possibly without much preamble, and Mollian kept a sharp awareness of the threads wound between his soul and hers, assuring himself that he wasn't too late, that she was alive.

His magic swirled through him in a wild and untamable current, a reaction to his *mehhen* being in danger. Like it somehow knew that without her, he wouldn't be able to hold all of it, and magic without a vessel, without someone to wield it, was inconsequential.

Mollian reached for her again.

She was there, latching onto his touch against her mind and pulling him in with a desperation that made him completely unravel.

Merriam had left the only home she'd ever known, had slain demons from a foreign world, had watched her love die in front of her, and had faced every trial ever placed in front of her. But Mollian had never felt her truly scared until now.

Fury raced through him, and he kept his awareness on Merriam's touch in his mind. *Hold on.* Mollian was still too far to Cast to her, but he kept the thought regardless, hoping she could feel his urgency.

The mercenaries branched off into the woods, angling away to sur-round the cabin that would soon appear through the trees. Mollian, with Kodi and Rovin on either side of him, slowed for a few moments, letting the mercenaries have a chance to pull ahead.

"Ferrick is mine," Mollian repeated, the only plan he had. The only part of him that could be considered calm was the part of his mind that reached out to Merriam. Everything else was a volatile, crackling energy.

Mollian kicked his heels into his horse again, expecting the Rangers to follow, and thundered down the path toward the cabin.

"She soiled herself, Captain. But I left her whole for you."

The voices pulled Merriam into consciousness, fear sitting heavy in her gut like a stone as her brain sluggishly placed who was talking. She hadn't been out long enough for her arms to go completely numb again, and she couldn't help the whimper that escaped her as her entire left hand screamed in blinding agony.

"Wake up, *Marshal*." Ferrick grasped her chin, shaking her head.

A wave of nausea pushed through Merriam at the sharp movement. There was nothing but bile in her stomach at this point, but her body convulsed, trying to bring it up anyway. Her good eye fluttered open, and despite the fact that she knew she was fully and completely at his mercy, Merriam glared at Ferrick with a pure, unadulterated hatred.

He laughed, infuriating her further. "Guess you didn't break her after all. I'm surprised, Commander." Ferrick turned to look at Eskar. "Pleasantly so." Her obedience and loyalty to him, in light of what very well could be considered treason, had his cock hardening in his pants. Her respect and acknowledgement of his power was intoxicating.

Ferrick turned back to the girl bound before him, an unamused smirk pulling at one corner of his mouth. "You never had to die, you know. If you'd only learned your place ... you've got no one to blame but yourself. How many times did I try to teach you to stand down? How many times did Rovin?"

Anger masked the betrayal that whipped through Merriam, stealing her breath, and she kicked out, connecting with Ferrick's knee.

The rage in his blue eyes almost matched her own, but instead of stepping back, he stepped into her, forcing a leg between hers as he gripped her jaw, tilting her head back as he leaned against her. "You never learn, do you? Instead, you challenge me at every turn. You turn *my men* against me. You pervert the laws of this land for your own agenda, contaminating the mind of the king ..." Ferrick's firm hold on her chin kept her head still and her eyes on him.

The weight of his thigh was uncomfortable against her groin, the crotch of her pants still damp, but Merriam didn't dare shift her hips to try to alleviate the discomfort. She could feel the stiff length of his erection against her abdomen, and terror crippled her as she realized the potential for a fate far worse than simple death.

Ferrick saw the light shift in her eyes, and he smiled, grinding against her. "Should I try one last time, Merriam, to teach you your place in this world?"

She pressed as far back against the wall as she could, unable to keep tears from filling her eyes. She wanted to spit on him, rake her nails across his face, and scream obscenities at him.

But she could do none of those things, and she knew with a cold, steady certainty that he was going to kill her, and she was powerless to stop him. So Merriam clenched her teeth against that Legends-damned gag, and she Cast to him with all of the rage and fear and betrayal in her being.

Molli is going to slaughter you.

"You've been warming Mollian's bed for so many years. I can't destroy him, obviously. I can only make him need me. But I will destroy what's his, and I'll tear your cunt open until it's gaping and bleeding, and you're begging me for death."

Ferrick's hand dropped down to her hip, and she did begin struggling, then.

Her broken hand screamed in protest at being jostled. Merriam wrapped her good hand around the rope above, pulling up and kicking her feet out, bucking her hips to try to dislodge him.

Ferrick laughed, her terror filling him with power until he was drunk on it.

Eskar stewed behind him. "Is it wise to draw this out, Captain?" she asked. She wasn't stupid enough to think that she was the only female Ferrick slept with, and she used him for power just as much as he used her. But she never had to watch or listen when he fucked someone else, and her stomach soured, wondering if she would think about this every time Ferrick called for her again. Merriam deserved to die, deserved to hurt, but this felt different.

Ferrick paused, turning to Eskar with curiosity. "Growing soft, Commander?"

Eskar bristled, hands fisting at her sides. "No, and you presume too much. This isn't about the girl, it's about the king. Mollian will have noticed her absence by now. We need to dump the body and be gone so that we aren't implicated in this."

"I presume nothing, Eskar. If you're so concerned about His Majesty, then go keep watch with the other two."

Merriam's heart thundered against her chest, Ferrick's erection still pressed to her stomach. Her body grew cold, knowing that whatever Ferrick had planned for her would grow exponentially worse since his subordinate had tried to interfere.

Then she felt a familiar brush against her consciousness and immediately latched onto it, unable to fake any lack of desperation as she clung to that feel of Mollian in her mind.

Hurry, hurry, hurry, she pleaded silently, tears spilling down her cheeks.

Feeling Mollian, knowing he would find her, renewed her determination. She pushed up onto her tiptoes, alleviating the strain on her arms, and closed her eyes. Ferrick would have a few last moments with her, but she would survive them.

Still pressed against her, Ferrick felt the change in her body and stiffened. "Something's wrong," he told Eskar, stepping back from Merriam.

He turned and walked out the door, Eskar following him with a curious tilt to her head.

As soon as the door latched behind them, Merriam wasted no time. If they knew they'd been discovered, they wouldn't hesitate to kill her and leave before they could be implicated.

Without giving herself a chance to hesitate, she pulled down on her left arm. A feral scream shredded her throat, the loose bone of her thumb shifting out of the way with a pain so bright, her vision blurred and her hearing diminished to only the rush of blood in her ears. But then her hand was free, and she cradled it to her chest, panting through her nose and shaking the rope off of her other hand.

The pain in her hand and her skull was incredibly disorienting paired with the heavy, desperate relief of Mollian's presence against her mind, but she thought she heard the thud of boots in the hallway. Her muscles threatened to freeze up, but she scrambled across the room, pressing her back to the wall beside the door.

The door swung open, and one of the Rangers who had tied her up took a step into the room.

Merriam swung her leg out, the toe of her boot sinking into his crotch. The Ranger hunched over, and she kicked again, this time at his face, and his nose split into a spray of blood with a satisfying crunch.

The Ranger dropped, dazed and in agony, and Merriam pushed the door closed, still holding her broken hand to her chest as she drove her heel down into his skull again and again and again.

She stumbled back, panting heavily and leg aching with the impact. The Ranger's skull was cracked, blood pooling on the floor below him along with small, gray chunks of brain matter. Bright drops of blood had sprayed across Merriam's pants, and she swallowed down against a surge of nausea before moving to the window.

Opening the latch, she boosted herself onto the sill, tumbling gracelessly to the ground below. Her head pounded a relentless rhythm with her heartbeat, and her hand hurt so badly she didn't even want to look at it, but she was free. Mollian was close, and she was free.

Merriam pushed unsteadily to her feet, ready to make a run for it.

Eskar followed Ferrick down the hall and into the common room. "Watch the front, Dirk," he ordered one of the two Rangers sitting at the old, rickety table.

Dirk tossed his playing cards down, moving to the window.

"What is it?" Eskar asked, watching the agitated edge of Ferrick's posture.

"The girl and the king are aware of each other's presence. Some sort of Keeper magic. If he's near, we need to calibrate, and quickly." He ran a frustrated hand over his jaw.

"What makes you think he's close by?" she asked.

"She stopped fighting, and I don't think it was because you tried to come to her rescue." Ferrick's lips lifted in a sneer as he glanced at Eskar, and he sat heavily in a chair, thinking. "We have to kill her. Take her body out of the cabin and make it look like we found her and are trying to bring her to the castle for help." He flicked his eyes to the remaining Ranger. "Bring her to me."

Ferrick propped his elbows on the table, flexing the muscles in his legs to keep his knee from bouncing. He was smart. He'd make it out of this. "You're supposed to be on assignment, so after we kill her, take off into the woods. There's an old game trail in the back of the ravine. Follow it north before you loop back in towards Umbra," he told Eskar.

"What about you?"

"I was with His Majesty for most of the day, and it doesn't matter what I was doing out in the forest, only that I found the girl. He should be so beside himself that he won't question anything immediately."

"What about me and Earl?" Dirk asked, turning from his watch.

Ferrick waved an unbothered hand through the air. "Bunk out here for the night, then return to Umbra in the morning." It was very possible the two of them would have to take the fall, but ... sacrifices were often required for the greater good. "Go see what's taking Earl so long," he told Eskar, unease making him irritated.

"Captain?" Dirk had resumed scanning the forest as Eskar left. "Someone's coming."

Ferrick sighed, standing and smoothing his uniform, adjusting the sword at his hip.

"It's the king." The fear in Dirk's voice was unmistakable, and it disgusted Ferrick.

"Let me throw him off the trail, then. Tell Eskar to finish the girl." It almost pained him knowing he'd likely be left with no choice but to pin the blame on her as well as the others, but he again reminded himself that it was all for the greater good. His good, at least.

As soon as Mollian saw the cabin, everything else dropped off of his plane of awareness.

He pulled his horse to a stop, dropping to the ground. "Pos!" he bellowed, his voice echoing off of the walls of the ravine.

Rovin and Kodi flanked their king, weapons drawn.

The front of the cabin opened, and Ferrick stepped out, his expression neutral. "Your Majesty, what an unex–"

"Let her go," Mollian demanded, pale green eyes blazing.

Ferrick blinked, his hand dropping casually to the hilt of his sword. "Pardon?"

Wrong answer, Mollian Cast to Ferrick, the words loud and reverberating through the male's head.

Mollian flung his hand out, the force of his magic spilling forward towards the captain. Power surged from inside Mollian, wild and violent, wrapping around the captain and anchoring into him as he drew his sword.

Magic seeped into Ferrick's pores, around his veins, into the knitting of his bones. Any words he had been about to speak were immediately lost as a pain brighter and more intense than anything he'd ever felt before threatened to shatter his mind.

Rip, Mollian's power whispered to him, curling deeper into the captain.

Ferrick's eyes bulged, his jaw clenched as he felt every part of his body straining to fit the magic trying to fill him.

Pull. Mollian's magic swirled, tightening its hold on the captain.

Ferrick's mouth wrenched open, allowing more tendrils of magic to dive down his throat, choking off the scream of terror and agony that spilled from him.

Tear, Mollian's magic ordered, desperate with his rage and fury.

So Mollian did, throwing his other hand out to better control his power, splayed fingers curling into fists. Sweat beaded against his tattooed brow, dripping down his face as he threw his arms wide with a single feral roar.

Shred. The magic that had braided itself into every fiber of Ferrick's being separated at Mollian's command, and Pos Ferrick split into hundreds of little pieces, his skin tearing, bones snapping, muscle ripping, a string of intestine connecting one chunk of torso to another. Bloody bits of flesh showered down around the place where Ferrick used to be, painting the ground with gore.

Kodi's mouth had dropped open, and he looked from Mollian to the bright patch of blood on the ground and back. "Legends out of fucking Hel," he breathed.

Rovin swallowed, completely unsure of what he'd just witnessed. Magic ... magic didn't do shit like that. Not outside of fairy tales. Not even any of the Legends had possessed a power that could shred a person into streamers.

Mollian was panting, hands falling to his sides as his magic slipped back into him, coiling in his core and settling, sated, in his veins. Movement at the corner of the building caught his eye, and he charged forward.

Another person spilled from the front door of the cabin, weapon drawn, but Mollian ignored them, knowing in the back of his mind that Rovin and Kodi would take care of it.

His only focus was Merriam. She ran, stumbling toward him, one hand cradled to her chest. A cloth was tied around her mouth, one eye black and blue and swollen almost shut.

Molli!

Mollian's heart shattered at the desperation of her voice in his head, a fresh wave of righteous indignation barreling through him. Others had been involved in this. They would pay.

But then Merriam was lifting her arms, throwing them around his shoulders as his own wrapped around her waist. Her good hand pressed against his back as the broken one dangled, throbbing and misformed.

Molli, she Cast again with relief, clutching herself to him. Her body shook from pain and adrenaline and exhaustion, tears falling down her cheeks.

Mollian's arms tightened around her, one hand smoothing down the back of her head. He caught the rag, magic ripping through the knot, and it dropped. She pulled back, ripping the cloth from her mouth and throwing it to the ground, gulping in air. Mollian gripped her shoulders, looking over her briefly before pulling her back against him, mindful of the misshapen hand she held to her chest.

Merriam, dizzy with adrenaline and relief, was half convinced she'd hallucinated Ferrick exploding, even though pieces of him scattered the clearing. "What happened?" she asked, Casting an image of Ferrick being shredded along with the question.

Mollian glanced over his shoulder sheepishly. "I got mad."

"Oh," she replied, resting her head against his shoulder and letting him take the brunt of her weight. "You found me." She smiled weakly, each of her freckles starkly contrasted against her pale cheeks.

"I'm sorry it took so long. I should have noticed earlier."

Merriam looked up, reaching to brush a curl from Mollian's brow. "Do not blame yourself for this." Emotion clogged her throat as she forced away thoughts of what else may have happened had Mollian not shown up when he did. Her eyes drifted past his shoulder, spying Kodi with his sword tucked against Eskar's neck, a thin dribble of blood slipping down his blade where it dug none-too-gently into her skin.

Rovin stood next to Kodi, sheathing a shortsword.

Merriam's vision tunneled when she saw him, hatred sinking into her gut and heating her blood. She launched past Mollian on legs fueled by vengeance alone.

Rovin's head whipped to her, brown eyes lit with concern at her appearance.

But Merriam was past registering his expression or the fact that he had come with Mollian. An animalistic scream tore from her chest as she jumped, knocking Rovin onto his ass. She threw her right fist into his jaw, sending him careening to the ground with stars dancing across his vision.

Merriam straddled him, letting out another anguished cry as she grabbed a handful of his hair and slammed his head back into the dirt again and again.

Hands grabbed her arms, pulling her off of the Ranger and wrapping around her. The familiar smell of spruce and plum brought her back from the murderous rage, and she devolved into sobs.

"He set me up, Molli. He wants me *dead.*"

"No, Ria, he wasn't part of this," Mollian soothed, tightening his arms around her middle as she tried to pull away and back to Rovin.

Rovin stood, looking at Merriam with a broken expression as he rubbed the deep bruise forming under the scruff on his jaw. "You really think, after everything, that I'm capable of something like this? Of doing this to you?" His voice broke, anguish bright in his eyes. Then they shuttered, and he swallowed, dropping his hand from his face.

Merriam stilled, tears spilling unencumbered down her cheeks. Confusion diluted the anger churning through her before her mind went numb, unable to process any more emotion in her over-tired, under-nourished state.

Rovin turned from her, binding Eskar's hands with iron cuffs and allowing Kodi to step back, wiping his sword across his thigh to clean it before sheathing it.

Eskar looked from Rovin to Merriam, blood dripping from her mouth as she laughed. "Don't look so dejected, Lieutenant. You chose to learn the hard way that she is the trash we warned you she would be."

Rovin bristled, ripping a strip from the hem of her shirt and tying it around her mouth, the fabric cutting into her cheeks as she bared her teeth at him. "You are nothing but a blight, poisoning everything you touch. The day I never have to look at your face again is a day I will rejoice." Rovin spit at the ground in front of her, walking to where they'd left the horses.

Merriam's body trembled, and she didn't even notice Mollian's magic slip through the tethers between their souls, the overflow of it settling inside her and melding with the magic given to her through his blood. It lent some healing properties to her exhausted body, but it could only do so much.

Her hand hurt so badly she wanted to scream, or laugh at the absurdity of being able to feel so much agony and still remain coherent. She turned into Mollian, resting her forehead on his chest and clutching her injured hand just below the wrist. "I wanna go home," she whispered, blocking everything else out.

"I know," Mollian replied. He didn't give himself time to examine any of his own feelings, not yet. Being present for her was the only thing that mattered right now. "We need to clear the cabin, though. Can I see your hand?"

Merriam stepped back, holding the broken appendage out to him and biting the inside of her cheek to try to distract herself. This was the first time she'd been able to look at it. Her middle finger was bent at an awkward angle and swollen to almost triple its usual size, and her thumb stuck out from her palm, jutting to the side.

"They did this?" Mollian asked lowly.

"I did the thumb myself, so I could slip out of the ropes," she answered, wiping the heel of her free hand across her cheeks to clear the tears there.

Mollian's stomach dropped, a shudder of equal parts horror and awe running through him. "Legends, Ria ..."

Merriam glanced up at him with a half-hearted smile and a shrug, eyes still shimmering with anguish. A clammy sheen covered her skin, her body unsure of what to do with all of the pain.

Mollian surveyed the rest of her, his gaze traveling up her arms, where her wrists were raw and angry, to the small scabs and bruising on her neck where Eskar had choked her with her necklace, to her swollen eye, red staining the white where a few capillaries had burst.

Merriam shifted uncomfortably as he looked down her body. "I don't suppose you brought any clean pants?" She forced out a laugh to hide the way her voice cracked, fresh tears clogging her throat.

Mollian's eyes hardened, and he glanced over Merriam's shoulder to where Eskar knelt on the ground. "She doesn't deserve to stand trial."

Merriam looked up at him, blinking against the exhaustion that tugged at her. "We need her ... to find the rest of Ferrick's fanatics."

Jasper walked up to them then, Aleah on his heels. "No one is left inside, Your Majesty. One tried to flee into the woods, but we caught him. Another was inside, but," he looked at Merriam, "I'm assuming you got to him first."

Merriam tipped her head in acknowledgement, swallowing past the lump in her throat.

"Are you okay?" Aleah asked, stepping close and grabbing her arms.

"I'm fine now. I feel weak and everything hurts, but I'm fine," Merriam assured her. She searched her eyes for a moment, amber meeting hazel, and dropped her voice to a murmur. "Thank you for coming. For helping Molli."

Aleah squeezed her arms. "Of course, Mer." She looked over at the bloodbath on the grass that Calysta was slowly picking her way through. "What the fuck happened there?"

"Ferrick," Merriam answered simply, then added, "Play stupid games, win stupid prizes."

Mollian looked away and pulled Merriam closer, still not ready to examine what exactly his magic had done.

Calysta joined them, handing Merriam a bundle of petals and herbs. "Ardorflower, for the pain," she said. After a cursory glance at Merriam's injuries while the girl chewed and swallowed, the nymph offered, "I can reset your thumb and splint the finger, but you need to see a medic."

"She won't have a choice," Mollian said with finality.

The ardorflower was working its way through Merriam's system, and she gladly gave herself over to it. Though the herb sat heavy in her otherwise empty stomach, the nausea that washed over her was a minor discomfort compared to everything else. Mollian's proximity was like a blanket of safety over her frazzled nerves, and the effects of Calysta's plants were pulling her down and away from the pain.

Seeing Merriam drift off, slumping into Mollian, Calysta took her hand, popping Merriam's thumb back into place with a quick, confident movement. Merriam yelped, flinching, but already the bright spot of agony had faded into more manageable, dull soreness.

Calysta's fingers ran gently over Merriam's finger, and she frowned before turning her black eyes up to Mollian. "This was not a clean break, and I can't tell if it's already started to try to heal. I can keep it immobile for the ride back, but I'm not comfortable trying anything with it. I don't want to make it any worse."

Mollian nodded. "Thank you."

Mollian and Aleah helped Merriam to the ground, Calysta running off to find something to splint her finger with. Merriam groaned as the wide patch of bark was secured to her hand, her arm secured to her chest with a sling to help keep it immobile. But after that, she was out, not waking again until she was laid on a medic's table in the south wing of the castle.

Her temple was prodded, eye forced open as a light was shone into it to examine any internal damage, finger rebroken, set, and splinted with the ones on either side.

The pain woke her up, and, forgetting where she was, she tried to fight them off. One medic received a boot to the face before Mollian grabbed her, Casting soothing words into her mind, and she gave herself back over to the ardorflower.

Up in their rooms, Mollian helped her bathe and get into clean clothes, and she was soon asleep in his bed without any more fuss.

Aleah had stayed to help, tucking the blankets up around Merriam's chin.

"Do you mind staying here for a bit? I need to update Bell and check on things with Eskar. I also need to find a new captain who won't try to kill everyone close to me, but that at least can wait until morning." Mollian ran his hands through his hair with a heavy sigh.

"You're good. You know that, right?" Aleah asked, hopping onto the bed next to Merriam and folding her legs in front of her. She'd found Merriam's axes in the cabin and set them on the bedside table within plain view and easy reach, figuring it would be a comfort for Merriam on the off chance she woke up alone.

Mollian looked at Merriam's sleeping form, a frown wrinkling the tattoo on his brow. "I would have torn the world apart to get her back."

Aleah tilted her head to the side, red strands falling over her shoulder. "You didn't, though. You could have torn apart anyone who questioned you or stood in your way, but you didn't."

Mollian shook his head. In a way he couldn't explain, he needed Aleah to understand, didn't want her to hold him on a false pedestal. "I almost killed Rovin."

"But you didn't," Aleah repeated, holding his troubled gaze.

"If Bellamy hadn't been here—"

"You could have killed him regardless of anyone being here. Hel, you could have killed Bellamy for getting in the way of your justice. You held yourself in check, though, Mollian. That's what matters." Aleah's eyes softened, and she brushed back a damp strand of hair from the deep blue patch on Merriam's face. "I'll stay here. Go take care of what you need to. She'll be safe."

Rovin was below the castle with Kodi, watching as Eskar was patted down and stripped of her belongings before being thrown into a cell.

One of the Guard handed Rovin her weapons belt along with Merriam's rings, which had been in Eskar's pocket.

Rovin closed his fist around the jewelry, his chest tightening with the memory of undiluted hatred on Merriam's face as she'd charged him. "You deserve less," he told Eskar.

She refused to look at him, keeping her head turned toward the far wall from where she sat on a cot.

"If it were up to me, you'd be strung up by your arms and left to suffer the same way she was."

Eskar tilted her head back against the wall, chuckling lightly. Her hands were clasped together in front of her with iron chains, but otherwise she had full freedom of movement. "Your sudden fascination with the prince's pet should concern you, young Ranger. You're so righteous in your indignation, but you didn't flip allegiance until you saw how high the human had climbed. You're lying to yourself if you won't admit you aren't also just after power."

Rovin snarled, but Kodi put a hand on his shoulder, pulling him back. "She's not worth it, brother. Let's go."

Rovin let himself be led up and out into the courtyard, the rings digging painfully into his skin. He opened his hand, holding them out and watching the moonlight sparkle against the smooth stones. "She thought I was a part of this, Ko." His voice was heavy and thick with emotion. "She thought I was capable of kidnapping her, torturing her, plotting her death." He dropped the rings into his pocket, slipping both hands into his hair as he squatted down and let the weight of his anguish flood him.

"Emotions were high. I'm sure it'll all be explained," Kodi said in comfort, resting his hand on the top of Rovin's head.

Rovin dug his fingers in harder, tears lining his eyes. "That's not the point. She honestly believed that I could have done this. After I tried to tell her how much I admire and respect her ... how much I want her in my life." A tear slipped down his nose, splashing onto his knee. He tilted his head back, folding his hands in front of him as he looked up at the sky. "I can't even blame her, because I did used to hate her that much. Whether that was fueled by Ferrick's twisted words in my ear or not, I used to hate her. I wanted to earn her trust, to have her view me in a different light, but ..." Rovin let out a breath, standing back up. "I have so much more recompensing to do. I may not have been responsible for this, but I have seven years of shit to make up for. And I have no idea where to start."

Rovin's shoulders were hunched forward, his countenance dejected, and Kodi could do nothing but walk beside him, offering silent support.

MERRIAM WOKE IN A panic, but the familiarity of Mollian's room, even in the dark, quickly calmed her. She sat up, grinding the heel of her hand against her good eye. A salve, once sticky but now dried to a flaky crust, covered the other, something to help bring down the swelling from her broken socket. Bandages had been wrapped around both her wrists, and her entire left hand was in a splint. Her thumb's dislocation had been clean, but the healers had instructed her to keep it immobile for at least a few days to give the ligaments and tendons time to heal properly.

Merriam slid from the bed, padding over to the bathroom to rinse her face. She studied herself in the mirror. Blonde waves fell messily over her shoulders and down her back. Her lips were chapped from lack of proper hydration, but she at least looked alive. The swelling around her eye had gone down, but a gnarly yellow and blue bruise covered almost the entire upper left side of her face.

Her injuries could have been a lot worse. She knew that, knew that she was lucky to be alive and relatively in one piece, but she couldn't stop the string of self-pity that wormed its way through her. Her eyes filled with tears as she looked at herself, tucked her hair behind her ears and bared her teeth at her reflection.

So human. So breakable. So weak.

No, she thought. *This didn't happen because you're human. You could be a Legend reincarnated and Ferrick still would have hated you for your relationship with Molli. This wasn't even truly about you, it was about him. Human you may be, but he needs you. Not them. You.*

Anger flared through her, then. They'd tricked her. Humiliated her. Abused her. When, in theory, they were on the same side, all in service to the Crown. But they weren't, not really. They were in service to power, hungry for every last morsel they could scrounge up.

That had been Ferrick's downfall. It would be Eskar's, too.

Merriam left the bathroom, heading out into the common room where Mollian sat working on the hilt of a sword. Aleah, surprisingly, was at his feet, resting on her belly and messing with a length of gold satin ribbon. They'd been quietly chatting when Merriam walked into the room, both of their heads lifting as she shuffled closer.

"Mer!" Aleah pushed up, sitting on her heels as the ribbon fell to the floor. "How do you feel?"

Merriam licked her lips, swallowing against a dry throat. "Thirsty, and a little like my head was smashed in a couple days ago."

Aleah laughed, standing and leading Merriam to a couch. "Here," she said, handing her a cup of water. "We have some food, too, in case you're hungry." She indicated the platter of bread and fruit.

Merriam smiled her thanks, bringing the cup to her lips and drinking deeply.

"I stuck around to make sure you made it through the night. You know how worried the guys get." Aleah waved a hand through the air as if shooing away a bothersome presence, but her hazel eyes glimmered with relief at seeing Merriam up and about.

"Oh, so not to talk my ear off and beg me to let you customize something, then?" Mollian joked, storing his little tools and baubles and walking over to sit on the short table in front of Merriam. He rested his hands on her knees, searching her face before giving her body a once-over.

I'm fine. "Really, I'm okay," she repeated aloud for Aleah's sake. "Give me a day to eat and hydrate, and you'll never be able to tell I was kidnapped."

Mollian gave her an unamused look.

"Too soon?" Merriam flashed an apologetic smile.

"Yep, you're exactly as fine as you ever were," Aleah acknowledged, resting on the arm of the couch with a yawn and gently tipping her head against Merriam's.

"It's late," Merriam stated, accepting the roll of bread Mollian handed to her and taking a large bite. "Have you guys been up all night?" The horizon was still dark, but dawn couldn't have been too far off.

Mollian shrugged. "I was too wired to sleep. Aleah was just keeping me company."

"I offered to fight him to burn some energy, but he said we'd probably end up breaking something," she mumbled sleepily.

Merriam smiled, finishing the bread. "Should I be concerned that I'm still so tired, even after doing little but sleeping for so long?"

"You've been through a lot; it's normal to be drained. The medics said there's not cause to worry as long as your energy levels are back to normal after a day or two of rest and nourishment." Mollian offered her more bread, but she waved it off, finishing the water.

"You can sleep in my room, Aleah. There are shirts and pants in the armoire, too, if you want something more comfortable." Merriam set the glass down on the table.

Aleah slid from the armrest. "That sounds lovely. I doubt I could even make it to Kodi's room at this point, much less down into Umbra." She pressed a kiss to the top of Merriam's head, waved goodnight to the king, and stumbled across the room through Merriam's bedroom door.

Mollian stood, holding his hands out to help Merriam up. "Bed, then?"

"Yes, please." She led the way.

As they lay together, Merriam's forehead resting against his arm in a way that felt more natural to him than breathing, Mollian tried to settle his mind. The fingers of one hand played in his hair, winding through a curl, releasing, winding again. His magic stirred gently through him, through Merriam, but it was hard for him to fully release the pure panic that had enveloped him when he'd realized she was gone.

More than that, he was still reeling from the sheer depth of power that had flowed from him when he'd killed Ferrick. Wrapping around a living thing like that should have required every ounce of concentration he possessed. Sinking into him, tearing him into thousands of tiny pieces should have been, by all counts, impossible.

But he'd done it.

And he'd liked it.

It wasn't so much that Mollian had liked the act of killing, though he would lose absolutely no sleep for murdering Ferrick after every horrible thing he'd done. It was the act of tearing him—tearing *something*—apart that had been like a breath of fresh air, like scratching an itch that had been impossible to reach and about to drive him insane.

Mollian's magic had craved the act, had sighed with relief at having finally accomplished the one thing it wanted.

Which was weird. Magic, as far as everything Mollian had read, wasn't sentient. Sure, he often referred to it as fickle, unwieldy, unwilling to dilute itself. Those were all more ways to describe the components of something that science hadn't quite been able to explain yet. But magic was always controlled, always a tool to be used by whomever possessed it.

His magic still felt like his, still felt like part of him. But in a way he couldn't understand, his magic knew its capabilities regardless of him ever having tried to test them. His magic had been whispering to him for over a year, begging for use that he'd never understood until he stood in that ravine with Ferrick.

The depth of that power—the hunger in it—scared him. He was never even meant to be born. A third Keeper should have been given only the scantest amounts of blood magic, so how had it happened that he'd been born with a bottomless well of it that seemed to follow the rules of the universe only at its whim? And the fact that it had so easily grabbed onto the living was an entirely different unsettling matter.

Mollian sighed, dropping his hand from his hair and rolling over to face his *mehhen*. She slept soundly, moonlight from the window highlighting the sickly yellow of the bruise on her face. He was lucky she was so strong. Lucky that she possessed every ounce of will and gumption required to be forever connected to him and the magic he was never supposed to have been given.

No, *not lucky*, Mollian thought as he drifted off, surrounded by her smell of rainfall and wildflowers. *Fated.*

In the morning, Merriam ate breakfast under the watchful eyes of Mollian and Aleah. They'd piled a plate full of food for her, more than she would probably need in an entire day. She rolled her eyes at their fussing, but dutifully ate until her stomach was full, setting the plate down in front of her.

Mollian looked it over as though he hadn't watched each time she'd taken a bite, finally giving a satisfied nod.

"I had a concussion and missed a single day of meals. You're being a bit dramatic, Molli."

"The medics said—"

"I *know* what the medics said. I'm listening to my body's cues, though. If something feels off, I'll tell you." Merriam turned to Aleah before Mollian could reply. "Want me to walk out with you?"

Mollian started, looking between them. He wouldn't forbid her to go, never in a million years would he think to try, but he couldn't help the fear that settled in his gut at the thought of Merriam wandering around with a pre-cracked skull and only one hand to fight with.

"Just to the gates." Merriam gave him a reassuring smile. "I won't leave the castle grounds, not today while I'm unsure how steady I am on my feet." *You'll be able to feel me the whole time.*

Okay, yeah. Sorry. Mollian's shoulders relaxed, and he resumed eating.

You know I love every nervous, worrywart inch of your pretty head, right?

Good.

"I might actually stop by the Ranger barracks and see if Kodi is on shift yet, but you're welcome to accompany me there," Aleah unknowingly interrupted the silent conversation, giving Merriam a tentatively insinuative glance.

"I'll come along to the courtyard, then," Merriam answered, standing up and ducking into the bedroom to grab her weapons belt.

"You sure?" Aleah pressed when she'd returned.

Merriam concentrated on buckling the heavy accessory around her waist with one working hand. "Yeah, maybe next time." Guilt sat like a stone in her stomach at how easily and entirely she'd turned on Rovin. She needed more time to process those feelings before she saw him again. If he even wanted to see her, that is.

"To the courtyard it is, then." Aleah nodded her affirmation, the end of her ponytail swinging against her neck. "Thank you for breakfast, Mollian. It was lovely."

"Anytime, Aleah," he answered, standing as well.

"Don't tell her that unless you want her here every morning," Merriam warned.

"If cinnamon buns are on the menu, I will absolutely be here," Aleah confirmed.

Mollian shrugged, pushing a curl from his face. "I don't see why that request can't be made. Though if I were you, I'd get in good with the kitchen staff. They're pretty appeasing when they've got a soft spot."

"They'll do what Molli wants because he's king, but he annoyed them too much as a child to be in their favor," Merriam teased.

"If your face wasn't broken, I'd throw a pillow at you," he retorted.

Merriam grinned, ruffling his hair. "I'll come find you when I'm done."

"I'll hold you to it." Mollian struggled to stamp down the fear that clawed its way up his throat as Merriam and Aleah left, and he focused on the blip of her against his consciousness to reassure himself that she was near.

Once in the main courtyard, the sound of the Guard training around the corner traveled on a soft autumn wind along with the faint scent of fallen leaves, no doubt being trampled underfoot. Merriam bit the inside of her cheek, her stomach knotting with anxiety. The smell reminded her so much of Rovin, and it was all too easy for her to imagine him leading training just around the corner.

Aleah grabbed her hand, giving it a gentle squeeze. "I'm glad you're okay."

Merriam pulled her into a gentle hug. "Thank you for being there. I know it couldn't have been easy, and it means a lot that you trusted Molli ... that you care about me that much."

A lump formed in Aleah's throat, and she laughed to cover up the onset of emotion. "He's not Chetney, Mer. Mollian's good. He'd have to be, if he shares a soul with you."

Merriam tightened her arms around the smaller girl before stepping back. "This is too much emotion for the morning. Go see your Ranger."

"Where are you going to go?"

Merriam swallowed, giving her a tight smile. "I'm also going to go see a Ranger. Or is it ex-Ranger? I've got some peace to make."

"Good luck with that, Marshal. Holler if you need me." Aleah lifted her hand, waving her fingers before turning around and heading off toward the barracks.

Merriam stood in the sun for a moment, eyes closed, just feeling the warmth on her face countered against the cool brush of the wind. *You were targeted because you* do *have power, regardless of what they want to think,* she reminded herself.

Opening her eyes, she turned away from the courtyard, heading around the side of the castle to where an entrance led below the main structure.

"Morning, Marshal," Evangaline greeted, posted outside the dungeon. She'd been practicing her footwork, but dropped her fighting stance when she saw Merriam.

"Evangeline, good morning," Merriam returned, stepping through when the young Ranger opened the weathered wooden door. She hesitated, turning back. "Eskar, is she …?" She paused, unsure of what exactly she wanted to ask.

"The comman—the prisoner is awake. Breakfast was at sunrise. She's cuffed in iron, last cell all the way down."

Merriam nodded, licking her lips and heading below the castle.

Two more guards, vetted by Rovin, were stationed at the bottom. They moved to stand when they saw her, but she waved for them to stay seated. Merriam pointed toward the back, and they nodded.

"Let us know if ya need anythin', Marshal," said one.

Merriam nodded in acknowledgment, walking down the hall. The soft thud from the heel of her boots sounded against the stones, accompanied by the murmurs from the guards' conversation.

"Surely Sekha's Marshal, the great demonslayer, isn't coming to visit little old me?"

Merriam came to a stop in front Eskar's cell, the fae sitting on the cot suspended from one wall.

Eskar had her legs folded in front of her, head resting back against the stones. Her wrists were clasped in iron, joined together by a short length of chain. She rolled her head to look at Merriam, giving her a smile that matched the cruel glimmer in her dark eyes. "Tell me, human, do you think they would still address you with the same respect had they seen you yesterday, covered in your own piss and bound by nothing but a measly rope?"

Merriam clenched her jaw. "You might have been too busy watching your lover get torn to bits to notice, but your measly rope *didn't* hold me. I got out of it and caved in the skull of one of your followers, even with a broken hand and no magic."

Eskar huffed, her eyes catching on the splint around Merriam's left hand, lips lifting in a sneer. "I should have done worse."

Merriam shrugged. "Could have, should have, would have, I'm sure. But you've lost the opportunity now."

"I know why you're here. Don't bother. I have accepted my fate."

Merriam raised a brow. "Oh? And why am I here, Eskar?"

"To gloat, obviously. Your little prince—"

"He is your *king*," Merriam interrupted with a hiss, anger heating her blood.

Eskar gave her a withering look, not bothering to correct her-self—what would they do? Sentence her to a second death?—and con-tinued, "—came and saved you, just like he always has."

"Where is your fucking head? Mollian showed up for me, he was always going to, but I got myself out of that house. You understand that, right?" Merriam was baffled.

"Minor details. Ferrick would have caught you in the forest and pulled you back."

Merriam scoffed, but her hand went behind her back, fingers curling around the end of her braid and pulling. The pressure at the base of her skull grounded her, kept her mind from going back to when she'd had the same thought.

"We're not that different, you and I."

Merriam waved a hand in front of her. "Please, enlighten me."

"We both want power, Merriam. Grandeur. Status. I chose to earn mine through fight and ambition. You were lucky enough to be attached to one destined for glory from the beginning."

"I'm not in a game for power, and I never have been. In case you don't remember, Mollian was never supposed to be king," Merriam pointed out, annoyance placing a sharp edge on her voice.

"No, I suppose he wasn't. But how fortunate things turned out for the both of you." Eskar sighed, stretching out her legs. "If I hadn't been in that cave myself, I would have suspected the two of you had offed Oren yourselves."

Fire burned in Merriam's eyes, her good hand wrapping around one of the iron bars of the cell as her lips curled. "What you will never understand, Eskar, is that it is possible to love someone, to value their presence in your life, even when they have nothing to offer you. What you will never understand is that there are things that power will never buy you. The strongest loyalties are not won through fear of retribution, but in the knowledge that you would be there for each other regardless of circumstances. You're so filled with mindless ambition, do you even know what you're clawing yourself toward?"

"Ohhh, something struck a chord. Is that guilt, Merriam? Your lover dies, but now your *mehhen* is king and the Ranger you're fucking probably well on his way to promotion. Tell me, how am I supposed to believe you when you're constantly surrounding yourself with people who have such a strong pull?"

Something like a snarl ripped its way from Merriam's throat.

Abruptly, she released the bar, taking a step back to calm herself. Eskar was riling her on purpose, and she was letting it happen. "You're wrong. I didn't come here to gloat," she said after a moment of silence. Merriam searched Eskar's face, wondering how it was possible to be filled with so much baseless hate. "I came to ask a simple question."

Eskar chuckled, bored with the conversation. "Ask, then."

"Why have you labeled me as an enemy all these years? Rovin and the others were young and impressionable, desperate for Ferrick's approval. But you were already a formidable Ranger by the time I showed up. Why did you choose to hate me?"

The chain between Eskar's wrists jingled as she shifted on her cot, looking away from Merriam with a sigh. "Does it really matter? You rose to the occasion."

Merriam pressed her lips together, giving a single nod before turning to walk back down the hall.

"Merriam?" Eskar called.

Merriam stopped, but didn't turn around.

"Before I die, whenever you schedule my execution, with my last words I will tell everyone gathered how easily you broke under my magic. How pitiful you looked, sobbing and pissing yourself after only a day of captivity. Chains or not, I still have the power to strip you of yours."

Merriam bit her cheek so hard she tasted blood as she stalked back up to the courtyard. *I will kill you.* Her promise to Eskar looped back through her mind as she broke out into the sunlight.

Chapter 28

A WEEK HAD GONE by since that night in the ravine, the time spent weeding out Ferrick's supporters and any of the Guard who harbored ill feelings about Mollian's reign or Ryddan's place in the kingdom. For all of Ferrick's ego, the number of true fanatics was smaller than Mollian expected, not even enough to make up half a detachment. Today, they would all be exiled.

All except for Eskar and Dirk, who would be executed for direct acts of treason.

Merriam flexed the thumb of her left hand, testing her mobility. The joint was stable, and any leftover ache was so small that she didn't register it once she turned her attention to something else. Her broken finger was still wrapped to the two around it, and would be for at least one more week, but at least she'd gained back some use of her hand. She would need it for what she had planned for Eskar.

She buckled her belt around her waist, smoothing down her shirt and looking at Mollian. "I'm ready."

"I don't think you should do this." Mollian ran a hand through his hair to keep from folding his arms across his chest like a stubborn child.

Merriam rested her good hand against the hilt of the sword sheathed on her belt. The weight of it, missing the balance of a matching weapon on her opposite side, was unfamiliar. The pull heightened her concentration along with her awareness of not just the weapon, but of everything around her.

"Don't you even dare say you have to." Mollian narrowed his eyes, aspen crown furrowing between his brows.

Merriam stepped up to him, placing a hand on each cheek and tipping his head down to rest his forehead against hers. *Tell me you trust me.*

You know I do.

Feel me, Molli. I have no doubts. I'm not scared.

Maybe that's what scares me.

"Nobody saw Ferrick die," she whispered. "Before you promote a new captain, your Guard needs to know that you won't tolerate treason. I'm your marshal, for better or worse. They need to know that I am capable of fulfilling all roles of that title. A simple execution won't prove anything. This is the only way to quell any doubts."

Mollian sighed, shaking off the surge of magic that swirled through him. "Don't drag it out, okay? No showmanship, Ria."

Merriam dropped her hands, grinning despite the heavy atmosphere. "Me? Showy?"

He leveled her with a cool green gaze. "I'm serious."

Merriam raised her hand, letting Mollian press his palm to hers, feeling the strength of the tethers that bound their souls together. "Fast and efficient, I promise."

Mollian dropped his hand, and they headed down to the castle grounds.

Ferrick had been a prominent figure in Sekha for over a hundred years, so the circumstances around his death had to be made public to prevent the spread of false rumors or questions about Mollian and his rule.

An amphitheater was set in the mountainside beneath one of the castle walls, and its seats were already packed with the citizens of Umbra and cities throughout Jekeida. The air was buzzing with the energy of people waiting to see the hand of justice.

People love a good execution, Merriam Cast, walking by Mollian's side. A guardsman cleared the way ahead of them, two following from behind. Her palm rested on the hilt of her sword, and she kept her eyes forward as they descended the steps to the stage at the bottom.

Eskar was on her knees next to the other Ranger who had been at the cabin, hands bound in front of them and a guard on either side. Her eyes were closed, face tilted up to the sky to absorb the last bit of warmth she would ever feel.

Cold, righteous anger burned low in Merriam's gut, and it took every ounce of her self-control not to tighten her grip on her sword. She dropped her hand instead, climbing the short stairs to the platform and gazing out over the crowd, not really seeing them.

Mollian stood center stage, shoulders back, sun shining against his white curls as he waited for the silence that quickly followed his arrival. "Eight days ago, Pos Ferrick set in motion an attempt on the life of Sekha's Marshal. While he did not live to stand trial, these two that kneel before you were not only privy to treason, but took an active role in it."

Mollian stepped in front of the prisoners, half turning to face them. "Do either of you deny your part in the kidnapping of your marshal?"

Silence.

A whisper of fury crossed Mollian's expression. Merriam could feel his magic stirring in her Bonded blood before it settled, and he spoke with a clear voice. "I, Mollian Stonebane, King of Sekha and Keeper of Nethyl, hereby charge you with treason. You are forthwith stripped of your rank and titles of Ranger and discharged from the Royal Guard."

Two guards walked forward, slashing deep cuts through the Ranger tattoos on the backs of their wrists.

"I ask again, do either of you deny your actions against the Crown or wish to plea for mercy?"

The male to Eskar's left swallowed hard, but remained silent.

Mollian turned back to the crowd, the air charged with an almost palpable energy as the citizens of Jekeida waited for their young king to name the punishment. "The sentence for treason is death. Marshal." Mollian turned to Merriam, his body tight with nervous energy that only Merriam could read. "Unless you speak for their mercy, it is your duty to fulfill the execution."

Merriam stepped forward. For every bit of nervous energy that flowed through Mollian, her own muscles sang with an energy of their own, an energy borne of confidence and retribution. "Eskar, if His Majesty the King will allow it, I would like to offer you a deal."

A few gasps from the crowd. None had been expecting this.

Merriam looked at Mollian, waiting for his nod of approval before continuing. "You told me that I have no power of my own. Now is your chance to prove that claim. I challenge you to a duel to the death. Defeat me, and you will win your life and the life of your companion, to be carried out in exile from Sekha."

"What are the terms of this duel?" Eskar asked, looking up at Merriam.

"It will be a fair fight. Your hands will be unchained and you will be given a sword, but the iron stays around your wrists. No magic, just skill." Merriam held Eskar's gaze, the calm of a fight falling over her like a sheet. No emotions, no crowd, just the will to wield a sword in a dance her muscles seemed to crave.

"I accept."

Eskar was hauled to her feet, chain removed from between her wrists. A sword was provided to her, and the ground in front of the stage was cleared to give room for the duel.

Merriam nimbly hopped from the stage, closing her eyes as the impact jostled the still-healing bone by her eye. Eskar would make that fragile point her target, no doubt. She knew Merriam hadn't had enough time to heal.

But Merriam was expecting it.

After Merriam's visit with Eskar, she knew the only way she would be able to carry out the execution was a fight to the death. She needed to displace any doubt in Sekha that she was not fit for her position, to publicly prove her merit, one final time.

Mollian had initially refused. Merriam hadn't recovered from her injuries. She couldn't even hold an axe with her left hand. But Merriam's right hand, her sword hand, was perfectly intact.

The axes were her favorite, an extension of herself at this point. With her axes, she was a lethal, unstoppable force. But she'd trained with the Guard for over a year and learned their sword movements. When she joined the mercenaries, Jasper had required her to train with a sword at least once a week, as well as many other common weapons. He had never allowed her to lose her sword skills. Favorites were fine, but she needed to be able to protect herself, to get the job done, with whatever tools were at her disposal.

Merriam unsheathed her sword, unbuckling her weapons belt and tossing it aside so the scabbard wouldn't knock against her legs and trip her up during the fight.

Eskar stood in front of her, gripping her sword in her hand, the back of her wrist dripping bright blood to the dirt. "You've got a death wish, merc."

Merriam smiled calmly, shifting her feet and raising her sword, point aiming toward Eskar's chest.

Eskar lunged, knocking Merriam's sword aside with a clang that rang through the air. Merriam kept her grip on the weapon and let her arm swing out with the force of the blow, not fighting the momentum, but carrying it through as she looped her arm down, swinging her sword up and turning her body into the movement to add force to the blow.

Eskar, who'd been about to strike again, clumsily pulled her sword back to block, stumbling a step backward as she absorbed the impact. Merriam pressed forward, her blade shrieking as she drew it down Eskar's and swung again toward the fae's side. On the defensive, Eskar backed toward the stage, blocking as Merriam advanced, her feet quick in the dirt, body twisting to add leverage behind each movement.

Merriam knew that the high fae relied on their magic, even when they didn't think they were doing so. Eskar had been taught to push her magic into every strike, every block. Arrogance in her superiority, in her class, had kept her from practicing the basic movement taught to the Guard. Furthermore, Eskar was now a commander. Even as a lieutenant, she'd been able to fall back to her weapon of choice: a bow and arrow. If she did still practice with a sword, it was seldom. She had long ago grown comfortable in her own style, and while it was formidable, it was dependent.

Dependency in battle—in any fight—was the quickest route to death.

Merriam feinted, then pulled back, letting Eskar see an opening. As the fae lunged, her weight moving forward, Merriam dropped, crouching low on one leg as she kicked the other out, knocking Eskar's feet from under her.

As Eskar fell, scrambling to catch herself, Merriam sprung back up, twisting the sword in her hand. She drove down, blade plunging into Eskar's chest with a wet crunch as it slid through bone.

Eskar hit the ground, head slamming the dirt with enough force to make her see stars, her eyes unfocusing momentarily. Merriam landed next to her in a crouch. "I expected more," she whispered before standing and wrenching the blade free.

Eskar coughed, blood foaming at her lips as she glared at Merriam. She opened her mouth to speak, but Merriam was already bringing down the sword, blade cutting deep into her throat before being halted by the muscles and tendons in her neck. Blood poured into the ground, spreading in a bright puddle as Eskar's hands fluttered up in an attempt to stanch the flow.

It was a messy kill, Merriam knew, but she didn't regret it as she stood straight, watching the fae's feet give one final kick in defiance of death.

Merriam's chest heaved, a bead of sweat dripping down her spine. She glanced up at Mollian, his face clear of emotion.

Fast and efficient, she Cast, setting her sword on the edge of the platform and jumping up after it.

One corner of Mollian's mouth twitched, and he averted his gaze. *Jokes already?*

A *trick of the trade.* Merriam wiped her arm over her brow to keep sweat from dripping into her eyes as she walked to the guard standing to the side, holding a large, heavy battle axe in front of him. She took it, walking up to where Dirk still knelt at the front of the stage.

Merriam killed him with a quick, precise blow to the back of the neck. The sharp blade and weight of the axe severed his head from his body, and it rolled across the wooden planks, landing on the ground next to Eskar.

The axe fell to Merriam's side, and she could feel the eyes of the crowd on her, but her gaze only strayed from the blood pooling across the floor to meet Mollian's.

Awareness of the audience was slowly creeping up through the adrenaline from the fight. These people, the people she was now sworn to protect, had just seen her kill. And that scared her.

Guards were hauling the bodies away, and Merriam stepped to the side, keeping her eyes down.

Mollian looked out over his people, the Royal Guard scattered throughout the crowd. "The following fae have been found guilty of conspiring against the Crown, and are hereby sentenced to exile." Mollian read the names from a list as the rest of Ferrick's followers were led onto the stage to have their tattoos slashed through. He wasn't sure if he was supposed to say something else once the act was finished, but he found he had no words, so he turned, exiting the back of the stage with Merriam close on his heels.

A guard came to take the axe from Merriam, and she gladly yielded it, slumping against the wall. "Why does a public execution feel so much different than a fight or even an assassination?"

"Because people you're sworn to protect now know, without a shadow of a doubt, that they should also fear you." Mollian leaned a shoulder against the worn wooden planks next to her.

Merriam frowned down at her blood-splattered boots. "Isn't that what I wanted?" she asked quietly. "To erase all doubt?"

Mollian pulled her to his chest, resting his chin on her head. *I don't know what I'm doing half the time. I know this was never what you wanted, either, this responsibility. This visibility. Neither of us was born for politics. But I couldn't do this without you.*

I would never ask you to. Merriam let the weight of his arms around her shoulders ground her, his smell of spruce and plum surrounding her in a plain, uncomplicated comfort.

Two days after Eskar's execution, Mollian stood at the head of the throne room, Merriam a few steps down to his right with Ryddan at her side.

The little prince looked every part the royal child, hair slicked to the side, clothes impeccably pressed. Lydia had done her best in wrangling him into submission, and he stood placidly next to Merriam with the promise of a trip to the confectioner's in Umbra if he could make it through the ceremony without fidgeting. He tipped his face up to her with a smile, clasping a folded golden cloak to his chest.

Merriam winked at him, placing a hand on his shoulder as the doors at the back of the room swung open.

Dio entered, walking down the aisle. The room was filled with Royal Guard. Higher-ranking officers stood toward the front along with the guildmasters, all watching the fae's purposeful approach.

When Dio reached Mollian, he dropped to a knee and bowed his head.

"Commander Dio," Mollian spoke, his voice ringing clear through the room. "Do you vow to uphold the laws of the Rangers and the code of the Royal Guard, to protect the people of Sekha, and to remain loyal to the Crown in all that you do?"

Dio, head still bowed, replied loud and clear, "I vow to uphold the laws of the Rangers and the code of the Royal Guard. I vow to protect the people of Sekha and remain loyal to the Crown in all that I do."

"Then rise, Kottor Dio."

Dio stood.

Mollian removed the badge from Dio's chest, handing it to Merriam in exchange for the shining aspen leaf of the Captain of the Guard. Mollian pinned it to the dark green dress jacket, again turning to Merriam.

She pulled a sword from her belt. The blade was bright and unmarred, reflecting the sunlight that shone through the windows. The hilt was made of a dark metal, aspen branches etched throughout and inlaid with gold. A smooth, supple leather had been woven together for the grip. The pommel had been hollowed out, a single aspen leaf suspended in resin in its center.

Personally, Mollian thought it was probably one of the most beautiful pieces he'd ever made, and he couldn't help the small smile that stretched his lips as he took it from Merriam, laying it across his palms. Mollian lifted his eyes from the sword to meet Dio's, holding his offering forward. "I, Mollian Stonebane, King of Sekha and Keeper of Nethyl, name you, Kottor Dio, Captain of the Royal Guard and gift you this weapon in thanks for your continued service to Sekha and to the Crown."

Dio took the sword from Mollian, bowing his head as he slid it into the empty sheath on his belt. "Thank you, Your Majesty. I promise to use it to serve you well."

Mollian motioned for Dio to turn, facing the hall. Merriam handed him the cloak Ryddan had been holding, and Mollian shook it out, clasping the dark golden fabric over Dio's shoulders. "Captain Dio, the Guard is yours to command."

Dio called the room to attention, the sound of boots snapping together in unison raising goosebumps on Merriam's arms. Dio saluted the Guard, and the Guard saluted back, holding the posture until Dio lowered his. He set the room at ease, turning back to Mollian to salute the king.

Mollian returned it, wholly unprepared for the depth of emotion that filled him at the gleam of respect in Dio's eyes. He felt suddenly young, and as the memory of his erratic emotions and his magic tearing through Ferrick washed over him, he was unsure if he'd earned it.

But he wanted to. He wanted to be a king that a male like Dio would respect and take pride in serving.

Chapter 29

More special, more rare

DONOVA WALKED UP THE stairs to the tallest point in the castle on the cliff side. Her long, black hair thumped lightly between her shoulder blades from where it was bound high on her head. "Good morning, Perran. I request an audience with Djuhl Dronin," she greeted the lesser demon by the door.

Perran wrinkled his nose up, only for a moment, before smoothing his expression. "One moment, warlock."

Donova's hand curled into a fist at her side as Perran disappeared. She longed to go back to her home hidden in the cliffs of the sulfur sea. There was so much pretense and politics here. So many people with power deep enough and strong enough to rival her own. It made her uncomfortable, not having the utter confidence that she was the most powerful being in the area.

But the djuhl could give her things she might never have been able to accomplish by herself. She could at least admit that. She had her dreams, her magic, her potions and wards and spells, but the stones ... she had never had an item so intrinsically connected to the fabric of the world as those stones, and she was almost positive she had found a way to wield them. Though many greater demons here possessed powerful magic, she was confident that none of them would ever have been capable of accomplishing this task.

Perran returned, holding the door open for her and bowing his head respectfully. "He will see you."

Donova walked into the large chamber, Dronin seated at a table in the center, his generals on either side of him.

"The dreamwalker graces us with her presence." Nevra smiled, forked tongue peeking between her teeth as she leaned forward and twirled a small knife in her fingers. "You look much more well-rested than last I saw you."

Donova met the demon's gaze, no emotion in her bright golden eyes. "I am, thank you, General."

Nevra laughed, tilting her head back and kicking out the chair next to her, offering Donova a seat.

Dronin sighed, lifting a piece of rare, bloody meat to his mouth. "If Lyvin and I took the opportunity to point out every time you showed up looking solidly fucked, we'd never get anything done."

Lyvin snorted, and Nevra shot him a withering glance before dipping her head respectfully to Dronin. "I meant no offense, My Djuhl."

"If you wanted to join in, I'm sure you could have just asked," Lyvin offered.

Nevra bared her teeth at him.

Dronin growled, snapping both of their attention to him. "If you want to bicker like spawn, do it elsewhere. The warlock isn't here to listen to the two of you prattle on all morning."

The two generals met each other's eyes once more, this time in silent, shared amusement. Dronin seldom let newcomers into meetings of the inner circle, and it was even more rare for him to take someone to bed while they were important in court.

Donova looked at Dronin, who dipped his head, waiting for her to speak.

"I know where the djuhlin is, Your Eminence, and I know when we can grab it."

"Where?" Dronin asked, leaning forward.

"The portal will need to be opened in the place Djuhl Charn died," she said simply, with a tone that vaguely indicated they were all idiots for not having thought of it sooner. "That is where their royalty resides. The female who killed him currently has possession of the djuhlin. Whoever is sent to retrieve it may have to deal with her."

Dronin waved a hand dismissively. "I have an entire realm at my disposal, sorceress. My byrds can retrieve the djuhlin. When?"

Donova folded her hands together in her lap. "In three days' time. I have dreamed that they will hold a celebration there. But across from here, a species that lives in the realm will be holding a separate rite, a more special, more rare gathering where they pour forth their magic into the veins that power their world. That concentration of magic will thin the barrier between us, and, with the stones you were able to give me, I can create a spell to open a portal."

She took a breath, examining her nails to hide the self-satisfaction gleaming in her eyes. "I've been experimenting and have succeeded in breaking into that realm already. Only momentarily, and the opening is small, but I can do it. Once whatever distance between us is minimized, I will be able to create a portal capable of letting the byrds through."

Dronin scraped his three dark claws over his chin, deep red eyes narrowed in thought. "I have no doubt about the byrds' ability to find the spawn. They will be able to scent its blood, but how long will you be able to keep the portal open?"

Donova's lips curled into her mouth, gaze dropping to the table as she thought. "It depends how long the non-demons practice their magic. If the barrier stays thin, I can hold the portal for longer, but when the space between our worlds thickens ... I am very powerful, Your Eminence, but the magic of the stones is unruly and does not enjoy being controlled."

"When my brother used the rings, he could only open a rift long enough to slip through. It never stayed open behind him."

"I've studied the properties of the stones against what I know of the magic of our realm. It's possible to create a more permanent portal, but it will require a vast amount of power," Donova cautioned. "If I'm going to open it, there is a very real chance I will only be able to do so once using my own magic. We will have only one chance to grab the djuhlin. We cannot fail." Her golden eyes leveled on Dronin.

"Get us into the realm, dreamwalker. I can take care of the rest."

Chapter 30

A MESSAGE ARRIVED FOR Merriam during breakfast three days after Dio's promotion. Rillak came into the common room, handing over a tightly rolled parchment.

"For me?" Merriam asked skeptically, reaching to take it.

"No offense to His Majesty, but there's only one o' you 'round here tha' goes by the name demonslayer." Rillak winked before returning to his post.

Apprehension clawed through Merriam's gut, a phantom ache spreading from her temple in memory of the last note that had been left for her. She unrolled it, the confusion on her face melting into a smile as she read.

Mollian watched her expectantly, unceremoniously wiping bacon grease from his chin.

"Shiloh's in town for the full moons festival!" Merriam hopped up, running to her room to grab her boots. "The performer from Do Lech," she threw over her shoulder at Mollian's confused expression.

Nethyl's moons only matched twice a year: in the spring, when they were both new, and in the fall, when they were both full. Festivals were held across Sekha during each occurrence, starting early in the morning and lasting through the entire night.

Merriam plopped down across from him, leaning forward to tie up her laces. "I'm going to go into town to meet with them. There's news from the south, I guess."

"Chetney?" Mollian asked.

"They didn't specify, but it's a safe bet." Merriam stood again, buckling her axes around her waist. "Want to come?"

Mollian shook his head. "I've got a full schedule today. Plus, what's that you're always saying? Plausible deniability?" He pointed to the crown across his brow. "I'll meet them at the festival, I'm sure." He paused, reminding himself that they'd eradicated anyone who wanted her dead. "Will you be out late?"

"I'll be back before supper." Merriam promised, and blew him a kiss before heading out.

The morning air was crisp; a gentle fog settled on the mountains. Beads of moisture dotted Merriam's cloak by the time she made it to the inn where Shiloh was staying.

She pulled off her hood, welcoming the fire-warmed air that brushed her cheeks as she glanced around for only a moment before spotting them.

"Merriam! So good to see you!" Shiloh stood to embrace her, motioning for her to sit. "I wasn't sure if you'd already eaten, but I have tea."

"Tea is lovely, thank you." Merriam poured a cup from a pot in the center of the table. "You should have let me know you were coming—we could have put you up at the castle."

Shiloh waved a hand. "Staying in town is better for business, and I don't want to impose. I heard you've been dealing with a lot since you got back." Their eyes drifted down to Merriam's splinted finger.

She resisted the urge to pull her hand into her lap, shrugging instead. "Comes with a life in politics, I suppose."

"I don't begrudge you it," Shiloh replied softly. They pushed their hair back from their face, pulling their teacup closer. "Speaking of politics and the giant asshats that go hand in hand, have you heard about the

Kinbriar heir?"

Merriam raised her brow. "What about him?"

"He's missing. No one has seen him since the night before your group left Do Lech." Shiloh took a sip, dark eyes watching Merriam.

"I'm sure Spiro and Larna must be very worried," she offered noncommittally, holding Shiloh's gaze.

A smile tugged at one corner of their lips. "They are. Personally, I hope they never find him, but they're starting to suspect that something unsavory might have happened. When I left, the overseers were still arguing over whether or not they should wait until after Do Lech's festival to head up to Umbra and present their concerns directly to the king."

Merriam stirred cream into her tea, intently watching the liquids mix. "Umbra is a long way to travel on mere suspicion."

"You're telling me, but from what I've heard, they think Illiziana's murder and Chetney's dissappearance are connected. There's been nothing to prove it, but Larna is sure that someone from your party had to have been responsible."

A knot of anxiety settled in Merriam's stomach, and she took a careful sip of tea in an attempt to appear unbothered. *Without a body, they can't prove anything.*

"There's absolutely no evidence to point to foul play where Chetney is concerned," Shiloh said, leaning back in their chair. "Personally, I'm a big fan of the theory that he's the one who offed Illiziana, then split town after. The overseers will come up here and whine to the king, but that's all they can do."

"I suppose so. Still not a great look, though," Merriam murmured. She tucked the information away, deciding to stop by the merc house on her way home to give them a heads up. Plus, Aleah needed to be prepared for the possibility of running into her grandparents.

Shiloh leaned back in their chair, dropping their eyes to the table for a moment. "There's something else I wanted to tell you, but ... It's probably dumb."

Merriam tilted her head to the side, waiting.

"There's some sort of strange blight affecting some of the plants down south. Not everywhere. It was just one small section I saw when I took a detour off the main road."

Merriam frowned in confusion. "What kind of blight?"

"I've been living in the south my entire life, Mer, and I've never seen anything like it. The leaves went gray. Not brown, not gold, gray. It looks like they're being eaten by some sort of mite or worm, maybe. But it looks wrong. It *feels* wrong." Shiloh stopped, pressing their lips together for a moment before continuing. "The area is right over one of the ley lines, too."

That got Merriam's attention, and she sat up straighter. "Maybe it's leeching?"

"I don't know ... isn't Nehyl's magic a source of life? Unless the leech is supercharging some sort of bug into devouring the vibrancy of the trees."

"I have a friend that might know about any insects down there with a long dormancy period." Merriam sighed, running her teeth over her lip. "I'll also ask Molli what he thinks. Maybe we'll find time after the festival to go take a look and shore up the warding."

The two moved on to brighter conversation after that, and Merriam took her leave, wanting enough time to talk to the mercenaries without her absence worrying Mollian.

Later that evening, Merriam lay on the floor of the common room she shared with Mollian, the lengths of her hair spread out above her head where she'd left it to dry hours before. Neither Calysta nor Aleah had been home when she'd stopped by the merc house, but she'd left all the information with Jasper and eased some of her nerves by babying Panic and annoying Leonidas.

She'd told Mollian about the blighted plants, which he'd made note to look into after the festival, and had since been steadily working away at the hilt of a sword. The soft scraping and scratching of his tools filled the room, along with an occasional hum of one tune or another.

Merriam had napped for a while, woken up and read a bit, and was now staring at the ceiling, book rising and falling with her breathing where it rested against her chest.

"Are you going to just lay there all night, or are you going to go talk to him?" Mollian finally asked.

Merriam scowled. "Forgive me if my recent kidnapping has me wary of approaching males."

Mollian glanced down at her with a disbelieving look. He was still struggling with the attack on her and could barely keep his anxiety in check when she was too far for him to feel in his mind, but Merriam had bounced back quickly. Her immediate return to work was a coping mechanism, he knew, but she'd never been one to let fear take root.

She turned her eyes from his with a huff. "I turned on him so easily, Molli."

"You'd been through an ordeal; I doubt he'll hold it against you."

"I promised I'd kill him."

Mollian had returned to his crafting, his fingers never pausing in their movements as he replied, "Not for the first time, either, if my memory serves me."

Merriam snorted, setting the book aside and sitting up. "I'm kind of a bitch, huh?"

Mollian shrugged. "A little bratty, maybe, but we love you anyway."

"Thanks for the confidence, Lord King." Merriam stood, reaching out to ruffle his curls.

She disappeared into her room, braiding her hair and buckling her axes around her waist.

"Let me know you're safe, will you?" Mollian said as she reentered the common room, worry creeping into his voice.

Merriam walked up behind him, wrapping her arms around his shoulders and resting her cheek against his head. "I will," she promised. *No one is ever getting the best of me again.*

You say that, but–

But nothing. Merriam interrupted him, straightening. *You were taken once, too, remember?*

Yes, and I've been under almost constant guard since, Mollian replied drily.

"Yes, and you're the king," Merriam reminded him. "I am but the lowly human who shares his soul." She dropped a kiss to his curls before straightening. *I love you, and no one is going to take me from you. I'll keep you close.*

With that, she left the room before she was able to talk herself out of it.

Apologize to Rovin. That was all she needed to do. Whatever came of it, she would deal with when it happened.

As she walked, Merriam flexed the fingers of her right hand, the left still splinted. The medic who'd looked it over the day before was confident she'd have full use of her hand again within a few days, as long as she kept the finger immobile until then, so she was patiently biding her time.

Biting her lip, Merriam pushed open the door to the Ranger's barracks. The few in the common room looked at her when she entered, and she raised her hand in silent greeting, trying not to let their attention heat her cheeks.

She walked across the room to the staircase that led to the upper floors, climbing to the third before stopping and taking a moment to catch her breath. As promised, she reached out for Mollian, a brief brush against his consciousness before she scanned her surroundings. Muffled noises came from a few of the rooms. It sounded like a card game of some sort was taking place a few doors down.

Merriam's fingers rested against the hilt of her axe, injured hand held to her chest, as she walked down the hall. Her heart thundered against her ribs, the fading bruise on her temple aching with the memory of being attacked the last time she was here.

But Ferrick was dead, along with Eskar. Their most fervent supporters were well on their way out of the country. And she had amends to make.

Merriam knocked.

And waited.

It couldn't have been longer than a few moments, but it felt like a year between each heartbeat before the door opened.

Merriam's gaze had been on her feet, and it dragged up over a pair of loose linen pants hanging low from narrow hips, to the tan skin of an exposed abdomen, to a muscular chest with a smattering of coarse, dark curls. Merriam's cheeks did heat then, and she forced her eyes up to Rovin's rather than let them follow the path of muscle over his arms.

Amusement glittered in his eyes along with the faintest hint of ap-prehension as he watched her, reaching above his head to rest his arm against the door frame. "This is a surprise."

Merriam licked her lips, resting her hands on the heads of her axes to keep from fidgeting. "I was hoping we could talk?" She silently cursed herself that it came out as a question.

Rovin's eyes flicked down to her weapons before meeting hers again. "Are you here to fight me?"

"I'd rather not this time, if it's all the same to you," she replied, holding up her injured hand. "I'm not quite battle-ready yet."

"Then welcome, Marshal, to my humble abode." Rovin stepped aside, sweeping his arm out to allow her to pass.

Merriam entered, reaching out again for Mollian to let him know all was well and pushing away his responding touch.

Rovin sat on his bed, one leg folded in front of him, and gestured toward the other end and then to the chair at the desk across from him. "Wherever you're comfortable."

She sank into the chair, folding her hands in her lap to keep from fidgeting.

Rovin frowned at her posture, her unease bleeding over into him. "I never expected you to show up here."

"I'm sorry I attacked you," she blurted.

"You did more than attack me," he said simply, sadness filling his eyes.

Merriam swallowed, staring at the floor. "Will you let me explain?"

He nodded, remaining silent.

"Remember the war room, when we were going over everything from Do Lech?"

Another nod.

"I decided then that I was done trying to run. Done avoiding what I wanted because I was scared of being hurt. When we were in the forest, you told me to come to you when I was ready to admit that there was—is?—something between us. But then you weren't around. I couldn't find you." Merriam took a deep breath, wiping her palms on her thighs. "A note was left for me with Molli's Guard, asking me to come see you. I was so fucking nervous and hopeful and ..."

"Then you were taken," Rovin said quietly, dropping his leg to plant both feet on the floor and face her fully.

Merriam chewed her lip, finally meeting his eyes. "Eskar told me it was you, and the thought that you had tricked me, that you'd tried to gain my trust only so you could get me out of the way, hurt so *much*. It hurt because I had finally admitted to myself, to Mollian even, that I care about you. I wanted to open my heart to you, and I thought you'd played me."

"Mer, I—"

She held up her hand, stopping him. "I knew I'd been brought there to die, and the only way I could keep myself whole in the face of that hurt was to bind myself with hatred. I promised myself I would kill you for what you'd done to me and how you'd made me feel." She paused, sawing her teeth over her bottom lip. "I'm sorry, though. I'm sorry I believed the picture Ferrick and Eskar had tried to paint me of your intentions."

Rovin rested a hand on either side of him, curling his fingers into the bedding. "There's a reason you believed me capable of such horrible things, Mer." He shook his head, chestnut waves falling over one side of his face. "I was so incredibly hateful toward you for such a long time. It was stupid of me to expect that a few words and one kiss were enough to erase all of your feelings from the past." He pushed his hair back, hand lingering. "I know I told you I would rather you look at me like you wanted to fight me than not look at me at all, but … The way you looked at me in the war room … I want it again. I crave it more than air."

"Why?" Merriam asked.

Rovin met her gaze, brown eyes softer than she'd ever seen them before. "You don't need me. You are resilient and strong, and your life is full of people who love you. But you looked at me like you wanted me to be part of your life, anyway. And there's something about knowing that even though you'd be fine without me, you still want to let me in that feels … good. Being wanted by someone like you is intoxicating."

Merriam stared at him, processing his words and trying to decipher the emotions battling inside of her because of them. Warmth spread from her chest, down through her stomach, and up into her head, making her thought process go soupy. She realized she was smiling, her cheeks warm, and she scowled. "This isn't fair."

He cocked his head to the side in question.

"You're shirtless."

A smile tugged at one corner of Rovin's mouth. "I didn't realize I was so distracting, pet."

She scowled harder. "You're not."

"Okay." He shrugged, letting her have it.

"You're infuriating," Merriam huffed, standing and crossing her arms.

"Then why did you come to see me?" Rovin asked, tilting his head up to look at her.

Her stomach somersaulted as she took two steps forward to close the distance between them, reaching out. Her fingers skimmed his forehead before sliding across his temple and into his hair. The strands were soft and warm, sliding between her fingers like silk. His eyes were on her face, but she refused to meet them, instead watching her fingers brush through his waves even as her chest tightened, making it hard to breathe.

"I came because I couldn't bear you thinking that I hated you or blamed you for any of what happened. I'm tired of fighting you, and as much as I sometimes despise it, I do, very much so, want you in my life," she whispered, finally meeting his eyes.

She started to pull her hand back, but Rovin caught her wrist, staring up into amber so warm it almost seemed to glow. The desire to pull her closer to him was almost stronger than his self-restraint, and his grip tightened around her, hunger flaring in his eyes. "Come to the full moons festival with me."

"What?" Merriam replied, her eyes focused on his lips and the feeling of his warm, calloused fingers over the pulse point on her wrist.

"There's still a lot of shit we need to work out, Mer. History like ours takes time to heal, but I'd like to heal it together. Spend tomorrow with me," Rovin murmured, thumb making a single pass across the sensitive skin on the inside of her arm.

Those damn butterflies were back by the hundreds, and Merriam nodded dumbly, squeezing her thighs together against the needy ache building between her legs with the intensity in his gaze.

Rovin brought her hand in front of his face, pressing a kiss to her palm before releasing her.

Her hand dropped, skin tingling where his lips had touched her. She stepped back as he stood, reaching around her to pull a shirt from the top of his desk and slide it over his head.

He leaned forward, dropping a kiss to her forehead. "I want to stay here and fuck you senseless, Merriam Demonslayer, but I'm already late for my shift."

Merriam blinked up at him, his words sending her heart into an unhealthy rhythm. "What?"

Rovin chuckled, stepping away from her to grab his weapons belt from a peg by his bed. "I think I like rendering you speechless. Something tells me it's a skill that not many possess."

"I didn't know you were working tonight." She folded her arms over her chest, shaking herself out of a lust-induced stupor even as the flex of Rovin's forearms buckling the belt around his waist threatened to send her right back into it.

"I can have my schedule sent to you, Marshal, if you need it for official reasons."

Merriam ignored the remark. "Tomorrow, though?" Then her eyes flew wide at the implication of his previous whispered statement. "The full moons festival, I mean," she added, cheeks heating.

"I have some Guard duties to take care of during the day, but I'll meet you there just before sundown," Rovin promised, throwing his arms into a jacket, sleeves marked with his lieutenant bars. "Walk down with me?" he added after a moment's hesitation.

Merriam's breath hitched. Walking through the Ranger's barracks at Rovin's side would remove any doubt that she'd been there to see him.

But even though it terrified her, she found herself nodding.

Rovin understood the weight of what he'd asked her, and her willing-ness to push through her fears for him, to step out of the acts that made her comfortable, made his heart swell. He wanted to kiss her, but he didn't trust that he'd be able to stop once he tasted her, so he held the door open, letting her pass before he shut and locked it behind him.

He took her elbow, directing her to the fire escape before letting her go to open the door. He propped it open with his foot, tucking his hands into his pockets.

Merriam looked up at him, both amused and irritated at his misdirec-tion, and stepped out into the cool night air. "This is more secluded than expected."

Rovin shrugged, his shoulder brushing against hers as they descend-ed. "Tomorrow will be plenty of public interaction."

"The *most* public interaction," Merriam agreed, nerves knotting in her stomach.

When they reached the ground, Rovin faced her, reaching out to brush his thumb under the lightest remnants of the bruise at her temple. "I'm sorry, Mer. For everything."

Merriam grabbed his hand, pulling it away from her face and squeez-ing his fingers. "We can't change our past," she said simply, then grinned. "Besides, maybe there's something to be said about the fact that we've seen the absolute worst in each other, yet still find ourselves here."

"Here? Outside of the Ranger barracks?" Rovin raised his eyebrows, looking around.

Merriam released his hand to shove his shoulder. "You're an ass, Rovin Arwood," she said with a laugh.

And Rovin thought he'd never enjoyed hearing his name as much as he did in that moment.

THE FULL MOONS FESTIVAL was in full swing, Merriam walking with Aleah on one side and Bellamy on the other with Ryddan perched on his shoulders. She glanced again to the west, watching the sun sink toward the mountains as nerves tightened in her belly.

Aleah let out a short squeal, dashing ahead.

"Is there another sweet roll vendor?" Campbell asked, rising onto his toes to peer over the crowd.

"I don't think it's food this time," Jasper remarked, catching sight of Aleah's bright red ponytail swing as she threw herself at Kodi.

"And of course he brought trouble with him," Campbell murmured, dropping back to his heels.

Merriam blushed, pulling her braid over her shoulder to twirl the end through her fingers. "Actually, um, we've made a peace ... of sorts." She watched Aleah and Kodi walk back toward their group, hand in hand, with Rovin alongside them.

All eyes turned to her, save for Bellamy's, whose lips twitched with the suppression of a smile.

"You and Rovin Arwood … are on good terms?" Leonidas's jaw had actually dropped.

"Panic is going to think your tongue is a worm." Merriam said.

Panic shifted his feet on Leonidas' shoulder, happy to be included.

"Don't let her fool you, they're on more than good terms," Bellamy said smugly, one hand on either of Ryddan's shins as the child looked about in wonder, not caring to listen to the conversation below him.

"More than?" Campbell raised his brows so high they almost disappeared under his thick brown curls.

"Can we please not make this weird?" Merriam begged as the Rangers approached them.

That was an impossibility, though, and they all knew it.

Those damned butterflies were back, and with reinforcements. Merriam bit her lip as she met Rovin's eyes, suddenly unsure of how to act.

"I'd rather listen to the two of you bicker all night than have to stand around while you awkwardly make eyes at each other," Jasper remarked, breaking the tension.

Merriam's cheeks heated, and she crossed her arms over her chest as she turned to him. "There's an entire festival, Jaz. Don't feel your presence is a necessity."

"Oh, she bites!" Leonidas put a palm over his chest, wincing on behalf of Jasper. He turned to Rovin with a friendly smile, dropping his hand. "If Mer says you're good, then it's all in the past, as far as I'm concerned." Rovin opened his mouth to reply, but Leonidas cut him off. "Panic, on the other hand, isn't too great about letting go of old feelings, so be mindful. That beak is perfectly shaped for plucking an eye out."

Panic, hearing his name again, tilted his head to the side, clicking the aforementioned beak once in agreement.

Merriam rolled her eyes, pushing Leonidas out of the way as Aleah snickered into Kodi's shoulder. "Ignore them," she told Rovin, letting her shoulder brush against his.

"I think I'd be more worried if they didn't tease," Rovin assured her.

"He's more than just a sharp sword and a pretty face, after all." Aleah winked at Merriam before pulling Kodi into the crowd. "Let's go get seats for the show before all the good spots are taken."

Show was a word that caught Ryddan's attention, and he perked up. "What kind of show?" he asked excitedly.

Bellamy glanced down at where Merriam's and Rovin's fingers had intertwined, a smile stretching the scar on his cheek.

"Typically, it's a play about one or two of the Legends, but I'm not sure which they've picked this year," Merriam answered the child after sticking her tongue out at Bellamy.

The group followed Aleah through the crowd to the amphitheater against the side of the mountain below the castle, making their way down the steps toward the front.

"Marshal, Lieutenant," the Guard at the front greeted them both by their rank, allowing the whole group to slide through. A rush of adrenaline went through Merriam as she passed him with her hand still in Rovin's, and she bit the inside of her cheek to keep from grinning like a fool.

"What?" Rovin asked, catching her expression when she glanced at him.

Merriam shrugged. "I'm just not used to being ... publicly affectionate," she explained with a breathy chuckle.

"Does it make you uncomfortable?" Rovin pulled his hand back, but Merriam gave his fingers a reassuring squeeze.

"No, it's okay. It's a good weird."

A vendor came by selling warm, salted popcorn, and Merriam happily traded him a few coppers for some large paper buckets to split between the group, dropping Rovin's hand to snack.

Ryddan had shifted into a large raven, he and Panic taking turns chasing each other around the amphitheater. Ryddan would occasionally swoop back in to pluck popcorn from the various tubs, happily croaking before flying off again.

"It's good to watch him be a kid," Merriam said.

"Definitely not a normal one by any means, but he needs this happiness and freedom," Bellamy agreed.

Mollian walked up, sinking down onto the bench between Merriam and Bellamy. "I hate you both for leaving me."

"Last time I checked, you're the only one with a royal title," Merriam pointed out. "Bell doesn't even have rank." Merriam had tried after Bellamy was assigned to protecting Ryddan, but rules were rules, and Rangers needed five years in service before they could be promoted.

"Last time I checked, you're only here because of me. My misery should be your misery," Mollian grumbled. He'd spent the morning greeting the citizens of Umbra and those who had traveled from across Jekeida to attend the festival.

"Believe me, Lord King, I feel your pain at my very core," Merriam joked, earning an elbow to the ribs.

After the show, Bellamy, with Lydia in tow, took Ryddan to the parts of the festival that catered to children, leaving everyone else to the more rough and rowdy festivities.

For the majority of the evening, Merriam competed in duels. Training swords only, but many of the Guard and a few citizens wanted to test their mettle against the demonslayer. Merriam was exhausted by the time the moons were high overhead, her arms and legs dotted in light bruises from fighting. Tendrils of hair had come free from her braid, dancing against her cheeks in the light wind.

And she was practically glowing.

Though Merriam hadn't won every fight, the friendly competitive nature of every duel had made her happy down to her soul. Moving, learning, bantering with her opponents, and watching others fight had been more fun than she'd ever experienced.

She'd participated in the duels during other full moons festivals, but never as much, and whether she'd called the challenge or a member of the Royal Guard, there had always been some level of animosity and agenda behind it.

This had been different. No one was trying to prove anything; every competitor had just been eager to test their skill.

Rovin, who'd also fought his fair share, could hardly take his eyes off of her. Merriam's amber eyes shone brightly, her cheeks rosy both from exertion and her wide smile. So much of him had wanted to challenge her, but the energy between them was too charged, and he knew many of his comrades would easily be able to see how badly he had it for her in the forced proximity of combat.

So he'd held back, even when Kodi elbowed him in the side and threatened to call a duel between Rovin and Merriam himself.

With the fighting drawn to a close, Mollian stepped down from his seat on the bleachers and walked over to where Merriam leaned against a wooden boundary post, guzzling water. "I think I'm going to head over to the evening show in the amphitheater," he told her, handing over her weapons belt that she'd taken off prior to the duels. *Bonfire was lit not too long ago.* He fought back an impish grin, eyes flicking to Rovin and back.

He'd seen the way the Ranger had watched her all night, but he also knew that Merriam would never suggest separating from him on her own. She would use him as an excuse to avoid being alone with Rovin, even though he knew that's what she wanted as surely as he knew his own name.

"Okay, I'll find you later?" Merriam held her hand up, and Mollian pressed his palm to hers.

Enjoy. He walked away.

Nobody likes a meddler, Merriam threw after him. She turned to Rovin, buckling her axes back around her waist. Concentrating on what her hands were doing, she asked, "Do you want to see the show? Or we could grab some drinks and head over to the bonfire." Task completed, she glanced up at Rovin, cursing her stomach for the way it flipped even as her lips pulled up into a smile at the easy happiness plain in his eyes.

"Bonfire and drinks get my vote."

"Did you catch where everyone else went?" Merriam asked as they walked toward a vendor selling mead.

"Aleah pulled Kodi away for food after her last fight. She said Calysta would be off doing 'her nymphy thing' for the rest of the night, and I'm not sure where the guys went off to." Rovin paid for the first round, and they found a patch of grass several paces away from the fire already grown large and reaching into the sky.

Lively music played from across the clearing, and several people danced near the flames, the entire atmosphere jovial and carefree.

Merriam sipped from her mug as she watched. The silence between her and Rovin was charged, but not uncomfortable. She turned to face him, folding her legs in front of her and placing the mug between them. "Want to play a game?"

Rovin leaned on one hand, pulling his gaze from the fire to look at her. "What do you have in mind, pet?"

"Shears, but winner gets to ask a question, and loser has to drink."

"What kind of question?" Rovin raised a brow.

Merriam shrugged. "Anything goes."

"Fair enough, then."

Rovin won the first round, holding his pointer and middle fingers out like a pair of shears, and miming cutting Merriam's fingers, which were stretched out flat like a sheet of paper. He rubbed the scruff on his jaw in thought as Merriam drank. "Anything goes?"

Merriam lifted her cup. "I will answer whatever you have to throw at me, Ranger-man."

"What made you decide to come here? To Nethyl, I mean." Mollian had originally told everyone she was from South Audha, and Rovin hadn't learned until last year that she was from a completely different plane of reality altogether.

Merriam rolled her lip between her teeth. "Opening with something pretty complex." She laughed lightly, eyes on her drink. "When we were kids, and I still lived ... on the flipside of Umbra, Molli asked me to come back with him. My parents weren't great, and he could see that even if I wasn't quite ready to accept it. My mom was rarely ever sober, and my dad was gone a lot for work. He had a temper, though, and he would hurt us when he was home." Her eyebrows pulled together with the memories of the shouting and being pushed up against the wall. "We moved away, and when Molli finally found me again years later, I knew whatever waited for me here was better than the life I had on Earth."

Disgust churned in Rovin's stomach at the climate he'd perpetuated within the Guard. She'd endured so much, only to come to Umbra and be put through even more. "And what awaited you was a bunch of battle-trained dickheads with a shared superiority complex."

Merriam laughed, her head tipping back. "Somehow, still worth it. Though I remain undecided about one or two of you."

Rovin accepted the jab, her easy laughter warming his chest. Unbidden, the memory of when she'd straddled him last summer, fury in her eyes and a threat on her lips as she'd cut a line down his throat filled his mind. He had the urge to challenge her again, insatiably curious about how that fire would feel when she wasn't trying to kill him.

He shook the thoughts away, holding out his hand again. "Next round,

Marshal?"

Merriam won, and she propped her elbows on her knees, searching Rovin's eyes with full seriousness. She licked her lips, brushing a stray lock of hair from her face. "If you were a bird, what would you be?"

Rovin let out a bark of laughter, the question nothing close to what he'd been expecting. "What kind of question is that?"

"An important one," Merriam deadpanned.

Rovin ran a hand through his hair, chestnut waves shining in the light of the distant fire. "I'd be a barn owl."

Merriam narrowed her eyes suspiciously. "Why?"

"They're a lethal predator—strong, silent, smart."

Merriam nodded, his answer satisfying something inside her, but she picked up her mug, smiling over the rim as she took a drink. "Cocky of you to assume those qualities," she teased.

"Oh? And what would you give me?"

Merriam took another drink as she thought. "A penguin."

"The fuck is a penguin?"

"They live in cold climates where I'm from. They're flightless, just waddle around over the ice and slide on their bellies," she spoke through a fit of laughter, wiping tears from beneath her eyes.

"Waddle?" Rovin repeated, incredulous at the comparison.

Merriam, still laughing, dropped her arms straight to her sides, hands flared out as she wiggled from side to side in pantomime. "This is you."

"You are deranged." Rovin shook his head, her laughter infectious.

The game continued, Merriam winning most of the time, and, when they were out of drink, she stood up, offering to get more.

Her good mood from all of the fighting had only grown, and she wondered at how easily she and Rovin joked with each other. It was as though all those years of purposefully annoying one another and acting on every irritation had made it incredibly simple to slip into a well-matched cadence of banter and teasing.

The fact that a majority of her most pleasant dreams had once included causing him bodily harm was not lost on her, but as Merriam neared the front of the line, she bounced on her toes, eager to return to his company.

BELLAMY WANTED A DRINK.

He watched Ryddan run through a miniature obstacle course with some other children, the little prince easy to keep track of with the moonlight bright against his white hair. The pure joy on Ryddan's face warmed Bellamy to the core, and the Ranger thought that there probably wasn't much he wouldn't do to keep him this happy forever.

But at his side stood Lydia, and she kept casting him dreamy, longing glances.

Most of the time, he was oblivious to her pining, but he'd noticed it when he'd stayed with Ryddan during Merriam's rescue, and that initial recognition had rendered him incapable of ignoring it further.

He sighed, folding his arms across his chest, but second-guessed that the posture was too imposing and dropped one hand to the hilt of his sword, then pushed his hair behind his shoulder with the other, not wanting anyone to think he sensed danger, clasping both hands behind his back, but feeling too formal, and finally letting his arms hang at his sides. "I'm fine watching him for the rest of the day. You can go hang out with your friends or see the rest of the festival if you want."

Lydia shook her head, eyelashes fluttering at him before she turned her face away, a blush crawling up her cheeks. "Thank you for the offer, but I'm content to stay with you—with you and Ryddan."

Bellamy pressed his lips together, nodding. His skin felt tight and itchy around his scar, and he rubbed the heel of his hand across it. He forgot it was there most of the time, but it was like it could sense when he was uncomfortable and wanted to add to it.

Ryddan ran up, slamming into Bellamy's legs, head tilted up to him. "Can we have sweets for supper?" His deep green eyes, pupils vertically slit, sparkled with an undiluted joy.

"Of course we can," Bellamy answered.

"No, you may not," Lydia said at the same time. Her eyes flew to Bellamy, aghast that he would agree to such a request.

Ryddan looked from Bellamy to Lydia. "Aleah said the full moons festival has all the best sweets, and that's all she eats all day long."

Lydia huffed, hands going to her hips. "Well Aleah is—"

"Absolutely correct!" Bellamy interjected, smoothing Ryddan's hair back from his face. "Should we go find something?"

Ryddan grinned, nodding enthusiastically. He grabbed Bellamy's hand, pulling him through the crowd.

"A growing boy needs *vegetables* and *meat*, Bellamy," Lydia insisted quietly as she followed.

Bellamy, his back to her, let his eyes roll so hard his vision blurred. "Which he had for supper last night, if I'm not mistaken, and will have again tomorrow. It's one day. A growing boy also needs *fun* and a little bit of autonomy."

Lydia tsked, but followed as Ryddan dragged Bellamy over to a vendor selling airy, puffed pastries dusted generously with powdery sugar.

The three drifted through the crowd, Ryddan sitting on one of Bellamy's shoulders as he ate, sugar dropping onto his lap and Bellamy's shirt with each bite.

Bellamy, one hand braced against Ryddan's legs, spied a small crowd gathering, and picked up the pace, heading to see what was happening.

A large stump had been placed at the corner of one line of stalls, and on it stood a fae. Four translucent wings fluttered at their back, moonlight shining through them so strongly they created prisms on the ground. Their dark hair was short on the sides, but long on top, draping over their eyes. They were dressed in a black vest, the pale skin of their arms almost completely covered in black ink, most of the designs so small he couldn't tell exactly what they were from a distance. Black pants, so tight they could have been painted on, covered their legs, and Bellamy's gaze drifted slowly down the curve of their ass and the muscle in their thighs and calves.

Catching himself, Bellamy jerked his gaze up to their face. They were watching him with an amused smirk, pulling a deck of cards from the pocket of their vest and beginning a fancy shuffle, but those dark eyes stayed locked on his while their fingers moved the cards in a complicated dance.

Shiloh winked, turning their attention to the rest of the crowd and flipping the cards in an extravagant arc over their head. Oohs and ahhs accompanied the act, and Shiloh launched into a well-practiced routine.

From the first time Shiloh pulled a card seemingly from thin air, Bellamy completely forgot about Lydia's existence. Aside from a part of his brain that still registered the child on his shoulder, making sure he didn't fall, all of his attention was focused on the fair folk who was capable of magic—*magic!* And not just moving things around like any high fae could do, but conjuring things from nowhere and reading people's minds.

It was the absolute wildest thing Bellamy had ever seen.

At some point during the act, Ryddan had spotted Dio's two small children, sliding down to the ground and joining them. Bellamy had watched his approach, and Dio, standing close by with his husband, caught Bellamy's gaze, giving the young Ranger a nod in acknowledgment that he would keep an eye on the prince.

Bellamy gave his captain a brief salute, turning his attention back to Shiloh.

After the act had finished, Dio walked up to Bellamy, placing a hand on his shoulder. "I can take Ryddan for a while. Relax, enjoy the festival."

"Sure, thank you, sir." Bellamy looked at Ryddan, leveling him with a look that clearly communicated he'd better behave.

Ryddan smiled, waving to Bellamy before running off through the crowd with Dio's daughters, his husband a few steps behind.

Bellamy walked up to Shiloh, hands in his pockets. They hopped down from the stump, shooting off a couple of thank-yous as people dropped tips into the container at their feet. As soon as Shiloh's eyes met Bellamy's, every coherent thought left his head. "You're magic," he blurted dumbly.

Shiloh laughed, bending down to collect their things. "I like to think so."

Bellamy fought back the flush of embarrassment that crawled up his cheeks, trying to regain his composure. "Can I, um. Can I buy you a drink?"

Shiloh raised a skeptical eyebrow. "That fae you were with gonna have a problem with that?"

Bellamy cocked his head to the side, brow wrinkling in confusion for a moment before it dawned on him. "Oh! Lydia? No, she's just Ryddan's nursemaid. Rydd's my ... he's the prince."

"You usually carry the prince around on your shoulders?" Shiloh asked, walking through the crowd.

Bellamy followed. "Only on special occasions."

Shiloh stepped into a large tent where a bar had been set up, sitting at a table while Bellamy got two flagons of ale.

"My friends would have loved your show, but I think they're at the fighting ring right now," he said as he sat.

"I've got a couple more on the schedule for tonight." Shiloh smiled.

"Mer would probably be able to guess a bit of what you do; she's pretty quick like that, but she—"

Shiloh's eyebrows shot up, and Bellamy stopped, wondering if he'd overstepped by insinuating someone could find out their tricks.

"The demonslayer?" Shiloh asked.

"Yeah." Bellamy was unsure whether to be pleased on Merriam's behalf that her reputation was so far-reaching, or worried about giving the impression that he'd been trying to show off how connected he was.

"Wait a second." Shiloh ran their hands into their hair, drumming their fingers against their head. "Don't tell me ... you're ... what was it? Benjamin? No ... Legends. Billlllll ..."

"Bellamy," he offered, a confused smile playing on his lips.

Shiloh laughed, clapping their hands once in front of them, wings giving a little flutter. "Yes! Bellamy! Merriam told me about you."

"Wait, you know her?"

"I met her in Do Lech. She told me you'd be a fan." They held their hand out. "Shiloh, sleight-of-hand expert and trickster extraordinaire. Pleased to meet you, Bellamy."

They sat at the table through a second round of drinks, and that was all it took for Bellamy to be completely infatuated.

"I've got another show to do. Will I see you around?" Shiloh slid from the stool.

"I hope so," Bellamy said honestly, not even caring if he sounded like a loon.

Merriam dropped to the ground, folding her legs and handing over a mug. The liquid inside had sloshed over her hand, and she unceremoniously dragged her tongue across it before wiping it on her pants. "What?" she asked with a smile, tilting her head to the side.

Rovin shook his head, eyes sparkling in the firelight. "Nothing, you just surprise me sometimes."

"Because I'm amazing?"

"Because you're a mess," he teased, nudging her knee with his.

Merriam snorted, but didn't bother trying to deny it. "Now, I believe you owe me an answer," she said after a sip of tart berry mead.

Rovin held an arm out. "Ask away."

"One of the most embarrassing moments of your life."

Rovin contemplated, bringing his drink to his lips. "Okay, remember last summer when we were on the way to Entumbra?"

Merriam nodded, perking up.

"I said something to you about needing to report to the Guard if you knew of someone putting a bounty on Mollian's head. As soon as it was out of my mouth, I felt like an absolute idiot. Mulled over that one for the rest of the day."

Merriam burst into a fit of laughter. "Legends, I'd forgotten about that!" She snorted, slapping her hand over her mouth. "That was a good one. And now I know what I can tease you about when the need arises."

Rovin scowled playfully. "I thought this was a safe space?"

Merriam shrugged, tossing her braid over her shoulder. "Lesson learned, Rov, never trust a drunk Mer."

"New round," Rovin prompted, lowering his drink to his lap and leaning forward.

A lock of hair had fallen over his face, and Merriam resisted the urge to reach out and brush it away, instead matching his stance and extending her arm, a challenging gleam in her eyes. "Your call, Ranger-man."

Rovin won, letting out a small, triumphant whoop.

"It's about time," Merriam laughed, sitting up straight. "This had better be good."

Rovin licked his lips, at a sudden loss. "Okay, um ..." His eyes roamed the clearing as he thought. Her knee was still touching his, and the contact was muddling his brain more than the alcohol. "Do you really share a bed with the king?" The question fell from his mouth without passing any of the filters in his brain.

Merriam didn't take her eyes from his, needing to gauge his reaction. He could not be threatened by Mollian if she was meant to be with him. "Most nights, yes."

There was no spark of jealousy in Rovin's expression, just an open curiosity. "It's not ... weird, ever?" He couldn't think of a better word, or any word, really, to phrase what he was trying to ask.

"Never, not once," Merriam answered, taking another sip before trying to explain. "Have you ever had a pet? Like a dog or a cat that slept in your bed? Cuddling Molli is like that. Warm. Comfortable. Safe. But never anything ... more."

"I've never had a pet," he admitted. "But sometimes, when I was young, I used to share a bed with my sister when I had nightmares or it was storming, and that brought those same feelings of comfort."

Merriam's eyes flew wide, and she almost choked on her drink. "Hold on, there is so much to dissect here. You used to be scared of rain? You have a *sister*?"

"Not rain, thunder, which is loud in the mountains in case you never realized. And yes, I have a sister. You've threatened to fuck her on more than one occasion."

Merriam cackled, full and from her belly. "I never knew she actually existed! I was just trying to get under your skin."

"Well, you succeeded." Rovin grinned from behind his mug.

"At least you know now it was an idle threat," Merriam offered.

"I'll sleep soundly with the knowledge," he joked.

"Unless it's raining, of course." Merriam tipped her drink back, setting the cup down between them and leaning forward, hands outstretched. "Another round?"

Rovin looked at the firelight dancing in her eyes, the easy smile on her face, and his chest tightened. He rose slightly, one hand on the ground between them to support himself, the other sliding into her hair as he slanted his mouth over hers.

She yielded easily, warmth flooding her as her mouth popped open and she slid her tongue over his lower lip. Her hands went to his arms, fingers digging into muscle.

Rovin pressed further against her, desire building in his chest and running down his spine, tightening at the base. Merriam whimpered when he bit her lip, and blood rushed to his cock.

The fire let out a loud pop, and he suddenly remembered where they were. He pulled back, opening his eyes to find Merriam's fluttering open to stare at him, slightly dazed, mouth still parted.

"Oh," she breathed. Her heart thudded against her ribcage, hunger heating her blood. She couldn't even find the wherewithal to care that he'd just kissed her in the middle of the festival. She just wanted his hands on her again. "You wanna get out of here?"

Rovin nodded, and they stood, leaving their drinks and walking into the trees towards the castle.

As soon as they were within the tree line, Merriam whirled around, her hands going to either side of Rovin's face as she slammed her mouth to his. Rovin caught her, pushing her up against a tree and hoisting her knee up over his hip. He ground against her, breaking the kiss to nip her neck. "Where?"

Merriam tilted her head to the side, letting her fingers slide into his hair. "The barracks?" she asked, pulling his mouth back to hers.

Rovin groaned, tugging her hips closer against him. "Thin walls."

"Presumptuous of you." Merriam smiled, letting out a small yelp when he caught her lip between his teeth. "I wish I had my damn rings." With her fingers bandaged together, Merriam had left her pieces of the Gate in her bedside drawer.

Rovin gripped her thigh, hoisting it higher on his hip. His other hand dragged up her side to her breast, his thumb dragging over her nipple.

The feel of him between her legs and his hands on her body like they'd always belonged there erased any last inhibition Merriam possessed. Her tongue swept over his, and he pressed against her again, the need in her core pooling hot and heavy. "Fuck it," she breathed against his lips. "My room."

The guards outside of her quarters—Mollian's quarters—would see Rovin enter with her, and by the next shift change, the entire Royal Guard would know that the marshal was sleeping with a Ranger lieutenant.

And she didn't fucking care.

Merriam held her body flush to Rovin's and let the depth of her emotions wash through her. After so many years of him living under her skin, constantly heating her blood, this release of tension felt more vital than air.

"You're sure?" Rovin whispered, his hand climbing into her hair. He knew what this meant for her, for him, too. Nothing stayed quiet in the castle for long, and things were about to go very public very quickly.

"Positive." Merriam pulled back, looking into his lust-drunk eyes, the brown dark and glittering in the bright moonlight.

Rovin leaned forward, dragging his nose against hers before claiming her in another deep kiss, knotting his fingers into her hair so that her head tipped back further. He pulled away, grabbing her hand and heading up to the castle when a sharp scream cut through the air.

It was followed by the clamor of many raised voices.

Merriam looked at Rovin with wide eyes before running back to the festival with him close on her heels.

They broke through the trees and into the clearing, Merriam's gaze going to the sky. A small ripple of light hung in the air, and creatures were flying through. They were larger than any bird she'd seen. Their beaks were long and pointed, and claws tipped their wings. Their legs, which extended as they dove toward the people gathered in celebration, were jointed twice, long and spindly. They were like something out of a nightmare.

She threw out her awareness, searching for Mollian. He was close, but it did little to quell the fear that completely erased every trace of lust in her veins.

"What are those?" Rovin asked, shortsword held at the ready.

Merriam shook her head, unclasping her axes. The left was held awkwardly, mostly with her pinky and thumb. "Fucking Hel." She slid it back into her belt. It would only get in the way. She looked across the field, seeing Mollian running toward the area where the creatures were appearing. "Watch Molli!" she called to Rovin, running forward to meet the king.

"On it," Rovin replied as he ran.

Mollian had a sword at his hip, but it stayed sheathed. His hands were thrown out toward that strange sliver of light, his eyes locked on it.

Merriam raised her axe, cutting into one of the demonic birds as it dove for her. She cut through its belly, and it fell to the ground with a shriek. "Molli!" she called, nearing where he stood.

He didn't turn to her, his gaze locked on the light. *It's a portal.*

His words filled her with dread, and she turned her back to his when she reached him, defending him from the swarm. *How is that possible?*

It shouldn't be. But I think I can close it.

Rovin was at her side, bringing down another of the creatures. They seemed to know that Mollian was trying to cut off their connection, half of the swarm aiming for him.

Mollian's magic slid through the open seam in the sky, but it kept slipping from the surface, unable to grasp it. He grit his teeth in concentration, forcing it to loop around the portal. He had no solid idea of what exactly he was supposed to do, but he knew—with some buried part of him, he knew—that he could seal it off. Starting with one edge of the streak of light, he squeezed, pinching it together until it fused and fizzled off into nothing.

That one act sent a surge of confidence through him, and he focused harder, blocking out the sound around him. There was nothing except for the portal, his magic pouring from his veins, and Merriam at his back. Even if he'd had the spare brain power to be surprised by his awareness of Merriam, he wouldn't have been. A reserve of his magic flowed through her, and even without it, the tethers between their souls seemed to surge with energy.

Bit by bit, Mollian sealed off the portal.

Merriam's head buzzed, her breathing labored. She slumped against Mollian's back, her brow furrowed. "Something is wrong," she panted. She felt completely winded, but she'd barely expended any energy.

Rovin glanced at her, his face splattered with black blood. "Are you okay?"

The air around Merriam's face grew cold, and she shook her head, raising her axe to continue fighting. "I feel like I'm about to pass out," she whispered, barely lobbing off the outstretched foot of a creature before it reached her. She forced herself back upright, blinking furiously to stave off the darkness at the edge of her vision.

"Mollian!" Rovin called over his shoulder, concern edging his voice.

Merriam shook her head. "No, he needs to close the portal," she said. And she felt it, then, the surge of energy running from her and into her *mehhen.*

Years of their connection, the bond between them strengthening and growing deeper, and she finally understood. Mollian needed her. Whatever magic he'd been gifted, the magic that his siblings had sensed, even if they didn't fully acknowledge it, needed more than what he could give to control it. Their destinies were tied together, their souls shared, because his power had needed two people to do ... whatever it was exactly that it did.

"Molli needs my strength," she whispered, willing herself to stay on her feet.

Fear flooded Rovin's blood when he saw how pale her face had grown, freckles standing out against almost bloodless skin in dark patches. Other members of the Guard were there, slashing swords through the air as the byrds took turns diving toward Mollian. Rovin looked to the one nearest him. "Stay with the king!" he ordered.

As soon as the guard acknowledged him, Rovin turned to Merriam, pulling the axe from her hand.

"No, stop!" She pulled back, but the weapon slipped easily from her fingers.

"You can't help Mollian if you're dead," he grunted, slinging her arm over his shoulder and taking her weight. He walked her from the thick of the fighting, keeping one arm around her waist and his sword raised. But the creatures were focused on Mollian, so Rovin sheathed his weapon and leaned down to scoop Merriam into his arms, running toward the trees.

"I can walk!" Merriam protested, glaring up at him. But her skin was cold and clammy, and she tightened her arms around his neck, her gaze drifting over his shoulder to Mollian, only his wild white curls visible through the fray.

Roughly half of the portal had been closed, and Merriam's head buzzed lightly, but her fatigue seemed to have plateaued. She was dizzy, but she would be able to stand. She was winded, but she could fight if she had to.

Merriam started to struggle, far enough away from the fighting to feel confident on her feet.

A sharp, terror-filled shriek cut through the air, ringing out even above the din of everyone scrambling to leave the area.

Rovin's arms tightened around her as he spun to face the noise. "BELLY!"

Merriam's heart stopped, gaze snapping up to the sky.

Three of the creatures had hold of Ryddan, talons wrapped around him as they flew toward the portal.

SHIFT! she Cast desperately, leaping from Rovin's hold and landing in a run, pulling an axe to toss at the creatures.

Rovin's arm went around her waist, pulling her back and sending them both tumbling to the ground. "You could hit Ryddan," he panted as she struggled to stand.

A disgruntled cry fell from Merriam's lips. She knew he was right. She was in no condition to throw an axe from any distance with guaranteed accuracy. She watched helplessly as Mollian closed off a bit more of the portal.

Bellamy raced through the crowd, brown curls streaming behind him as he lept over discarded chairs and baskets.

The creatures soared toward the portal over Mollian's head, abandoning the attack to slip back through.

"DADDY!" Ryddan shrieked, eyes wild with terror and small fingers outstretched toward Bellamy. Not even a heartbeat later, he was gone, and the portal winked closed.

Mollian dropped to his knees, brow drenched in sweat.

The Guard made quick work of the remaining creatures left behind when the portal closed, Bellamy joining the fight with a feral cry, unsheathing his sword and slicing clean through an attacking byrd.

Merriam struggled to her feet, still winded, but she could feel that her energy was once again hers. She ran for Mollian, sliding to the ground in front of him. "What was that? What happened?" she panted, grasping his hands.

Mollian raised his eyes to meet hers, exhaustion shining brightly in the pale green depths. "I couldn't do it, Ria," he whispered.

Bellamy threw his sword down, grabbing Mollian by the front of his shirt and hoisting him to his feet. "Bring it back!" he shouted, eyes wild.

Mollian held Bellamy's hands, shaking his head. White curls stuck to his brow, a bead of sweat dropping from his temple. "I can't."

"They took Ryddan." Bellamy's voice cracked, his hold tightening around the fabric of Mollian's shirt.

Rovin was behind Bellamy, grasping his shoulder. "Bellamy, not here."

Bellamy realized where they were, who he was grabbing, and immediately let go of Mollian, taking a step back and bumping into Rovin.

Mollian snapped to at the same time as Bellamy, locking down his panic and despair to take control. "Rovin, gather the Guard, make sure the people are okay. Help the vendors if they need it. If you find Dio, tell him to meet me in the war room."

Rovin nodded, rounding up the Guard nearby and setting off.

Mollian reached out for Bellamy's wrist, holding him there. *Are you okay?* he Cast to Merriam.

She nodded, her head clear and her fatigue now minor.

"Try to find a body that's intact and take it up to the study. We need to figure out what these things are and where they came from," he instructed the Ranger.

"Molli," Merriam started, eyes drifting over the bodies scattered through the clearing. "They took Rydd. Other than when you started trying to cut off the portal, they didn't target anything else." It had been a full year without any activity pointing to the demons she'd earned her moniker defeating. After so much time, she'd been confident that killing Basta had eradicated that threat.

But now ...

Merriam ran a shaky hand over her hair. "These things ... the black blood ... they're demons." Another realization hit her the second she said the word, as though naming the creatures uncovered a detail that had fallen to the wayside with everything else that had happened last summer. "Basta's rings," she breathed, her knees threatening to buckle. "I left Basta's rings."

"No." Mollian shook his head in denial. "No, Basta didn't know about him, and demons can't wield the rings."

"What else could they be? Why else target Ryddan?" she asked.

"Why?" Bellamy's voice broke. "After all this time, why?"

Merriam looked around the clearing, wiping the back of her hand across her mouth. "The demon that wore Basta wanted portal magic.

If they learned of Ryddan's existence, if they knew whose child he was, they would want him. We have to find out where he's from."

Mollian curled his hands into fists and took a deep, shuddering breath. "We need to go to Entumbra."

MOLLIAN PACED THE HALL of the war room, white curls even more wild than usual from how often his hands ran through his hair. Only Dio, Bellamy, and Merriam were with him.

"I'm going to Entumbra. This isn't an attack on Sekha or even on Nethyl. There's only one reason those demons would have come for Rydd. We need to find him, and fast." Mollian stopped his pacing, eyes drifting over the people seated at the table. "I will not sit here idly while everyone else goes."

"I agree, Your Majesty," Dio said. "My only council would be that you sacrifice the time to set up a proper chain of command before you leave and make the preparations to bring the proper people with you. It's been many years since Umbra was left in the hands of anyone other than a Stonebane, and the last thing Sekha needs is more chaos."

Merriam rested her chin on her knees, which were hugged to her chest. "I've been to the demon realm. I can get back, right? The Gate will take us back?"

"In theory," Mollian answered, but he was distracted, his mind going in a thousand places at once. He felt so incredibly young and ill-equipped to deal with what very well could mean the end of the world as he knew it, and feeling so inadequate made him sick. He flung a hand out behind him, magic blindly wrapping around the back of a chair, which he swung at a wall across the room with enough force to shatter it.

A chunk of wood skittered across the floor, knocking against the leg of Merriam's seat. She stood, walking over and pressing her palm to his back. *Breathe, Molli.*

I think I'm going to pass out. Mollian couldn't hold on to one single thought long enough to process it. His skin was tight, his muscles burned, and he wanted action.

Merriam leaned against him, feeling every one of his muscles tensed and coiled. *That's fine. We're here. Just breathe.*

Mollian shook his head, pressing the heels of his hands to his eyes as he tried to sort through all of the thoughts and emotions running through him, all while keeping a hold on the magic that surged in his veins, searching for an outlet.

Give it to me, Merriam Cast. She knew she should also be freaking out, but something about Mollian's state kept her calm, collected. She needed to give him what he couldn't do himself.

Mollian shuddered, but loosened his hold on his magic. It slid into Merriam through the tethers between their souls, mixing seamlessly with her Bonded blood. She stifled a gasp, unprepared for the pressure of its volume against her veins.

With the surge of his power lessened, Mollian pushed from the wall, smoothing a hand over Merriam's hair in silent thanks as he stepped back toward the table. "Dio, can you gather the guildmasters? Let them know to bring anything pressing that will need my attention before I leave. Then we'll figure out some sort of chain of command for matters of state that may arise in my absence."

"Yes, Your Majesty."

Mollian rested his hands against the table, looking over the map. "You can assign an escort from the Guard, but keep it small. Large groups are too slow to travel with." He raised his eyes to look at Bellamy. "You and Rovin will accompany me and Merriam through the Gate."

"If only the four of us are going through, why wait for the Gate at all? Why not Travel directly there? Merriam and Rovin went when they killed Basta," Bellamy said.

"It's not that simple," Mollian said. "Unless we're going to a parallel realm, Travel takes a lot of effort and very calculated concentration. And we have to be sure of where we're going if we don't want to risk overexertion."

Merriam chewed on her lip, still against the wall where Mollian had left her. "Basta's blood took me there last time. The intention, the location, was all his. Traveling there shouldn't have worked, not when I had no clue where I was trying to go. Using the rings to go back is dangerous. There are a thousand different worlds we could end up in, and if we got stuck over there ..." she met Bellamy's gaze apologetically. "It's safer to use the Gate."

"What about one of those creatures? Can't you use their blood?" Bellamy pressed.

"We can use what we learn about them to better pinpoint which world we need to go to, but their blood can't communicate with the stones." Mollian looked at Bellamy with an apologetic shake of his head before turning to Merriam. "Ria, get with Rovin and start compiling everything you remember about that world. The more, the better. Even the most minute details could be helpful. Bell, you know Rydd better than any of us. Anything you can remember about his demon nature could also be helpful in locating him. In the meantime, I'll be working with Dio to prepare everything in Umbra for my absence." Mollian tapped his fingers against the table with a definitive nod. "As long as everything is able to be taken care of tomorrow, we'll leave the morning after."

By the time Merriam and Mollian crawled into bed, the sky to the east was turning light with the impending sunrise. Mollian would need to be up in a few hours to start organizing things for his departure, but he knew he should try to get some sleep in before then.

He lay there, his mind restless as he replayed the events of the night. He focused on the feel of Merriam pressed against him, letting her presence keep him grounded as his emotions stayed on the brink of unraveling entirely. "I've been having dreams when you're gone."

Merriam's brow furrowed. "What?" she mumbled.

"I don't remember them, not really, but the *feel* of them ..."

Merriam opened her eyes, pulling herself back from the brink of sleep. She glanced up, looking at Mollian as he stared at the ceiling.

"I'm in a place, but not a place. Like it's outside of everything. And my magic calls to me, and I wake up trying to fight for control of it, to settle it, because it wants something that I can't give it."

Merriam sat up, wiping a hand across her eyes. "How many times have you dreamed this?"

"A few," he replied quietly. "I meant to tell you, but things have been so hectic."

"It's okay, Molli." She smoothed the hair back from his face. "Everything is stressful right now; it has been for a long time. But we're together again."

"It's not just that." Mollian looked up at her, the shot of brown through his one iris a deep, glittering void in the dark. "When I ... when I tore Ferrick apart? My magic *wanted* to. It knew what to do, and it spoke to me then, too. That release—using it that way—it felt right." He shivered. "I didn't even give it a second thought, Ria."

Merriam held his gaze, still brushing her fingers over his soft white curls. It struck her then how young they were, how much they'd already seen and endured that never should have been.

"I wanted to do the same to Eskar," he admitted, looking back up at the ceiling. "I wanted to rip her into a thousand tiny pieces like I did to Ferrick. The whole time you were fighting her, I kept thinking about how easy it would be. How simple to just reach out, wrap her in my magic, let it sink into her pores and seep into her bones and just ..." he trailed off, making a popping sound with his lips. A tremor ran through him as his magic remembered what it had felt like for her to be gone.

"But you didn't," Merriam offered.

"No, I didn't." But Mollian wasn't appeased. "What's wrong with me? Have you ever heard of a fae being able to manipulate the living that way?"

Merriam shrugged. "The wild nymphs—can't they manipulate the living?"

Mollian frowned. "Nerves, synopses, muscular impulses, yes, but I've never heard it described the way my magic feels."

"You said it talks to you?"

"Not in words, but in feelings. It wants to rip, to pull things apart. It doesn't make sense, not on the scale that I feel it inside of me. Sometimes I think I'm going crazy."

"You are crazy, Lord King," Merriam said with a small smile.

"With Ryddan gone, with the threat of demons back in play—" Mollian paused. *I'm scared to be alone, Ria. To be away from you.* She was the only thing keeping him held together, and he couldn't find it within himself to be ashamed of that dependency.

I won't leave you, she promised, feeling the agitation in his magic as it cycled through her.

I can't hold it without you. I don't know where it takes me in my dreams, but it wants something, and I'm not sure if I'm supposed to comply.

Merriam laid back down, settling into the mattress on her side. She studied the planes of Mollian's face in the near-darkness for a moment, the steady rise and fall of his chest. "You're *good*, Molli," she told him. "You always have been. Your magic, whether or not you were ever supposed to have possessed it, is inherently part of you, and I will never be convinced that any bit of you is made of malice."

Mollian turned his head to look at her, and she smoothed the wrinkle from between his brows with a finger.

"Your magic is different. It's strong. But you're both those things, too. We'll figure it out together." Merriam reached down to clasp his hand. *You will never have to carry this alone.*

Merriam and Rovin met in the library after breakfast the next morning with the goal of making a sort of checklist for what to look for in Entumbra's records. The library there held accounts of every world a Keeper had ever visited, some more detailed than others, and there would be a lot to dig through. Any semblance of a roadmap to make that search easier would save valuable time.

Merriam was already seated at a small table when Rovin entered, sliding into the chair across from her. "How are you holding up?"

The open concern in his eyes pulled at something in her chest. Because he wanted to take care of her, but he wasn't caging. Nothing about him read protective, just supportive. Merriam knew in that moment that he would never try to hold her back, would never treat her like she couldn't hold her own or try to fight her battles for her. Not because he didn't care, but because he respected her ability to take charge. An unnamed emotion swelled with the realization, and she stamped it down, swallowing and forcing her gaze to the table. "I'm sick with worry over Ryddan, but we'll find him. And I'm okay. Whatever magic or strength Molli needed from me yesterday replenished before we'd even reached the castle." She flicked her eyes back to him with a reassuring smile, pushing some paper and a pencil toward him.

"Has that ever happened before? Where he's had to pull from you?" Rovin asked.

Merriam shook her head with a small shrug. "He's never had to try to close a rift like that before, though. If someone has ever broken through from another world like that on purpose, it hasn't happened in hundreds of years."

He picked up the pencil, twisting it in his fingers with a wry grin. "Gotta love whatever twist of fate decided we would be the lucky ones having to write the rules of conduct and procedure for war with demons."

She snorted, sitting back in her seat. "Here's to hoping we don't royally fuck it up."

They slipped into a comfortable silence, both writing everything they remembered about the demon realm separately before checking it against each other to compile into a single list.

Merriam had replayed a lot of moments in her head over the past year, but one thing she'd never really dwelt on was Rovin's presence when she'd followed Basta. She knew that she probably would have died if he hadn't been there, but she'd never spent much time thinking about how he'd known what she was about to do before she Traveled or why he'd lunged for her, grabbing on just before she slipped from Nethyl.

She peeked up at him now, biting her lip in contemplation. "Rov?"

He lifted his head, the question in her eyes giving him pause.

"Why did you follow me to the demon realm last summer?"

"I couldn't let you go alone," he said after a moment of contemplation. "I knew that you weren't going to let Basta get away, and I knew that you were about to risk your life to make sure he could never hurt Mollian again. And I wanted to help you … because I've never once seen you falter in the face of fear."

Merriam was equally as unprepared for the depth of his answer as she was for the way he looked at her when he said it, like he was warring between wanting to worship her and wondering if she was mentally well. "I can't quite tell if you're into that or not," she joked in an attempt to dilute the charge between them.

"I admire the shit out of you for it," he said, completely undermining her efforts.

The door to the library opened, one of the Royal Guard poking his head in. "Pardon the interruption, Marshal, but there's a nymph here to see you. Says it's important."

Merriam pushed her list across to Rovin. "Here's what I've got so far. See if it jogs anything else loose for you. I'll be back." Her fingers drifted over his arm as she walked past him to the door. He reached up to squeeze her hand when she grazed his shoulder, and then she was gone, trying to calm the flutter of her heart and following the guard downstairs.

Calysta was waiting in the courtyard, her arms folded over her chest in an attempt to comfort herself. A cool breeze caught the long strands of her hair, crossing the worried pull of her brows over tired black eyes. She looked like she hadn't slept much, either.

"What's wrong?" Merriam asked, leaving the guard at the doors and hurrying over.

"I need to talk to you." Calysta searched Merriam's face for a moment before averting her gaze, looking off toward a small copse of trees.

"Are you okay? Has something happened?" Merriam rested her hand on the nymph's arm, her olive green skin warm despite the chill in the air.

Calysta shook her head, needle-sharp teeth dimpling her lower lip for a moment as she gathered herself. "We used to hold a rite during the full moons. Once every ten years, nymphs would gather in great numbers to honor Nethyl and the magic that connects us to her." She shivered, flicking her gaze to Merriam again before studying her feet, bare toes curling into the grass. "Such a ceremony hasn't taken place in over a hundred years. Like I told you on the way down to Do Lech, Illiziana found a way to outlaw them. She was the biggest champion for those regulations, though, and with her dead, we were free to pour our magic back into Nethyl again ..."

Merriam's mouth popped open. When she'd first learned of Illiziana's death, the overseer's name had felt familiar, but she couldn't quite place it. The pieces were slowly coming together now, though. "The nymphs hired Aleah."

Calysta nodded, fingers twisting into the folds of her skirt. "I didn't know, not until afterwards, but, Mer, I—" she broke off, swallowing and finally lifting her eyes to meet Merriam's gaze. "It's been so long since the folk were able to perform the ceremony with any large gathering, and ... when we tapped into the ley lines, I think—I know—it messes with the source magic. It touches the Gate." Calysta pushed her fingers into her hair, frustrated with how much she was struggling with the words. "I think the full moons rite let the demons break through."

It was the nymph's blood, combined with pieces from the Gate, that created the first Keeper. But nymphs were connected to nature, not the Gate itself. Merriam searched Calysta's face, still trying to decipher everything. She grabbed Calysta's arms. "This is not your fault."

Calysta's musical voice was laced with distress. "But if we somehow made the Gate's magic flare, made it easier for them to reach us ... I'll never forgive myself if Ryddan is hurt because of us."

"I left Basta's rings behind when I killed him. They had pieces of the Gate in their possession this whole time and have probably been trying to figure out how to use them. Your people have been holding these ceremonies for millennia and nothing like this has ever happened before. If anything, knowing the demons inadvertently had your help can be a good thing if it means they don't have the magic to break through on their own."

"But now they have Rydd, and his magic is strong enough for that," Calysta said quietly.

Merriam pulled her into a hug, holding her tightly. "We'll figure it out." She didn't say anything else, turning this new information over and not sure how it would affect or change the course of action.

Bellamy was not well.

Every fiber of his being was a live wire, energy coursing through him and rendering him incapable of sitting still, much less sleeping.

Captain Dio hadn't scheduled him for any shifts. Not only was he due to leave for Entumbra in the morning, but Dio also knew he was in somewhat of a fragile mental state with Ryddan's abduction.

Fragile was putting it lightly.

Bellamy spent the morning after Ryddan's disappearance restlessly wandering the castle grounds, out of his mind with the need to do something, when he finally found Dio in his office in the barracks.

"Your job right now is Ryddan. Don't worry about anything else," Dio told him, his expression empathetic.

Bellamy clenched his teeth together, giving a brisk nod before walking back down the hall. He sank into a chair in the common room, hands clasped between his knees. There was nothing he could do until they were in Entumbra.

"You okay, Bell?"

Bellamy glanced up to see Evangeline in a seat next to him, curled up with a drawing pad on her lap and her dark hair spilling over her shoulders.

She gave him a tentative smile. "Your leg."

Bellamy moved a hand to his knee, which he hadn't even noticed was bouncing. "I think I need to expel some energy. You, uh, want to go run some drills?" He stood, scooping his hair back to tie up.

"I've got less than an hour before duty, or I would. Do you want me to try to find someone to swap shifts?" she asked. In all the time she'd known him, she'd never seen him this agitated and out of it before.

"No, it's okay." Bellamy stood and waved a hand over his shoulder, walking from the barracks.

His mind was still in a spiral, and he ended up outside of Ryddan's room from muscle memory. His breath caught in his throat as he reached for the door, but he turned around, almost smacking right into Lydia.

"Sorry," he mumbled, stepping past her.

But she reached out, grabbing his hand. "Wait."

He stopped, turning to face her.

Lydia bit her lip, moving closer to him. "I know you'll find him." Her hand moved up his arm.

"What are you doing?" he asked, his voice flat.

She blinked up at him, her hand lingering. "You were always so good with him. This is a scary time, but we can ... we can be there for each other."

"Don't," Bellamy said quietly, looking down at where she touched him.

"Bellamy, I—"

"Don't," he interrupted, jerking his arm away. "Don't do this."

Lydia gave him a wounded look, and it took everything in him not to roll his eyes. "Is it Evangeline?"

"What the fuck?" He blinked at her, incredulous.

"I won't get in the way of your relationship, but I need you to know how important you are to me, and—"

Whatever self-control, whatever thread of sanity had been left in Bellamy snapped, and he threw his arms out. "What is wrong with you?!"

Lydia flinched back. She'd never heard Bellamy raise his voice before.

"Ryddan is *gone*. He has been *taken*. What about this situation makes you think that I want to kindle a relationship?" Agitation wound tight through his chest, swirling through the gray-blue of his eyes as he glared at her.

She swallowed, tucking a lock of hair behind her ear. "I didn't think—"

Bellamy interrupted with a snort. "Fucking *clearly*. Legends be damned, Lydia." He stormed off, leaving her standing open-mouthed in the hallway.

He went down to the training room, needing to move. To burn off energy.

Two groups of Royal Guard had come and gone, and Bellamy was still running through sword drills and tossing knives at targets. His shirt was plastered to his back, sweat dripping from his face by the time he took a break, guzzling water.

The room felt stuffy, the walls like they were closing in. Bellamy dropped the training sword, moving toward the door. Before he pushed it open, he turned back around, picking up the sword to properly store it. The impulse irritated him, so he dropped it again, bursting out into the courtyard before he could go back for it a second time.

A strong wind rolled down the mountain, lifting the edges of his hair from his shoulders and instantly cooling him as the sweat dried on his skin. Bellamy looked up at the sky, stars just appearing in a vast distance that made him feel cold and alone.

Ryddan was out there, somewhere.

Bellamy knew he wasn't anywhere in this galaxy—that's not the way that portals worked—but the sentiment felt the same. Ryddan was just as unreachable as the stars whose light had probably taken hours, maybe even years, to reach him.

Bellamy swallowed, a shiver traveling down his spine as he heard Ryddan's shriek again.

Daddy.

That single cry had torn right through his soul.

He was, in many ways, still just a kid himself. He knew that. He hadn't even been a Ranger for two full years yet. Bellamy had never really thought about children or having any of his own one day. It had always seemed like something so far off in the future, a hundred years away, if not more. But he *knew* without a shadow of a doubt, that whatever depth of protectiveness and love he felt for Ryddan couldn't have grown any deeper if the kid shared his blood.

And he'd been taken. Not even ten steps away, he'd been snatched up into the air.

Bellamy had let that happen.

Guilt and anger churned in his gut—thick. Heavy. Sickening. He had let those creatures take Ryddan, and Legends only knew where he was now.

Bellamy pushed his fingers into his hair, gritting his teeth against the cry of anguish that wanted to rip from his chest. Pulling the tie free from his curls, he twisted them into a bun, securing his hair again before launching into a run.

Bellamy sprinted through the courtyard, out the back entrance that opened into the forest behind the amphitheater. It only opened one way, so he'd have to go back in through the main gate, but that didn't matter. He didn't even have a destination. He just ran, trying to give his mind something to concentrate on other than his complete and utter failure as a protector.

The wind picked up, gusting across Bellamy's face and blowing dark, angry clouds over the mountains. It didn't take long for them to open up in a torrential downpour.

Despite the rain, Bellamy ran until his lungs burned, the muscles in his legs weak and jittery. His throat was raw from how heavy he was breathing, and spirals of hair had sprung free from his bun, slicked against his neck and cheeks. Rainwater poured over his face as he hunched forward, hands on his knees and catching his breath.

I should have brought the damn sword, Bellamy thought, wanting to swing at something. He was afraid to stop moving, afraid to rest, afraid to think.

Resting his hands on his head, he turned toward the lights of Umbra, not quite ready for the long walk home, but not sure what else to do with himself.

Bellamy trudged through town, his legs burning at the uphill slope toward the castle. Emotions swirled through him in an indecipherable cyclone, muddling his mind until everything went numb. He leaned against an awning to catch his breath. His chest was tight, and he was struggling to breathe in. His hand wrapped around a wooden post, nails digging into the grain.

"Bellamy?"

He turned his head, a violent shiver racking his body as the wind blew cold against him.

A small circle of red glowed from the shadows before Shiloh stepped forward, a joint burning in their fingertips as they blew a cloud of fragrant smoke into the air above them. "What are you doing down here so late?"

Bellamy stared at them, fingers still gripping the post, panting shallowly.

"Hey, are you okay?" Shiloh rested a hand against his arm.

A drop of rain mixed with sweat rolled into Bellamy's eye, and he blinked at the sting of salt, wiping the back of his hand across his forehead. He was still struggling to breathe, but so much of his concentration now went to where Shiloh was touching him, their skin warm and soft. "I don't ... what?"

Shiloh licked their fingertips, pinching the end of the joint to put it out before tucking it behind their ear. They wiped their hand against their pants to clear the ash before grabbing Bellamy's shoulders, holding his gaze. "What are you doing out here? It's freezing."

Bellamy looked from Shiloh to the street, streams of water running over the cobblestones. Another shiver shook his frame, his teeth chattering.

"Come on, let's get you warmed up." Shiloh slid their hands down Bellamy's arms, his skin cold and wet. They grabbed his hand, pulling him inside.

Shiloh's touch was grounding in a way that Bellamy didn't understand. He was so aware of their presence, and the warmth of their touch lingered on his skin, leaving a trail of heat down his arms. He still couldn't sort through everything else that was raging inside of him, but he grasped onto that warmth, noticing nothing else as he was led upstairs and into a room.

Shiloh disappeared to run the tap to the shower, and Bellamy shrunk even deeper into himself with every second they were gone. Cold droplets fell from his hair and clothes down to the floor, and he was standing in a small puddle by the time Shiloh returned.

"Legends, Ranger." They shook their head, wings fluttering at their back in a mix of exasperation and sympathy. "Look at me, Bellamy." They put their hands on either side of his face.

The pressure of their thumb against his scar is what pulled Bellamy to the surface. He blinked, beginning to register the warmth of their skin against his cheeks.

"You're freezing. I can put you in the shower, but it'll be best if we start your clothes drying now." Shiloh still held his face, and he let his cheek lean into their hand, increasing the pressure on the bottom of his scar, the raised tissue itself void of feeling, but the skin around it and the muscle beneath it making the touch more than readable. "I can help you, but I need you to acknowledge me."

Bellamy shivered, the cold seeping into his bones, and blinked again. He was so cold, and their hands were very warm.

"I'm not about to be arrested for stripping a Ranger of the Royal Guard." Shiloh drummed their fingers against his cheek. "You can go in there in your clothes, but then you'll be wet for a good long while."

Their words finally sunk in, and Bellamy, teeth chattering, nodded. He closed his eyes when Shiloh dropped their hands from his face, trying to hold on to the warmth that lingered there. He raised his arms with more effort than it should have taken, bending forward slightly to allow Shiloh to peel the drenched fabric from his body.

Goosebumps raised across his skin as cool, dry air washed over him, his hair still dripping down his back.

Shiloh knelt in front of him, unlacing his boots and lifting first one foot, then the other, to take them off. They stood, tugging the laces of his pants. "Usually I would offer to buy you dinner first," Shiloh joked, not expecting Bellamy to respond, but more out of habit. They needed to bring down the tense atmosphere. Everything was so stiff and cold, and they knew they'd have to pull Bellamy from that headspace.

Clothes discarded on the floor, Shiloh led a naked Bellamy into the bathroom and under the warm spray of the shower. "I'll be right back, okay? I'm going to see what can be done about your clothes."

Bellamy stood, steam billowing around him and pinpricks lighting across his extremities where the water flushed away the cold, bringing feeling back to his toes and fingers. He flexed them, letting his head tip forward. His hair fell around his face, curls matted together in a solid curtain as water streamed down them. He braced his palms against the tile beneath the showerhead, letting the thunder of water against his head and back drown out everything else, letting his mind go blank.

"I'm here." Shiloh's voice filtered through the void. "When you're ready to come out, I'm here."

Bellamy opened his mouth to acknowledge them, but he didn't have any words. So he closed his eyes, tipping his face up to the water and giving himself over to the heat and the semblance of oblivion it provided.

He couldn't have said how long he stood there, but he slowly started to come back to himself, and he blinked, taking in his surroundings. Embarrassment crept up his cheeks, knowing how numb he'd gotten, how helpless Shiloh had seen him.

Bellamy turned the tap off, and his eyes flicked to motion just outside of the tiled shower area as Shiloh hopped down from the counter they'd been seated on, grabbing a towel to offer him.

"If you're okay in here, go ahead and dry off. I'll run down to the tavern and grab some stew." Shiloh backed toward the door.

Bellamy held the towel in front of him. He'd spent enough time in the communal showers in the barracks not to feel self conscious about his body, but standing in front of Shiloh felt different. Maybe because of how raw the fae had seen him, but part of him wanted to shield any perceivable weakness. "Shiloh," he called as they turned to leave.

They stopped, looking back at him and meeting his gaze.

"Thank you."

Shiloh smiled, waving him off as they opened the door, steam drifting from the small space.

Bellamy leaned forward, squeezing as much water out of his hair as he could before toweling off the rest of his body. He wrapped the towel around his waist and walked into the main room. Shiloh had wrung out his clothes, then draped them over a chair next to a small fireplace to dry. They were still incredibly cold and damp, so Bellamy sat on the bed, folding his hands in his lap and twisting his fingers together, anxiety starting to creep back over him.

Shiloh returned shortly, two steaming bowls of stew and a loaf of bread on a tray. They set it on the bed, sitting down on the other side of it. "I would offer you some clothes while yours are drying, but—" They gestured down at their narrow hips, then to Bellamy. "I'm not sure if you've noticed, but your thighs are like tree trunks. You can wrap up in a blanket if you want, though."

Bellamy chuckled, their joking easing something in his chest. "I'm okay, as long as you're not uncomfortable." The air in the room was warm now that he wasn't soaked and already freezing.

Shiloh ripped the loaf in half, setting one portion next to the bowl closest to Bellamy, and began eating.

Bellamy wasn't sure if he was hungry. He hadn't had much of an appetite since Ryddan's disappearance, but once he took a bite, he was ravenous, and devoured the stew without finesse.

Shiloh didn't ask Bellamy to talk, just sat comfortably across from him as they ate. The calmness of their presence, the lack of expectation, was like a weight off his shoulders.

Bellamy set his empty bowl down on the tray, and, without making a conscious decision to talk, words fell from his lips. "I've been the head of Ryddan's guard for a year now," he said softly. "Both of his parents are dead, and I … I'm not presumptuous enough to claim him as my own, but I love him like he is."

"Do you know what it was that took him?" Shiloh asked.

Bellamy swallowed, picking up a cup of water and running his thumb over the rim. "Demons, like the ones responsible for Oren's and Gressia's deaths." He blinked. "He shares their blood. The demons, I mean. But he's not like them."

Shiloh put their hand on his leg, at a loss for words, but wanting to be of comfort.

Bellamy finally looked up, meeting their eyes. "He's not like them, and I'm scared for what that means, now that they have him."

"You think they'll hurt him," Shiloh voiced the fear that Bellamy had left unnamed since Ryddan's abduction.

Bellamy tightened his grip on the cup, the wood groaning slightly with the pressure before he released it. "He's just a kid. He's smart, and his magic is strong, but he's just a kid."

"It's not your fault, you know that, right?" Shiloh asked softly.

Bellamy's eyes were flat and morose as he looked at them, a shiver running through his body. "Isn't it?"

Shiloh tilted their head to the side, something in their expression going hard as they scoffed. "No, it's not. Is this self-deprecation going to help get Ryddan back?"

Bellamy blinked in surprise at the shift in their tone. "No, but—"

"No." Shiloh folded their arms across their chest. "Unless you called forth those demons or were given advance notice of their attack and didn't tell anyone, that's the last I want to hear of you trying to claim fault. Be sad, be mad, be scared, but don't make this your fault. That isn't going to lead anywhere productive."

Bellamy swallowed past the lump in his throat.

Shiloh moved the tray to the floor and turned to face him more fully. "You love him, that's what's important. That's what he'll hold on to. He'll know you're going to come for him."

Bellamy nodded, at a loss for words.

"Here, I want you to have something." Shiloh leaned back, opening a drawer in the bedside table. They handed Bellamy a large sliver of purple stone, white cracks running beneath its polished surface. "This is amethyst. It's good for protecting, purifying, and a few other things. Most importantly, it'll act as a totem. When you start to slide back into that cloud of despair, hold it in your hand and picture all of those dark emotions spilling into the stone. Acknowledge those feelings. Tell someone they're there, but don't let them overtake you, okay?"

"Amethyst." Bellamy set his cup on the floor to turn the stone in his palm. "It's magic, like umbrite?"

Shiloh smiled, closing his fingers over it. "Not in the same way, but perception is often stronger than reality."

Bellamy looked at where their long, slim fingers lay over his, hiding the stone from view. He could feel the cool weight of it against his skin, and it, too, was a comfort. He turned his eyes up to meet Shiloh's, their gaze open and free of judgment. "Thank you," he whispered, a different sort of tightness squeezing his chest.

MOLLIAN WAS MUCH MORE relaxed after spending the day preparing to leave. Even though handing over matters of state to different guildmasters and setting up a chain of command to keep the country running smoothly in his absence was stressful, he still felt better with a plan in place. Even knowing the nymphs' full moons rite might have assisted the demon's breakthrough seemed to further calm him. Information and knowledge had always been his comfort, and each new circumstance around Ryddan's abduction that came to light only added to his confidence that they would be able to save the young prince. While he was still worried, he had quickly regained his ability to think through things with logic instead of just emotion.

But Merriam was antsy. They would be leaving in the morning, and she was way too wired to sleep. She couldn't stop thinking, and with nothing productive to put the thoughts toward, she kept circling around what-ifs that became darker and more dreadful with each play-through.

The weather seemed to match her mood, rain lashing against the side of the castle as the wind howled.

She threw on a cloak, shoving her feet into boots that she didn't bother to fully lace. "I'm going for a walk," she told Mollian, who was sitting at the desk, going over a few final statements that would need his approval before they left.

"I can go with you," he offered, pushing back his chair. With Ryddan gone, the memory of her own abduction was ever-present in his mind, and his magic rushed through him, carried by anxiety at the thought of her leaving.

Merriam walked over to press her palm to his, feeling his surge of agitation. "No, I'll be fine. I just need to move."

But she needed more than just to move. She needed to be distracted, and her old habit had always been to find someone to divert her attention. Without making a fully conscious decision to do so, she ended up outside of the Ranger barracks.

Merriam wrapped her cloak tighter around her, water streaming from her hood, and bit her lip before slipping inside and up the stairs to the third floor. She knocked on Rovin's door, and he answered after a moment, a look of surprise on his face.

"Mer?"

She slipped past him, and he closed the door behind her.

"Aren't we leaving early in the morning?"

Merriam nodded, unclasping her cloak and letting it drop to the floor before stepping into him and wrapping her arms around his waist. Her head settled against his chest, listening to the steady beat of his heart as his warmth soaked into her.

After a moment's surprised hesitation, Rovin hugged her close, his chest tightening with the knowledge that she'd come to him for comfort. He pressed his lips against her hair, breathing in her smell of petrichor and wildflowers.

Merriam tilted her head up, eyes fluttering closed as her mouth found his. She kissed him, pulling his bottom lip into her mouth and running her tongue across it as she melted further against him. Desire chased everything else from her mind—desire for *him*, and if she had the where-withal for a coherent thought, the strength of her hunger for him might have irritated her. But she didn't process anything past recognition of

Rovin's body flush against hers, still not close enough to douse the need that sparked in her core.

His hold tightened around her, one hand traveling up to the back of her head as he deepened the kiss. His tongue swept into her mouth, and her resulting whimper made his pants grow uncomfortably tight.

Her hands dragged from his back around to his stomach, sliding under his shirt. Merriam's fingers were cold, but a wake of heat followed where her nails raked across his skin. Then her fingers were at his belt, slipping it free of the buckle, and Rovin's hands dropped to hers, halting her.

He broke the kiss, but trailed his lips across her jaw, not wanting her to feel rejected. "You can talk to me," he whispered against her neck, pulling away to look her in the eyes.

Merriam tugged against his grip. "I need you," she pleaded.

"You're not okay." His thumbs brushed over the backs of her hands, and he pulled her over to the bed.

She glowered at him. "Do you want to talk, or do you want to get your dick wet?"

Rovin's brows lifted at her crassness, and he shook his head with a chuckle. "I think *you* need to talk." He sat, attempting to guide her down next to him.

Merriam pulled back, and this time, he released her. She crossed her arms over her chest. "I'm not here to talk. I can talk with a dozen other people if I wanted to talk."

Rovin searched her face. "You can talk to me, too."

"But I don't *want* to fucking talk. I need a release." Merriam dug her fingers into her sides.

"I'll go to the training ring with you. We can fight it out if you have pent up energy," he offered.

Merriam scoffed, throwing her hands out. "I don't want to fight, Rovin, I want to fuck. I didn't think it would take that much convincing."

"I want to be here for you. The fact that you came to me means more than you even know, but fucking you will mean something to me, and I won't do it for the first time knowing it's just a release for you. Talk to me, vent all of your feelings and frustrations, but whatever relationship we have ... I don't want to just be a distraction to you. Let me be more than a physical crutch."

Merriam set her jaw, frustration tightening her throat. "Oren never made me talk about my feelings."

Hurt flashed through Rovin's eyes. "I'm not Oren." He stood, letting out a rueful laugh. "I know that you loved him, and I would never ask you to deny that or pretend it didn't happen." He searched her face. "But I'm not him, and if you're going to compare us, then I may as well end things now before I keep coming up short."

Merriam's stomach plummeted. "I'm sorry, I wasn't thinking." She reached for him, but he pulled away.

"I'm not patient or just or kind. I will push you out of your comfort zone, I will aggravate you, and I won't always give you what you want."

Merriam bit her lip, again wrapping her arms around herself.

"I want to be here for you and show up in every way I can. But I need you to trust me with your feelings, like I intend to trust you with mine." He ran a hand through his hair, looking away from her. "I can promise to be the best of myself, but ..." he trailed off, leaning against the edge of the small desk. His throat bobbed as he swallowed, meeting her gaze. "If this is going to work, we need to be partners. Equals. And that includes you having just as much consideration for my feelings as I do for yours. I don't care what Oren needed from you, what Mollian needs from you, what Bellamy or Jasper or Ryddan need from you. This"—he gestured between them—"is its own thing. And I need communication."

Merriam took a small step closer, reaching out again. This time, he stayed still, letting her touch his arm, her fingers drifting down to grab his hand. "I'm sorry, Rov." Her voice cracked. She knew she was being selfish, even if it hurt for him to call her out on it.

"What do you want from me, pet?" he asked.

Merriam closed the distance between them and slid a hand into his hair, brushing it behind his clipped ear and curling the ends around her finger. Her throat tightened, unsure how to answer. "I don't know."

"That's not good enough." But he didn't pull away from her.

Merriam released his hair to trail a hand down his chest, resting her palm over the steady beat of his heart. "Solace," she breathed, flicking her eyes up to him. "Give me solace."

Rovin exhaled, cupping her face in his hands and resting his forehead against hers. "Merriam."

"I'm not good at this," she said, curling her fingers into the fabric of his shirt. "At talking, at *feeling*. What I know right now is that I'm scared, and I don't want to be. I'm scared for Ryddan and for Molli and for Bellamy. I want something to fight, to slaughter, for making me feel this way, to *move* and forget everything that's out of my control. But I also want to feel centered and focused ..." Merriam brought her other hand up, closing her eyes as she felt his breath ghost across her face. "And I want you. Nothing else is right right now, and I can't fix any of it, but *you're* here and that feels right and that's what I want to focus on. That's *all* I want to focus on for a while."

Rovin's thumb brushed across her cheek, across her lips, and her mouth popped open with a shaky inhale.

"I want you, Rovin," she said again, her voice soft as she leaned back to look up at him. "Not as a distraction. Not as a release. Just you."

Rovin slid his nose against hers, a hesitant touch that made her stomach flip. Then he claimed her mouth, and there was nothing hesitant about it. His arms circled her, pulling her flush against him, one hand dragging down her back to squeeze her ass. He sucked her bottom lip into his mouth, his canines pricking her skin.

Merriam whimpered, sweeping her tongue across his as she rolled her hips against him, one hand sliding up his chest and tangling into his hair.

Rovin broke the kiss, trailing his lips across her jaw. "Thin walls, pet," he murmured against her skin.

Merriam slid her hands to the hem of his shirt, pulling it up over his head and meeting his eyes, the intensity of the lust in those brown depths making her stomach plummet deliciously, desire winding, undeniable and aching, in her core. "Presumptuous." Her voice came out light and breathy, and she tried to smirk at him but couldn't quite manage it, teeth sinking into her lip as she placed her hands on his chest.

Her eyes drifted from his gaze to watch the path of her hands, his muscles tightening underneath skin scattered with light scars, a fresh bruise visible on the deep tan skin over his ribs. Her fingers ran across it, and she flicked her eyes back up to his, hands finally settling against his hips.

Merriam brushed her lips up his neck to his jaw, tracing the same spot, now unmarked, where she'd cut him with her axe the year before.

Rovin shivered, his arms tightening around her, one hand gripping her braid at the base of her neck, tilting her face up to reclaim her mouth.

Merriam's fingers dug into his shoulders, her leg hooking around his thigh as she pulled herself closer to him. Rovin lowered them to the bed, and Merriam pushed him back, crawling on top of him. She felt his heart thundering in his chest, the ridge of his cock stiff against her thigh. He ground into her, and hot, heavy desire consumed her, the need to be filled now pulsing between her legs. She laughed softly in partial wonder.

"What?" Rovin asked, a smile tugging on his lips.

Merriam stroked her fingers down his face, tracing the bones of his cheeks and jaw, brushing his hair back from his temples. "I used to hate you," she whispered, trailing her lips down his cheek. "I used to hate you so. Fucking. Much."

Rovin caught her mouth in a kiss, dragging one hand down her back and digging the fingers of the other further into her hair. "And now?"

Merriam searched his eyes, his pupils blown wide with lust, but also something softer, something that both terrified her and simultaneously melted her insides, and she wanted nothing more than to lose herself in him. "Sometimes I wish I still did."

Rovin tipped his face up to her, trapping her bottom lip between his teeth. She whimpered, her fingers digging into his throat, and his cock throbbed between them. "You can pretend you do." He dipped his face into her neck, nipping at her skin.

Merriam rocked her hips against him, her hands dragging down his chest to work the laces of his pants.

Rovin sat up, pulling her shirt over her head and getting rid of her bra. He groaned, trapping a nipple in his mouth before pushing her to her feet to yank her pants down her legs, ripping her boots off and tossing them across the room.

Merriam stood naked in front of him, and his hand subconsciously moved to his crotch to adjust himself. Rovin pulled her back to him, his fingers digging into her hips. His cock was painfully hard, pressing against his pants, his heart pounding as need and lust surged through him. Every shadow of muscle, every scar, every stretch and mark and curve of her skin begged him for touch, for worship.

Merriam saw the hunger deepen in his eyes, and, holding his gaze, loosened the tie of his pants, sliding the fabric down his hips before climbing back on top of him.

"*Fuck,*" he whispered, pulling her closer. His hands spread over her back, pressing her against him. She rolled her hips, sliding against his length. He captured her mouth in a bruising kiss, biting her lip as he gripped her hips, lifting her. Moving one hand to grab his cock, he ran the tip through her wetness and fit it against her entrance.

Merriam sat up and dug her nails into his shoulders, sinking down onto his length. He stretched her, filling her, and a moan escaped her. Her head fell back, and she raised up before dropping back down, pleasure coursing through her.

"So fucking tight," Rovin growled, his fingers digging into her waist as he drove up into her.

She moved with him, and he gripped the inside of her thigh before pressing his thumb over her clit, circling. "Rov," she gasped, her fingers scratching down his chest.

"You'll have to dig a little harder than that if you want to hurt me."

Merriam met his gaze, the undiluted hunger there begging her to lose control as she rocked her hips, his thumb keeping rhythm. "Don't you dare stop, or I *will* hurt you," she panted, pleasure tightening through her abdomen, her breaths coming faster.

Rovin watched her, his eyes roaming her body, her mouth swollen from his kiss, small breasts bouncing as she moved with him. He wanted to take one of her pert nipples into his mouth, taste it, bite it, but he felt her tighten around him, and held back, not wanting to break her pace. His eyes dropped down to where they met, watching as his cock disappeared into her glistening heat, and his balls tightened. "Shit, Mer," he grunted. His own pleasure was coiled tightly at the base of his spine, and the noises coming from her were too fucking pretty.

He moved his hand from between her legs, and she whimpered at the loss of touch. He pulled her from on top of him, tossing her onto the bed and crawling between her legs.

Merriam sat up on her arms, but before she had a moment to speak, Rovin's mouth covered her cunt, tongue lapping at her entrance before his lips locked around her clit, and he sucked. She cried out, her legs tightening around his head.

Rovin bit the inside of her thigh. "Quieter, pet," he reminded her, his breath ghosting across her wetness.

"Rov, I can't—" her protest devolved into another whimper of pleasure, and she slapped one hand over her mouth, the other fisting in his hair as he licked her, his tongue diving inside of her before he focused back on that bundle of nerves that screamed for attention. She rocked her hips up to meet his mouth, the scruff of his beard scratching against the inside of her thighs.

Rovin peered up at her, an animalistic hunger in his eyes as he watched her come undone underneath him. He pushed two fingers inside of her, curling them against her front.

Merriam dug both of her hands into his hair, one strangled "fuck" escaping as the pleasure in her core exploded through her entire being.

Rovin kept his fingers inside of her, pressing his thumb to her clit as she pulsed around him, and he moved up her body, greedily taking the tip of a breast into his mouth.

Merriam's heart thundered against her ribcage. She lifted one leg, pressing her thigh purposefully against the solid ridge of his cock.

Rovin trapped her nipple between his teeth, tugging lightly as he thrust against her. Then he slipped his fingers from her, bracketing her head with his forearms as he leaned over her, kissing her neck.

"Needed a break, Lieutenant?" she teased breathlessly, tilting her head to allow him more access.

"Just a snack," Rovin said against her skin. He wrapped an arm around her, lifting her and flipping her onto her stomach. He pushed her knees up, shoving a leg between them. "Bite the pillow if you need to."

She looked back at him, ready to retort, but he slammed into her, his fingers curling against her thighs as he hissed. "So warm," he groaned. "So fucking wet."

Merriam pushed back against him with a whimper, relishing in the way he handled her. "You did this. I need more."

"So greedy." Rovin thrust into her, holding her steady.

"For you." Merriam gripped the sheets, gasping as he pounded into her. "Fuck, Rov. You feel so—ah—so good. Use me." Her voice was high and pleading, but her only focus was on the way she stretched around him, unable to speak when he dragged against that spot inside of her.

He leaned forward, pressing his lips to her shoulders. "I fucking love the dirty things that come from your mouth." He wrapped an arm around her, sliding his fingers over her still-sensitive clit.

Merriam did pull his pillow to her then, burying her face into it to muffle the noises that she couldn't hold back. Rovin had no fear of breaking her, and his animalistic need to take her was electrifying, a second orgasm curling tightly in her belly.

His fingers kept moving over her, and each thrust went so fucking deep, it wasn't long before she tipped back over the edge, coming un-done around him.

Rovin's eyes fluttered closed, his hands moving to anchor her hips.

"Legends, woman." The whisper escaped his lips as his entire body tensed at the feel of her squeezing him. He slammed into her a final time before pulling out as everything tightened inside of him, and he gripped his cock, catching his own release. Rovin rested against her back for a moment, both of them catching their breath. He kissed her spine, his other hand squeezing her hip before he rolled from the bed, moving into the conjoining bathroom where he quickly washed up and wet a towel to bring back to Merriam.

She still lay there, a thin sheen of sweat on her skin. She took the towel, smiling sheepishly in thanks. "Is the bathroom ... will someone walk in from the other side?"

"You can lock it from the inside." Rovin sat next to her.

Merriam pushed up, Rovin watching her unabashedly as she disappeared, closing the door. He threw the pillow back to the top of the bed, pulling the blankets back. That felt presumptuous, and he stood there for a moment in indecision. He heard the bathroom door open behind him and made up his mind. "Stay for a little bit?"

Merriam closed the door, locking it from their side before slipping past Rovin and crawling beneath the blankets.

He climbed in after her, and they lay on their sides, facing one another. Rovin brushed the back of his fingers across her cheek, tucking a stray lock of hair behind her ear.

"Come here often?" she asked, tucking the blankets up under her chin. They smelled like him. The musk of fallen leaves and fresh, bright notes of apple and, barely perceptible, the sweet silk of caramel underneath it all. Her stomach flipped, the intimacy of the moment hitting her. The way the warm brown of his eyes was so soft and vulnerable compared to when he'd been ravaging her.

"I like to consider myself a regular," Rovin replied, playing along with her joke.

"Mmmm," Merriam hummed, blinking sweetly at him. "And are you often accompanied?"

"Here?" Rovin clarified with a smirk. "My most frequent company has a penchant for blood and violent creatures and isn't quite my type."

Merriam laughed. "Kodi doesn't count."

"Then, no, I'm not often accompanied here." Rovin rolled, half leaning over her. "It's pretty exclusive admittance." He brushed a kiss across her lips.

Merriam smiled. "I like exclusivity."

Rovin dropped back to the bed, laying on his back, but his head turned to look at her. "You have mine."

Merriam's stomach flipped again, and she scooted closer, fitting herself beneath his arm to press her body against him and rest her head on his chest. She'd almost forgotten they were naked, and the feeling of his skin against hers affected her more than she wanted to consider. "You have mine, too," she whispered.

Rovin's thumb brushed over her arm twice before stilling, and he held her against him, marveling at how content he was to just be here with her.

"Tell me a story," Merriam requested. "Something from before you came to Umbra."

As they talked, sharing tidbits from childhood and teenage years in quiet voices, Merriam lazily ran her fingers through the hair on his chest, the warmth of his skin against her cheek soothing in a way she'd never expected to feel again. She wondered what it would be like to sleep next to him, if he would hold her through the night or if he would roll away, preferring to rest untethered. She bit her lip, drawing a pattern between his pecs. Would he expect her to stay tonight? Would she want to?

They would be leaving at the crack of dawn, and—

Merriam groaned, slapping her hands over her face. "I never started packing." *You never checked on Molli, either,* she chided herself. He hadn't been back to Entumbra since he'd been crowned, and she could only imagine what emotions he was suppressing in the interest of staying strong for everyone else. Guilt flooded her at having left him so quickly, and she scrambled from beneath the blankets, grabbing for her clothes.

"I'm so sorry," she told Rovin, pulling her shirt over her head. "I have to check in—"

"Mer," Rovin said with a laugh, and she stopped, looking at him. He sat up, his hair an alluringly disheveled mess around his face. "It's okay," he said, and she pulled up her pants, sitting on the edge of the bed to shove on her boots. "We've got nothing but time."

She bit her lip, the deep brown of his eyes sparkling with something so insanely soft that she had to look away for fear she would physically melt.

"I'll see you in the morning." Rovin grabbed her hand, pulling her into a lingering kiss.

"Have a good night, Ranger-man," Merriam whispered against his lips, running her fingers down the stubble on his cheek before standing to leave.

"Tell your *mehhen* I'm grateful he let me steal your time," Rovin joked, knowing her urgency could only be linked to Mollian.

Merriam gave him a playful glare before she turned to leave. "I will be doing no such thing."

MERRIAM WAS WIRED AND ready for action by the time they reached Entumbra. After two days of traveling by horseback, her skin was buzzing with the need to move. She wanted to head straight down to the Gate and test their luck using what she and Rovin had compiled with Bellamy's knowledge of Ryddan's demon side, but Mollian insisted it would save them time in the long run to cross-reference the information with the notes kept in Entumbra's library, that way they could more accurately pick their destinations and be better prepared for what they would face once they arrived there.

Regenya had seen their approach and was waiting at the base of the stairs when they arrived. A raven had been sent ahead with news of Ryddan's abduction and their plans to search for him using the Gate. She threw her arms around Mollian as soon as he'd hopped down from his horse, then smoothed his curls away from his face as she tried to fight back tears.

"I'm fine, Mother," Mollian assured her, returning her hug before gently pushing her back.

Matted white curls blew around the Keeper's face, crossing the aspen leaf crown that matched Mollian's. Her skin seemed to sag from her cheeks, and the dark circles under her eyes further emphasized her exhaustion. "How did they get through?" Regenya asked. "There wasn't a leak from here. The wards have been solid, and I've felt no disturbances."

Merriam stepped up to Mollian, holding her cloak around her against the cold wind blowing through the courtyard. "Our best guess? They used Basta's rings."

Regenya's brow furrowed, her bright green eyes turning to Merriam. "But the blood—"

"I think they used some sort of spell magic," Mollian interrupted. "The portal was only open long enough for them to take Ryddan and leave, and it stayed open the entire time. It wasn't Traveling, it was ... like they'd forced a hole between the two worlds. Unlike anything I've ever seen before. If they use Ryddan to hold something like that open ..." Mollian trailed off.

Regenya's face went ashen despite the cold, a hand rising to her lips. "They cannot take Entumbra," she whispered fearfully.

"The idea is to get Ryddan back before they have a chance to launch an attack," Merriam said.

"He must be so scared." Tears lined her eyes again, and her gaze lifted to the sky as she struggled to remain composed. "You have to find him, Mollian. Come, Darius has pulled some resources from the library. Every demon realm we have knowledge of." Regenya turned, leading the way up the stairs. Mollian followed, Merriam and Bellamy on his heels.

Rovin held back to help the Guard that escorted them get settled, leading the group to the stablehouse to show them where they could set up for the duration of their stay.

Darius was waiting for them in the library, and Merriam started in on the stack of books and papers he'd laid out. Bellamy and Mollian tried to help narrow down the pile, having profusely studied her notes, and set their possibilities to the side for her to glance over. Once everyone had settled, the former regents left to attend to other things around Entumbra that required attention, though Merriam suspected their absence was more because Regenya didn't want to be seen in such a fragile state.

It was slow going. Merriam remembered the heavy smell of sulfur, the indigo sky, the lightning that jumped from cloud to cloud. She remembered the smooth gray stone that stretched as far as her eyes could see.

But there was no way to know for sure that the whole world was made of the gray stone, or that the area closest to the Gate would be. There was no way to know that the lightning wasn't a passing storm or a seasonal phenomenon. Merriam chewed on the inside of her lip as she looked through the information spread in front of her, hesitant to rule out anything that had even one of the environmental qualities or seemed to have a creature in any way similar to any of the demons she'd seen.

She wanted to scream at the impossibility of it all. She'd been so confident that the Gate would read what she wanted in her Bonded blood and lead her right to Ryddan, but now that she'd seen the enormity of what an endless amount of realities truly meant ... she sighed, setting aside a stack of notes on a world she was fairly confident wasn't what they were looking for.

Bellamy glanced at her, and she gave him a reassuring smile. He'd been quiet the whole trip, and she couldn't blame him, but she didn't want to stress him out by voicing her fears. She could only imagine how much he blamed himself for Ryddan's disappearance, and her heart ached for him.

Don't give up hope, Mollian Cast.

Merriam looked up, meeting pale green eyes that watched her with concern. *What if I'm remembering all of this wrong? I was so hopped up on adrenaline. What if none of these details are helpful?*

They are. Don't second guess yourself, Ria. Trust your gut, it's not usually wrong.

Quit being so sage. Merriam peeked up at him from the book she was reading, a small smile on her lips.

Mollian winked, turning his attention back to the work in front of them. Truthfully, he was nervous, too. He was in no way prepared for a full-on war, and he knew that was exactly what he'd get if the demons were able to make it to Nethyl. The Gate had to be protected at all costs, or the fate of all life was at risk.

He was also worried about his nephew. He shared Bellamy's fear that Ryddan was too much a fae, too much a Keeper. If they were to hurt him ... he clenched his jaw, forcing his breathing to remain even as magic churned through him. He would tear every last one of them apart if

Ryddan was harmed.

The door to the library swung open, everyone glancing up as Rovin walked in.

Merriam turned away first, her teeth sinking into her lip as she focused on the writing in front of her.

Rovin pulled out the chair next to her, his arm brushing hers as he sat. "How can I help?"

Merriam pushed the stack of hopefuls his way. "Look through these and order them by priority, which realms are more likely to be what we're looking for. Just use your intuition."

"Sir, yes, sir," Rovin replied, not maliciously, perusing the paper on the top of the stack.

His elbow still touched Merriam's, and she made no move to push him away.

Mollian tipped his head to the side, curling his lips inward to keep the grin from spreading across his face. *You fucked him?*

Merriam felt her face flush and tucked her elbow against her side. Then, realizing the absurdity of the action, lifted her arm to scratch at the back of her neck, replacing it in its original spot next to Rovin's. *Yep.*

Mollian nodded demurely, his gaze falling back to the book in front of him. *So are you, like, a thing now?*

Merriam looked up at him with a scowl. *Is this really the time to be having this conversation?*

You had two days of travel to talk to me about it.

Sorry if my mind was otherwise occupied. I didn't know you'd want to hear about my latest escapades.

Flirty eyes on the road are one thing, but all this touching in public is another all together.

This is hardly public, Merriam retorted.

Elbow to elbow, all comfy cozy, Mollian teased.

I'll shove my elbow up your ass if you don't quit it.

Mollian choked on a laugh, which manifested as a sort of snort.

Bellamy's head lifted, looking first at Mollian, then Merriam. "It's creepy when you two have silent conversations."

Merriam glared at Mollian pointedly.

"What? You're the one who brought butt stuff into this."

Merriam threw her hands up in exasperation.

Rovin looked up. "Butt stuff?"

"Don't get excited, Arwood. My butt," Mollian said.

"Legends above." Merriam dragged her hands down her face.

"Why are you guys talking about sex, anyway? That doesn't—" Bellamy looked from Merriam, arms folded angrily on the table and amber eyes fixed on Mollian, to Rovin, watching Merriam curiously, to Mollian, meeting Merriam's death glare with a jubilant grin, and understood. "*Ohhh.*"

Merriam turned that fierce amber gaze toward him. "Bellamy, not a fucking word."

"I didn't even say anything!" he defended, raising his hands in protest.

"So heated," Mollian teased.

Merriam took a deep breath, turning her attention back to the books. "I refuse to let you goad me further," she said with finality, straightening her shoulders.

"Very well." Mollian dipped his head. *Just let me know if you'll be sleeping in my room or his.*

Merriam tossed a pencil at his head.

"May as well just say it out loud at this point. We all know this is about Rovin," Bellamy said, lifting a book in front of him to protect any potential assault from Merriam.

"Why are you talking about me and butt stuff?" Rovin asked warily.

Merriam dropped her head to the table with a groan as Mollian's laughter filled the room. "You're such a fucking child."

"If I'm a child, you're a child, and you shouldn't insult your king," Mollian said primly.

Merriam peered up at him. "Elbow. Ass. I swear."

"In that case, you're not invited to bunk with me. Rovin, she's yours for the duration of our stay."

Merriam held her hand up before Rovin could speak, a bewildered but amused gleam in his eyes. "Don't egg him on, please. Just let it go."

Rovin looked from her to Bellamy, who shrugged, holding back a smile. "Sir, yes, sir," he repeated his early statement.

"Does she make you call her that in bed?"

"Molli!" Merriam's voice was roughly three octaves higher than normal.

"Sir Marshal, actually," Rovin answered casually, flipping a page.

Bellamy and Mollian dissolved into laughter.

Merriam rolled her eyes, but a smile played on the corners of her lips.

Rovin pressed his leg against hers, mouthing a "sorry."

"Why did I expect you to stop making my life difficult?" she asked, shaking her head.

"There's a question with no fathomable answer," Rovin replied.

They eventually settled back into a comfortable silence, making quick work of the rest of the references.

Even though Bellamy's insides were still knotted with worry for Ryddan, being with his friends, interacting with them while they actively worked on finding the prince, helped ease some of those nerves. Shiloh was right, he didn't have to bear any of this alone, and it was good for him to be with people who would understand his pain. People who cared about him.

They had a solid list of realms sorted into what Merriam and Rovin felt most resembled the place they'd Traveled to before, and Mollian tucked it into his pocket, nodding solemnly as he stood. "Alrighty, then. Let's go find our princeling."

Merriam's hands drifted to her axes, fingers playing over the handles as they walked down the stairs to the belly of the castle. Mollian split off to inform his parents of their plans, catching back up before they started down the tunnel that led deep beneath the mountain.

Merriam and Mollian took the steps side-by-side, both familiar with the route and comfortable in the damp, dimly lit tunnel. Merriam could feel the magic of the Gate running through her, through Mollian's and Oren's Bonded blood, the tattoos on her back itching with the proximity.

Mollian's blood was also reacting to the presence of the Gate. He hadn't been back since he'd been crowned, stones from the Gate crushed into dust and mixed with the ink that crossed his brow. Subconsciously, he let his magic flow into Merriam, circling through the two of them as they neared the source of not just a Keeper's power, but the source of all energy for all worlds, all realms, all realities.

Rovin stayed close behind the two, unable to help thinking back to his first visit down to the Gate. It had been shortly after they'd discovered Gressia's death, when they'd first brought Ryddan to Nethyl from the world where Gressia had been hiding him. The air had been tense then; he and Merriam nothing more than reluctant allies against an evil deeper and darker than anything he wished to experience again. He forced back a dark chuckle at the thought. If those demons had found a way to Travel to Nethyl outside of the Gate, he knew they'd be back, and in greater numbers. He'd barely survived last time, and the thought of fighting more of them—of an all-out war—chilled him to the bone.

Despite having a few visits to Entumbra under his belt and having Traveled with Merriam or Mollian on multiple occasions, Bellamy had never been below the castle. A sense of excitement filled him the further down they went. A large part of it was action, doing something to search for Ryddan and bring him home, but he also knew he was about to see something that not many were privileged to see, and he was about to visit worlds that no one from Nethyl outside of Keepers, the Stonebanes, had ever seen before. It would be dangerous—he had no misconceptions about that—but he couldn't help the curiosity-fueled sense of adventure that pushed out any fear he felt.

Further down the four of them went, the air damp and cold, lit by strips of light along the floor, until the tunnel opened up into a massive cavern. The Gate was at its center, orydite and umbrite sparkling in the light as they wrapped around each other.

Rovin set his teeth against the eerie vibrations in the air. The fact that the Gate held more magic, more power than anything else on this planet—or any other—was indisputable. Energy radiated palpably from the stones, even without any of its properties in his blood.

Bellamy's eyes were wide, filled with awe as he stared at the arch. "It's so much … smaller than I expected," he said softly. For something that clearly held so much magic, he'd expected it to be gargantuan. But he would be able to run a hand over the uppermost part of the arch, even if he couldn't reach the top of the stone as easily. The opening in the arch was only a few heads taller than him.

"Shh, don't offend it," Mollian said, digging their list from his pocket to look over once more.

Merriam rolled her eyes. "It's not sentient," she assured Bellamy.

Mollian pulled a knife from his belt, cutting a shallow line across three of his fingers, squeezing them into a fist to bring his blood to the surface. "Remember, stay together and don't engage unless we have to. We're just doing reconnaissance right now."

Rovin grabbed Merriam's hand, threading his fingers through hers in an act of comfort. She squeezed, tugging him half a step closer. "Just like last time, only less perilous," she joked.

"Sure, just like last time." He shook his head as Mollian swept his hand over the arch, eyes closed in concentration. "When you were almost possessed, and I was thrown around like a ragdoll."

"Don't forget the demon that almost ripped your arm off," Bellamy added helpfully.

"I said *less* perilous," Merriam reiterated, turning her attention to the Gate.

The air inside vortexed, and Merriam was reminded of the way the sky looked when high on mushrooms. She shivered, meeting Mollian's gaze with a nod and letting go of Rovin's hand to rest her fingers against her axes. The free movement of her left hand, no longer splinted, was incredibly reassuring.

"Mind your face," Mollian reminded her, a flash of worry in his eyes as he scanned her temple, the bone healing but still fragile, before he stepped through. The air moved around him without any resistance. For a moment, he felt the almost heavy pressure of nothing, then he stepped through, the air thick with humidity around him, making him feel instantly sticky. "Well, they got the sulfur right," he coughed, eyes watering as everyone else came through.

Bellamy's eyes were almost comically wide, a soft wind blowing his hair back from his shoulders. He brushed a curl out of his eyes, the other hand resting on the pommel of his sword.

The ground was gray, rocky, and pitted with vents that spewed a strange, greenish steam. Merriam stepped forward cautiously, looking around and up to the sky, a lavender hue with three small suns shining through the haze.

"Is any of this familiar?" Mollian asked, wiping a tear from his cheek before scratching his neck. His skin was reacting negatively to something in the air.

Merriam shook her head, brows furrowed. "Yes, and no. Come on, let's go further."

As they walked, Bellamy would occasionally pull a chunk of white chalk from a bag at his belt, drop it to the ground and, with a slight press of magic, drag it across the stone before lifting it back up into his hand with a flick of his fingers, marking their way back.

Goosebumps covered Merriam's skin despite the warm environment. "Why is it so lifeless?" she asked quietly.

The only sound for the duration of their hike had been the scuffle of boots against rock and the soft hiss of steam from the strange vents.

Mollian scratched his forearm. "There's gotta be something we're missing here." He pulled the paper from his pocket. "Why didn't we write down what sort of life to expect?"

Bellamy shrugged, lifting his hair off his neck. "We only looked up places with demon-like inhabitants. Seemed kind of redundant to keep reiterating it."

Mollian frowned thoughtfully, shoving the paper back into his pocket and walking over to one of the vents, a round hole in the ground with a slightly raised lip where the gray stone had been broken open. He tried to push the steam back, throwing a flare of magic at it, but the particles were too small to grab onto, brushing out of the way, but not moving enough to be helpful. Tentatively, he reached out a hand.

"Molli, stop!" Merriam hissed, jerking him back. "You can't just touch the weird green steam."

Mollian gave her a withering look. "Well, I wasn't going to shove my face into it without testing to see if it was harmful. Besides, it's filling the air. If it were that bad, we wouldn't be able to breathe by now." He scratched his arm again, blinking heavily.

"I'm no medic, Your Majesty, but I think you might be allergic to it," Bellamy said.

"I think whatever lives here might be under the surface. Thought it might at least be worth a check." Mollian brushed his hair back.

"Let me." Bellamy walked up to a vent, tentatively reaching a hand into the steam, waggling his fingers around a bit. Satisfied that it wasn't going to eat away at his skin, he set his feet, leaning over the hole and peering down, blinking to keep his vision clear. "There are tunnels down there!"

"Oh, fuck," Rovin whispered.

Merriam turned to look at him, but he was facing away from the others.

"This isn't it. It's not the place." He turned around, reaching for Merriam. "We need to leave *now*."

She gave him a confused look, then her eyes caught movement behind him, and her face drained of color, mouth popping open in shock.

"Mollian, Bellamy," Rovin called, grabbing Merriam's hand.

"Who the fuck wrote the account for the creatures that live here?" Merriam asked as Rovin pulled her back toward the Gate.

"One of my aunts or uncles at some point down the line," Mollian answered unhelpfully, right on her heels with Bellamy beside him. "Maybe when that thing was just a baby."

Off in the distance, just visible on the horizon, was an absolutely gargantuan creature lumbering across the vast expanse of rock on two thick legs. From this distance, she guessed that, were the four of them to stand in a circle holding hands, they wouldn't be able to reach even halfway around one of those legs.

Its arms were thinner, two hanging at its sides and two propped up in front of it, and its head was basically indiscernible, but presumably at the top of the long, slender neck that looked fairly prehensile. "How fast do you think it is?" she asked.

Rovin squeezed her hand, peering at it. "I sincerely hope we don't have to find out."

It didn't seem like it had noticed them, continuing to amble along, but they hurried back regardless, not wanting to catch its attention or allow it to get any closer.

Bellamy haphazardly scuffed at the chalk marks as they passed them, trying to obliterate them without wasting much time. "How often do you think it rains here?" The thought of that monster stumbling through to Nethyl raised the hair on the back of his neck.

They made it back to the Gate, which, in this world, was just a vague arch-shape raised against a large rock. When Merriam grew close to it, she could feel the orydite and umbrite, but faintly, as if it weren't quite *in* this world, but just outside of it.

They pushed through without preamble, the energy in Mollian's blood flaring as they passed back. He let out a sigh as the cold air brushed his skin, cooling the moisture that seemed to coat it. "There's one off the list," he said, scratching the back of his hand. "What was it, twenty? Fifty more potentials?"

Bellamy threw a cloak at Mollian. He'd discarded it before going through, so its surface was free of the other realm's air.

"Thanks." Mollian wiped the fabric across all of his exposed skin, ruffling his hair and brushing off his clothes for good measure. "None of you were absolutely miserable there?"

Merriam shrugged. "I've heard the skin of royalty is typically more delicate."

Mollian flipped her off before pulling the paper out again and checking the next location. "Are we all good to go?" They nodded, and he again cut open his hand, opening the Gate to the next location.

They repeated this three more times, exploring each for a while before deciding it was safe to rule out. Twice they had ended up attacked by some sort of animal, but so far they had yet to encounter a being with any sort of operative intelligence. Several hours had gone by at this point, and the group trudged up the stairs to eat, deciding they would try more after supper.

"Anything?" Darius asked as they appeared in the dining room. Regenya sat next to him, looking at Mollian with enough hope in her eyes to send a punch through Merriam's gut.

Mollian shook his head, a curl spilling over his brow. "No, but there are still many more worlds to search."

Dinner was a dismal affair, though the food was good. Regenya and Darius offered to search, either with their group or on their own, but Mollian waved his parents off. "How long has it been since either of you was in a fight?"

"Your father is an expert swordsman, Mollian."

Darius put a hand over his wife's, caramel brown eyes crinkling in the corners as he smiled at her. "I *was* an expert, my love. And while I could still lay him on his ass in a spar"—he winked at his son—"Mollian is right. Our presence is best served here. We can continue the research, make sure there's nothing they missed. And when they do find where Ryddan was taken, we'll be ready. We can help then."

"I'm just so worried about him. He's still so young." Regenya hugged herself, hands running up and down her arms.

"We'll find him," Bellamy said quietly, eyes on the food in front of him.

"So much rests on his shoulders," Regenya sighed. "Life is already so unfair to him."

Merriam tilted her head to the side, indignation in her eyes. "*Nothing* rests on his shoulders. He is a *child*."

Regenya met her gaze, shock at Merriam's tone winning out over any other emotion. "I beg your pardon."

"He's a Stonebane prince, but he was not born into a predetermined line of succession for the Gate *or* the throne. Mollian can produce an heir. Hel, with how much Stonebane blood runs through my veins, *I* can probably produce an heir—"

Rovin choked on his food, coughing quietly and bringing a cup to his mouth to try to cover up the disturbance.

"So Ryddan has *no* forced responsibilities. He's in the same position Molli was: an anomaly born with no set destiny. When he is grown, he can choose his own path. If he wants to be in line for the throne, he has a claim. If he wants charge of the Gate, this is his home. But nothing will be forced on him while he's six fucking years old." Merriam's nostrils flared, fire in her amber eyes. She could feel Mollian's magic, agitated with the Gate's proximity, swirling in her veins, and not for the first time, she wished that she could wield it, if only to further punctuate her point.

Bellamy was watching her with adoration in his eyes. As it was, he would never have been able to speak to his former queen in such a way. But he was reminded once again that Ryddan had people who loved him and would stand up for him, and his chest tightened with thankfulness that he had found his way into this circle of chosen family who would protect each other at all costs.

Bellamy noticed Rovin also staring, his brown eyes heated with something much different than the emotion in Merriam's. Bellamy subtly kicked the lieutenant, fighting back a smirk when Rovin's gaze shot to him, at first irritated and then embarrassed, a slight flush crawling up his neck.

"You have always been so freely vocal, Merriam." Regenya's words were short and clipped. "Stonebane blood may run through your veins, but—"

"Mother," Mollian cut her off smoothly, his voice even. "Don't say anything you may come to regret. Merriam speaks with my authority. Always. As my *mehhen* and as Sekha's Marshal."

Regenya leveled her gaze at her son, and they stared each other down for several moments.

Bell's right, the whole silent conversation thing is creepy when you're not privy to it, Merriam Cast to Mollian, ripping a chunk from a loaf of bread and dipping it into a bowl of soup.

Mollian snorted, breaking eye contact with his mother. *She tries, you know. But she is so used to being a regent.*

Probably grates endlessly on her that the female who shares your bed is anything but regal.

And won't provide me any heirs.

Merriam gagged jokingly and dropped her bread, pushing her bowl away. *And now I've lost my appetite.*

Mollian laughed, and Rovin watched her curiously. Bellamy rolled his eyes. "Creepy," he sang at them under his breath.

Darius gave them all strange looks, standing and offering a hand to his wife. "Mollian," he started, then stopped, taking a breath.

Mollian glanced up at him.

She only tries to help, his father Cast. *I know you never saw eye to eye, but she loves you, and she's scared for your youth and the youth you fill your council with. But she does trust you.*

Possibly it was from the lack of sleep or the added exertion from how much he'd used his magic already that day, but anger flared in Mollian, racing through his blood like a flame over tinder. "Do you?" he asked out loud, dropping his gaze to his mother. "Do you trust me? I know you didn't raise me the way you raised Oren. I know you never expected me to wear this crown, but it's *mine.* For better or worse, I rule Sekha." Mollian's hands shook, and he curled them into fists on the table.

"You speak of youth like five years really makes such a difference in this lifespan, as though the entire guild of masters isn't the same as the ones you left me with, as if the captain that *you* placed in charge of the Royal Guard didn't try to murder my *mehhen* so that he could get closer to me." Mollian shook his head in disgust. "You speak of youth like the decisions I make lack wisdom because I haven't lived as long as others. You judge me for naming Merriam marshal, but *she* is the one who killed Basta. She, *as nothing but a mercenary,* rid this planet of the greatest threat it has seen in millennia.

"You think I surround myself with people who lack experience, but Rovin has fought and killed more demons than any other member of the Guard—*without magic.* He went with Merriam to Basta's realm, determined to keep her and his country safe—*without magic.* And Bellamy, with less than a year as a Ranger, took on the responsibility of guarding Sekha's prince. Without batting an eye, he dedicated his time and energy to making sure Ryddan stayed safe and happy. More than that, he stepped in to fill a role that nobody else bothered to worry about. Not you, not me, not Merriam. Ryddan thinks of Bellamy as a *father.* Did you know that? All the times he's brought Ryddan to see you? That *he* is the one raising the prince, not just making sure he's safe and cared for, but making sure that he *feels* safe and cared for and knows that he always has someone to turn to. Twenty fucking years old, but Bellamy saw an orphaned child and opened his heart to him."

Mollian dropped his eyes to the table with another shake of his head, lips pinched together. "I understand that years can bring wisdom, but I also understand better than most that nothing can replace loyalty and trust, and those things cannot be bought. My inner circle is filled with people who would give their life for me without hesitation, not because of the crown on my brow, but because they know that I would do the same for them."

He pushed his chair back, standing up and tossing his napkin to the table. "Now, if you will excuse us, we need to find my nephew and save the universe from certain doom." Mollian walked to the stairs without turning around.

The cacophony of wood scraping against wood filled the dining room as the others moved to follow their king.

Darius stood silently, his hand holding Regenya's where she was still seated. Merriam fought the urge to turn and bow to them, not wanting to steal any of Mollian's thunder nor undermine his words with the admittedly childish pettiness.

Bellamy caught up to Mollian first, following him into the belly of the castle. "Molli." He put a hand on his shoulder.

Mollian stopped and reached up to rest his hand against one of the many arch supports. He took a breath, turning to face Bellamy and ready to apologize for outing something so personal in a fit of anger. But as soon as he turned, Bellamy's arms went around his shoulders, hugging him tightly.

"Thank you," he said softly, his chin resting on Mollian's shoulder and a lump in his throat.

Mollian blinked in confusion as he returned the embrace, meeting Merriam's eyes. She watched him with a small smile on her lips, arms crossed in front of her.

"I hope you know I never would have forced that acknowledgement. I have never expected anything for it, and I never will. But thank you for validating it, regardless." Bellamy squeezed him again before releasing him and stepping back.

"That kid adores you, Bell," Mollian said, placing a hand on his shoulder. "It's easy to see how much he looks up to you, how much your approval means to him. And you handle his fits and tantrums with more patience than I could ever muster. You've been more than just head of his guard for quite a while now. And you should claim him. If you want, I mean. I can grant you guardianship."

Bellamy faltered, taking a step back. "I ... what?"

Mollian smiled with a casual shrug. "Plenty of other Rangers have families."

"Molli, I," Bellamy swallowed, shaking his head. "You would let me claim him as my ward? Officially?"

Mollian grasped Bellamy's face in his hands, pressing their foreheads together. "Let's go find your kid, Bell." He stood straight, passing the other two to head toward the tunnel. "You got anything touchy-feely to say, Arwood?" he teased.

Rovin shook his head, one hand holding Merriam's. "I'm thankful to have earned your trust, Stonebane."

Mollian glanced down to their clasped hands. "You saved her, even when you were still at odds. I'll never forget that." He met Rovin's eyes again, unable and perhaps unwilling to communicate that he couldn't have gone on without her.

Merriam saw it, though. *You have me forever,* she promised him. *My soul is inseparable from yours, so you don't have much of a choice.*

The corner of Mollian's lip pulled up into a smile as he turned to lead the way down to the Gate. *You're a twat.* A brief pause. *And I love you.*

There was a stronger, renewed sense of companionship between the four of them as they stepped up to the Gate. They would find Ryddan, whatever it took, and they would be better for it because they were together.

Merriam felt an ache in her heart at the thought of the mercenaries and how much danger she'd waltzed into with them at her side. This was a similar feeling, knowing she could trust these people with her life.

She bit her lip, glancing at Rovin as Mollian opened the Gate. *How the tables turn,* she thought, moving her focus and stepping through.

It was night here, or she thought it must be. The sky was filled with blues and purples of every possible hue, sparkling with swirls of thousands and thousands of stars. Merriam tipped her head back, eyes wide as she stared.

Bellamy's expression matched hers, hand dropping from the hilt of his sword as he took everything in, eyes shining with wonder. "This might be the most beautiful sky I've ever seen."

Merriam silently nodded in agreement.

They were at the edge of a forest, some sort of black evergreen dotted the gently sloping land in front of them with large stone buildings in the distance. This was the first world they'd visited that appeared to house some sort of civilization.

Merriam brushed her fingers over the carved grooves on her axes. "So how do we play this, then? I don't suppose we walk up and ask if they've recently stolen a prince?"

"While wielding our weapons, preferably. Let them know we're a threat," Mollian said sarcastically.

"We should find a place to stake out. Watch for life, for a person. If they seem similar to the demons we fought last summer, then we can head back to Entumbra and do more research on the place," Rovin suggested, looking at Mollian in deference.

Mollian nodded. "We'll have more luck finding someone if we head further in toward the city, but lie low."

They hid in the trees, watching for any signs of life. It was hard to tell how much time had passed. No large celestial bodies were floating across the sky, just endlessly swirling bands of stars, like galaxies hanging over the atmosphere. Merriam stretched her legs out, one and then the other, massaging the muscle above her knee when Mollian spotted movement.

A jaguar, fur so dark its spots were just visible, was running down the hill to the city. Its coat was shiny, muscles rippling in the light from the stars.

That doesn't look like our kind of demon, Merriam Cast to Mollian, but her mouth dropped open when, mid-stride, the jaguar shifted into a person before walking between two buildings. Her hand went to her axe, and she looked at Mollian. "He shifted," she said quietly.

"He looked so much like us, though," Rovin pointed out. "None of the demons we saw had our skin, not even the one in Basta."

"Ryddan looks like us," Bellamy said. "If he has a fae form, any other demon may be able to shift into one, too."

Merriam bit her lip. "I don't know. Rydd is a Keeper, that's a powerful blood magic. He's never not looked like himself outside of when he's an animal."

"Let's go back to the Gate. We'll mark this place down as a potential and look deeper into it," Mollian decided.

A thread of hopelessness worked its way through Merriam as they hiked away from the city. With an innumerable amount of realities, how would it be possible to locate a single, specific one before it was too late?

THEY TRIED TWO MORE worlds after the one with the shifter, but none looked even remotely as established. By that time, they were all tired and a little disoriented from crossing through so many different realities.

"Let's get some rest," Mollian said, running a hand through his hair with an exhausted sigh. "We'll head out again at first light tomorrow." He caught Merriam's eyes, and she nodded. "Can you guys make it back up on your own?"

"It's one tunnel, Molli. I think we can manage." Bellamy rolled his eyes, but his expression was soft with understanding, and he turned to Rovin. "Lead the way, Lieutenant."

Rovin glanced at Merriam, confused. "You're not coming?"

She bit her lip, twisting the end of her braid through her fingers. "In a bit. There's someone we need to see first."

He understood, then, giving her a small smile before following Bellamy out of the cavern.

Mollian led her through the narrow passageway that opened up into the crypt that held the remains of all the past Keepers. It had been over a year since he'd visited, and he was unprepared for the depth of pain that washed over him when he saw where his siblings lay. The soft blue glow from the bioluminescent moths reflected off his curls, making him look almost ethereal as he approached Gressia's grave.

"You raised a smart kid, Gress," he said. "He keeps us all on our toes, but I can't imagine life in Umbra without him anymore." His voice caught in his throat.

Merriam wrapped her arms around his, leaning her head against his shoulder.

"They took him," Mollian choked out. "I tried to protect him, but they came for him, and they took him." A feeling of inadequacy, of failure, washed over him, and his magic reacted to the agitation with a forceful surge in his veins. He pushed a hand through his hair, taking a breath that was as equally shaky as the movement. "I'll get him back, Gressia. I promise we'll bring him home." He squeezed Merriam's hands with one of his.

She released him, letting him step forward to rest his fingers against the lip of the alcove. His despair was thick in the magic that coursed through her, but she stood back, knowing he needed to work through it on his own and knowing he knew she was there if he couldn't.

He eventually pushed away, turning to where his brother's body rested as he wiped the back of his hand over a cheek. Tears still glittered in his eyes as he blew out a heavy breath.

Merriam rested her shoulder next to the head of Oren's grave, trying to hide the concern that was plain on her face.

"I'm not sure how much of that you overheard, but I'm kinda fucking up your country, and I don't know if I'm qualified to be fixing it."

Merriam's brow furrowed, and she shook her head. "Don't—"

"But Ria's fucking a Ranger, and I think that's probably a lot more shocking," he interrupted her.

Her mouth dropped open, and she couldn't stop the surprised chuckle that bubbled from her chest. "What the fuck, Molli?"

He shrugged, an unrepentant smile playing at his lips. "Figured I'd go ahead and get it out in the open, save you the awkward beating around the bush."

You're an ass. But she knew he'd broken the mood for her sake, refusing to let her sink into any amount of guilt at moving on. "I like him, O," she admitted, looking down at her boots. "I'm not even really sure when it happened, but ... I like him." She paused, letting the familiar wave of grief wash over her with his memory. Her eyes closed, and she pushed away everything else until she felt his magic running through her blood, reminding her that he was always there. She opened her eyes with a soft sigh, gripping the edge of his grave. "Your meddling brother has plenty to catch you up on, I'm sure, so I'll leave him to it." Mollian grinned, and she thumped the center of his chest.

He pulled her to him, planting a kiss on the top of her head. "I'll be up soon."

She nodded, letting him have the time alone. "I still miss you," she whispered before she left.

Breathing got easier the further she climbed, the weight of the magic in the Gate and her blood lessening with distance. As Merriam trudged up the spiral staircase that led from the belly of the castle, movement in the atrium caught her eye when she passed, making her backtrack. "Rovin?"

He stood from the chair he'd been sitting in, tucking his hands into his pockets as he walked over to her.

The fact that he'd waited for her tightened in her chest, and she bit the inside of her cheek to force back the wave of emotion that crashed against her psyche.

"I think we do pretty good at this team stuff," he said.

Merriam rolled her eyes, but smiled up at him. "I'm saving that judgment until after our next trip into peril. Maybe we only fought well together when we wanted to be the ones to rip out each other's throats."

"You might be onto something there." Rovin chuckled.

Merriam bit her lip, her stomach flipping under the intensity of his gaze. "I'm glad you're here," she whispered. She took another step forward, lifting onto her toes to kiss him.

Rovin slid one hand free, grabbing her by the back of the neck and pulling her closer. Merriam's hands flew up to his chest as she moved her mouth with his, biting his lip and running her tongue across it. Rovin groaned, his hand tightening in her hair before he pulled back, breathless. "Where are you sleeping?" he whispered against her lips.

Merriam smiled, snaking her arms around his neck, her body flush to his. "With Molli, but you're welcome to join us."

Rovin chuckled, running his nose along hers. "Being watched isn't my thing, pet."

She stepped back. "Well, that's a relief, because watching isn't Molli's."

Rovin caught her hand, running his thumb across the back of her fingers. "You're okay, right?"

Merriam met his gaze, offering a small shrug. But he'd asked her for communication, and she'd promised to try. "I think so. It's hard working through what exactly I'm feeling right now, because it's not just about me. There are bigger things that I have to focus on, and I am absolutely going to use it as an excuse not to examine my own shit." She looked down to where his hand still held hers before peeking up at him again. "But I am glad you're here. I want you here."

Rovin tugged her closer, pressing a kiss to her temple. "I'll be wherever you want me, Mer."

She tilted her face up to him. "That's quite a declaration."

"Sleep well, Marshal." He stepped away.

She pulled him back in for another kiss. "Good night, Rov." Merriam headed upstairs and slipped into Mollian's room, ready for a quick shower and feeling half asleep on her feet. She had just gotten out and was drying off when Mollian came in, ripping off his shirt as soon as the door closed.

"I'm still itchy from earlier," he complained, examining his chest and back in the mirror for hives.

"You look fine," she laughed, rolling her eyes at his dramatics.

"Well, I feel miserable," he grumbled.

While Mollian showered, Merriam brushed out her hair, letting the repetitive motion soothe her. She was in bed by the time Mollian was out and dried, but she scooted close as soon as he crawled in next to her, pressing her forehead against his arm. "I still miss him so much," she whispered.

Mollian grabbed her hand. "Me, too."

"Do you think ..." she trailed off, swallowing. "Oren would have brushed my hair tonight. He would have tried to soothe all of my worry over this. But Rovin is also supportive. He looks at me like I'm strong and capable, but also like he wants to ride into battle at my side, and I ... I like the way that feels." Merriam blinked, her lashes tickling Mollian's skin. "Do you think Oren would be upset with me, for ..."

"For finding comfort in someone else?" Mollian finished.

Merriam swallowed.

"No, Ria." He rolled onto his side, pulling her into his chest. "He would be happy knowing you had found someone. He never would have wanted you to carry the weight of everything alone."

"I have you."

"You need more than me. You always have."

"Are you calling me needy?"

"Incredibly." Mollian smiled. "Oren would never begrudge that you moved on. If anything, I bet he's eternally amused that you're in bed with the enemy."

"He would get some sick enjoyment out of where my feelings have taken me, wouldn't he?"

Mollian released her, moving to his back. "I meant what I said earlier. Rov's good, and he proved that before he had feelings for you. Forget what Oren would have thought—I'd never let you latch onto someone bad for you. Your soul is still mine. I'm personally invested in protecting it."

Merriam's eyes dropped closed, a smile twitching at her lips. "So possessive, Lord King."

"Always," Mollian replied.

Mollian opened his eyes, a sense of dread immediately filling him at the nothing that filled his vision.

He was back in the darkness, and his magic woke in his veins, rolling through him with a hum.

It was happy, eager to be set free.

Mollian, exhausted, let it take control, flinging his hands out and letting it pull into the darkness. He'd done it so many times at this point that sinking his magic into the dark fabric took almost no concentration.

Pull, it whispered to him, and he did.

Rip, it whispered, and he threw his arms apart, widening the gap until bright, colorful light spilled free above him.

Tear, it whispered.

Mollian curled his hands into fists, dropping to the ground with a cry as the blackness fell away completely.

The tendrils of light spun through each other above him, and he panted, climbing back to his feet. "What are you," he whispered.

Shred, his magic pleaded.

Mollian licked his lips, reaching out a hand. His magic curled around a shimmering green cord, and he tried to trace its path above him, following it over and around others until it disappeared below him.

He picked another, shining gold, following it the same way, and again it ended underneath him. Another, and another, and all the same.

Mollian wrapped his magic around a blue cord almost hidden by the others in front of it, tugging curiously. It bounced slightly, but resisted his pull. He tightened his hold on it, tilting his head to the side as he tried to work his magic into the cord. A curl spilled over his forehead, his brow furrowing as he raised his other hand, tongue poking from the corner of his mouth in his concentration.

Slowly, he found a way through, his magic sinking into the tendril. Something was moving through it, streaming, pulsing with—

"What the fuck." Mollian dropped his hold, stumbling back in realization.

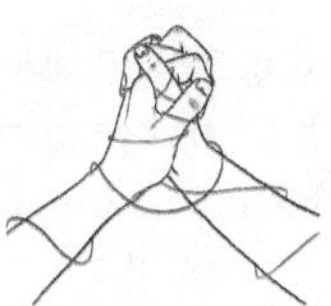

Merriam woke, arms flung out in front of her. She tucked them under her chin along with the blankets that had slid down her torso. There was a chill in the room, and she felt the cold along her spine. She scooted back with a sigh, searching for Mollian's warmth.

Her eyebrows pinched together, and she slid a hand back, patting around the mattress.

He wasn't there.

Merriam tucked her hand back in front of her, disgruntled at the inconvenience. She tried to go back to sleep, thinking Mollian had gotten up to go to the bathroom, but she was too awake and aware of the cold. *Fire, since you're up?* she Cast sleepily toward the bathroom.

No response.

She sighed, reaching out for him. Maybe he'd gone to get a snack.

But she didn't feel him.

Merriam sat up, rubbing the heel of her hand against an eye as she looked around, confused. She reached for him again, and felt a slight ping in her mind, but it was different, weaker than she'd ever felt it before.

Like he was there, but ... not.

She shivered, sliding out of bed as panic started to crawl up her throat, her heart rate speeding up. She reached up to the aspen leaf at her neck, sliding it across its chain as she forced even breaths. "Molli, where are you?" she whispered, looking around and reaching out again. The presence she could usually feel against her consciousness was there, but muffled, like it was covered by a blanket.

The wound tethers of their souls weren't stretched like when one of them Traveled, the distance between realities pulling them taut. They were still relaxed, but this almost scared Merriam more. Where was he?

She walked toward the door, intending to search for him and needing to move before the panic took over. She was about to reach for the handle when she was pushed forward, a wave of magic slamming into her back. Merriam threw her hands out to catch herself, a surprised cry leaving her mouth.

The sound of objects toppling to the floor filled the room at the same time, and she spun around, hair flying across her shoulders, the brush across her arms overstimulating in her shock, disorienting, and she stumbled back against the wall. "Molli?"

He was sitting in the bed, propped up on his elbows. His pale green eyes were wide, chest rising with heavy breaths. "Ria, what are you doing?"

Merriam shook her head, pushing her hair behind her shoulders. "Where were you?"

He blinked, looking up at her as she walked over, confusion clouding his eyes. "What? I had the dream again, I—"

"You Traveled," Merriam interrupted him, climbing onto the bed and tucking her legs underneath her. "I woke up, and you weren't here, Molli. You were *gone*."

Mollian licked his lips, dragging his hands through his hair. The details of the dream had once again faded, and he lashed out, tossing a lamp to the floor. "Fuck."

She reached for him, worry erasing her earlier panic. *Breathe.*

"I figured something out, Ria. There's something ..." He ran his hands down his face, shaking his head. "That place, I know what it is, but as soon as I wake up, I can't fucking remember. It all just ... I can't remember."

Merriam's mouth dried up as she watched his hands, and she reached out, pulling them from his face. "Molli, where are your rings?"

He glanced up at her in confusion. "I put them on the nightstand. I don't like the feel of them when I'm sleeping."

Merriam jumped up as soon as he'd started talking, moving to his side of the bed and searching the floor. She saw a glint of silver under the frame and reached out with a shaky hand, picking up the orydite from where it had fallen when Mollian's magic hit it. The umbrite was close by, and Merriam clasped the rings in her palm, looking up to meet Mollian's curious gaze.

"I'm not kidding, Molli," she said, sitting back on her heels. "You were gone when I woke up. You were gone, and then you were back in bed a second later. You *Traveled.* How is that possible? You weren't even wearing the rings."

Mollian took the jewelry from her and examined it in his palm. His mind raced, reaching for details that evaded him, sinking further away the more he tried to grasp them. "I need to remember. That place ... There was something about that place. I know it, Ria."

"Is sleep-Traveling even a fucking thing?" Merriam asked.

He laughed, the sound slightly manic. "If anyone could, I suppose it makes sense that I'm the third-born freak capable of it."

She crawled up next to him, grasping his shoulders. "Your magic has been stronger since you were crowned, more agitated. I've felt it. Have you told anyone else about the dreams?"

"Just Bellamy," Mollian answered.

Merriam chewed her lip, a million questions running through her head. "I felt you," she finally realized.

"What?"

"When you were gone. I could still feel you in my head. Muffled, but there."

Mollian's brow furrowed, and he shook his head. "No, that's not possible. If I were in a different ..." he broke off, a detail from his dream flickering just out of reach. "I figured it out before I came back. I know I did."

"Does Nethyl have another parallel, aside from Earth?" Merriam asked. She already knew they couldn't feel each other across that barrier, but maybe there was a closer world.

"No, Earth is the only flipside. There are realities that are close, but none as connected. If I can't feel you there, I shouldn't be able to feel you from anywhere else."

"You've only been there in your sleep?"

Mollian nodded.

"When you're stressed?"

He nodded again, watching the wheels turn in her head.

"You told me before your magic knew this place?"

"Yes," Mollian's heart started to pound, details slowly coming back to him. "I've never known what to do there. My magic just pulls for it." At the word, it began to swirl in his veins, and he shivered. "My magic takes me there. When I'm too preoccupied to keep a hold on it, it takes me there." He stood, rings toppling to the floor as he pushed his hands into his hair and paced. "It isn't *mine*, though. It's Keeper magic. The Gate's magic." He stopped, the feeling of touching that strand of light rushing back to him. "You felt me?"

"Yes," Merriam answered, holding her breath like Mollian held his. Their hearts pounded in sync.

"I don't think I was anywhere, Ria. I think I was between everywhere."

"THE LITTLE SHIT BIT me," Lyvin growled, shaking out his hand. Dark blood dripped down his fingers, spattering on the floor.

"Wrap it up, you are making a mess," Dronin told him.

"Someone should tell him not to pick fights with people who can rip his head from his shoulders," the greater demon muttered, licking the blood from the wound at his wrist and up his fingers. He pressed it against his shirt to staunch the blood flow, holding his arm to his chest with an annoyed glare.

"The djhulin posing a challenge for you, Lyvin?" Nevra stepped into the room with Donova at her heels.

"Did you get me any of *his*?" the sorceress asked, looking briefly at the faint stain of blood on Lyvin's fingers before flicking her gaze to his eyes.

"No, I did not get you any blood. I was too busy trying to keep all of my fingers without killing the bastard," Lyvin hissed.

Donova turned her gaze to Dronin. "I need his blood, Your Eminence. I have to have enough time to alter my spells before you launch your attack."

Dronin stood with a discontented sigh. "I will deal with him. Nevra, head back to the training grounds. Tell the other generals to prepare their legions for war."

"As you wish, My Djuhl," Nevra bowed low, waiting for him to pass so she could follow him from the room. "If I may, Dronin," she spoke as he began walking down the hall toward where the tiny part-demon was being kept.

The djuhl stopped, looking over his shoulder.

"The spawn is, mostly, one of us. He is young, impressionable, and he never knew Charn. A little bit of … softness could go a long way." Nevra's mauve eyes held his gaze evenly.

"Softness. Right." Dronin smirked, continuing down the hall. He opened the door, looking around the sparsely furnished room. His eyes narrowed, vertically slit pupils expanding slightly in the dim light. "It would do you well to come out, djuhlin."

Ryddan was huddled under the bed in the form of a pine marten, pressed tightly to the wall. He understood that the demon was not speaking Common, but the words still made sense. It was similar to the way an animal's calls and noises made sense when he took their form. Like an instinctive knowledge.

But he was not whatever creature those huge, taloned feet belonged to. So why did he know what it said?

"You do not have to be afraid." Dronin's voice rumbled through the room. "We are kin, djuhlin."

Ryddan shivered, pressing tighter into the corner.

"Your father was my brother. I know those others took you before he had a chance to raise you. Those others, the ones you have been with? They killed your father. Do you not think they are more dangerous to you than I would be?"

Ryddan shifted back into his fae form, green eyes glaring from the darkness. His tongue formed sounds that had never come from his mouth, but he didn't stop to question it. "Basta was evil. He killed my uncle and my mother, and he wanted to take over all of Nethyl."

Dronin lowered into a crouch, great wings flaring behind his back to keep balance. "Your father was Djuhl Charn, djuhlin, and he was a great warrior, only trying to better the world for his people." Lies, but they were sweet on Dronin's tongue when he saw the hesitation flicker through the spawn's eyes. Charn had been a fool, and now he was dead.

"You're wrong," Ryddan insisted, his voice small but angry.

"Come out from under the bed, young one." Dronin sat back on his heels. "If I was going to kill you, you would be dead already, and that flimsy piece of furniture would not save you, regardless."

Ryddan was scared, but it was stuffy under the bed, and he figured it would be easier to shift into something big and dangerous if he were out in the open. He pulled himself forward, climbing onto the mattress and bringing his knees up to his chest.

"Like it or not, this is where you belong. This is what you were bred for."

Ryddan scowled. "No, I'm a Keeper. I belong on Nethyl." Defiance flashed in his eyes.

Dronin was pleased with the spawn's spirit. Nevra was right; he was young, and there was hope that he would play to their side. Dronin just had to find the right words. "A Keeper? Is that what your mother was? That is where you get your magic?"

Ryddan lifted his chin. "Yeah."

Dronin fought back a snort at Ryddan's attitude and complete lack of deference. Anyone else who dared to speak to him in such a way would have their throat slit on the spot, but there was no denying the royal blood that fueled Ryddan's small body. "You have the eyes of a greater demon, though, so do they make you deny that you are also djuhlin?"

"Why do you keep calling me that?" Ryddan demanded. He was confused and scared and hungry, and all of it was making him irritable. He wanted to be held and comforted. And he wanted Bellamy. His throat closed up at the thought of his guardian, tears springing to his eyes. He blinked them back, digging his fingernails into his shins and forcing deep breaths the way Merriam had taught him to.

"That is what you are," Dronin said simply, watching the emotion in the spawn's eyes with guarded curiosity. "I am a djuhl. I rule this realm, every being under my power and at my command. My brother, Charn, was also a djuhl. As his spawn, you are a djuhlin and heir to all that was his."

Ryddan turned the words over in his mind, distracting him from the pang of homesickness. The meaning of the words sunk in, and he looked at Dronin with slightly less fear than before. "I'm an heir here, too?" He knew that word, and he knew it meant he was important. They couldn't hurt him if he was important.

"Yes," Dronin answered, watching him.

Ryddan picked at the leg of his pants, trying to make everything make sense in his mind. He no longer felt terror, but he was still sad, wary, and he was struggling to keep all of his emotions from spinning out. Something told him the demon wouldn't hold him, regardless of whether or not they shared blood. "I don't want to be an heir. I just want to go home." His bottom lip pushed out, trembling as he again wished for Bellamy. For Merriam or Mollian. Even Lydia, with her rules and restrictions, would be a comfort at this point.

"You have yet to even see any of this realm. How do you know you will not like it better?"

"Because I won't."

"You do not want to even give it a chance?"

Ryddan shook his head, squeezing his eyes shut.

Dronin's patience was running thin, and he grit his teeth, lips lifting in a silent snarl. "You bit my general." He wasn't sure why he said it, but he watched for Ryddan's reaction.

"He tried to grab me." Ryddan opened his eyes, still hunched over his knees.

"How did you manage to get the better of him?" Dronin asked.

"I was a wolf."

Wolf. This word was unfamiliar to Dronin, but he was entirely intrigued. "Show me."

In the blink of an eye, a large gray wolf stood on the bed, hackles raised and teeth bared.

Dronin ran a sharp talon along his jaw. *Interesting.* "Can you change into many forms?"

Ryddan, still as a wolf, nodded.

"You truly are a djuhlin, then." Dronin shifted into a wolflike form of his own, only his was three times the size of Ryddan's, with dark black fur, tall spines along its back, and a long, narrow mouth filled with needle-sharp fangs.

Ryddan crouched low, his ears flat against his skull. Then he cocked his head to the side, bright green eyes traveling over the creature in front of him, and shifted.

Ryddan's version of the demon was smaller than Dronin's, but otherwise the same. The room was overcrowded with both of them, and Dronin resumed his natural form, a smile splitting his lips despite himself. "That magic, the one to transform into any beast you desire, was a gift from your father, djuhlin."

Ryddan shifted back, glaring at Dronin. "That's not my name."

"What is, then?"

"Ryddan." He licked his lips in thought, peeking up at Dronin. "My father was your brother?"

"He was."

"And the shifter magic, that's his?"

"It is."

Ryddan nodded, not sure how he felt about all of this new information. He sat back on the bed, looking toward the door. "I still want to go home. I'm tired and hungry, and I want Belly." He folded his arms over his chest, half a vain attempt at physical comfort, half defiance at the attempt to build common ground.

Dronin had little tolerance for whining, and grit his teeth together as he forced back his annoyance. He needed the youngling's blood, then he could leave. "Your mother possessed portal magic—that is what she passed on to you?"

"Yes, but no one taught me to use it yet. It's different than shifting."

"There is a warlock here who can help, but she will need some of your blood to figure out how it works. I can take some to her so she can learn how to reach your other home, and I will have food sent to you on the way." Dronin approached the bed.

Ryddan's heart sped up in his chest, but he'd only heard home and food, and he would do anything for the former. He nodded, holding Dronin's gaze.

Dronin pulled a vial from the pocket of his pants, holding a hand out toward Ryddan.

Reluctantly, Ryddan held out his arm, watching with wide eyes as Dronin took it, pressing a sharp, black talon to soft brown flesh and slicing it open with ease. A searing pain raced up Ryddan's arm, and he whimpered, but watched as Dronin held the small glass tube to the wound, collecting the blood that dripped from it.

Without another word, Dronin stood. The clack of a lock latching behind him filled the room. Ryddan, still bleeding, fell onto his side, curling into a ball as loneliness and longing filled every inch of his small frame, and he cried.

"BETWEEN EVERYWHERE?" MERRIAM REPEATED, tipping her head to the side.

"The Gate connects everything, right? Feeds life and energy to every other world that exists?"

"I'm following."

"Presumably, if it connects everything, it has to have a place *where* it all connects. I think that's where I've been going in my dreams. I think that's where this place is. It's between everything else, where everything connects to the source." Mollian began pacing again, flexing his hands at his sides.

"Has anyone been … between … before?" Merriam moved back against the headboard, pulling the blankets up over herself.

Mollian walked to the fireplace, stacking logs and tinder. "I've never heard of it, no, but I felt it tonight." As he lit the flames to ward off the chill in the room, he explained everything he could remember, small details coming back to him in flashes. "I think each cord runs to its own universe, and, like we already knew, Nethyl and the Gate are at the center of it all. The magic that runs through those cords is the same magic that runs through the Gate."

"The same magic that runs through your veins," Merriam murmured, watching the flames lap at the logs across the room.

"Yours, too," Mollian reminded her. He sat on the edge of the bed, worrying his lip with one elongated canine. "I want to try to go back."

Merriam glanced at him in alarm. "What?!"

"I want to see if I can slip between worlds when I'm conscious, if I can decide to go there or if I'm just at the mercy of the Gate's magic." Phrasing it that way, as if the magic in his veins wasn't his, felt right. He wasn't heir to that power, he was simply a conduit, someone able to wield it. But it was greater than him.

"Molli, no." Merriam shook her head frantically, reaching out to keep him in place. "You're exhausted. What happens if you get caught somewhere bad or slip into some universe that doesn't actually have any planets, you just end up floating in space and get ripped apart by the vacuum of it?"

"I wouldn't get ripped apart." Mollian rolled his eyes. "At worst, I'd asphyxiate or freeze to death, possibly rupture my lungs."

"Oh, well, if that's all," Merriam replied drily. She squeezed his arm, tugging to pull him further onto the bed. "Just rest, please. There's a lot going on, and I'd ... I'd feel better if someone else knew what you were planning. Someone who could help if something went wrong."

"Merriam Demonslayer," Mollian grinned. "Are you requesting the presence of my mother?"

"Being as she's the only other full-blooded Keeper left, yes," Merriam acquiesced. "Just wait, please. We can try more in the morning. We don't even know why you're being pulled there, anyway."

Mollian tucked her hair behind her ear, dropping his hand to his lap. "Okay, sleep first."

They laid back down, Merriam pressed into his side, afraid he would disappear again. But the day had been long, and they soon slipped away, wrapped in the safety and comfort of each other.

Breakfast was a simple affair, with only the four of them eating in the dining room. Merriam knew they'd have to talk to Regenya about Mollian's dreams soon, but she was thankful to put it off for a while and focus on finding Ryddan.

Rovin sat close to Merriam, which Mollian and Bellamy teased him for, but the banter settled all of them and gave them a sense of normalcy. And when she shifted to press her leg against his while she ate, like it was the most natural thing in the world to want to be near him, Rovin's entire body lit up. He knew he would put up with any amount of teasing for the rest of his life if it meant he could feel her coming undone around him again. He adjusted the front of his pants, pulling his thoughts to the day ahead.

Back underneath the mountain, they marked six more worlds off their list of potentials, and one as a possibility.

"One more and then supper?" Mollian could feel exhaustion heavy in his blood with the amount of world-jumping he'd done in the past couple of days. Merriam had taken them to a couple of the worlds, but opening the Gate took a greater toll on her than Mollian, so he was determined to shoulder most of the burden. They'd stopped once for a small snack, but had skipped lunch. There was still so much ground to cover and so little time to cover it.

"What's next?" Merriam prompted in agreement.

Mollian checked the list. "Tymecht," he read aloud, filling his mind with the other details as he prepared to take them there.

When Merriam stepped through the Gate, humid air pressed against her skin and goosebumps erupted across her flesh. She swallowed, looking up at the dark indigo sky thick with clouds and watching as lightning flashed across it. The smell of sulfur burned her throat as she breathed in, and she reached for Mollian's hand, halting him as he stepped forward.

"This is it," Rovin said from behind her, the same expression of realization on his face.

Merriam nodded. "This is the world Basta brought us to. I'm sure of it."

Bellamy looked around, knowing they weren't geographically near to where Ryddan had been taken, but searching for a sign of him, regardless.

Mollian reached out with his mind, Merriam pinging loudly next to him, but no one else that shared his blood. He closed his eyes, pushing harder.

Nothing.

"He's not close," Mollian said, meeting Bellamy's eyes.

Bellamy nodded, hand wrapped around the hilt of his sword. "That would've been too easy, I suppose."

"Let's go back," Merriam urged, eyes scanning the horizon for the telltale oily smoke of unformed demons. "We know which place this is, so let's learn what we can and plan a rescue."

"Maybe we should split up," Rovin suggested. "Do a little scouting here to cross-reference with the information already gathered. Hel, we brought an escort from the Guard with us. Maybe their stronghold is close enough that we can march on them now. They won't be expecting an attack."

Merriam chewed her lip, knowing there was some logic in the plan, but uncomfortable with it nonetheless. "They know where the Gate is," she said. "Basta would have known, and I'm willing to bet he told others. They've probably avoided coming through because one, they can't open it alone, and two, the iron in Entumbra is a deterrent. But what if they patrol close by? Basta was dumb, but he wasn't an imbecile. It's a fair guess that whoever planned Ryddan's abduction isn't, either. They'll be watching the Gate, expecting us to go after him. And we may have a small group of fighters, but that's nothing compared to the army they're likely to have. Remember how big those creatures were last summer? We'd be marching to our deaths."

"She's right," Bellamy surprised himself by saying. He'd slipped the shard of amethyst from his pocket, squeezing it tightly and letting it ground him. "We shouldn't risk it, not with Ryddan being nowhere close, and not when Mer is the only one of us protected from possession."

Merriam's fingers brushed against the iron chain at her throat, remembering the way the demon had recoiled from her the last time she'd been here. "Protection and research first," she affirmed.

They climbed back up to the castle proper, more than ready for a good meal. They'd just started eating when one of the human attendants came running down the stairs.

"A bird has come from Umbra," they said in their human tongue, holding out a small scroll to Mollian.

"Thank you," he replied, unrolling the paper. His eyes scanned quickly before moving over the words a second time.

"What is it?" Merriam asked, sensing the shift in him.

Mollian's fist curled around the note, his jaw set. "We need to go back."

"Back?" Bellamy questioned, wondering if he meant to Tymecht.

"To Umbra." Mollian's voice was flat, but his eyes were lit with energy, and it coursed through him, all of his muscles wound tight. He looked at Merriam. "You were right, they're planning to launch an attack. Demons were found in the city."

"What?" Merriam pushed back from the table, hands flying to the axes at her hips like demons might come spilling down the hallways at any moment.

"Two of those giant birds, plus one demon, unformed. Leonidas was able to dispatch the creatures, but the other got away." Mollian stood. "We're going back tonight. Rovin, Bellamy, brief the Guard. They'll stay back to help my parents protect the Gate." The two Rangers nodded, leaving the table with their food hardly touched. Mollian turned to Merriam. "I need to tell my parents what's happening. Go to the library, grab what you can on Tymecht to take back with us. We need to know as much as we can about what we'll be fighting."

Merriam hesitated, feeling his agitation as his magic swirled through her veins.

"I'm fine, Ria," he insisted, and she knew he wasn't. "Go."

She gave him a final look of concern before racing up the stairs with her heart in her throat. Whatever had him so discomposed was immediately enough to terrify her.

Merriam threw open the door to the library, eyes scanning the rows and rows of books and papers, looking for anything on the demon world. It took her longer than it should have to gather everything. She kept dropping things in her frenzy, and once she had everything stacked on a table, she couldn't find a basket or satchel to carry it all in. After throwing open multiple drawers in the desks throughout the room, she finally found one, trying not to shove everything into it too haphazardly, and ran for Mollian's room.

The disconcerting sounds of destruction echoed down the hallway, the unease already in Merriam's stomach doubling.

Opening the door, she picked her way carefully through the splintered remains of furniture. She could feel Mollian's power churning discontentedly in her own veins, the disquiet growing the closer she got where he crouched on the floor.

"Talk to me," she said softly.

Mollian pulled his hands away from his face, his eyes looking around the wreckage of the room. "I can't do this."

Merriam's brow furrowed as she reached down to run a hand across his back. "What can't you do?"

"Be the king Oren would have been," Mollian's voice broke, and he brought his tear-filled gaze up to meet hers. "I was never raised to lead wars and strategize and make decisions that could have a catastrophic effect on the balance of the universe. I've been playing at being a leader, but this isn't playtime anymore. People are going to *die*, and it's going to be my fault. My own Guard kidnapped you and almost killed you. And now demons? I didn't stop them from killing Oren. I didn't stop them from taking Ryddan ... how am I supposed to stop them from invading?"

Merriam's heart broke as she watched her *mehhen*, the pain clear in his eyes. She sank to her knees in front of him, wrapping her arms around his shoulders and cradling his head to her chest for a moment before pulling away to search his gaze.

She traced the tattoo across his forehead with her thumb, eyes never leaving his. "This is *your* crown, Molli. You are king. This is your rule, not anyone else's. I know you never asked for the weight that's on your shoulders, but you do bear it well. Nothing that's happened in the past matters, because you make every decision with the interest of Sekha at heart. It doesn't matter what Oren would have done. He always knew you were your own person, and he would never want you to try to be him. You're Molli—kind and wild and intuitive—and he would be so proud of you for the way you have stepped up to run this country while still keeping yourself."

"I'm a murderer, Ria."

"Likewise, Lord King." A smile tugged at her lips.

Mollian pulled her hands from his face, shaking his head even as he fought his own amusement at her casual acceptance of the title. "Killing Ferrick, ripping him apart that way ... I didn't do that to protect Sekha. I did it because the thought of something happening to you made me lose control. I let my magic take over. It was the first time in so long that whatever power runs through me had felt truly content. How am I supposed to feel about that? And in conjunction with my dreams, wherever it is I've actually been Traveling to this whole time ... I can't handle this. Ryddan is gone, demons are once again attacking our home, the possibility of inter-dimensional war is on the horizon for the first time in the fucking history of the world and ..." Mollian paused, dragging his hands down his face before running his fingers into his hair, further mussing the snow-white curls.

"I'm just me," he said defeatedly. "Just one third-born Keeper who just happens to be responsible for the fate and future of life as we know it. I don't know how to do this."

Merriam pulled him into another hug, smoothing down his hair. "You put too much pressure on yourself, Molli. All of this is unprecedented, but we've always been good at ingenuity and thinking on our feet. And this burden is not yours alone. You have me. You have Captain Dio, the Guard, dozens of advisers, and the mercenaries at your disposal, too."

Mollian relaxed, the erratic nature of his emotions starting to settle. He didn't move from her arms, though, but took selfish comfort in her warmth, her strength, her calm.

"And look on the bright side. If we are somehow unable to keep the demons from overtaking this realm, pretty soon it won't be our problem anyway, because we'll be dead."

You're not okay in the head.

I think I'm doing quite well, all things considered. Merriam stood, pulling Mollian up after her. "Let's go home, Molli. We've got a realm to save."

Chapter 40

MOLLIAN BRIEFLY EXPLAINED THE situation to his parents and told them he would send a full detachment of Guard to join their escort as soon as they were home. Then he and Merriam met Bellamy and Rovin in the courtyard.

The light of the moons shone on the small group as they huddled together beneath the large stone castle. Then they were gone, flipping through reality to an abandoned warehouse on Earth, buried next to countless other hangars and storage facilities at the edge of the Denver International Airport, where Earth's Gate resided miles below the tarmac.

Mollian quickly found a human to glamor for the drive south and into the mountains, turning the two-day trip from Umbra to Entumbra on Nethyl into a couple of hours. When they Traveled back, they were just outside of the castle gates in Umbra, and, even though they knew the danger was only beginning, all four of them could breathe a little easier now that they were home.

"First things first," Mollian said, wiping his hands on his pants. His palms were sweaty with the nervous energy coursing through him. Whatever was going to happen, he had the undying sense that they would only have one chance to make it to the other side victorious. The grace period for mistakes and oversights had become practically nonexistent. "Ria, go to Tymecht. If you see anyone, come back immediately. The demons cannot be aware that we've discovered their realm. See if it looks like they could be keeping Ryddan close by."

Merriam nodded, pulling a small knife from her belt and cutting the back of her forearm. "Back by a hundred count?"

"I'll come after you if you're not," Mollian replied.

Merriam dragged her umbrite ring through her blood and struck them together. As soon as she disappeared, Mollian started the count. She was back before he made it to forty, breathing heavily and reaching an arm behind her to scratch between her shoulder blades. "Nothing but a bunch of rocks," she reported. "If they had a camp set up, they didn't stick around long after they took Rydd. I didn't see any life, either. If they left scouts, they're not out in the open."

"We'll plan to fight them on our turf, then." He looked at the Rangers. "Rovin, have a detachment sent back to Entumbra. They need to leave first thing in the morning. Bell, find Captain Dio and have him meet us in the war room." The two Rangers nodded before running off, a sense of urgency in their steps. Mollian turned to Merriam. "Send a bird to the mercs. Leo saw the initial attack—I'll need to speak with him." He paused for a moment, looking toward the castle with a frown. "Calysta, too."

They parted ways, Mollian heading straight for the war room, digging through the desk in the office at the back of it. It didn't take him long to find what he was looking for, the map folded neatly in a complex way that he would probably never be able to return it to. He took the map back out into the main room, gently shaking it open, the paper almost as big as a bedsheet, and laid it over the table.

It was a map of Sekha, but instead of the territories and cities that were shown on the map carved into the top of the table, it was marked with lines, branching out and spreading from one focal point. They were ley lines, and Mollian had a sinking feeling that his hunch was right.

Captain Dio showed up first with Bellamy and a couple of the commanders on his heels. Rovin and Merriam arrived one after the other, and the commanders gave each other curious looks when Rovin slid into the seat next to Merriam's.

"Were you able to find the demon?" Mollian asked Dio, standing in front of his seat at the head of the table.

Dio shook his head, running a hand through his slicked-back hair, a few golden blonde strands falling loose over his forehead. "I have patrols monitoring the streets, but if it's still in Umbra, it hasn't been making any trouble. We're still looking."

Mollian dragged a hand over his face, pale green eyes solemn. "I don't want to create a panic, but we need to find it. Start having your men test the citizens. Just having them hold a piece of iron should be enough. The demons are more susceptible to it than even the high fae." He didn't want his people to feel threatened or unsafe, but he didn't know what else to do.

"Yes, Your Majesty." Dio didn't argue, and his eyes held no judgment or misgiving.

Leonidas and Calysta walked through the doors then, and Mollian's shoulders sagged with relief at the sight of the nymph. She would be able to help. "Leo, Calysta, thank you for coming on such short notice," he greeted them both before focusing his gaze on the human. "What happened?" The note had been brief and to the point.

"They came from the south," Leonidas started without preamble. "It was those long-necked, freaky-legged birds first. Panic took one of them down, but the other managed to swipe at a couple citizens before I dispatched it. They're fine, no casualties, but a demon—unformed, just as that weird, roiling black cloud—came after them, and I lost sight of where it landed. It's possible it's not even in Umbra anymore."

Mollian's eyes were on the map spread over the table, pointed canine working over one corner of his lip as he attempted to pull all the pieces together. "Calysta, what do you know of the ley lines that run south of Umbra?"

Calysta stepped forward, running her fingers over the lines on the map. She tilted her head to the side, petal pink hair spilling over her shoulders and down her back, black eyes following the lines up to where they centered in Entumbra. "The line that runs by Umbra and down to the southern coast is deep." She turned her gaze to Mollian. "It's a main line, many others throughout Sekha branch from it, and much of Nethyl's magic flows through it."

Mollian pressed his lips closed, brows drawing together. "The Gate's magic is what connects everything, every reality and world. What if ..." he trailed off, brushing a curl from his forehead and turning his gaze to meet those around the table. "This line runs extremely close to where the full moons festival was held. The nymphs held a ceremony that night?" Mollian asked Calysta.

She nodded uneasily. "It was only a small gathering here. The larger one is always held further south, away from the major cities. This year's was ... big. More nymphs gathered at once since before your time. There has been legislature in the past that hindered our movements, but it wasn't renewed. We fed the line quite heavily." Calysta's musical voice was soft, quiet, her eyes turning back to the table.

"I think the barrier between our world and others is thinner over the ley lines due to the nature of the magic and might have grown even more paltry during the ceremony," Mollian said. "Typically, that wouldn't necessarily be an issue. But those demons have orydite and umbrite. It's possible the pieces of the Gate paired with the thinner distance and whatever magic they're capable of themselves is what enabled them to come through and steal Ryddan."

Merriam frowned. "But that's not how the rings work. We've never been able to hold a portal open, and even when we do Travel, that's a single passenger situation. Dozens of those creatures came through, and we're not remotely close to where the majority of the nymphs gathered."

"Just because we've never figured out a way to hold open a rift doesn't mean it's not possible," Mollian countered, looking at Merriam. "It makes sense that the magic should be able to be used that way, but there's never been a reason for a Keeper to learn it. Think about it, we have the Gate if we need to bring multiple people with us, but even that is rare. We only Travel to distant realms to learn, to document. We've never researched how to open separate rifts because our whole ideology is to keep the fluke ones from even opening in the first place. Why would we ever concentrate efforts on doing the opposite?" The question was accompanied by a dark, ironic chuckle.

"They've taken our magic and perverted it," he continued. "They want more, and now that they have Ryddan, it will only be easier for them to break back through. I don't think they'll go through Entumbra. They're so susceptible to iron, even Ryddan was uncomfortable at the castle. They need the Gate, but breaking through there would weaken them while they still have to fight. There are wards around Entumbra to keep random waves of magic from seeping out, but the magic doesn't just stay with the Gate, it flows through all of Nethyl, all of Sekha. In theory, if a Keeper got in touch with a ley line, they could tap into that power to Travel."

Calysta brushed her fingers over the map. "The nymphs also feel the magic that runs beneath Nethyl's surface. We are born solitary creatures, but we gather where the magic is. Like yours, King, our magic is of the world. We may not be able to wield it the way you do, but there have been times when the magic has let us see into other places. You're right, whatever separates us from other realms fades because of the Gate's power. Many nymphs have told stories of different worlds they've seen in their minds while tapped into the ley lines."

Mollian sat back in his chair, a look of resignation on his face. "When the demons come back to attack, they'll come through where it will give them the least resistance. Those other demons came from the south?" Mollian looked to Leonidas.

Leonidas nodded. "Panic's been acting dodgy, too. Always dipping southward like something is pulling him there. I'd thought it was some sort of delayed migration instinct, but what if he was sensing something else shift in Nethyl?"

"And what Shiloh saw on their way to Umbra," Merriam added. "The plants are dying. What if that's where the demons live, where they're practicing trying to break through? Nothing on this planet has ever caused the sort of reaction they told me about."

"I think it's worth a look heading south. If the demons are going to bring a fight to us, we need to meet them where they come through and not let them gain any ground," Mollian said with finality.

"How do we prepare?" one of the commanders asked.

"We need to use every advantage we have," Mollian said. "We need to prepare the Guard to head south, set up a war camp away from any towns and cities. And everyone should wear iron, too."

The commanders sat up, looking at each other in shock. "Your Majesty, we have always trained with our magic. We use it to fight."

Rovin scoffed, shaking his head. Dio gave him a warning look, but Rovin ignored it, leaning forward. "*Some* of you do. There are plenty of fair folk in your ranks. Those of us without magic have trained to fight the same as you, and we've managed just fine."

Dio frowned. "Lieutenant Arwood is right." He took a deep breath, the wheels of his mind turning before he looked at Mollian. "How much time do you think we have?"

"There's a question, Captain. It sounds like they were testing their reach, but I'm not sure how long it will take them to perfect it and figure out how to use the Keeper magic correctly. It could be days, but it could very well be hours." Mollian shrugged, the casual gesture in complete contrast to his bleak and serious expression.

"Fuck," Dio muttered.

Merriam chuckled. "I agree with you, Captain."

A smile twitched on the corners of Dio's mouth. "I can say with full honesty that I never imagined myself in charge of strategy for this type of warfare. But whether we have days or hours, we'll use all the time we can to prepare." He turned to his commanders. "Outside of patrols, everyone trains. Every high fae wears iron. They need to get used to wielding weapons without the use of their magic. In the meantime, we need to find a blacksmith." Dio looked at Merriam. "Your necklace is what saved you from possession, correct?"

Merriam touched the aspen leaf around her neck, rubbing the pendant between her thumb and forefinger. "Yes. Granted, I'm no expert, but every instance of possession I've seen, the demon enters through the mouth." She dropped her hand, gaze on the table to try to hide some of the pain in her eyes. "Oren's wrists were bound in iron when he was taken. The iron burned his skin, and there's a chance it would have chased the demon out, but the chains were dropped so quickly. I think my necklace being so close to the entry point and not letting it have a chance to get in and grab hold in the first place is what made the difference."

Dio nodded. "We need as many iron necklaces as we can get. Last summer, the demons already had vessels from Sekha. That won't be the case now, and everyone needs to be prepared. We don't have much time, but we'll use what we can."

Merriam chewed her lip, turning things over in her mind. "There isn't time," she whispered, her eyes unfocused. She glanced up, meeting Mollian's gaze. "I can get iron. They'll never find enough here. And the time it would take to forge it down? We need to go south soon. We probably don't have days. Bell and I can get what we need in just a few hours."

Rovin watched her curiously. But her mention of Bellamy brought to his mind something she'd said last year: "*I need someone who can glamor.*" And he understood she meant to go to Earth. "How difficult will it be to make necklaces out of what's available?"

Merriam looked at him, a glimmer somewhere between amused and cocky lighting her eyes. "Prepare to have your mind fucking blown."

Mollian curled his fingers into his leg, swallowing against the panic rising in his chest. She hadn't been out of his reach since she'd been kidnapped. The dip to Tymecht didn't count, because she was still geographically close in that other realm. But if she was going to be wandering Earth ... "When do you need to get the materials?"

"It's probably less risky now, while it's night."

He took a deep breath, settling himself and the magic in his blood. She was safe, Ferrick was gone, and she was more than capable of protecting herself. "Go, we'll take care of things here." *Be safe.*

Always. Merriam stood, barely resisting the instinct to push Mollian's curls back from his forehead. He was now completely in charge of so much and held more authority than anyone else in the country, but in times like these, he was still Mollian, and her habit was to pull comfort from him the same as his was to pull from her.

Mollian raised his hand, and she pressed her palm to his, Bellamy standing to follow her from the room.

Rovin watched her leave, a tightness in his chest that he realized came from admiration. Merriam was strong and ingenuitive, and it was not lost on him that this would be the second time she would have a direct hand in saving the fate of more than just their world. And, after everything, she had chosen *him.* He felt a gaze searing into his cheek and turned to see Mollian staring at him. Rovin felt warmth crawl up his neck, abashed at being caught.

But Mollian saw the admiration there, and shared a small, conspiratorial smile with the Ranger. He hadn't thought it would be so easy to forgive Rovin for everything he'd done, but watching him look at Merriam like that ... it didn't erase the past, but it was clear that he'd grown and that none of those old feelings and resentments remained in him.

"How can we help?" Leonidas asked, pulling Mollian's attention back to the meeting at hand.

"Would you mind helping the Guard train? If Captain Dio is okay with it. You all have experience fighting the demons." Mollian looked to the captain, who nodded, beginning to draw out a schedule.

"Where are we going?" Bellamy asked, following Merriam out to the courtyard.

Merriam reached back, grabbing his hand to pull him down the steps to the ground. "We're going to the land of all things crafty." She grinned, facing him.

Before he could question her further, she threw her arms around him, sliding her rings together and taking them to Earth.

Bellamy was well aware of what was expected of him at his point, and set off to find them a ride. On the other side of reality from Umbra was a small gas station off one of the mountain roads, and it usually never took too long for someone to stop by. When a man pulled up in a truck, Bellamy walked up, pushing out a glamor as he asked the man to drive them into town.

The whole idea of cars was still wild to him, as was a majority of the things about Earth. He looked at the one moon with a small smile, as if they shared the secret knowledge that there wasn't a single part of him that belonged in its world.

With the car secured, Merriam and Bellamy settled in for the ride into the city.

"What does crafty things mean?" Bellamy asked, head leaning against the window and eyes on the sky.

"We're going to Joann's."

"Who's Joann?"

Merriam tilted her head to the side. "You know, I don't actually know. But I used to be a big fan of her store."

"She's a smith?"

"No, no." Merriam laughed. "Mostly textiles, but also materials for building jewelry, painting, and other creative ventures."

Bellamy lifted his head, looking at Merriam in surprise. "That's so many things. Weapons, too?"

"No weapons, weirdly, but there's an idea. I have picked up a couple of things from Joann's in the past for Mollian's weapon beautification, though." Merriam pulled her braid over her shoulder, curling the end over her finger. It was still tied with the string that Oren had given her, and she brushed the pad of her thumb over it, a pang of bittersweet longing filling her. *You would be so proud of how Molli is handling all of this.*

"Does she have magazines?" Bellamy asked, sitting up suddenly at the prospect of the new information and pictures he could bring back.

Merriam dropped her braid. "They do, but I'm not sure how sciencey of a selection they'll have."

The car pulled into the empty parking lot, the dash flashing 11:47pm. "Do you think you can get him to wait around?"

Bellamy frowned thoughtfully. "I can try." He leaned forward, putting a hand on the man's shoulder. The pressure in the car increased as Bellamy conjured up his magic, his voice dripping with something sweet and savory that pulsed around Merriam's head. "Look at the moon. Isn't it the most beautiful thing you've ever seen? You should keep looking at it. Watch the moon until you can't see it anymore."

"It's so pretty," the man mumbled, tipping forward in his seat to get a better view.

Bellamy sat back with a shrug. "Let's hope that holds."

They got out of the car, walking up to the storefront. Merriam brought them back to Nethyl, moving a few paces through the forest before Traveling back to Earth on the other side of the locked glass doors.

"Does Joann sleep upstairs?" Bellamy asked as Merriam searched the front of the store for a light switch. Bright fluorescents flickered to life, and Bellamy's jaw dropped as he got a good view of the rows and rows of merchandise. "This is so much bigger than the store outside of Umbra."

Merriam stepped up next to him, pointing to a camera in the corner. "Can you unplug that? Along with any others you see?"

Bellamy reached out with his magic to render the camera inoperable and followed Merriam as she grabbed a cart.

"Go on, take a look around, but be quick."

Bellamy scampered off, and Merriam fought back a laugh at his childlike excitement. He would count as a seasoned warrior at this point, and was for all intents and purposes raising a prince, but when he didn't have to be a Ranger or a guardian—when he could just be Bellamy—he reminded her of a nine-year-old boy.

Merriam looked up at the signs hanging over the aisles and followed them to jewelry. It didn't take her long to find spools of thin iron chain, and she pulled every last one of them from their peg, dumping them into the cart. She moved down the row, grabbing several packs of O rings and lobster clasps and every pair of needle-nose pliers.

From there, she moved to the front of the store, where she found a couple of large canvas bags to transfer her wares into, biceps burning from the weight. "Bell!" she called.

His head popped from an aisle, curly hair falling over his shoulders. "Wait, I just need another moment!" He disappeared again.

"We have to go before your glamor on our ride wears off," Merriam insisted.

A disgruntled moan floated from somewhere in the stacks, and Merriam burst into laughter as Bellamy appeared, arms loaded with boxes and items. "I found things!"

"I see." She tipped her head to the side with a little shake. "What is all of that?"

Bellamy walked up to the checkout counter, dumping everything down. "There's science kits! Look, Molli and Rydd will love all of this, too. Things with magnets, and this one is electricity, and this one—"

"Okay, okay, just throw them into a bag. You can tell me about them in the car."

Bellamy began neatly stacking his prizes into canvas bags. "Wait, do we need to pay Joann? This is a lot of stuff." He looked at Merriam with concern in his eyes.

"Joann isn't really a person, Bell. It's a corporation, and they have insurance. But I appreciate your morals."

"What's a corporation?"

"Like, this store is owned by a company that has hundreds of these stores."

"So we shouldn't leave any coin?"

Merriam shrugged. "We can, but it won't make it to the people who are in charge, anyway." She dug around in the small pouch on her belt, pulling out a gold coin regardless and leaving it on the counter. Maybe someone from the opening shift could pawn it.

Bellamy nodded at the gesture, satisfied.

Bags in hand, Merriam turned off the lights, handing the haul to Bellamy so she could get them out of the store. By the time they'd Traveled to Nethyl and then back again to the parking lot, Merriam's vision swam, the tattoos on her back itching and her head light. "Fuck." She stepped away from Bellamy, leaning her hands on her knees. "Well, at least we know the chains are truly iron." Even though it didn't fully block the Keeper magic since the properties of it were bonded to her blood, which also held iron, such large quantities of the metal still put a damper on it.

"I mean, yeah, I could have told you as much." Bellamy smirked, walking toward the car. "Let's head back up the mountain, buddy," he suggested to the man, voice thick with glamor.

The ride back went by quickly, Bellamy telling Merriam about the different things he found. He felt optimistic and solid, like saving Ryddan was never a question. Of course it would happen, because how could it not? Failure wasn't an option—it wasn't even a word.

Chapter 41

MERRIAM AND BELLAMY WALKED into the war room, dropping their load of iron chains and other accessories onto the floor. "Go round up some of the Guard, anyone who's available for grunt work. We've got a lot of necklaces to make. See if you can find any other pairs of pliers, too. I'm sure the stablehands might know where some can be found."

"Pliers and bodies, got it." Bellamy left, and Merriam went to work, unwrapping the spools of chain and organizing their supplies. She tucked Bellamy's bag of assorted prizes into the office at the back of the war room and had only a few moments to settle herself before members of the Guard started to arrive. She was still slightly woozy from Traveling with so much iron, but she also attributed it to a lack of proper food and hydration. As soon as she ate and had a little rest, she'd be good as new.

Merriam demonstrated how to make a necklace, a simple enough task. Cut a length of chain, add a clasp, repeat. She had to bite her cheek to keep from smiling at the absurdity of watching several trained warriors bent over the delicate chains and claw clasps, making jewelry for their comrades as they sat scattered around the floor.

She felt the touch of Mollian against her mind, beckoning her. After double checking the Guard would be okay on their own, she reached out for her *mehhen*, the tattoos on her back itching in her slightly drained state as she followed his pull out to the courtyard.

"What are you doing out here?" she asked.

"I want to try to go back."

Merriam's heart dropped, and she shook her head. "It's late. You're probably tired, what if—"

"There's no time." Mollian grabbed her shoulders, searching her face. "I'm at least on ground level in case I end up somewhere else, but that's all I can give you, Ria. I have to know what this place is. I have to test our theories so we can more accurately plan."

Merriam swallowed, staring into pale green eyes, moonlight shining off of his hair. "What if I can't come after you?"

"You won't have to."

"You can't know that," she pleaded.

Mollian's fingers tightened around her, and Merriam felt his magic stir in her veins. "There's something here," he insisted. "If I can just figure out what it is, I could fix everything. I feel it."

Merriam pressed her lips together, every selfish part of her screaming to make him stay.

"There's a reason I'm here. There's a reason I have the magic I do. It's the same reason I think I have you, the reason I need you." Mollian slid his hands down her arms, finding hers and lifting them so he could press their palms together.

Merriam closed her eyes, concentrating on the swell inside her as her soul quieted, recognizing the proximity of his and the rightness of it all. "If you get lost, I'm throwing your entire weapons decorating kit into the middle of the ocean just to spite you," she promised.

Mollian laughed, even as his chest tightened with recognition of how truly lucky he was to have her. "Deal." He took a deep breath, stepping back from her and dropping his hands. "You can feel me there, remember? Nothing to worry about."

She folded her arms over her chest, fingers curled into fists, but nodded.

Mollian closed his eyes, rolling his head over his shoulders as he relaxed and let his mind free. He felt his feet planted against the ground. He felt Merriam's presence, anxious, but still reassuring, anchoring. He leaned into that, focusing on his connection to her, that unbreakable bond between them that had only grown stronger through the years. He let his magic slide along the tendrils that wound between them, examining the strength of each and knowing without a doubt that he would always find his way back to her.

Mollian reined his magic in and took a deep breath, clearing his mind of everything except for the feel of his power. Nothing happened, just a breeze blowing a curl across his cheek. His face twitched as he fought off a scowl, keeping his breathing even as he kept his focus inward. Traveling was second-nature at this point, but even though he never thought about it, it still activated the magic in his blood. He conjured that feeling, the slight fizzle in his veins when his power woke.

And then he fell.

Merriam gasped despite herself. One moment, Mollian was there, and the next, without even touching his rings, he was gone, like he'd been nothing but an apparition that had blown away in the wind. She curled her hand against her chest, reaching out for him. Just like in Entumbra, she was able to get a faint sense of him. Close, but untouchable. She bit her lip, holding onto that connection. She stood like that for long enough that her feet started to hurt, and she shifted her weight, looking up to the sky.

"Mer? What are you doing out here?"

Merriam jumped at Rovin's voice. She'd been so heavily concentrated on Mollian that she hadn't even heard him approach. "I'm ..." she trailed off, unsure how to finish.

"Sick and tired of unprecedented situations?" Rovin joked, slipping his hands into his pockets.

One corner of Merriam's mouth pulled up. "Extremely so. Namely, because they all seem to involve the stuff of nightmares and having to fight them."

"Thinking of letting someone else win the title of demonslayer?"

"Not a chance." Merriam stepped closer, leaning into him.

"Atta girl." Rovin's arms went around her without hesitation, his lips pressed to her hairline. "But you can't slaughter demons if you're exhausted. Could I interest you in sleep?"

Merriam closed her eyes, letting him take the brunt of her weight. His smell—fallen leaves and crisp apple—filled her head, and something in her relaxed with it. "Are you inviting me to your bed, Lieutenant?"

"If yours is preferred, I'm not picky." His voice rumbled through her.

Merriam tilted her head up to look at him, hands tucked against his chest. "You never much struck me as a cuddler."

"Even after I carried you—*twice*—through the streets of Umbra?"

Merriam lifted a hand, stroking the stubble along his jaw. "There was movement there, a purpose for it."

Rovin held her gaze, his eyes dark and depthless, but the emotion in them clear. "True, but I wouldn't have offered a second time if you hadn't fit so well against me the first."

She smirked, brushing her fingers up into his hair and down the back of his neck to twirl one of the silky locks. "You were playing the long game?"

His hands slid lower on her waist, anchoring her against him. "Then? No, the only thing more annoying than having to spend my night off keeping you out of trouble was ending that night with the knowledge that I didn't hate it when your body was tucked against mine."

"My deepest apologies, then, both for the trouble and the revelation." Merriam lifted onto her toes, brushing her lips over his.

Rovin pulled her in, the kiss soft, slow. "I really was just proposing sleep, pet."

She chuckled, uncurling his hair from around her fingers and sliding her hand back down his chest. "I know, but I'm waiting for Molli. You should rest, though. There might not be much more opportunity for it."

"What do you mean? Where is he?" Rovin pulled back, looking around.

Merriam chewed the inside of her cheek, contemplating. "He's ..." she blinked, her vision blurring. She pressed her palms against Rovin's chest, shaking her head to clear it. She felt Mollian's magic being pulled from her, rushing down the tethers that bound their souls together. Her vision darkened at the edges, and she raised a hand to her head, her skin cold and clammy and the strongest feeling of vertigo overwhelming her.

She collapsed against Rovin, her face pale.

"Mer? Mer!" Rovin held her to his chest as her body went limp, and he sank to the ground, fear coursing through him.

Mollian knew without opening his eyes that he was back. The air was completely still around him, devoid of any discernible temperature or movement. Blinking, he was slightly shocked to find that the layer of dark that typically covered the thousands upon thousands of shimmering threads was missing. He saw everything that connected life, bare before him.

"Now what to do with it," he muttered, pushing his hair back from his forehead. His other hand was planted on his hip as he stared above him, eyes narrowing.

He remembered touching the thread, recognizing the Gate's magic that ran through it. Raising a hand, he threw his magic out, letting it slide through the many twisting veins that connected somewhere below his feet. He latched onto one without much thought, curling his fingers into a fist as he drove his magic into it. The surface resisted his touch, and he raised his other hand, concentrating on finding any crevice to slither into.

Mollian pushed, sinking in further until he could sense the magic flowing just below his touch. His skin crawled, a feeling like he shouldn't be messing with this energy coming over him, so he spread his magic over the tendril instead of digging further, testing to see how he could manipulate it. He tugged, and it moved only marginally before pulling taut.

A bead of sweat pearled on his temple, sliding down his face with the effort of holding the vein that very much wanted to be left alone. He pulled from a deeper reserve of his magic, tightening around the energy and trying to pinch it off, disrupt the flow even just momentarily.

His teeth clenched together, arms shaking with effort as he pulled them down, but he felt that flow of magic slowly thinning beneath his touch.

Rip. Tear. Pull, his magic begged, and Mollian, with a final burst of strength, forced the gap tighter, the magic flowing through the cord reduced to barely a trickle.

What am I doing? Alarm rolled through him, and he instantly let go, pulling his magic back in, back toward Merriam.

In the blink of an eye, he was standing in the courtyard, Merriam and Rovin on the ground in front of him.

Merriam was brushing Rovin's hand from her face, clearly trying to tell him she was fine. Her eyes found Mollian, and she pushed herself up further. "Did you make it? Did you figure it out?"

"What happened?" Mollian fell to the ground beside them, anxiety coiling tight in his chest as he reached for Merriam, examining her for injuries.

In a move that surprised all three of them, Rovin pulled Merriam further against his chest, putting as much of himself between her and Mollian as possible. "What the fuck were you doing?" he growled through clenched teeth.

Mollian blinked, his head tipping to the side in shock as he regarded the Ranger in front of him, his entire posture protective and brown eyes bright with suspicion.

Rovin Arwood was protecting Merriam. From Mollian.

The sheer absurdity of it all bubbled from his chest in a sardonic burst of laughter, and he sat back on his heels, raising a quizzical brow. "You understand she's literally my soul, right?"

Merriam was also looking up at Rovin with a form of confused wonder. "I think we fell into a different reality," she said, though neither of the males looked at her, their gazes locked on each other.

"Just because she's your *mehhen* doesn't give you the right to use her like a fucking power bank." Rovin glared.

Mollian frowned in confusion. "What are you talking about?"

"The same thing happened the day Ryddan was taken, only this was worse." Rovin's arms tightened around Merriam, the perceived injustice spurring a need to guard her.

"I'm fine," she huffed, pushing against Rovin's hold.

Mollian still held Rovin's glare, his own eyes wide as he drifted back to the festival, to feeling that reserve of power and pulling from it as he tried to close off the portal, the same reserve he'd dove into tonight without a second thought. "Fucking Hel," he breathed, the realization slamming into him.

Every time Merriam's presence had settled the magic in his veins, every time it had been too much and he'd off-loaded it onto her ... he'd never even really had to think about it, almost as though she was an extension of him. Because, in a way, she was.

His eyes finally flitted down to her face, color returning to her cheeks. "Ria, I—"

"Don't, it's okay. You needed it." Merriam's eyes were soft, and she reached out to brush a curl from his forehead.

Rovin looked from Merriam to Mollian, his turn for confusion to cloud his features. "You didn't know?"

Mollian shook his head, eyes still on Merriam. "Why didn't you tell me?"

She sat up fully, dropping her gaze to her lap. "I just assumed you knew."

"You thought I would knowingly pull from you without your consent? Without talking to you about it first? Testing the reactions and effects?" His voice was pained.

"Molli, it's *your* magic that runs through my blood. *Your* soul that is tethered to mine. Of course you're free to take what you need when it's needed. We're one," she soothed, raising her palm.

Mollian pressed his to it, the flow of energy between them almost imperceptible, but the same steady connection they'd always shared. "I would never have done it if I knew it hurt you."

"Excuse Rov's theatrics." Merriam rolled her eyes good-naturedly. "It was fine, I promise. I just got a little lightheaded. It's been an exhausting day, and it all happened much more dramatically than it should have."

"What about during Ryddan's abduction?" Rovin countered.

"I'd had a couple drinks, and I didn't pass out then." Merriam cut him a glare, a clear request for him to drop it. She turned back to Mollian. "You made it?"

"I made it." Mollian wet his lips, looking from Merriam to Rovin. "And I think that place between is the key to everything."

Chapter 42

RYDDAN STOOD ON A large balcony looking out over the dark, choppy waves of the ocean below, their surface tinged yellow with sulfur. He shivered even though the air was warm against his skin.

Warm and *wet*. Why was the air so *wet*?

He wrinkled his nose, crossing his arms over his chest. A smooth pink line broke the light brown of his skin, a cut freshly healed where Dronin had taken more of his blood. "You said I could go home." Ryddan could hear the whine in his voice, and he barely reined in the urge to stamp his foot against the ground in frustration at being so childish. He needed them to see him as a prince, not a little whiny-willow kitty-baby.

"You do not think you belong here?" Dronin asked, his great wings open and tilted against the breeze blowing from the sea.

Lightning flashed through the sky, and Ryddan steeled his little shoulders, looking up at the djuhl. "No."

Dronin looked down at him, amused at the defiance in Ryddan's deep green eyes.

"My blood runs red," Ryddan stated. "*Bright* red."

"Do you eat raw meat, djuhlin?"

Ryddan frowned, shaking his head. His hair was tinged purple, reflecting the light from the sky, but each flash of lightning shone pure and white.

"Why not?"

"It would make me sick."

Dronin hummed, turning his back on the sea and looking down at the spawn. "What about when you are a creature? Do you ever hunt your own food?"

Ryddan pressed his lips together, unsure where this line of questioning was going and growing wary.

"You can eat raw meat without sickness when in another form, can you not?" Dronin pushed.

"Yes," Ryddan answered, curling his fingers into his shirt, nervous.

"How do you know, then, that you are *fae*, as you call it, and not demon? Perhaps you share so many of your mother's features, not because that is your truest form, but because that is the form you were raised to choose?"

Ryddan gave a small shrug, unsure how to defend himself or whatever inside him told him that this was who he was. "I've never been a demon."

"But you know our tongue, and in all your forms, you have our eyes."

Anger cut through Ryddan's confusion, and he puffed his chest out, raising his chin as his fists fell to his sides. "No, I have my uncle's eyes. Everyone says so." His little voice was laced with conviction.

"Your uncle has the pupils of a predator, then?"

Ryddan's stance faltered.

"You are a greater demon. Be one."

Ryddan shook his head, taking a step back.

Dronin narrowed his eyes, that deep, dark red gleaming. "Be what you are, djuhlin."

"I *am* what I am!" Ryddan cried, the whine back in his voice.

Dronin bent forward, baring his teeth in a snarl. "I am losing my patience."

"I'll run away," Ryddan threatened, his lower lip beginning to tremble.

"That would be a very unwise choice," Dronin advised. "Change into what you are."

I'm already me! Ryddan wanted to scream, but something kept the words trapped in his throat. Anger and fear and that cold shred of loneliness swirled through him, and he squeezed his eyes shut, putting his hands over his ears. He wanted to be a dragon. He wanted to be a sea snake. He wanted to be any great creature that could wrap around Dronin and rip off his wings and toss him into the ocean, holding him under the stinking waves until all of the breath bubbled from his lungs.

Ryddan's blood, heated with too many heavy emotions for his young mind, rushed through his veins, the magic it carried agitated. The smell of sulfur burned his lungs. The humidity in the air lay heavy against his skin. Every part of him was so uncomfortable, and he screamed internally for his magic to take him home.

But Ryddan's blood held two different magics, and though Mollian and Regenya were slowly beginning to teach him how to wield a Keeper's magic, the magic given to him by his father had only ever been self-taught, and he was still too young to fully comprehend all that it was.

It was his father's magic that heeded him now.

From one heartbeat to the next, everything around Ryddan seemed to quiet. The air no longer stifled him. His heart rate slowed.

"Look at me, Ryddan," Dronin commanded.

Ryddan opened his eyes, confused by the look of satisfaction on the demon's face. But he started to recognize the differences as he lowered his hands. He was no longer fae, and he didn't need to see himself to know it for certain.

His hands and feet were each tipped with three sharp claws. His skin was dark gray, thicker, and more suited to this climate. His hair was still short, but more coarse, a shock of black falling over his forehead between two nubs of horn. Sharp plates of dark bone grew from his back, running down to a tail that was thick at the base and tapered to a point tipped with two spikes.

Ryddan swung the tail around in front of him, his tongue brushing over the long fangs in his upper and lower jaws. He was just as comfortable maneuvering in this body as he was any other, the weight and balance of the tail just as second nature as the wings of a bird or the long body of a marten.

A peculiar look washed over Dronin's face as he watched Ryddan. "You look like your father."

Ryddan blinked up at him, trying to decipher Dronin's emotions. He was used to people telling him he reminded them of the dead. He'd never stopped to think about how strange a thing that was to tell a child. It was just a normality with so many expired relatives, and famous ones, at that. But Dronin's acknowledgement felt different than when Merriam would brush the hair out of his eyes, a soft smile on her lips, or when Regenya would watch him from across the table at supper, bringing a hand up to press over her heart.

Dronin's gaze was much more calculating than that, comparing this tiny version of his brother to the one who'd died a year ago.

Ryddan didn't back down from that look, straightening his shoulders and watching back.

"Well, well, would you look at the little djuhlin." Ryddan stiffened, whirling around as Nevra approached. She stopped a few paces from him, a playful smile on her lips. "I can teach you how to wield that death trap like a true conqueror." Her eyes flicked to the barbs on his tail.

"Ryddan does not want to be taught, Nevra. He wants to go back to the fae." Dronin crossed his arms over his chest, his voice mocking.

Defiance flared through Ryddan, immediately wanting to push back against anything anyone decided for him. "I never said I didn't want to be taught!" He glared, the deep green of his eyes eerie in the dark features of his demon face. Nothing in Tymecht was that vibrantly colored. "I like battle training."

Nevra and Dronin shared a smile over the spawn's head. "Do you know how to fight, djuhlin?" Nevra asked, lowering to one knee so that she could more easily meet Ryddan's eyes.

"I was taught by the best." Ryddan's chest puffed up with pride. "Belly and Ria practice with me sometimes."

"Oh?" Nevra prompted, tilting her head.

Encouraged, Ryddan leaned forward as if sharing a secret. "A lot of the Guard won't say it out loud, but they all watch Ria to learn from her. They call her demonslayer."

Nevra's eyes flicked to Dronin, who tucked his wings against his back. "And you trust these fae who have killed so many of your own kind?" he asked.

Ryddan turned to him, some of the surety leaving his expression. The question was too deep for his child's brain to fully pull apart in the moment, so he said the only thing that came to mind. "Ria's not fae, she's human."

Nevra's dark eyes widened, a wicked smile stretching her lips as she stood. "Of course she is."

Dronin wanted to laugh, but he held back the dark glee that warmed his blood. "Ah, yes, the same human demon slayer who killed your father."

"The demons were attacking. They were going to take over and—"

"Oh no, young one," Dronin took a step closer, cocking his head to the side and watching Ryddan with sorrowful eyes. "My dearest brother was killed *here*, in his own realm. She chased him here, this human."

Ryddan's brow furrowed, and he curled his hands into fists, claws pricking his skin. He looked down, unclenching his fingers to see beads of dark blood welling in his palms. "But—"

"It is true," Nevra said. "I saw his body with my own eyes, his blood splashed across the rocks to the north."

Ryddan's stomach churned, a tremor running down his spine as his mind bucked against their implications.

"Does she wear her name with pride, Ryddan? Does she enjoy being called demonslayer?" Dronin asked, voice softer than Ryddan had ever heard it.

"Well, yeah, but—"

"And are you not a demon?" Dronin prodded.

"No, I—"

"No?" Nevra interjected. "You look every bit a greater demon to me. I can sense a djuhl's power in your blood from here."

Ryddan swallowed, his emotions threatening to rise up and overwhelm him again. Merriam didn't see him as a demon, he knew that. She was always warm toward him and had never once looked at him with disgust.

She's never seen me look like them.

As soon as he thought it, Ryddan rejected the notion. She was his family, she'd told him as much many times. "I don't want to think about this," he whimpered, curling into himself. He was scared and confused and alone again, and he hated it.

"You do not have to." Nevra opened an arm to him. "Come eat, then maybe we can train with Lyvin while our djuhl talks to Donova about getting you back home."

Ryddan watched her for a moment, then walked over, letting himself be tucked against her side. His head barely came to her waist, but her hand on his shoulder was a basal comfort that he'd missed, and his body started to relax.

"Now you have four teeth made to bite him with—how fun is that?"

Ryddan didn't know whether to grimace or smile. "Is he mad?"

"Lyvin is used to rough play, djuhlin. It is our way," Nevra assured him, escorting him from the balcony. She cast one last look at Dronin as she left, and he nodded his thanks to her before stepping onto the balcony railing and falling over the side.

He flew to another, smaller balcony on the other side of the castle, relishing the swell of air against his wings. He landed on the wide stone railing and folded them in as he stepped down, pushing open the doors.

"It is courtesy to knock before entering private chambers." Donova sat across the room, her back to him.

Dronin walked over, wrapping her ponytail in his fist. "Every part of this castle is mine," he said, pulling her head back and leaning down to drag his teeth over her neck.

"I have spells to prepare," she reminded him curtly, but she hissed in pleasure when he captured her bottom lip in his mouth, tugging on it before he straightened, releasing her.

"How is your progress?"

Donova returned to the table in front of her, sliding her fingers over a volume of text. "The properties of his blood have taken a while to decipher. His blood manipulates the stones as expected, but is also partially of the stones. The spellwork required is rather complicated, but I think I have found something that will work."

"Good." Dronin lowered himself onto her bed.

"Keep your warriors at the ready, My Djuhl." Donova walked over, standing in front of him. "But I will need more blood from the youngling."

Dronin placed his hands on her hips, the points of his claws pressing into her skin. "Nevra was right, the beast. We might be able to turn him."

Donova pushed her fingers into his hair, her claws scraping against his horns as she allowed herself to be guided between his legs. "I suppose he is young enough."

"He is Charn's spawn. If we can raise him to be a conqueror, it would only make it easier for us to dominate other realms." Dronin hooked one claw into the neckline of Donova's gown, ripping it down the middle with one swift pull. His eyes traveled down the alabaster skin now exposed to him, and desire flooded his system.

Donova tightened her fingers in the dark strands of his hair as his lips pressed to her skin, awakening a heavy need in her core as her magic danced under his touch, craving the proximity of his own. "That will take time."

Dronin lifted her from the backs of her thighs, pulling her forward so that she was straddling him. "Once we take Nethyl, once we take the Gate, we will have nothing but time. And he will learn through action." He bit her neck, sliding the ruined fabric from her shoulders. "And in the meantime, I have you."

Donova smiled, challenge flaring in her golden eyes as she ground against him. "You are confident in that, are you?"

Dronin slid one hand between them, nothing about his movements gentle as he touched her center. His cock ached with the pressure of his leathers, and he was almost mad with the desire to bury himself in her. "You know you are well past the point of leaving, sorceress."

She didn't bother denying it, freeing him from his leathers and giving herself over to the call of her power to be melded with his, her body begging to be filled.

Chapter 43

Little hellion

IT TOOK MOST OF the night and half the next day to prepare the Royal Guard to march. A detachment had been sent to Entumbra, and another left behind to guard the castle, but outside of that, the entire army went south.

Shiloh had marked the location where they'd seen the dying trees on a map. With a prospective destination set, Merriam had told them to stay behind, but they refused.

"I know I'm not a fighter, Mer, and I have no delusions of grandeur. But I do know my way around plants, and I'm a quick learner. I can help in the med tent, even just to sort and run supplies."

"You have no obligation to this," Merriam said, meeting their gaze. "Battle isn't pretty, and it's not fun. Stay in Umbra."

"I'm aware, and I wouldn't offer if I didn't mean it. Let me go."

Merriam had seen the sincerity in their eyes, but still felt unsure about letting a civilian tag along, regardless of how much she liked them. She'd sent Shiloh down to the medics, who'd thankfully accepted the help, knowing they were likely to be stretched thin in the midst of the fighting and happy to have an extra runner.

The march to the spot where the demons might be breaking through took almost four days. Each day, Merriam Traveled to Tymecht to scout the area, but other than a couple of small villages in the distance, she hadn't seen anything worth reporting, and she'd never been able to get a sense of Ryddan close by.

On Nethyl, though, the caravan had come across a couple of lesser demons and a handful of byrds along the way, but nothing that put up too great of a fight. The creatures' presence solidified that Sekha's army was on the right path and that they weren't wrong in assuming the demons were planning an invasion.

Merriam rode with Mollian at the front of the group, the sun dipping low against the horizon as they crested a hill. She stopped her horse dead in its tracks, her mouth falling open.

"I think we've found where they're getting in," Mollian said, his voice even despite the dread that chilled his blood.

The forests they'd traveled through had all been vibrant with the colors of fall: brilliant yellows, deep oranges, and vivid reds. But every tree on the horizon was gray—leached of color—including the leaves littering the forest floor.

"That's where the ley line runs?" Merriam asked.

Mollian nodded as Calysta came up to them, shortly followed by Dio. "Can you feel it in your blood? It's the same hum as the Gate's magic."

Merriam was too unsettled to fully separate what was anxiety and what was the physical proximity of raw magic, but she nodded anyway.

"The trees ..." Calysta pressed a fist to her chest, eyes wide as she took it in. "This is unnatural. Whatever is eating them, it's not of this world. I'll go talk to them. And I'll put out a call for the other nymphs to join the fight. Nethyl needs us."

"How have we not had more reports of this?" Dio asked, disbelief in his voice.

"We've broken from the main road. It's possible not many have traveled this way," Mollian offered before turning to Merriam. "Did Shiloh make it sound this bad when they told you?"

Merriam shook her head. "They said a few trees, but that was before the demons had Ryddan. Maybe they've been testing their boundaries more now, pushing for the limits of what their spells can do mixed with his magic." She caught Mollian's eyes. "I'll go take a look, see what we might be dealing with."

He pressed his lips together, swallowing against the fear that threatened to choke him. *Stay out of sight*, he cautioned.

Merriam gave a brisk nod, sliding from the saddle and preparing to Travel. She was growing more comfortable with the way Tymecht's distance pulled at her strength. It still left her a little breathless, but she expected it now, and landed in a crouch in the demon realm. She took a deep breath, sulfur burning her lungs. Like much of the demon realm's landscape, this area was scattered with large boulders. She slowly rose to peek over the edge of one, and her heart dropped into her stomach.

The sharp edges of the rock cut into her palms as she pressed her hands against it to help steady herself. She was on the edge of a mountain, which dipped away sharply into a sprawling plain below. A vast sea stretched out to one side, and a giant castle hewn from the same stone as the landscape sat on a cliff at the sea's edge. At the base of the castle was a swarm of organized activity.

The demon army.

Merriam's mouth went dry, eyes wide as she took in their numbers, weighing them against Sekha's forces. She watched for a moment longer before Traveling home. "This is it," she told Mollian and Dio. "This is where they're planning to break through."

A shiver ran down Mollian's spine before he steeled himself. "We'll set up camp at the base of the hill. Captain, prepare your Guard. We'll go over strategy this evening."

"Yes, sir." Dio turned to give instruction to the commanders.

"Let's go try to shore up warding along this line. It won't stop them from breaking through at this point, but it can possibly slow them down." Mollian smiled grimly, leading Merriam down into the valley.

They spent the afternoon discussing everything Merriam had seen and running through potential plans while adding runes through the trees. Merriam's skin crawled each time she drew her blood across the bark. Something unnatural was eating away at them. There was no question about it.

When they'd done as much as they could, they returned to camp, Mollian squeezing her hand in comfort before leaving her to find Dio and discuss how to stage and move the Guard during battle.

Merriam went to a training ring that had been set up in the center of camp, happy to let her body move from muscle memory for a while as she sparred with some of the Guard, iron necklaces around their throats to force them to fight without magic.

The camp was fully set up by nightfall, wired with a nervous energy from the knowledge that battle was imminent.

Merriam was eating supper with Leonidas and Campbell when Jasper and Aleah showed up.

"Miss me?" Aleah grinned, dropping to sit between Leonidas and Merriam and stealing a strip of meat from the marshal's grasp.

"Gonna tell us what held you up in Umbra?" Merriam asked, leaning her head against Aleah's shoulder as Jasper sat across from them. Neither had shown up the morning the caravan left, but had sent a message with the others that they would catch up as soon as they could.

Aleah flicked her gaze to Jasper before focusing on her feet. "My grandparents."

Merriam straightened, looking at Aleah in surprise.

Campbell choked, turning to Jasper for confirmation.

Panic stood in the dirt in front of Merriam, tilting his head to and fro with his eyes trained on the meat in her fingers.

"They arrived right before you got back from Entumbra," Aleah started slowly. "At first, they were determined to see Mollian, but once they heard he was planning to leave the capital, they held back." She met Merriam's gaze with a grim smile. "Spiro figured he'd have more of a chance of being heard if he presented his suspicions to someone without such a personal connection to one of their potential suspects."

Merriam's heart lodged in her throat, but the faintly amused glimmer in Aleah's hazel eyes kept her blood from running cold.

Panic let out a soft chirrup, still watching Merriam's food.

"I went to see them," Aleah continued as Merriam ripped off a strip of beef to toss to the falcon. "You don't have to worry about any of that shit with Chetney falling back on you, Kodi, or us."

"Legends, red, you didn't kill them, did you?" Leonidas asked.

Aleah laughed. "Don't worry, even I'm not crazy enough to take out the patriarch of the second most powerful family in Sekha. I just gave them a choice." She shrugged, tucking her hair behind her clipped ear. "Either they could go back home and accept that their eldest son skipped town of his own volition, or I could go back for them, accept my new title as heiress, and let everyone know exactly why I disappeared for so long and the complicit part they played in it. They wisely picked the option where Aleah Kinbriar stayed a ghost."

"Are you okay?" Merriam asked, squeezing Aleah's hand.

Aleah squeezed back. "Seeing them again after so long was weirdly ... empowering. With Chetney gone, I don't have anything to be afraid of anymore. Hel, you should have seen Larna's face when I showed up at their door. *She* was scared of *me*." She shook her head in partial disbelief.

"We're clear from the Illiziana job, too. They won't push it," Jasper added.

Aleah looked around. "Where's Calysta?"

"She went to plead our cause to the nymphs and try to enlist them in the fight," Campbell said.

After they'd all eaten, Aleah left to find Kodi, and Merriam checked in with Mollian before slinking from camp. He was still deep in strategy talks with Dio and the commanders of the Guard, and she needed a moment away from the noise, away from all of the people. A cold breeze blew down the hillside, and she held the edges of her cloak tight as she climbed.

Merriam sat beneath a copse of unblighted trees at the top of a hill, legs tucked to her chest and chin resting on her knees. Her gaze was on the sky, the reflection of stars shining in her eyes and her bottom lip tucked into her mouth. The camp and dying woods across from it were at her back, the land in front of her unmarred by demons. She hoped they could do enough to keep it that way.

Footsteps sounded in the leaf fall behind her, announcing Rovin's presence before he sat next to her. Merriam leaned into him, curling her fists in the folds of her cloak. He propped a leg up, resting his forearm on his knee. "How do you feel?"

Merriam looked at him, searching his face for a moment before answering. "Good, I suppose."

He brushed a thumb over her lower lip and the indents left in it from her teeth. "Your mouth would beg to differ."

Merriam nipped at him as he dropped his hand. "I only mean I think I should feel a lot more frazzled than I am. We don't even really have a foolproof plan, but somehow I'm just ... ready for action. And not even in an antsy way." She shrugged, resting her head against his shoulder.

"Maybe it's because I know they'll be here, and I know there's only two outcomes. However we get there doesn't really matter."

"What are the outcomes?" Rovin asked, pressing his lips against the top of her head as she tucked herself closer against him.

"Either we bring back Ryddan and block off Tymecht, or they kill us all."

"That's it? No second chances, rebellions, or long, drawn-out wars that we eventually win?"

"I mean, sure, it won't be an automatic be-all end-all, but think about it. We'd eventually exhaust ourselves. We can't protect everybody. What happens when the demons start possessing people? Will the common folk be able to kill their friends and neighbors, even if it isn't really them anymore? We'd put up a Hel of a fight, sure, but if they kept pouring through, eventually they'd take over. And from there, who knows? Complete and utter destruction is my bet." Merriam's gaze traveled across the sky as she grabbed Rovin's hand and pulled it into her lap.

He snorted. "That's dismal."

She tipped her head up to look at him, a smile playing at her lips. "That's why we're not going to fail."

"You're something else, you know that?" Rovin's gaze slid from her eyes to her mouth, so close to his, and his stomach flipped with the realization that he could kiss her. That the two of them were in a place where the act would be welcomed and reciprocated. It made him dizzy to think about and filled his chest with considerable warmth.

Merriam matched the intensity of his gaze, her stomach tumbling over itself. "Are you gonna do something about it?" she challenged.

He cupped her cheek and slanted his mouth over hers, pulling her lower lip between his teeth as his hand ran over her hair to grip the back of her neck. He smiled as he kissed her, her body turning to him and her hands fisting in his shirt as she pulled herself closer.

"What's so funny?" she asked breathlessly.

"I just like you," he answered, wrapping his arms around her and pulling her onto his lap. "And your smart mouth is so damn kissable."

Merriam's hands went into his hair, fingers tangling in the thick brown waves as she wrapped her legs around him and locked her ankles behind his back. Her tongue slid along his, and a needy whimper escaped her.

Rovin gripped her hips, grinding against her. His cock strained against the seam of his pants, his own desire coiled tightly at the base of his spine as Merriam pulled at his hair, sharp pricks of pain lighting across his scalp.

Her hands roamed down his back, sliding underneath his shirt. Desire pounded in her blood as she pulled herself closer against him, rocking her hips to create friction where she craved it—where she craved *him*.

Her fingers were cold against Rovin's skin, but her touch sent fire burning through him, and when she rolled her hips against his erection, all coherent thought fled him. "*Fucking Hel*," he growled against her neck, running his teeth against her throat before biting her shoulder, pulling at the laces of her pants and wedging a hand between them. He glided two fingers through her arousal before pushing into her. "You're already so ready for me, pet."

Merriam grabbed his face, crashing her lips back to his in a kiss that was full of tongues and teeth as she rocked her hips against his hand. A strangled sound of need crawled up her throat.

Rovin pressed the heel of his palm against her clit as he curled his fingers inside her, matching the movement of his wrist to the movement of her hips. His other hand was under her shirt, moving across her skin with a possessive pressure that almost made Merriam forget to breathe. He gripped her ribs, thumb brushing over her nipple through the thin fabric of her bra. The touch was light and sent a ripple of pleasure down Merriam's spine.

Rovin continued to drive his fingers into her, and her hands moved from his face to his shoulders, using him as leverage to grind against his hand. "Rov—Rovi," she panted.

Rovin was painfully hard, and hearing her beg for him as she clenched around his fingers made his balls tighten. "You're so fucking pretty when you come." He matched her movements, swiveling the heel of his hand against her clit. "Do it for me."

The command was simple, measured, but he dragged his fingers over the front of her inner walls as he said it, and she couldn't have denied him if she'd wanted to. Merriam bit down on his lip, which did nothing to stifle her whimper as she convulsed around him. As her orgasm faded, she moved her hands back to his cheeks, fingers scraping against the stubble on his jaw, and rested her forehead against his.

Rovin, still holding her ribs, could feel her heart pounding, and a small, self-satisfied smile tugged at his mouth. He leaned back, holding eye contact with her as he pulled his hand free. Her arousal coated his fingers, which he brought to his mouth, sucking them clean. Then he kissed her, letting her taste how much she wanted him.

"Take off your pants and fuck me," Merriam ordered breathlessly, brushing her lips back over his.

Rovin's cock twitched in his pants. "Sir, yes, sir." He smirked when she smacked his shoulder, but then her other hand snaked between them, palming his length. Rovin's eyes rolled back, and he thrust into her hand.

"You like it when I tell you what to do, Ranger-man?" she whispered huskily.

Rovin nipped at her neck. "I fucking hate it. Drives me mad."

Merriam smiled, tilting her head to give him better access as she continued to stroke him through his pants. "Too bad that shit gets me off."

Rovin licked up the column of her neck, and she shivered. "Of course it does. Fucking little hellion." She pulled his laces loose, and he almost sighed at the release of pressure on his cock. But then her hand was back around him, and he sucked in a breath as he pumped into her grip. "Fucking. Little. Hellion."

Merriam sucked on his bottom lip, running her tongue across it. "I need you inside of me. *Now.*"

Rovin's answer was just a growl, and he lifted her from his lap before standing and pulling her to her feet with him. He kissed her, hands roaming her body as he backed her against the trunk of a cypress, the breath leaving her lungs in a short gasp as he shoved her against it.

Rovin's fingers curled around the waist of her pants, just beginning to slide them down when the clatter of boots stomping through the forest reached them.

"Put your dick away, it's family time," Kodi called, announcing his arrival.

"Go back to camp," Rovin retorted.

"Sure, but we'll all know you're up here fucking."

The familiar presence settling her soul broke through the lust and desire clouding Merriam's mind, and she rose onto her tiptoes, peering over Rovin's shoulder. She settled back down, meeting his gaze apologetically. "Later?"

Rovin pressed a final, chaste kiss to her lips in answer, retying the laces of his pants as Merriam fixed her own clothes. She twined her fingers through his as their friends appeared through the trees.

"A year ago, I'd expect to find one of you up here bleeding out after being left alone," Aleah teased.

"I might prefer it that way," Mollian added, wrinkling his nose in mock distaste.

Merriam rolled her eyes.

"Shiloh brought a deck of cards," Bellamy said. "We could play a game."

Campbell walked to the edge of the trees, spinning on his heel and sitting. "I know getting drunk and stupid isn't going to happen with imminent doom on the horizon and all that, but there's no reason we can't uphold the rest of our Odds tradition." He smiled up at Leonidas, holding out a hand to pull the man down next to him.

Chapter 44

Battle braids

SOON THEY WERE ALL arranged in a circle, knee to knee, and Merriam bit her lip, her heart swelling with fullness at the people around her. Mollian, her constant, was at her right and Rovin at her left. The mercenaries, who were still more her family than any she'd ever had, filled out the rest of the circle along with Kodi, Shiloh, and Bellamy on Mollian's other side. So many people she cared about. When had her circle grown so big?

Bellamy's scar glowed pale in the moonlight, cutting over one gray-blue eye and down his cheek as he explained the rules of the game. A knot formed in Merriam's stomach, remembering the demon who'd given him the wound. She had so much to lose if things went south. They all had so much to lose.

She glanced at Mollian, who met her gaze with an encouraging smile. *We've got this.*

Do you even know what you're supposed to be doing between worlds?

Merriam toyed with the aspen leaf at her throat.

Does a goose know why it flies south for winter or enjoys the water? It's instinct. I have to trust that my magic will guide me.

Merriam fought back a snort, rolling her eyes. *I'm sure all of Sekha will rest well knowing their king has equated himself with a goose.*

"And if the rest of us are done having silent conversations, we can begin," Bellamy said loudly.

Mollian grinned, raising his hands in front of him, palms out. "I promise there was no talk of butts this time."

As they played, Campbell and Aleah explained Odds to the Rangers and Shiloh. "Before any job where there's liable to be a lot of casualties, we each pick who we think will end with a higher body count," Campbell said. "The only rules are no picking yourself, and be able to defend your decision."

"Typically, we get absolutely blasted while doing so. Makes arguing your point a lot more fun," Aleah added happily.

"That's pretty dark," Shiloh said, glancing over the cards in their hand. "I like it."

Aleah nodded definitively. "You can stay. Welcome to the cool kids club, membership by invite only."

"Who put *you* in charge of who's in or not?" Leonidas raised an eyebrow, tossing out a card into the center of the group.

Anyone who could play off him also threw their card in.

"I found Cam and Calysta," Aleah said, tapping a finger against her chin as she looked over her hand. "And I would even argue that I found Jasper, too. Really, this whole group wouldn't even exist without me."

"That's a stretch." Jasper pulled a card from the center before tossing in two more.

"No, she might have a point." Calysta added her own card, pushing Jasper's back to him. "She did find me and Campbell, and Kodi would have never hung around without her. And who was always hanging around Kodi?" The nymph's gleaming black eyes slid to Rovin, her pointed teeth showing as she smiled.

"Rovin and Mer were at each other's throats long before Kodi was at Aleah's," Campbell pointed out, making a play.

Mollian added to the pile of cards in the middle. "But if Rovin was with Kodi, and Kodi was with Aleah, and Aleah was with Ria, then that would force Ria and Rovin together." He looked up, winking at the half-fae. "I'm with Aleah on this one."

"I would argue, but I think I lost the strand somewhere," Merriam laughed. "How did we get here?"

"Shiloh is part of the group now," Aleah reminded her before turning back to Shiloh. "Unfortunately, that means you'll have to stay in Umbra. Sorry, rules are rules," she chirped without remorse.

"I don't know how any of you can even read these damned things," Kodi muttered, squinting at his cards in the darkness.

"My odds aren't on the blind one," Calysta intoned. "I think I'll throw them on Rovin."

Rovin glanced at the nymph in surprise, then caught himself. "I'm saying Aleah, and there's a strategy here." He tossed a card into the center of the circle and explained while the others played from it. "We all know Kodi is a bloodthirsty animal in a fight—" Kodi saluted. "—and we can safely assume that he'll go even harder than usual, now that he's got Aleah to impress. But I'm guessing that you're going to be trying to one up him the whole time." Rovin looked at Aleah as he finished his statement, pointing a finger emphatically. "And I'm willing to bet that your competitive nature is going to win out."

"How very perceptive of you." Aleah flashed him a smile, baring pointed canines.

By the time they finished doling out their choices for who would make the most kills, the wind had picked up, running up the side of the mountain and blowing the cards across the center of the circle.

Bellamy fought with his hair while he leaned to pick them up, tendrils flying across his face. When he sat back down, the others still conversing about possible outcomes and whose strengths would prove better in which situation, Merriam stood.

"Should we move this party to the camp?" she suggested with a little shiver.

"Fire sounds lovely," Campbell agreed.

The group packed up, heading back down the mountain to the clearing where all of the tents had been set up.

Calysta peered further into the valley, her eyes running along the ground where she knew the ley line rested. Nerves, or maybe anticipation, thrummed in her veins, and she wondered if any of the surrounding nymphs would answer her call.

"You okay?" Merriam asked, resting a hand on the olive green skin of

Calysta's shoulder.

Calysta leaned into the familiar touch, recognizing the absurdity that it grounded her more than the ley line's proximity. She, a nymph, with such strong connections to those without Nethyl's magic. Even all these years later, it still felt novel. "Did we make this worse?" she responded in question. "My people, I mean. Did we let the demons come in?"

Merriam squeezed Calysta's shoulder, shaking her head. "They had Basta's rings, and that oversight was *mine*," she reminded her.

"Our ceremonies made it easier, though."

Merriam shrugged. "If they hadn't, would we have known to check whether the area they were coming in through was over a ley line? Would we know where to expect the fight? Maybe it had to happen this way for a reason. But nobody blames you or the nymphs. Molli doesn't blame you any more than he blames me."

Calysta understood the message meant to quell her unspoken fear: whatever the nymphs' unknown involvement in thinning the barrier between their worlds, Mollian wouldn't repress them again.

They sat around a fire, the wind here much calmer than it had been higher in the hills, and Merriam saw Bellamy pull the tie out of the top half of his hair, toying with his curls to try to regain some order after the wind's assault.

"May I?" she asked, walking up behind him and running her fingers over his head.

Bellamy tilted his face up, meeting her eyes with a small smile. "Sure."

Merriam gently and methodically separated clumps of curls, starting at the crown of his head and braiding everything together. She pulled the woven strands taut, making sure that his hair wouldn't get in the way during the impending fight, and tied off the end. He squeezed her hand in thanks, knowing this was a moment bigger than words.

Aleah sank down next to Bellamy. "Me next?" Her hazel eyes gleamed in the firelight, soft and vulnerable in a way Aleah almost never allowed herself to be.

Fear wound itself into a tight, cold ball in Merriam's gut. Whatever they were about to face would be bad, and it was very likely—Hel, even probable—that they all wouldn't make it to the other side. She released Bellamy's hand, running her fingers through Aleah's hair.

Merriam gave the half-fae two braids, again taking the time to make sure everything was secure.

"Shit, if we're all doing battle braids, I want one, too." Kodi came over, arms loaded with bread and fruit.

Aleah took the food, doling it out to the group as Merriam tilted her head, contemplating Kodi's mohawk. She ended up weaving a small braid along one end, his curls just long enough for her to work with.

Calysta, who had never in her life tied up her hair, allowed Merriam to add one chunky braid draping down the side of her head, and her fingers kept drifting over the pale pink plait the entire time Merriam loosely wove the tight twists of Jasper's hair together.

Leonidas' hair was nowhere near long enough to even attempt, and Merriam barely managed to pull Campbell's curls into a tiny braid over one of his ears. Shiloh even sat, though they wouldn't be fighting, and let Merriam braid back the top of their hair, ending in a small bun at the crown of their head. Merriam steeled herself against the prick of grief she expected to pierce her heart, Shiloh's hairstyle so similar to what Oren had always worn.

Her throat grew tight, but the memory of him warmed her chest, and in the same way she knew that he would be so proud of Mollian and everything that he'd done for Sekha, she knew that he would be proud of how much she had allowed herself to outwardly feel, of how much she was willing to show others that she cared, regardless of the potential pain it made her vulnerable to. Tears pricked her eyes. *A lesson learned too late.*

He would be happy to see you allowing yourself to love so freely. Mollian's voice wrapped around her, more comforting than the heat of the fire.

"What about you, Lord King?" she asked, clearing her throat and blinking to clear the tears from her eyes.

Mollian brushed a curl from his forehead. "But what will I do with my hands if my hair isn't in my face?"

"There's a sex joke to be made there if you were anyone but you," Aleah said.

"Sorry to throw a wrench in your humor." Mollian grinned, folding his legs in front of him as he sat before Merriam. "Only because you're you," he told her.

Merriam set to work on his silky, white curls, his scent of spruce and plum enveloping her. She wove braids on either side of his temple, tying them together at the back of his head. When she'd finished, she tilted his face up to hers, her thumbs stroking the spots where the aspen leaves faded into his hairline. "Now your crown isn't hidden. When you walk around this camp, when you're out on that battlefield, everyone will know you are their king."

"And the demons will know precisely who to target," Mollian replied sarcastically, but he leaned his head back into her hands in silent thanks for her constant support.

"Not many people out there with your white hair, Your Majesty. You'd be an obvious target even without that tattoo," Kodi pointed out.

"I guess it's a good thing I have other places to be, then."

Merriam wrapped her arms around his shoulders, resting her cheek against the top of his head. "Don't make me come looking for you, okay?" Her tone was joking, but that knot of fear in her stomach doubled. She still had the undying sense that where Mollian saw the inner workings of the universe was a place she wouldn't be able to follow, regardless of his magic running through her veins.

They sat together for a moment, back to front, the conversation around them returning to the normal jokes and arguments. Merriam closed her eyes, focusing on those threads that wove between her soul and Mollian's. There was no telling what was hers and what was his, they were just one. Selfish relief at knowing he wouldn't be in the thick of the fighting eased some of the pressure in her chest.

But something else kept her lungs feeling compressed, a different kind of fear than just knowing people she loved would be in peril. It was a fear of loss, a fear of suffering that was so strong and deep and still so unfairly familiar to her.

Merriam opened her eyes, forcing the dark thoughts back as she looked at Rovin, who stood a few paces away. The flames shone auburn against his hair, one arm slung over Kodi's shoulders as he joked with the others. His eyes met hers, and his expression softened.

The beat of Merriam's heart fluttered against Mollian's back, and his hand tightened around her arm in solidarity. Biting her lip, Merriam extended an open palm to Rovin.

He stepped over, and she lifted her cheek from Mollian's hair, her *mehhen* brushing his hand down her arm before moving closer to the others and sliding into their conversation without missing a beat.

"Would you like a battle braid, Lieutenant?" A swarm of butterflies now orbited that knot of fear in her stomach.

Rovin, who'd taken to leaving his hair down as a way to hide the mark that told the world he wasn't high fae, saw the vulnerability in those amber eyes, and the depth of that emotion almost sent him to his knees. He wanted to cup her face, hold her to him, and never let go. She'd had her fingers in everyone's hair, had touched them all with the comfortable ease of friendship, but he knew this was different. He didn't understand why, didn't understand that Merriam had offered to do Oren's hair only once. That it had been before a fight that had ultimately led to his death. Rovin didn't know that, in those moments fixing the hair of the male she'd loved, Merriam had decided she wanted to make her relationship public, had decided she could live with the potential hurt it would expose her to. That it was worth the risk.

Rovin didn't know any of this, but he'd known Merriam for eight years, and he knew her facial expressions and her body language well enough to understand that this meant something to her. He knew that, in meaning something, it scared her. But she was still offering it.

To him.

And that small bit of knowledge filled him with more adoration than anything else ever could. For him to be the recipient of this vulnerability, this act of intimacy that he admired the strength of without having to be privy to its full depth, solidified in him that she would be it for him. He was hers.

She was still kneeling, hand outstretched, and he took it, sinking to his knees in front of her and brushing the backs of his fingers across her cheek. "Thank you," he whispered before turning around to sit.

The force of emotion that swelled through Merriam tightened her chest, and she licked her lips, searching for something sarcastic or biting to say to lighten the mood, but nothing came. So she went to work sectioning off his hair. She stayed quiet, her fingers steady even though that cold fear still churned through her. It threatened to choke her, almost paralyzing in its depth. But she closed her eyes, swallowing past the lump in her throat and choosing to stare down that darkness and what she was so afraid of. "I don't think I can lose you." Her voice was so quiet it was almost drowned out by the crackle of the fire a few paces away.

Rovin's heart constricted. "You can put a leash on me if you'd like, pet."

Merriam cracked a smile, the pressure around them easing. She took a deep, full breath, the fear no longer threatening to overwhelm her. Like having voiced it had rid it of its harsher shadows. "I'll trust that you have a good recall," she said as she tied off his hair. Only half was pulled back, the bottom brushing over his shoulders. She'd left enough down to still cover his ears, knowing the security blanket it was for him.

"Mmm," Rovin leaned his head back into her touch, eyes closing as her fingers combed through his hair. "I have been trained well."

Merriam leaned down, brushing his hair behind his clipped ear and gently taking the tip of it between her teeth. "Say what you want about Ferrick, I suppose, but at least he did that right."

Rovin choked, a shiver running up his spine at the brush of her breath over his cheek. "How about you don't talk about that asshole while you're touching me in ways that make me want to ravage you."

Merriam laughed, burying her face in his neck as she wrapped her arms around his shoulders, one hand dragging down his chest as she leaned into him. "Oh? And here I always thought you'd had such a hard on for him."

Rovin grabbed her wrists, shrugging his shoulder up to his ear as she tried to trail kisses along his neck. "Legends, you're not right in the head." He tried to wrestle her off of him, but each time he tried to move away, she darted around his reach to touch him further, breathless laughter shaking her chest as she teased him. He stood, still holding her arms over his shoulders so that she dangled down his back, and walked over to Mollian, swinging her into him. "Take your pet, Your Majesty, she's gone mad."

Mollian held his hands up, stepping back. "You riled her up, that means she's your responsibility."

Merriam wriggled free from Rovin's grasp, dropping to the ground and turning on Mollian. "I'll have you know, Lord King, that I am no one's responsibility, and I can just as easily become your problem."

"You really want to roughhouse after you just spent so much time doing everyone's hair?" Mollian blocked her attempts to poke him in the ribs.

"Is that a challenge against my braiding skills?" Merriam asked, firelight dancing in her amber eyes.

"Wait, are we dueling?" Aleah asked, and Campbell perked up.

Merriam grinned, and Mollian and Rovin shared an exasperated but endearing look over her shoulder.

"Form a ring," Rovin called, his voice carrying across their section of the camp.

"The demonslayer is asking for action!" Kodi added, drawing the attention of the other members of the Guard. The mood shift in the camp was palpable at the opportunity to burn off nervous energy and spar with Merriam, the mercenaries, or possibly some of their commanding officers.

It was the kind of physical release that would strengthen the camaraderie of the camp. One people. One goal. They would dance with each other and their weapons tonight, and they would be ready to meet the demons with blade and bloodlust when the time came.

Chapter 45

MERRIAM WOKE WHEN MOLLIAN rose from the bedroll they shared. A discontented squeak left her as the cold air of the morning hit her back, erasing the warmth Mollian had provided. "Where are you going?" she mumbled, shifting the blankets further under her chin.

"To see about breakfast. Show my face around camp. Be an inspiration and all that." Mollian pulled a fresh shirt over his head, sitting on a low stool to don his boots.

Merriam rolled, peeking an eye open to watch him. "Breakfast is good."

"I'll bring you some if you want to rest longer." Mollian looked up, raising a hand to brush the hair from his eyes out of habit. But the braids along his hairline held everything neatly in place.

"No, I should get up. A king at war needs his marshal and all that." Merriam closed her eyes, burrowing further into the blankets. She'd been up late, fulfilling the promise of *later* with Rovin until the wee hours of the morning.

If you say so. Mollian's voice rolled through her, light and teasing and warm.

I'll be right behind you. Merriam Cast the image of a salute, giving herself a few more moments to relax.

She opened her eyes, shooting up from the blankets an indiscriminate amount of time later. A line of drool wet her cheek, and she brushed it off with the heel of her hand, which she wiped on the hem of her shirt as she looked around, her heart rate slowing. Sunlight streamed through the tent, the loose flap drifting in the breeze. A plate of food rested beside the bedroll, along with a cup of water.

She folded her legs in front of her, pulling the plate into her lap and digging in.

Merriam was just about finished when a shadow fell over the entrance, Aleah poking her head in. "Oh good, you're up!" She plopped onto the other end of the bed, plucking a berry from the plate. "A few of the commanders want to go over the strategy a final time. Mollian's been holding them at bay to wait for you, but they're getting antsy."

"Why did no one wake me?" Merriam gulped down the water, wiping the back of her hand across her mouth and looking around for fresh clothes.

"Our fearless king was under the impression you needed sleep. I'd say he was right, judging by the depth of those pillow lines." Aleah stole the remaining berries before rolling away and jumping back to her feet. "They're in the main tent when you're ready."

Merriam rubbed her fingers against her cheek, setting the dishes aside and hurriedly taking care of basic hygiene before changing into battle gear. She buckled her weapons belt around her hips as she walked, eyes on the simple mechanism that refused to slip into place.

An arm slung over her shoulders, redirecting her out of the way of a group of guardsmen that were marching through the camp.

Finally, the buckle caught. "Thanks, Kodi."

He dropped his arm, tucking his hands into his pockets as he walked with her. "My pleasure, demonslayer." He stopped when they reached the tent. "Brass only, so this is where I take my leave," he started, scuffing the toe of one boot through the grass. "I'll be briefed on whatever my role is by my commander later, but um ..." he swallowed, meeting Merriam's gaze evenly. "You've got special shit planned, right? You and Mollian?"

She nodded.

"Are the mercs involved?"

"They're just here to fight, that's all. No special missions," Merriam assured him.

"Ah, great." Kodi took a step back, relief relaxing his shoulders. He knew Aleah could hold her own, but it was easier to breathe knowing he'd at least be able to keep her in his sight. "Have fun in there."

"I'll do my best." She ducked into the tent.

"Ah, Marshal, thank you for coming," Captain Dio greeted genuinely, motioning for her to step forward. They'd set up a table with a map of the area, little markers showing their camp and where it sat next to a thick vein of magic. "Do you mind running through everything once more?"

"Not at all." Merriam stepped forward, resting her hands on the table. "I'm sure Captain Dio has already briefed you all on formations and positions when it's time to fight the demons. You and your men have the most important job of this battle: holding the front lines and keeping their attention. While you're fighting here, I'll be taking two Rangers on a rescue mission for Prince Ryddan. I don't think they'll have the balls to bring him back to our world without defeating us first, so we'll be sneaking into their realm. The hope here is that it will be a quick in and out, where we'll then join the fight on the front lines." She'd already told Bellamy and Rovin where to meet her when the battle began.

"In the meantime, I'll be working to close off the portal they'll have opened between our worlds," Mollian said, stepping up to her side.

Merriam had only planned to take Bellamy, but Mollian and Rovin insisted a third should go. The chances of Merriam's strength being sapped while Mollian tried to cut off the demon world were high, and it would be smarter to have someone else there in case Ryddan also needed assistance. Mollian had selected Rovin, knowing he could trust the Ranger to keep Merriam's best interest in mind even when Merriam wouldn't.

The commanders talked more strategy and asked further questions, but it was all typical battle planning, where to set up which detachments and whose command each would fall under.

After the meeting ended, Mollian walked from the tent with Merriam, a tense set to his shoulders as he guided her away from most of the activity. He crossed his arms over his chest, watching the camp movements over Merriam's shoulder as he concentrated on settling the agitated churning of his magic. "I've been thinking about everything we have planned ... and I'm scared, Ria. I can't stop thinking about Ferrick taking you, and I know this isn't like that, but you'll still be out of my reach. I can't protect you when you're in Tymecht, and that terrifies me. I almost lost you once, and I don't think I could come back from that a second time."

"Molli." The pain in his face squeezed Merriam's heart. "You said you'd always find your way back to me, and you have. But that bond works both ways. I will *always* come back to you." She cupped his face in her hands, searching his eyes. "Every measure of fight and gumption I possess is mirrored within you. It always has been, whether or not you've seen it." Merriam pressed a palm over Mollian's heart. "You are going to save the world, Molli, and I *will* be here when you return from it. I promise."

Mollian pressed his lips together, blinking against the tears that lined his eyes. "You can't promise that."

"I just did." She smiled, tears filling her own eyes.

A chuckle that was half a sob tore from his chest, and he pulled her against him, resting his chin on her head. "I love you."

"I love you, too." She wrapped her arms around his waist and held him. "I'll get our prince back, and we'll all be together again on the other side of this."

They pulled apart as Evangeline walked up. "Captain Dio is asking for you, Your Majesty. More of the Guard have arrived."

Mollian pressed his palm to Merriam's before turning to the Ranger. "Lead the way." He had had birds sent to the outposts around Sekha as well as other kingdoms of Nethyl before they left Umbra, letting them know of the possible peril so that they could prepare themselves should the worst happen. A few of the closer units had marched to aid the fight and were now getting settled with the forces from Umbra.

Merriam found the mercenaries gathered with a group of the Guard, Shiloh in the center of the circle performing. They seemed right at home amid the warriors, confidence and sass saturating their features as they correctly picked cards, pulled coins and jewelry from pockets, and won over even the most devout of the skeptics in the crowd.

After the performance, they split off to train. Calysta and Shiloh worked with a few of the medics to create a stockpile of herbs, poultices, and tinctures for the wounded. Bellamy had gifted Shiloh a knife and taught them a few fancy moves, but they'd never been a fighter, and the time to learn was not moments before battle.

All day, tensions were high in the camp, everyone sparing occasional glances out into the field and the dead forest beyond, watching for any sign of a disturbance.

The sun went down, and Merriam found herself by a fire, seated between Rovin and Leonidas, the rest of the mercenaries scattered around them along with Kodi, Bellamy, and Shiloh. Mollian had been pulled away by Captain Dio.

The group slipped into their usual darkly humorous antics. Everyone was tense, ready to spring into action at the first warning call, but there was comfort in the pretense of normality.

Merriam leaned her head against Rovin's shoulder, closing her eyes as the heat of the fire danced over her face. "Stay with me tonight?"

Rovin's hand tightened where it held her knee pressed to his. With how late they'd been out last night, he'd assumed that she'd want to stay closer to Mollian.

"In Molli's tent. I just want you near me." Her throat closed up after that, unable to finish the thought. *In case we don't have more time.*

Warmth filled Rovin as he brushed his thumb over the inside of her knee, pressing a kiss against her temple. "I want to be near you."

Mollian soon joined them, and in a turn of events that really should have surprised nobody, the whole group was invited to bunk in the king's tent. "It feels like a necessary part of tradition, same as Odds. Why tempt fate by breaking protocol?" he pointed out.

Nobody could argue with that logic.

So they retrieved their bedding, laying it out in one giant palette of cushions and blankets on the floor of the tent, and drifted off to sleep surrounded by family.

The demons struck in the dead of night.

Merriam slept with her face tucked against Mollian's shoulder and her feet resting against Rovin's legs. Her head shot up when the alarm sounded, and she was alert as soon as her eyes opened. She sprung to her feet, leaping over the scattered bedrolls to shove her feet into her boots, quickly lacing them up before standing to grab her weapons belt, axes accompanied by a small assortment of knives. Her fingers shook slightly as she worked the buckle, and she forced herself to slow down.

The rest of the tent had also erupted into motion. Rovin caught her eyes as he laced up his own boots, only the tick of his jaw betraying how unsettled he was. He gave her a brief nod, signaling he'd be close behind her.

Merriam spun, her eyes finding Mollian's in the commotion.

Be safe. Run if you need to.

Promise. She smiled at him, unlatching the clasps of her axes and ducking from the tent.

Aleah and Kodi were right on her heels, eyes already bright and both of them buzzing with the need for battle.

"Legends-loving fuck," Aleah breathed, her eyes on the sky.

A large rift, the edges glowing a bright, ethereal blue, cut through the swath of stars in the sky. Cloud after oily cloud poured from it, slamming to the ground and materializing into creatures of every nightmarish shape and size. Byrds flew around them, their cries creating a bone-chilling cacophony.

"That'll do it," Merriam stated, acknowledging the fear that coursed through her veins. She let it run through her, then let it run out, and solidified her mind into the cool, calculating calm of a fight. "See you on the other side." She held up an axe, and Aleah knocked the flat of her sword against it.

"See ya," Aleah replied, exploding into motion a moment later. Kodi winked, flashing Merriam a feral grin before taking off after Aleah, and Merriam ran in the other direction, pulling her other axe free.

She ran through rows of tents, breaking free into the clearing.

Merriam had seen war depicted in many movies and tv shows when she'd lived on Earth. It was violent, brutal, yes, but had always been shown to have some sort of order, unspoken laws that each side followed to create a flow and make things easier to follow.

But what was happening in the meadow was nothing short of chaos.

Most of the demons were in the form of creatures, but a few looked like people. The greater demons fought with weapons, though their hands and feet were tipped in large claws that glinted in the moonlight.

They fought alongside the creatures, and it took every ounce of Merriam's restraint not to run to the aid of the Guard who fought them.

She had a job to do.

Merriam raised an axe, slamming the blade down into the flat head of a demon that ran through the fray on six stumpy but agile legs, its mouth open, baring pointed teeth in preparation to attack. She wrenched her axe free, not slowing her movement through the clearing.

She slashed through the spindly legs of another demon as she passed, leaving it lopsided and lilting for the fae who fought it. A serpentine creature shot towards her, and she swung at it, the blade of an axe catching its side before she leapt over the rest of its thick body, landing in a run on the other side.

Merriam had almost made it into the woods, attacking whatever demons stood in her path, but not slowing to finish them off, when a searing burst of pain tore through her arm. She hissed, whirling to find a greater demon standing a few paces away, arm cocked to throw another sharp metal disc. Blood leaked down the back of her arm where the first had cut into her muscle.

The demon loosed the sphere, and Merriam barely reacted fast enough to knock it aside before launching herself towards him. She dropped into a roll when he threw another, slamming the back of an axe into the side of his knee as she sprung up, drawing the blade of the other up into his side.

The demon roared in pain, his fully black eyes shining with unadulterated rage. He lifted a mace from the holster on his back, the spiked block that topped it larger than Merriam's head.

She didn't give him time to set up for an attack, darting to the side and swinging toward his arms.

He was faster than Merriam expected, blocking the attack with the grip of the mace while taking a step back. He swung for her, and Merriam jumped back before rushing in closer, aiming low with her axes to attack his legs. She ran by the demon, then whirled on one foot to face him again, already swooping in for another attack as he was turning to face her.

Sweat dripped down her temple as she attacked again, and she blinked furiously to clear it from her eyes. The demon was ready for her this time, the mace slamming into the head of her axe with enough force that it almost slid completely from her grip. Merriam danced back, adjusting her hold on her weapons.

The demon advanced on her, and she blocked a couple of swift attacks before another anguished, enraged cry ripped from his throat. He whirled, yelling a string of what could only have been profanities in a guttural language.

As soon as the demon turned, Merriam ran forward, slamming one axe into the base of his spine before springing up to drive the other into his neck. He crumpled forward, and she pulled her weapons free. Bellamy stood on the other side, face spattered with black blood and the blade of his sword dripping with it.

She nodded at him in thanks, and they both ran for the trees. "Have you seen Rovin?" she panted when they were well within the foliage, watching the battle below. Sweat rolled down her spine, and she fell back against a tree to rest.

Bellamy shook his head. "Not since the tent." He wiped his blade against a pant leg, cleaning it of gore as he scanned the fighting. "Wait, there he is."

Merriam stood straight, lifting onto her toes to increase her view. Rovin fought his way toward where they stood, his short sword in one hand and a dagger in the other. His progress was slower, his path zigzagging so that he could lend his weapons to as many of the Guard as he could.

"Stupid, heroic asshole," Merriam said, dropping back down to her heels.

Bellamy shifted uncomfortably, wondering if he should have taken more time to help his comrades as he'd pushed through the fighting.

"Ryddan needs us." Merriam rested her hand on his arm, sensing his discomfort. "The sooner we get him out, the sooner we can get back and help. And the sooner we can end this."

Bellamy nodded, setting his shoulders. His face was grim, the scar that ran down one side of his face adding to his solemn expression. "How many of them do you think are left over there?" The clearing was now filled with demons, and the number coming through the rift had dwindled down to almost nothing, though it looked like the byrds came and went as they pleased.

Merriam slid her axes into her belt. "I'm hoping not many."

"At least we're all trained in stealth, should your hopes fall through."

Rovin was close now, darting up the slope of the mountain.

Merriam smiled wanly. "At least we have that," she agreed. "You ready?"

Mollian watched Merriam leave, Kodi and Aleah practically chasing her out. His *mehhen* had never been one to hesitate in the face of danger, and the possible end of the world was no exception.

Rovin caught his eyes, the Ranger strapping his weapons belt around his waist.

Mollian knew it was selfish, knew that, as king, he had no right to demand it in light of every other priority necessary for today's victory, but he formed the words in his mind and, with great effort, Cast them anyway. *Keep her safe.*

If Rovin was surprised at hearing Mollian's voice in his head, he didn't show it. He nodded once in acknowledgement, slipping from the tent with shortsword in hand.

Wild fear iced Mollian's veins, and he stood still as the tent emptied out, trying to settle the magic that ran rampant through him, urging him to run into the battle, to follow that other portion of his soul and defend it. He felt the soft blankets underneath his bare feet, looking down at them as he breathed evenly.

"This had better fucking work," he said before walking from the tent, not even bothering to shove on boots but grabbing a spare sword on his way out. He twirled it in his arms, letting his muscles wake up. He needed to see what they were up against before he slipped away on his own.

Mollian broke through the line of tents, looking out over the fighting in front of him. The rift the demons had opened up floated above the ground, unformed demons spilling through in liquid-black clouds and crashing onto Nethyl's surface. A few tried to force their way down throats of the Guard, but Merriam's necklaces were effective, each cloud tumbling back and forming into some animalistic creature or another.

A smaller, catlike creature ran for him, leaping with claws out-

stretched. He brought his sword up to block it, and a Ranger was instantly at his side, driving her own sword through its ribcage before ripping
the weapon free.

The demon fell to the ground, and Mollian slammed the point of his
sword through its skull for good measure. "Thanks, Evangeline," he said.

"Anytime, Your Majesty." She ran off into the fray, a wholly different
Ranger than she'd been a year ago.

Some of his nervous energy expelled, and having laid eyes on the
portal he would attempt to close, Mollian took a step back, leaving the
sword protruding from the demon.

As he moved, he filled his head with images of the black nothing,
thinking of the strange feel of completely neutral air against his skin, the
lack of smell, the lack of sound. With a deep breath, he concentrated on
the feel of the magic in his veins. Then he closed his eyes and fell.

Aleah and Kodi fought in tandem, their rhythm explicable only by their
acute awareness of one another. They pushed forward, cutting through
demons until they reached the center of the fighting.

Directly underneath the rift stood a greater demon almost twice
Kodi's height. He flared his wings, meeting Kodi's gaze. His eyes were
vertically slit, and a deep, dark red that glittered with challenge in the
light of the moons.

Kodi cocked an eyebrow, raising his sword as a feral grin split his face.

Dronin was used to being revered and had never had anyone challenge him outside of Lyvin or Nevra, but even they only ever did so with
humility and respect. The fae in front of him was splattered with black
blood, muscles coiled like he was ready to spring. Thrill surged through
Dronin's veins, a rush of bloodlust that he hadn't felt in years. He pulled
a greatsword from a sheath at his back and lowered it to the ready.

Motion from the side caught him off guard, a flash of red streaking
toward his side.

Kodi's grin grew wider. Dronin had been so focused on him, he'd completely missed Aleah's small form, her head barely passing his hips, as she rushed in. She dropped, sliding on her knees and swiping for Dronin's ankles. While Dronin's attention narrowed on Aleah, Kodi sprung forward to attack.

Lyvin and Nevra fell through the rift, forming as soon as they hit the ground. Nevra lunged, catching Aleah's ribs with the top of her foot and sending the mercenary tumbling back down the hill.

Aleah yelped, releasing her hold on her sword to protect her head as she rolled. She slid to a stop, the exposed skin of her arms smarting from the friction with the ground. Her earlier momentum and the angle of Nevra's kick had saved her from any major injuries, and as soon as she was able to suck air back into her lungs, Aleah sprang to her feet, pulling two daggers from her belt and racing back up the slope, slicing through demons as she went.

Without missing a beat, she jumped, latching onto Nevra's back, pressing her knees into the demon's sides as she buried the blades up to the hilt.

Nevra screamed, whirling around and spitting out a stream of curses in a guttural language.

Aleah's legs slipped free with the centrifugal force of the turn, but she kept her grip on the hilts. Her weight ripped one out, then the other, deep rivulets of dark blood instantly soaking Nevra's back.

Aleah landed on her feet, crouched to attack again.

Nevra twisted to face her, readying her sword and calling something to the greater demons behind her.

Kodi was keeping Dronin busy, Dio at his side, the captain's hair wild and unkempt for the first time Kodi had ever seen. He spared a quick glance in Aleah's direction, but before he could worry about her, Jasper dropped to the ground next to her, lance in hand. The grass beneath the demons' feet grew, tangling around their claws. Calysta rose from her crouch, long strands of hair whipping around her face in the wind that rolled through the hills, her black eyes glittering with power as she tapped into the ley lines beneath them. Leonidas and Campbell ran up on either side of her, storming Lyvin as he knocked one of the Guard to the ground.

If Kodi and Aleah had slid into a formidable rhythm while fighting, it was nothing compared to the well-oiled machine the five mercenaries made. Their knowledge of each other's fighting styles and years spent training together was undeniable.

Kodi, Dio, and the rest of the Guard shared a training regimen, but they'd never fought together in the same way the mercenaries had, and it was obvious. The group moved like battle was a choreographed dance.

Leonidas and Campbell pressed Lyvin, Leonidas keeping the demon's sword busy while Campbell circled to his unguarded side, slicing down his torso before spinning away and bringing his sword up to block Nevra's attack on Aleah, allowing her to duck forward on the offensive.

Jasper filled in Campbell's absence, taking Lyvin's attentions from Leonidas, who cut down a reptilian lesser demon that threatened Calysta, her focus on manipulating the plants to help.

Dronin saw their compatibility, and though Lyvin and Nevra also fought as one, they were still outmatched. "Separate them, draw them away!" he ordered, his language indecipherable to the fae. Dronin threw out a powerful kick that caught Dio in the thigh, his claws raking through the captain's pants and leaving a trail of bright blood in their wake.

Dio cried out, scrambling to stand from where the force of the attack had sent him sprawling, and Dronin drove into the center of the mercs, breaking through their synchronized movements with a roar. Lyvin and Nevra pushed against one half, driving them deeper into the battlefield and herding them away from Dronin.

Lyvin sheathed his sword across his back, dropping onto all fours and running at the nymph with a snarl on his lips. He wrapped an arm around her, raking her from the ground and sprinting down the battlefield.

She shrieked, raking her own claws down his skin, but he shook off the sting, tossing her into the air and catching her olive-skinned arm in his mouth. He dragged her beneath him as he ran.

Calysta reached into the folds of her short gown, pulling out a knife and driving it into the demon's chest. He dropped her, ripping it free with a growl and turning on her.

Calysta lay on the ground, her arm shredded and leaking sparkling blood as she scrambled back, digging her fingers into the earth to call for her magic. But the panic running through her blood muddied her communication with Nethyl, and her command of the plants was sluggish.

Lyvin stood over her, her dagger looking ridiculously small gripped in his three-clawed hand as he leaned forward, his dark eyes meeting hers with animalistic glee. He plunged the blade into her chest as Campbell leapt forward, his sword sheathed across his back to not hinder his run as he barreled into Lyvin.

Campbell's antlers pierced the side of Lyvin's chest, one of the prongs tearing open the wound Calysta had caused. The two fell in a heap, rolling with the force of Campbell's momentum. Pain and anger washed through Lyvin in a dangerous combination, and he reached for the fae with his claws, but Campbell had already pulled free, pushing away from Lyvin's massive form and scrambling to stand, drawing his sword as black blood dripped from his antlers into his hair.

Nevra and Leonidas were close behind, rejoining the fight with fervor.

Each of Calysta's breaths was agony, and they rattled from her chest with a disconcerting wetness. She raised a shaky hand to where the knife protruded from her and felt blood foam up around the blade when she exhaled. Gritting her teeth against a strangled whimper, she blinked past the fog of pain and terror that clouded her vision, trying to convince her body that she wasn't about to die. Trying to conjure her magic.

Calysta felt the spark of it at her fingertips, the plants responding to her call. But movement to the east caught her attention before she could help her friends.

Spilling from the forest came hundreds of nymphs, more than Calysta had ever seen in a single place at once, and her heart clenched in her chest. "They came," she whispered.

MOLLIAN OPENED HIS EYES, the noise of battle gone. Nothing but cold, still silence. Every single tether was once again visible, lighting up the area with color and flares of light as energy and power surged through them. Like the last time he'd Traveled between realities, whatever black shroud had previously covered everything was nowhere to be seen.

Mollian shook his head, looking at the millions of strings of light above him. He was here; now he had to figure out how to find the demon realm and how to separate it from his friends. From his home.

Mollian cracked his knuckles, raising a hand and sending his magic out into the ether. For the first time in his life, he let it go, following its pull rather than fighting it or pushing it in a specific direction. He let it roam, doing his best to empty his own consciousness, following the feel of the Gate's power as it slid through the tethers of worlds. His mind clear, Mollian started to catch a sense of each reality as his magic brushed past it, and once he noticed it, it was easier to pick up on the subtle hints that pulsed from each world.

With a better understanding of what he was doing, Mollian urged his magic, and it eagerly responded, roaming faster through the strings of life until he felt something familiar, something heavy with a hint of sulfur and leather and lightning. He would never quite be able to describe how he knew that this was Tymecht; it was just an inherent sense. An intrinsic knowledge.

Once he found it, Mollian curled his fingers into a fist, wrapping his magic around the cord and working into the fabric of it. It sank in with almost too much ease, but from there it pulled from him wildly, and he struggled to regain control, falling forward onto his knees in unsteady surprise.

Mollian grit his teeth, sitting back on his heels as he fought to regain control of the magic that pulled from him so fast it left him breathless. He felt it halt, surrendering to him, but still eager.

Pull, it whispered.

Mollian slowly forced his hands apart, feeling the thread stretch slowly beneath his magic.

Rip, it requested.

Mollian forced it to sink down, digging through the fabric of its containment until he felt the power that flowed just under his reach.

Tear.

Mollian's lip lifted in a feral snarl, and he threw every ounce of his awareness into separating that cord, bit by bit.

Merriam dipped a ring into the blood that dripped down the back of her arm just as Rovin reached them, grabbing Bellamy and closing her eyes, concentrating on Tymecht and letting the feel of the world fill her mind as she swiped the stones across each other.

"We made it."

Merriam opened her eyes, peering up at Bellamy with a smirk. "You doubted me?"

"Only slightly. You've never taken a passenger this far before." Bellamy unsheathed his sword, crouching low behind a crop of rocks.

"That was the easy part." Merriam winked, taking a deep breath. *Home.* The thought filled her, and she Traveled back to Nethyl. "Took you long enough," she joked to Rovin, wrapping her arms around his waist. Her fingers were still wet with her blood.

"Instinct is a hard thing to override." Rovin pulled her closer. "You're hurt."

"Just a flesh wound," Merriam assured him. She took a deep breath, instantly surrounded by his smell of leaf fall and apples, and she had the urge to tilt her face up and bury it in his neck, blocking out everything else. Her brow furrowed in concentration, and she conjured up the smell of sulfur and the feel of heavy, stagnant air. When the picture was clear in her mind, when she could taste it on her tongue, she struck the stones together, transporting them to Tymecht. She stumbled back, pushing away from Rovin to slump against a rock. The tattoos between her shoulder blades itched, but even the maddening feel buried in her skin was hardly noticeable compared to the headache that bloomed at the base of her skull, spreading up into her temples.

"Are you okay?" Rovin stepped forward, resting a hand on her shoulder.

"I'm fine, just a little winded. We're far from home, and you guys are heavy." She blinked, shaking her head.

Bellamy ripped a strip of fabric from the hem of his shirt and tied it tight over the gash on the back of her arm. "Don't want that getting infected."

Merriam smiled her thanks, pulling herself up to peer over the rocks. The castle stood at the edge of a cliff, and the rift between their worlds stretched across the sky further down. "Let's go." She led them up to the castle, keeping a watch on the windows and parapets, but nothing stirred.

"Did they really leave their home unguarded? They know you can Travel," Rovin said quietly as they approached two massive doors cut from solid gray stone. An intricate design was carved into each slab, beautiful but chilling.

Merriam tilted her head back, craning to look up at the structure in front of her. "Maybe they didn't think we'd have a reason to come here.

We're not the ones trying to invade, after all."

"But they have Ryddan. They have to have known we'd come for him." Bellamy stepped forward, placing a palm against the door.

Merriam bit her lip, pressing her back against the opposite door. "Then let's be prepared for a fight." She slid her axes free, nodding for Bellamy to open it.

Bellamy pushed, the muscle in his arm flexing as he braced against the weight of the door.

It didn't budge.

Merriam straightened, dropping her weapons to her side.

Bellamy's cheeks heated in embarrassment. He removed the iron chain from around his neck, tucking it into his pocket as he again placed his hands on the door. His eyes narrowed in concentration, and he wrapped his magic around the slab of stone, planting his feet against the ground as he pushed again, magic straining.

"Did we ever stop to think about the castle maybe being, I don't know, locked while all the warriors are off conquering other lands?" Rovin asked.

Bellamy pushed away from the door with a frustrated grunt, taking a step back. "It's not going to open."

Merriam secured her axes back into her belt, a self-assured gleam in her amber eyes that made Rovin's stomach plummet.

"No." He shook his head.

Merriam blinked at him, the expression of innocence if not for the mischief still in her eyes.

"Mer." He leveled his gaze at her, his chest tight.

"Your worry is heartwarming, Lieutenant, but unnecessary."

Bellamy watched them, confused until they both glanced up the side of the castle. "We're going to climb in?"

"No," Rovin and Merriam answered in unison, but Merriam shot him a look before continuing. "*I'm* going to climb in, then I'll open the door for the two of you."

"You can't go in there alone. You don't know the layout or what you'll be facing," Rovin insisted.

Merriam smiled in pleasant surprise, resting her hands on her hips. "Oh, is that what you're worried about?" She'd expected him to think she wouldn't be capable of the climb, and something about his faith in that one well-honed, partially innate talent of hers warmed her. "Rov, I'm excellent at remaining undetected. Would call it my second-best skill, even." She frowned for a moment. "Maybe my third, because I am also *very* talented with the axes."

Rovin shook his head in exasperation. "Can you refrain from being a cocky little shit for a moment?" His tone was harsh, but his eyes glimmered with worry. "Legends, I'm reminded why I used to want to throttle you at every turn."

"Don't subject Bell to your kinks, Rov, we can explore them later," Merriam teased. Then she dropped the shit-eating grin, stepping forward and reaching out to him. "I'm sorry," she squeezed his hands. "I know this is serious, and I promise I understand the gravity of the situation. But we have to save Rydd. You may know how to climb trees, but when was the last time either of you free scaled? Even on a climbing wall with proper holds?" Merriam dropped his hands, turning her gaze to Bellamy. "I know there could be warriors in the castle, but contrary to the image I project, I am capable of staying hidden and not provoking a fight from every enemy I see. This is the best option we have," she insisted.

"Why don't you Travel?" Bellamy asked. "You could just walk a couple paces to the other side of the door."

"It's not that simple," Merriam shook her head. "For one thing, we're very far away from Nethyl, so it's taxing to Travel that distance, and I need to save my strength. Even if I did make it back, we're not in a parallel world, distances aren't exactly the same. I could possibly go to Tymecht's parallel realm, but I've no knowledge about what it is or what might be there, and—" Merriam broke off, repeating the head shake and biting her lip. She could feel Mollian's magic in her blood, awake and ready for action, but she could also feel that it wasn't her it was attuned to. She reached out, and that half sense of Mollian lit in her mind. Close, but not, and she understood that he would need every drop of that magic he'd shared with her. "The climb will be easy," she insisted. "We can figure out the rest."

The two Rangers nodded, and Merriam cracked her knuckles, approaching the wall.

Aleah watched Leonidas and Campbell chase after Lyvin for only a moment before turning her attention back to Dronin, taking a step closer to Kodi.

The greater demon smiled languidly as Jasper tossed his lance through the air. Dronin jumped over it, beating his wings twice and throwing out his arms.

When he came back to the ground, he was no longer in his usual form. Four paws tipped in claws as long as Aleah's forearm landed heavily in the dirt. Aleah's mouth dropped open, and she grabbed Kodi's arm in support as she stumbled back, eyes traveling up the massive form in front of her.

A dragon stood in the center of the battle, a deafening roar splitting through every other sound as Dronin tipped his head back on a thick, serpentine neck. He swished his tail, knocking over a few of the Guard as he raised a foot to swipe for Kodi and Aleah.

They lunged out of the way, regrouping further back.

"How do we fight a fucking dragon?" Aleah asked breathlessly, staring up at the three massive horns coming from his head.

"Together." Aleah whipped around to see Dio at Kodi's side, his blonde hair splattered with the same black blood that soaked his clothes and hastily-tied field bandages around his thigh. "He's still a demon, same as the others. Team up and go for the weak points."

"You want to play bait, Captain?" Kodi asked, shooting Dio a lopsided grin. "Keep him distracted, and I'll go for his underside."

"Do you have any other fliers?" Jasper asked, pulling another lance from a strap on his back. The other was underneath Dronin. "I can lead an assault from the sky, but with all the creatures flying around, it won't be very productive without backup."

Dio nodded, grabbing the attention of another Guard to send him off for any of the winged fair folk as Aleah darted forward, breaking free from the group to hold Dronin's attention. She was small and fast, mostly taunting him as she darted in and back out with no real intention of trying to wound him, just keeping him busy.

Dronin tracked Aleah's movements, deep red eyes following as she dove for him. He huffed, amused, leaning down with his jaws open to grab for her.

Pain sparked from his back leg, and he whipped his tail forward, Dio barely jumping over the tip as it swiped at him. The captain darted around the front, joining Aleah in feinting attacks.

Lyvin had already sustained many injuries, and Campbell's antlers had pierced something inside of him that leaked uncomfortably. The pain was almost euphoric, though. It had been too long since he'd been in true battle, and he thumped a fist against the wound, sending white-hot bursts of agony through his body as he grinned at the mercenaries standing before him.

Leonidas rushed forward, raining down heavy blows that Lyvin blocked with his sword. But Leonidas was gaining on him, Lyvin yielding ground with every blow.

Campbell had turned his attention to Nevra. Lyvin's blood clung to his antlers, his hair a matted mess. He smiled, beckoning Nevra with a curl of his fingers.

She lunged toward him with a snarl.

But she'd been focused on Campbell, unaware of Calysta behind her, one hand curled against the knife in her chest, shimmery blood coating her arm and staining her clothes, the other buried into the grass, weaving the blades together around the demon's feet.

Nevra fell forward, tearing the grass from the ground. She hissed, flipping onto her back, but Calysta fought her at every turn, wrapping grass and brambles around the general's arms and torso. More vegetation hindered her progress every time Nevra broke free of the others.

Campbell took the opportunity, raised his sword up to drive down into Nevra's chest.

He was halfway through the motion when a lesser demon flew in from the side, slamming into him so heavily Campbell sailed through the air, landing in a roll and tangling with the demon that was part bird, part lizard. It had feathered wings that ended in clawed hands it used to help it move, its head reptilian and sharp fangs in its mouth.

Campbell dropped his sword as he struggled with the lesser demon, wrapping his hands around its throat more in an attempt to keep its jaws away from his face than any real effort to choke it. He tried to kick its body away from him, but its clawed back feet dug into the ground on either side of him, holding firm.

Then the demon screeched and went limp, falling heavily onto Campbell. Pain bloomed in his chest where a couple of ribs had been bruised on impact and now shifted. He rolled the demon off of him to see Evangeline standing over him, panting heavily, with black blood dripping from her sword.

She held a hand out, and Campbell took it, letting her help him up before they both ran back toward where Leonidas fought with Lyvin and Nevra, Campbell scooping his sword up along the way.

Calysta did her best to help from the sidelines, but her skin had a sickly gray tint to it, and the black of her eyes was dull with pain as she wielded her magic.

A few other demons were trying to break through, but Campbell realized with surprise that a barrier had risen around their small group—more than Calysta would have been capable of without exhausting herself.

Campbell glanced over the battlefield, peeking between the overgrowth of shrubbery. Other nymphs had rallied toward the fight, blocking the greater demons from accessing each other, separating them to make it easier for the Guard to take them out.

Perran was walking through the castle, swallowing down agitation. Though warriors had been sent north to the location of the Gate in case of retaliation from the Keepers, very few had been left behind, and he thought it was a major oversight.

The warlock was confident that the battle wouldn't last long, though. She'd dreamed it, she'd said, and so Perran's interjections to leave extra protection behind had been ignored.

"Stay back and watch the djuhlin," he muttered, his eyes on his clawed feet. "You're no warrior, Perran, so stay behind and watch our prized possession with no help at all in case you undergo attack." He scoffed bitterly as he headed down toward the kitchens. If he had been asked, he would have told his djuhl that the warlock was more trouble than she was worth, that she was using him to fuel her own power.

He hadn't been asked, though. He'd served Dronin faithfully for his entire life, but his opinion was of no consequence. What could a lesser demon possibly know that the others hadn't already thought through?

Perran rounded the corner, coming face-to-face with a creature of pale skin, golden hair, and wide amber eyes that reflected his own surprise. His black eyes grew even wider as he realized this person must have come from Nethyl. Perran blinked, a self-satisfied grin spreading across his face. Looks like he'd been right after all.

Merriam was on him before the smile could finish stretching his lips, one arm wrapping around him, pinning his arms to his sides as she pulled him back against her chest, the other pressing the point of a dagger into his ribs.

"*Sukh vey kuuf, odn oei tau,*" she hissed into his ear, standing up on her toes to reach. *Call for help, and you die.*

Perran's muscles tensed. He didn't understand Common, but the threat was clear enough. He wasn't nearly as large as Dronin or even Lyvin or Nevra, but he was still built to fight, and he tried to calculate how to break free with all of his innards intact.

Sensing his indecision, Merriam pressed the knife further into his side, the tip piercing his soft flesh. "*Kyo na,*" she invited. *Try me.*

Again, Perran didn't have to understand the language for the sentiment to come across. He weighed out his options and decided that compliance would be the easiest course for now. He swallowed, not moving.

Merriam sank back to her heels, pulling the knife back slightly. Black blood welled from the wound, running down Perran's skin. She kept her hold on him, pushing him forward until they reached the front entrance.

"*Ifod eq.*" She released him, pushing him toward the door. *Open it.*

Perran considered charging her, then, but as he glanced over his shoulder, he saw the dagger had been slipped back into her belt, two axes now gripped in her hands and her feet already set to fight him. Weaponless aside from the claws he'd just filed that morning, Perran turned back to the doors, removing the large wooden beams that held them shut. He looked behind him again, one hand wrapped around a large ring embedded in the stone. A cold sliver of fear settled in his chest. What if she'd brought an army to their door? He wanted Dronin to see that he'd been right about wanting to keep more warriors here, but he didn't want his home taken over, and he certainly didn't want to die.

"*Ifod eq*," Merriam repeated, gesturing with her chin.

Perran swallowed, lifting a heavy bar and swinging one of the doors open.

A flash of lightning backlit the two Rangers standing at there, weapons at the ready.

Rovin was about to jump forward and run his sword through the demon in front of him when he glimpsed Merriam standing behind him. "Wait! He can take us to Ryddan!" she whisper-yelled. "Flank him, and keep your guard up. I think he's been contemplating a fight."

Perran held his hands up as Rovin and Bellamy stepped up to him, but his black eyes stayed on Merriam, sensing she was the one in charge.

"Where is the prince?" she demanded, spinning one axe in her grip.

The demon's focus flicked to the weapon momentarily as he shook his head. An almost exasperated burst of guttural clicks and grunts fell from his lips.

"You stole a child from us." Merriam held one hand out, indicating Ryddan's height. "Where are you keeping him?" She'd already reached out for him, searching for his proximity in her mind. The effort had rewarded her with a splitting headache and an insufferable itch between her shoulders that she'd scratched on a corner of a wall, but she'd felt him. He was here somewhere.

Perran sighed, muttering something else in his demon language.

"He doesn't understand," Rovin pointed out.

Merriam scoffed, taking a step closer and tapping the edge of an axe blade to his chest. "He understands enough," she insisted, her gaze narrowing on the lesser demon. "Take us to Ryddan, or I will split you in half, demon filth," she hissed.

Recognition flashed in Perran's eyes at Ryddan's name, and a deep understanding that he had royally fucked up sunk in for the first time. Dronin would kill him if he lost the djuhlin. These otherworlders would kill him if he didn't give him up. Perran regarded the female in front of him, nothing but cold calculation burning in her eyes. *She will probably kill me regardless*, he thought.

Perran grabbed the handle of the axe at his chest, wrenching it to the side as his other hand swept out, claws angled to rake across Merriam's eyes.

She kept hold of her weapon, but spun into the momentum as it was yanked, dancing away from the deathly sharp claws even as Bellamy swung his sword up in a powerful arc.

A flash of searing pain washed up Perran's arm, everything below his elbow hitting the floor with a disconcertingly wet *thud*. He bared his teeth in a snarl, pulling Merriam closer as he dove for her throat.

But she'd turned, pulling his arm out with her and crashing the blade of her other axe into it. She hadn't had enough strength behind the blow to slice through bone, muscle, and tendon, and the blade stuck fast halfway through Perran's arm.

He shrieked, a completely inhuman sound that pierced Merriam's eardrums, but she kept hold of her weapons, yanking the one from Perran's grip and wrenching the other from his arm. Rovin rammed his shortsword up through the lesser demon's back, tearing it free and preparing to thrust again when Perran sank to the floor, his keening turning into a gurgling wail as he choked on the blood that filled his lungs.

Merriam swung an axe through the top of his skull, abruptly cutting off the noise. The force of the impact reverberated up her arm, and she released the handle to flex her fingers and shake her hand out. Perran slumped forward, and she braced her foot against his shoulder to pull her axe free. The metal squealed against bone, blood and brain matter spilling from the gash with a wet splat.

"Legends." Bellamy turned away with a wince, fighting the lurch in his stomach.

"Guess we'll be searching on our own." Merriam wiped her blades off on the lower leg of her pants. "And we'd better do it quickly. There's no way everyone else left didn't hear him."

Merriam led them back to the staircase, hoping that their castles were laid out similarly to the ones on Nethyl, with sleeping quarters on the upper floors. She reached out with her mind again for a sense of Ryddan, hoping to gauge his location.

She thought she could feel a ping from him, but then her vision clouded over, and she slowed, pressing a hand to the wall and blinking furiously.

"Mer." Rovin stopped beside her, grabbing her waist.

She tried to shake him off, sharpness returning to her vision. She could feel the magic in her blood swirling agitatedly, seeping from her in a steady trickle. "I'm okay," she assured him, standing straight. She squeezed his arm before sliding from his grip, continuing down the hall.

Rovin watched her, worried.

"It's Molli," she said as they continued. "It's not an issue. I was just trying to use too much of his magic, and he needs it." She bit her tongue to keep from adding another *it's fine*, knowing that would further convince him that it was anything but, and they plowed ahead.

They spread out, keeping in each other's sights, listening at every door before opening it and peering inside. They'd gone up another flight of stairs before Bellamy noticed something towards the end of the hall.

"That door is barred from the outside," he breathed, sprinting headlong for it.

Rovin and Merriam were right on his heels as he removed the mechanism holding the door closed. "Rydd?" he called, swinging the door open.

A small demon was curled in a ball on the bed, his head raised. Bright green eyes blinked at the group, disbelief shining in them.

"Buddy." Bellamy stepped slowly into the room, unsure of what Ryddan had been through or what might startle him. The fact that he had a demon form barely registered. Seeing him alive and unscathed was a wave of relief over Bellamy's senses.

Ryddan sat up, unfolding his limbs. His throat squeezed shut. They were here. They'd come for him. "Belly," he choked in a small voice, holding out his arms.

Bellamy's heart shattered at that cry, and he rushed forward, pulling the child against his chest as it welded back together.

Ryddan buried his face against Bellamy, and every ounce of emotion that had built up in him over the past days poured out, his small fingers digging into Bellamy's shirt as he sobbed.

"Oh, buddy." Bellamy held him tight, his arm tucked between the spines on Ryddan's back. "It's going to be okay now. We're going home."

Ryddan sucked in deep, gasping breaths, trying to calm himself, and pushed away, looking over Bellamy's shoulder at Merriam. Tears spilled down the gray skin of his cheeks, his lower lip trembling. "You still want me in Umbra?"

Merriam walked over, smoothing dark hair behind small nubs of horn. "Of course we do. What kind of question is that?"

"The djuhl—my uncle—he told me you only want me there because I'm fae, that it's only because I look like Oren and my mother."

Merriam knelt down, meeting Ryddan's gaze evenly. "Do you really think I would have dragged Rovin's grouchy ass all the way across realms because I thought you looked cute walking around the castle? I love you, Ryddan. Molli and Bell do, too. We love *all* of you."

Ryddan let out a shuddering sigh, fighting back a fresh wave of tears as he clung to Bellamy.

"We have to go, okay? Once we're home, we'll have all the time to talk about everything." Bellamy stood, Ryddan still in his arms.

Rovin led the way back down the hall, their pace hurried.

"If we just get to the ground floor, I can move us from there," Merriam said.

"Wait, they have Keeper rings!" Ryddan said.

Merriam stilled, thinking. "Do you know where they are?"

"Donova has them in her chambers. They were trying to figure out how to use my blood to get back to Sekha." Ryddan wriggled free of Bellamy's grasp, dropping to the floor.

A surge of dizziness washed over Merriam as Mollian pulled more magic from her, and she locked her legs to keep from swaying and hoped that Rovin hadn't noticed. "We need to look for them." She knew Mollian was working on closing the portal, but she didn't know how permanent of a closure it would be. She blinked, everything coming back into focus. "Where are her rooms, Rydd?"

Ryddan furrowed his brow, trying to remember. The past few days had been such a whirlwind of confusion and information. "One floor up, on the other side of the castle."

Merriam nodded, looking down the hall as she bit her lip, thinking. "Bell, go look for the rings. Stealth mission, don't start any fights. Rov, I'll take you back to Nethyl, then come back and send Ryddan to you through the rift the demons created. Then I'll meet back up with Bellamy and, hopefully, we won't be too far behind you."

Rovin was already shaking his head. "I don't think it's smart to split up."

"We don't have much of an option," Merriam countered.

"She's right. We shouldn't waste time." Bellamy placed a hand on Ryddan's head, smoothing over his hair as the little body leaned against his leg. Getting him to safety was the most important thing. "I've got magic—I can use it to distract, grab the rings from across the room, possibly even glamor. Fast and easy." He nodded to Merriam, taking a step back. "Go," he told them, pushing Ryddan toward Merriam.

"Daddy, no!" Ryddan wrapped his arms around Bellamy's leg in panic as fresh tears spilled down his cheeks. "Don't leave me."

Bellamy's throat closed, feeling Ryddan's plea like a punch through the chest. He dropped to one knee, hugging him tight. "You've got to go with them, buddy. I'll follow in just a little bit, but you've got to go now."

Ryddan sniffled, nodding.

Bellamy kissed his forehead. "I love you." Then he stood, running off down the hall.

"Let's get you home." Merriam grabbed Ryddan's small, three-clawed demon hand, heading down to the ground floor.

Rovin's brow furrowed as he followed, his promise to Mollian at the forefront of his mind. They ducked behind the staircase, out of view of Perran's corpse. Before Rovin could object again and offer a new plan, Merriam grabbed his hands.

The cold of her fingers shocked him, but she gripped him firmly, her eyes on his. "I know you don't like this, but Ryddan is our first priority here. If Bellamy and I can't find the rings right away, we'll come back without them, okay? I promise."

Rovin swallowed against the rebuttal rising in his throat and nodded.

Merriam turned to Ryddan. "Stay here; stay hidden. I'll be right back."

"Okay." Ryddan huddled into the corner, eyes wide.

Merriam removed her dagger, cutting a short line across her forearm and swiping the orydite through the blood that welled from the wound. Then she grabbed Rovin and tipped them back to Nethyl.

The effort took the breath from her lungs, but her vision was clear, so she took that as a good sign. She rolled her shoulders against the itch of the blood-infused ink in her skin. They were behind the thick of the fighting, partially obscured by a copse of sickly gray aspens. The portal floated through the sky above them. Merriam purposefully kept her eyes from scanning the battlefield, instead focusing on Rovin. "I'll send Ryddan through the portal. Shiloh is in one of the med tents. If you go around the thick of the fighting, you can take him to them. They can take him further from the battle. Tell them to head west, up into the mountains so they have a vantage point. If things look … if things look like they're not going our way, send them north to Entumbra. Hopefully Regenya can come up with a contingency plan."

"Sir, yes, sir," Rovin replied, his chest tight.

"Be safe," Merriam murmured, stepping away from him.

Rovin caught her wrist, running his thumb over her pulse point. "Come back to me, pet."

Merriam bit her lip, nodding as he released her. Then she ran her rings together and disappeared. The effort of going back to Tymecht again had sapped more of her energy than she wanted to admit. *Of course, it couldn't have been one of the neighboring realms that wanted to invade,* she thought morosely.

Ryddan was right where she left him, and she reached for him, kneeling down to his level. He threw his arms around her neck, his little body trembling. Merriam held him, her heart clenching. He'd endured so much more than he ever should have had to, and still she had to ask him to be brave again. "Listen, I need you to be a bird, okay? There's a portal outside that leads home. Fly through there and head east towards the trees. Rovin is waiting there, and he'll take you somewhere safe."

Ryddan took a deep, shuddering breath. "Okay."

"There will be a lot of noise, sounds of fighting, but just head into the trees and Rovin will find you."

"I don't want to go alone," Ryddan said, his voice small.

"I know, but I can't go with you."

"Take me back like you took Rovin!" he pleaded.

Merriam squeezed him tighter, a lump forming in her throat. "I can't. I don't have much energy left, Rydd." Her heart thudded against her chest, and her head felt strangely light. So much of the magic in her blood, magic that had been a part of her for so many years she barely even registered its presence, was gone. Part of her worried that she wouldn't have enough left to take Bellamy back, but that was a problem for later. "You can do this," she assured the young prince.

Ryddan reluctantly let go, letting Merriam lead him outside. She cringed as they passed Perran, but Ryddan didn't even flinch. Another painful reminder that this child had seen far too much. They stood just below the portal, and Merriam ran a hand through his hair.

"Go directly east," she reminded him.

"Okay," Ryddan visibly steeled himself before shifting into a hawk, taking flight and heading for the rift.

I love you, kid, she Cast to him, watching him disappear before hurrying back inside to find Bellamy.

The lack of guards at the stronghold was suspicious, and she had both of her weapons out, peering carefully around every corner before moving through. But there was no one around to question her. *Dumbasses,* she thought, springing up the last few steps to the floor above the one where they'd found Ryddan.

Chapter 47

MOLLIAN WAS DRENCHED FROM head to toe in sweat as he knelt between worlds. His brow was furrowed in concentration, his teeth set together, and the muscles in his arms visibly quivered as he forced his magic deeper and deeper into the tether that connected Tymecht to the Gate.

He'd felt small tears break over its surface, and he knew with a sudden and infallible certainty what his magic wanted.

Life and energy passed from the Gate into every world, every universe, every reality. It was the most basic bit of common knowledge he'd ever possessed. The Gate connected everything together.

If Mollian could break the tether between Tymecht and the Gate, rip it free, not only should the portal between their worlds close, but Tymecht should also drift free, unable to ever break into any other realm again.

The fact that, without the Gate's magic feeding it, Tymecht could very well wither away into nothing wasn't even a consequence in Mollian's mind. His priority was the greater good of not just Nethyl, but all realms. If Dronin were allowed to succeed, life everywhere would be impacted and changed forever.

So Mollian bore down, a dull ache spreading from his knees as he forced his magic tighter around that cord. Tendrils of power slipped into that stream of magic flowing between the world and the Gate, trying to suck Mollian's magic free, but he held on, wrapping around the tether and trying to force it apart.

He could feel it starting to give, but it was exhausting him.

A blood vessel popped in his eye, red spreading out along the slash of brown that cut through the pale green of his iris. Green, like every Keeper since Orym, the first, millennia prior. Never had a Keeper had any eye color other than green.

But one of Mollian's eyes was cracked with brown. And now, as magic coursed through every fiber of his being while he fought to do the impossible, that slash of brown glowed amber.

Mollian dug deep, pulling from the well inside him, that place where Merriam was connected to him, holding the excess weight of his magic that would have otherwise overwhelmed him. He took it easily, a flicker in his mind to hold steady, to not take more than was necessary.

She needed enough to make it back to Nethyl. He reached out for a sense of her, but with so much of his concentration focused on ripping at the cord, he couldn't tell if she was still in Tymecht, only that she *was*.

He blinked, a drop of sweat falling into his eye, another tickling his cheek as it rolled down his skin. His breath pulled through his teeth.

Mollian felt another snap in the cord as a portion gave out.

Pull. Rip. Tear, his magic whispered as it coursed through him. *Shred.* The King of Sekha obeyed.

Donova had stayed behind. She was no warrior and had no interest in participating in barbaric bloodshed. She preferred to stay behind with her spells and potions, sitting with her legs folded in front of her on her large mattress.

Her eyes were rolled up into her head, a sparkling, flame-red crystal carved from once-molten rock perched in the palm of one hand. She watched the fighting from the eyes of the byrds, a multi-faceted view that would be enough to make a common demon's head spin. But she had no problem deciphering the maelstrom of visual information.

These fae were much more skilled than Dronin had expected, and they'd been prepared. Dronin's strongest strategy had been to possess as many of the warriors as possible. They would lose a handful of lesser demons that way, but the fae would also be taking each other out, which was well worth the sacrifice as far as the djuhl was concerned.

But the damned fae had protected themselves against possession by wrapping iron around their throats, the full force of their numbers focused only on the demons.

A noise outside of her bedchamber pulled her back to her body, and she slipped quickly from the bed, pressing her back to the wall as she watched the door swing partially open.

Nothing happened at first, but then a fae stepped into the room, and she ducked behind a tapestry hanging against the wall. She had no death wish.

Bellamy stepped toward the desk after a quick glance around the room. Something felt off, but he'd been on edge for days, so he didn't heed the instinct. The desk drew his attention, littered with stones and herbs and poultices. Movement by the window caught his eye now that he was in the room, and he whipped his head to the side.

From this vantage point, he had a perfect view of the rift torn between Tymecht and Nethyl. Lightning danced across the sky behind it, lighting the bright blue edges. He shivered, looking back to the desk and the smooth wooden bowl in the center. It was clear that whatever magic had opened the portal had been cast from here.

Bellamy dropped his gaze back to the bowl, searching for the familiar orydite and umbrite stones. The rings were to the side of the bowl, and he picked them up, watching the light glint off their surfaces.

Scratches marred both stones, bits shaved off to complete the spell. He dropped the rings into his pocket and turned to leave.

Donova watched him, her heart rate spiking as he stole the rings. She almost revealed herself then, dove toward his open back to sink her claws into his flesh and tear him down, but just as she stepped from behind the tapestry, an image flashed across her mind.

She was seated at Dronin's throne, the djuhl and his generals locked away on some other world. And she ruled Tymecht, the most powerful being in the realm.

Donova licked her lips, stepping back behind the curtain. Dronin may have set his sights on a full universe, but maybe she could be content with holding all the power in a single world.

Bellamy whirled back around, sure that he'd heard something by the window. He narrowed his eyes as he watched the tapestry flutter. *Wind?* he thought.

But the air here was stifling and stagnant, causing the shorter curls on the nape of his neck to stick uncomfortably against his skin. He swallowed, stepping further into the room, his hand moving to the hilt of his sword.

"Bell?"

He turned, seeing Merriam on the other side of the door. With one final glance at the window, he slid from the room, shutting the door behind him.

"Did you find them?" she asked.

"Package is secured," Bellamy affirmed, and they moved down the hall.

Merriam ran down the stairs, the air around her face feeling unsettlingly cold, and her fingers beginning to tingle. The sound of her blood rushed in her ears, and she grit her teeth. *Just make it to the ground.*

She rounded the corner, her eyes going wide as two large, catlike creatures pulled their muzzles from Perran's remains, fur and teeth matted with black blood. "Oh shit," she raised her axes, setting her feet. She felt Bellamy run into her back, and a second later all of the air in her lungs and the warmth in her body was sucked free as the remnants of Mollian's magic fled with a vacuum effect. Her vision went dark, and she collapsed.

Sweat ran in rivulets down Aleah's back, half-dried blood creating a sticky coating on her arm from a gash on her shoulder. Her lungs burned, but she didn't stop moving. Jasper and a few other fae dove from above, and Aleah sprinted forward, ducking beneath Dronin and leaping to draw her sword across his belly.

He roared in anger, and she darted from underneath him as he moved back, searching for his attacker. She dropped, letting her momentum roll her a few paces away before springing back to her feet.

"This isn't working," Kodi growled in frustration, joining her just out of the dragon's range to catch his breath and reevaluate. "His scales are too damn thick."

"Look under his jaw, it's so pliable there. If Jasper could just dip in. It would only take one solid blow from his lance to—" Aleah watched Kodi's expression change, a fresh light of challenge gleaming in his eyes, and her words caught in her throat.

Kodi slipped his fingers beneath the iron at his neck, giving a sharp, strong tug. The clasp broke free, leaving an angry red line against his skin. "I'm going to need my magic."

"What the fuck are you doing?" Aleah demanded in alarm.

"I'm going to climb him. Keep him grounded for me, yeah? And try to let Jasper know I'll want that fancy stick of his when I get to the top." Kodi dropped the necklace to the grass, pulling two daggers from his belt.

"Kodi, that's a suicide mission."

"Is that concern in your voice, little merc?" he asked, brushing a swift kiss over her lips before running towards the dragon.

"Fucking fae bastard," Aleah muttered, watching his departure. She twirled the sword in her fingers, loosening her wrist as she charged for Dronin.

Kodi took a running leap, blades slamming deep into the meat of a back leg. Adrenaline raced through his blood, his magic running strong through his muscles and his grip on his knives. He pulled one free, reaching up and slamming it home before removing the other, kicking off with his feet and repeating.

Dronin whipped his head toward Kodi, but before he could bite at the Ranger, Jasper dove in toward his neck, and he returned his attention to the sky, shaking his back leg. Kodi held on, biceps burning as he fought to keep his body close to the dragon and avoid being thrown free. He continued his climb, trusting the others to keep Dronin busy.

Bellamy watched in horror as Merriam crumpled in front of him, one axe skittering across the stone floor toward the demons. "Fucking Hel." He stepped over her fallen body, pulling two knives from his belt and tossing them, wrapping his magic around the blades as they sailed through the air, keeping his aim true.

They sunk into the chests of the demons, and they both raced forward, angered growls filling the anteroom. Bellamy threw his hands back, yanking the blades away so that their wounds bled freely and unsheathing his sword. He rushed forward to meet them with a wild cry, dropping to his knees to cut across the belly of one.

It lowered its jaws to snap at him, and he raised his sword to block the bite. The blade cut into its tongue as its teeth clamped down, and it quickly released it, shrieking as blood poured from its mouth.

Bellamy rolled from underneath it, jumping to his feet just in time to pull away as the other swiped at him, its claws raking across his shoulder. He grit his teeth against the sting, but swung for another attack.

Suddenly, it dropped back, heading towards Merriam. Before Bellamy could react, a cloud of liquid-black smoke came barreling toward him. In a heartbeat, he remembered removing the iron chain from around his neck before entering the castle. In the next, he dropped his sword as his hand reached toward the pocket of his pants, pulling out the necklace and shoving it into his mouth just as the formless demon slammed into him.

Across the room, Merriam felt the cold kiss of stone against her cheek. Through nothing but luck, she'd landed on the right side of her face and not where her skull was still fragile from her abduction, and she felt a small trickle of warmth where her temple had split on impact. In that same instance, her fingers twitched, and her lungs filled with air as she sucked in a breath.

Get up.

Her heart skipped a beat at the voice that flooded her, warmth returning to her veins. A large part of her screamed to stay still, to bask in the familiarity of a presence she'd never expected to feel again.

GET UP.

Her eyes flew open at the forceful command, fingers curling around the handle of an axe and swinging it upward as she rolled, bringing her other arm across the top of her chest to protect her throat on instinct.

The blade of her axe cut deep into the pad of the feline demon that swiped at her, blood splattering across her face as the axe cut through flesh and knocked it away. Merriam's heart thundered against her chest, eyes wide as she jumped to her feet, spitting acrid blood from her mouth as adrenaline sent tremors through her body.

As Merriam regained consciousness, the other demon hit the iron on Bellamy's tongue, the sulfurous taste of it threatening to choke him as it made a wordless hiss, trying to force its way down his throat only a heartbeat longer before retreating. Still shapeless, it poured through an open window. If it returned to its natural form now, it would bleed out, and its sense of self preservation was too strong.

Bellamy coughed, spitting the necklace into his palm as tears streamed from his eyes. The other demon was backing Merriam into a corner. Her own blood dripped from a gash on her temple, mixing with the black splatter on her cheeks into a chillingly dark mauve.

Bellamy ran, jumping to land on the demon's back. Gripping the course flanks with his legs, he wrapped his arms around its throat, grasping one end of the chain in each hand and pulling back. He grit his teeth, sawing the chain back and forth to force it into the demon's thick pelt.

Bellamy knew the instant the iron touched its skin.

It reared back with an ear-piercing shriek, tossing its head and trying to buck him off. Bellamy leaned against it, the muscles in his arms on fire as he locked himself around its throat, crushing its windpipe.

Merriam pulled the dagger from her belt, and when the demon lifted onto its back legs to dislodge Bellamy, she lunged, slamming the knife almost directly into the wound that Bellamy had left. Grasping with both hands, she threw herself to the ground, ripping the blade down its chest with the force of her weight.

Blood spilled to the floor, and she scrambled back as the demon's fight got weaker and weaker until it fell to the side with a final whimper.

Bellamy slid from its back, panting as he stared at her. "What happened?" he rasped.

Merriam shook her head slowly, at a complete loss for words. Mollian had taken the last of his magic. She knew that for a fact. The sudden loss of that presence had shocked her body, but she'd come back, and as she focused inward, she could still feel the Gate's magic running through her blood.

Oren.

Her throat closed painfully, a pang piercing her heart. She held her arm out in front of her, looking at the blood-splattered, colorful aspen branch that covered most of it. "I have more than just Molli's blood," she whispered, raising her gaze to meet Bellamy's.

She felt a faint brush of Mollian against her mind, and though it was still only that half-presence, the urgency in it was clear.

"We need to go, *now.*" She reached for Bellamy. He ran to grab their discarded weapons as she dragged her umbrite ring through the fresh blood on the side of her face.

Merriam's body, not built for using so much magic and unused to the punishing toll of it, was exhausted, but she wrapped her arms around Bellamy, her cheek pressed against his chest, and begged of it once more to use that which had been given through no motive but love.

Chapter 48

A CIRCLE OF PLANTS and water had been created around Campbell, Leonidas, and Evangeline. Calysta was half buried in it, propped against a blue-skinned water nymph while she called on her magic to aid in the fight. Blood seeped slowly around the knife still in her chest, each shallow breath dragging the blade against her ribs. The bite wound on her upper arm was still leaking blood, too, and that would have terrified her if she'd given herself a moment to think about it. All of the magic she possessed, all of her awareness, went to keeping the protective barrier around her friends intact. Everything else was secondary.

Lyvin was quickly fading, though the fight in his dark eyes was still bright.

Leonidas pushed forward, blood dripping down one leg where Lyvin had caught him, but he could tell he was close. Leonidas watched the demon's haggard breathing, and he made a clumsy swing for his side, leaving himself wide open to attack.

Lyvin, desperate, took the bait, driving toward Leonidas, who lifted onto his toes and spun, pressing his back to Lyvin's front and driving his sword up and into Lyvin's chest before pulling away and ripping the weapon free.

Lyvin choked, black blood spilling from his lips as he fell to his knees.

Leonidas didn't wait to watch him fully fall, immediately turning to help Evangeline and Campbell finish off Nevra.

They had her pretty well pinned, though, and he would just get in the way. "Make me an opening!" he called to Calysta.

She did, letting Leonidas slip through the brambles, water splashing over his face as he broke through. A lesser demon met him, and he fought. A Ranger ran over to help him, and together they dispatched it. Leonidas nodded his thanks, but before they could run off to another opponent, the Ranger was speared through the chest by the pointed leg of a lesser demon.

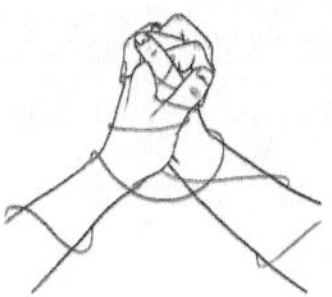

Blood had joined the sweat dotting Mollian's brow, sliding down his skin. The force of the magic inside of him was wearing at him, tearing him apart slowly.

But he was close. So fucking close.

Just a little more, and he could tell the tether was ready to give.

Another snap, inaudible, but it radiated down the presence of his magic as another split formed in Tymecht's cord.

One corner of Mollian's mouth lifted, his entire body buzzing with the effort he'd exuded. His magic started to slip, and his lips pressed together in a grimace. His arms trembled as he held onto the tether, muscles burning as he strained to rip it in two. With a quick pant, he threw more magic into his grip, everything he had focusing on whatever was holding Tymecht to the Gate.

His eyes closed as he focused. The sheer amount of magic he wielded was unheard of, and more blood pearled onto his skin as he forced control over it. His concentration was so severe, he didn't even realize he'd taken every last drop that he'd ever given to Merriam.

Another give in the tether. And another.

Those snaps and tears started to come more rapidly, and Mollian's heart thundered against his ribs as he realized just how close he was.

An ache in his soul, the tendrils woven between him and his *mehhen* pulling taut for a moment, pulled him back, but he couldn't let go now. He threw out his consciousness toward Merriam with urgency. She was there, somewhere, but he couldn't tell *where*.

He ground his teeth together, jaw aching as he held his magic in place, not letting it slip, but not forcing apart. *Make it home, Ria.* For three long breaths, nothing moved aside from a quiver in his muscles, then couldn't hold it anymore. Mollian threw his head back with a wild cry and forced his arms apart.

His magic was so deeply wrapped into the tether that it ripped deep gouges into the fabric of it as he pulled. It resisted, but Mollian held on, and finally, it snapped apart.

The ground underneath the battlefield on Nethyl rolled with enough ferocity to send fae and demons alike sprawling as a deep rumble echoed through the planet. Kodi almost lost his grip on the dragon, barely managing to hold on as Aleah collapsed onto Dio, almost impaling him in an effort to right herself.

Darius and Regenya woke in Entumbra, rushing down to the Gate as it sent ripple after ripple of maddened power through the castle, knocking stones free from the ancient foundation.

On Earth, tall buildings shook with a thunderous roar, the blaring of car alarms filling the night as lights turned on with panicked cries.

In Nessium, a world Merriam had once conjured from the Gate, the gigantic trees shook with such fervor the large, colorful flowers hugging their bark fell free, drifting down to the mossy floor below.

The large city under the dark sky full of swirling galaxies trembled, the rumble echoing across the dark forest as a flock of startled owls launched into the sky.

In a world even further away, a fae was knocked to her hands and knees, palms scraping in the dirt. She glared up into the boughs of a tall magnolia tree as the ground quaked, anger simmering in her purple eyes at whatever injustice this was.

Bottles and vials rattled from Donova's desk, dropping to the floor and shattering as the entire castle shook. The last of the djuhlin's blood she'd collected spread over the dark bricks. The warlock pressed her back against the wall, not even noticing the loss as fear stilled her heart. Her golden gaze was locked out of the window, where the portal she'd created between Tymecht and Nethyl winked from existence.

Across every universe and reality, realms trembled, a thunderous rumble echoing throughout as the very fabric of one world was ripped free from its source of energy.

If Mollian hadn't already been on his knees, the force of magic that poured from the shredded cord would have knocked him to the ground. He sat back on his heels with a gasp, hands dropping to the ground to steady himself.

Magic—life—energy—poured from the broken tether in a fast, urgent stream.

Without really understanding, Mollian reached out. His own exhausted magic dipped into it. His magic, which was the Gate's magic. The power bleeding from that broken tether recognized itself, and, now without a home, rushed to meet his.

Mollian sucked in a breath, pulling in his magic, but also all of the magic that poured free from Tymecht. It sank into him, knocking him back with the force of its weight and swirling through his veins in a powerful surge.

His entire body vibrated, his head light as energy flooded him, fell into him, learned him.

He blinked, every ache and pain fading as more power than any creature, person, or god from any universe had ever known coursed through him and tried to find space to settle inside of him.

On instinct, Mollian focused on that inherent connection to Merriam, alerting the magic in him to that bond. It spilled over, filling this new vessel with relief as it stretched, too compressed in Mollian's body.

With some of the excess pressure offloaded, Mollian stood, stretching out his muscles even though they no longer ached. He closed his eyes and, with a single deep breath, slipped back to Nethyl.

The cacophony of battle was an instant assault on his ears, the tang of blood and sulfur filling his nostrils. He opened his eyes, brushing sweat and blood from his forehead as he looked around.

Merriam collapsed onto the dirt, her knees barking with pain, but back on Nethyl. *Home. I made it home.* The thought filled her, clogging her throat with relief. The ground beneath her rolled, a tree falling somewhere behind her with a loud crash. *That can't be good.* As the world settled, the sounds of battle came from down the hill, and she raised her gaze to meet Bellamy's.

The Ranger had somehow managed to keep his feet despite the exhaustion gleaming in the stormy-blue depths of his eyes. Exhaustion and resolution.

Merriam lifted a hand for Bellamy to help pull her to her feet. "Let's go finish this thing," she said with a wince.

Bellamy wanted to caution her against joining the fight. She'd almost died, had been completely sapped of magic save for that small reserve from Oren, which had been used to get them back to Nethyl. But he could see it in her eyes. She knew, but she wasn't going to give in to her body's request for rest.

Merriam was about to say something in an attempt at inspiring when her gaze finally landed on the center of the battlefield.

"Is that a fucking dragon?" she asked, cold disbelief running through her entire body.

"Molli closed the portal," Bellamy breathed at the same time, noticing its absence.

They looked at each other, nodding resolutely as they ran down the hill into the fray, momentum carrying Merriam more than anything.

As she ran, Merriam felt a small trickle of energy flow through her, her fingers tingling. At first she thought it was just Mollian sending his magic back down the bond, but then a flood of power, pure and unadulterated, rushed into her, and she tripped, falling to the ground with a yelp.

Bellamy skidded to a halt in front of her, a small cloud of dust rising from around his boots as he turned. "Mer!"

Merriam blinked, her body vibrating. She looked up at Bellamy, eyes bright, as she climbed to her feet and dusted off her hands and legs.

"Are you okay?"

Merriam shook her head no. Mollian had shoved this power into her. She had no doubts about that, but this magic was not his. It felt similar, but there was none of Mollian in it. "Let's go slay demons," she said instead of voicing any of the fear that coursed through her. Even if she could sense that, buried beneath this new flow of power, her body was still completely drained, she had energy, and she might as well use it.

When Nevra saw that Lyvin had been slain, she screamed, the sound filled with rage and frustration instead of the anguish and heartbreak expected by one who'd just lost someone so close to them. She weighed her chances against the two in front of her, vines reaching forth to wrap around her legs.

With another wild cry, Nevra flipped her sword in her grip and whipped it at Campbell, barely waiting for it to leave her fingers before she leapt at Evangeline.

The Ranger squeaked in surprise, her weapon piercing Nevra's shoulder, but the demon's weight knocked her off balance, pushing the blade up and out with only superficial damage to the muscle.

Nevra gripped either side of Evangeline's face, her claws pricking skin. Before Evangeline could even open her mouth to scream, Nevra gave a violent twist. Then she dissolved into an oily black cloud, launching into the sky.

The snap of Evangeline's severed neck rocked through Campbell, who'd only barely dodged Nevra's sword. His blood pounded loudly in his ears as he watched the young Ranger's body fall to the dirt, her head rolling to an unnatural angle. Bile surged up his throat, and he tore his gaze from the corpse, forcing it down with a measured breath. The air was heavy with the scent of blood, sweat, and sulfur, and his stomach rolled again.

Campbell was thrown to his knees as the ground lurched beneath him, the echo of the tremors under the planet's surface almost deafening. He pushed to his feet and whipped his head around, wiping blood from his eyes with the back of his hand. "Where's Leo?"

Calysta drew in a rattling breath, letting her portion of the wall drop. "He went to fight."

He faltered next to her, dropping into a crouch and scanning the thick blanket of blood that shimmered over her torso. "Calysta ..."

She gave him a wan smile. "I'll be fine, go—" She coughed, specks of blood flying from her lips. "Go help Leo."

"I've got her," the water nymph assured him.

"The med tents are on the west side—try to get her there," Campbell said, squeezing Calysta's fingers before running off. He tried not to think about how cold and weak her hand had felt in his as he scanned the fray.

Campbell spotted Leonidas a short distance away, watching as he dispatched the demon in front of him. Leonidas turned just as another ran for him, but before he could raise his sword in defense, the demon lunged, arms outstretched.

"NO!" Campbell yelled, sprinting forward as long, impossibly sharp claws made contact with Leonidas' chest

Mollian felt strangely calm.

Merriam was close. He could feel her against his mind, and with that assurance, his attention was on the clearing. A flare of surprise flickered through him as his gaze landed on the giant dragon, surrounded by warriors, Kodi clinging to its neck by two daggers.

Mollian walked towards the group that was fighting it, mud made from blood-soaked dirt squelching unpleasantly beneath his toes.

A demon, crablike and moving fast on eight pointed legs, rushed him. Mollian threw his hand up, the newly gained magic in him easily wrapping around the creature and crushing it.

Blood and guts exploded from the cracked pieces of its shell as it crumpled to the ground.

Mollian's eyebrows lifted. *Well, that was impressive.*

He continued toward the dragon, dispatching the demons fighting with his Guard as he passed. Crushing them. Ripping limbs free. Twisting their bodies. The power he wielded whipped from him with ease, heeding his call to destruction with only the slightest coaxing.

Mollian raised a hand, fingers spread wide as he grabbed onto the dragon with his magic.

Dronin fought against his hold, but the power Mollian controlled stuck fast to his scales.

A trickle of unease dripped down Mollian's spine. Magic had never wanted to hold to life before. It was always slippery, unwilling to touch sentient energy.

But this required almost no real effort.

Mollian tipped his head to the side, pressing the dragon down into the dirt.

Dronin resisted, snarling as his gaze landed on the king.

Mollian raised his other hand, spreading out Dronin's wings and forcing them flat.

Pull. Rip. Tear, the magic whispered.

Mollian's heart rate sped up, his eyes wide as he realized how much he wanted to use every measure of the power he now possessed. Adrenaline dumped into his bloodstream, and he set his teeth against the buzzing in his body.

Dronin lurched forward, coming for Mollian.

Kodi crawled higher up the dragon's neck.

Shred, the magic pleaded.

Mollian felt where one wing was attached to Dronin's back, and his magic slipped around it, sliding beneath scales and digging into flesh.

Dronin's head whipped back, and an anguished screech rent the air.

Mollian flicked his hand as if waving off a fly, and the wing tore free. His stomach rolled, nausea crawling up his throat in equal parts terror and exhilaration at what he was so easily able to do.

Dronin fought harder against his hold now, and power *sang* in Mollian's veins. His head light, he explored its limits, letting the magic slide around and under all of the scales, slowly popping some free while other tendrils of magic sank into tender flesh.

Kodi continued scaling Dronin's neck, slamming a dagger into a new hold where a thick tendon connected jaw to neck. His thighs ached with the effort of gripping the slick scales, and his arms were almost completely shot, but adrenaline kept him moving along with the knowledge that he was so close to ending this. He looked up, a shadow floating over him as Jasper swooped in, dropping his lance.

Dronin, half-blind with agony and fury, whipped his head to the side.

Kodi almost lost his hold, one hand outstretched to catch the lance, but Dronin's jaws closed around Jasper.

A scream from the ground was the only sound Kodi heard as he dug the sides of his feet into Dronin's neck, pushing off as he pulled up on one of the daggers. Aleah's cry, not of physical pain, but of anger and anguish, was the only sound he heard as he planted his foot against the other dagger. It ripped downward with the force of his weight as he jumped from it, raising the lance.

With a feral yell, he slammed it through the ear canal on the side of Dronin's head, using his magic to drive it deep within the dragon's skull.

Dronin's mouth fell open with a roar, and Jasper tumbled free, barely forcing his wings open in enough time to slow his descent.

Kodi dropped, one hand grasping the knife and dragging it a little further down Dronin's neck, the other reaching for his sword. Kicking his feet to swing his body around, he pulled his magic back from the exhaustion of his body, focusing it as he drove the sword straight through the soft flesh below Dronin's jaw and wrenched it sideways.

The sword hung halfway out, but a torrent of black blood poured from the wound. Kodi's grip slipped, and he slid down the side of the dragon, pushing himself away to land free of the greater demon.

Kodi's landing was clumsy, his back slamming into the ground with enough force to drive all of the air from his lungs and a sickening crunch that sent a wave of excruciating pain through his entire body.

Dronin swayed with a strange keening noise, garbled from his slit throat, and he flickered before shifting back into his greater demon form.

Jasper's lance ran straight through his skull, and Kodi's sword fell to the ground with a clatter. Dronin sank to his knees, blood pouring from his throat and down his back where his wing had been ripped free.

The djuhl was dead before he hit the ground.

Calysta felt cold all over, and the world swam in her vision. She took a shallow breath, fingers flitting up to the blade in her chest. The water nymph had dragged her to the edge of the trees, trying to provide some cover. He knew he would never make it to the medics across the battlefield. He knew Calysta wouldn't, either.

Nethyl had settled, both nymphs sensing the strange lurch in the magic that ran from the Gate, but unable to decipher what it meant. Even the noise of the battle was muffled in Calysta's mind compared to the dull ache that seemed to fill her, radiating from her chest. "My ... friends?" she choked out, looking up at the nymph who held her.

"I think they're going to win," he told her.

Her eyelids fluttered with exhaustion, and she coughed up more blood. "Can you ..." A rattling breath. "Help me?" Her fingers feebly grasped the hilt of her knife.

"You'll bleed out," he protested.

Calysta smiled weakly, but it didn't touch the pain in her eyes. "I already am." Another cough, waves of agony that darked her vision, the salty tang of her own blood coating her tongue. "Please. I don't want ... them to watch ... me die." Only the shallowest of breaths passed her blood-spotted lips.

The water nymph saw how ashen her face was, heard the agony in her whispered words. Heard the truth in them, too. She had already lost so much blood, the magic that would have tried to heal her given to the fight. Her eyes met his, pleading for this one last mercy. And he obliged, pulling the blade from her chest.

Calysta cried out, albeit faintly, but an immense pressure left her as she was rolled onto her side, letting her blood spill freely to the ground and reducing the amount that would inevitably flood her lungs.

She closed her eyes, feeling the warmth of the other nymph's hands against her skin as her own grew colder. *Protect them,* she prayed, blood soaking the ground beneath her. *Protect them, and when they see your beauty, let them know that I am there. And that I loved them.*

Calysta felt a rush of pain as her lungs seized, unable to draw in air. But her body was already so weak, so much blood lost. Her heart thudded in her ears, loud but incredibly sluggish. The time between each heartbeat seemed to be doubling. Or maybe it was just her connection to time that no longer seemed of consequence.

Her fingers curled into the ground, claws digging shallow rivulets in the soaked earth. Then she drifted. Down ... down ... down ... until all that was left of her dissolved into the ley line of life-giving magic beneath Nethyl's surface.

The dragon made the most horrendous noise Merriam had ever heard, and she whipped her head to look. One of its wings ripped free, and she felt a shiver run through her, the magic in her blood echoing with a satisfied purr. It made her skin crawl, but she turned back to the battle, slamming her axes into the flesh of demons, her back against Bellamy's as three feline types surrounded them.

Bellamy turned his head, confirming that he and Merriam may well and truly be fucked. "What's our plan, Marshal?" he called, raising his sword.

Merriam licked her lips, sensing the electric hum in her blood and deciding to test it. "Follow my lead."

The three demons leapt in unison, and Merriam whirled, throwing her arms around Bellamy and taking them to Earth.

She immediately grabbed his arm, running him a few paces to the side and Traveling back before he could get too absorbed in his surroundings. She felt dizzy, but at the same time exhilarated, the unfamiliar power in her begging for use that she was incapable of. The demons had ended up scuffling with each other, turning in confusion to look for their lost prey.

Merriam and Bellamy rushed to meet them, wielding their weapons with deadly accuracy.

They finished off that group and ran towards a greater demon close by when a deafening roar shook the clearing.

Merriam slowed her run as she watched the dragon shift back into a demon form and fall to the ground. As soon as the greater demons felt the presence of their djuhl fade, they fled. The lesser demons, more primal in nature, still fought, but started to scatter once they noticed others retreating.

The battle was won.

Merriam panted, blinking furiously to clear her vision of both blood and sweat. Exhaustion pulled at her body, warring with the strange power that surged restlessly through her blood. Demons streamed into the forest, Bellamy joining the fae chasing after them. She longed to follow, but knew that her body had already given everything it had to give, despite the pressure of magic in her blood begging for more.

Wiping the blades of her axes against her legs, Merriam let her eyes flutter closed for a moment and reached out for a sense of Mollian. He was close, so loud in her mind she almost stumbled back. He latched onto her with such possessive force, Merriam almost turned and ran to him, whatever was in her blood trying to answer to his call.

"NO!" The scream tore through the air, overpowering the diminishing sounds of battle. A wordless wail followed, and Merriam whipped toward the sound.

Campbell was on his knees in the bloody grass, crouching over a body.

Mollian pulled his magic back in, cold fear filling him with the realization of what he'd done.

He may not have been the one to kill Dronin, but he could have. Easily.

He'd let this magic take control of his conscience, had been more interested in how he might be able to dissect instead of dispatch and move on.

And it had felt so *good*.

That terrified him, and he was overcome with the sense that the magic he'd taken from the broken tether was not meant to be possessed. It belonged to the Gate.

But so does your magic.

He didn't know if the thought was his own or the strange power inside of him, and he couldn't deny how energized, how alive he felt.

Merriam brushed against his mind, and he reached back, pulling her into him. She was safe. She'd made it home.

The relief that flooded him knowing she was okay mixed with the heady buzz of magic in a disorienting combination. Mollian whirled, looking for her. He needed to find her.

"Your Majesty, are you alright?" Dio ran up to him, sheathing his weapon.

Mollian blinked, the world coming back into focus. "The portal?"

"Closed," Dio said. "It snapped shut a few moments before you showed up."

Good, Mollian thought. "We need to track down the rest of the demons. Find Leonidas, have him send birds to—" Mollian stopped, magic flaring from him in a ripple.

Dio rocked back on his heels against the force of it.

"Merriam," Mollian whispered, taking off across the battlefield.

Chapter 49

Please

MERRIAM'S HEART DROPPED INTO her stomach, and she stumbled into a run as she watched Panic dive from the sky, landing with a screech. She slid to the ground at Campbell's side, a small cry escaping her when her already torn-up knees made impact. "No, nonono," she whispered, reaching out to touch Leonidas' shoulder.

Campbell cradled the man's head in his lap, choking down another wail as he turned wide eyes to Merriam. "Help." The word fell from his lips, tears and terror shimmering in his indigo gaze.

Merriam looked slowly over Leonidas' body, bringing a shaking hand to her lips. Claws had raked across his torso, the white bone of his ribs gleamed in the moonlight, and blood seeped from his abdomen.

Leonidas' eyes opened, a low groan escaping him.

"Leo? Leo! It's gonna be okay." Campbell brushed a hand down his face. "It's gonna be okay."

Merriam stripped her shirt over her head, pressing it to Leonida's chest in a feeble attempt to staunch the flow of blood.

The man's face had gone pale, but his lips twitched in some semblance of a smile. "Ca ... m ..." Panic pushed his head against Leonidas' hand, but his fingers barely moved.

Campbell looked up, frantically searching the battlefield as tears streamed down his cheeks. "Calysta! Calysta, help! Medic! We need, we need—" Campbell's shouts faded off into nothing as he choked on a sob.

Leonidas' gaze had been focused on Campbell, but it faded out, his eyes slipping closed as another labored breath shook his body.

The tan of Campbell's hands looked even darker in contrast to the paleness of Leonidas' face. "Hold on. I love you. Hold on."

Merriam sat up on her knees to look for help, but everything was still so chaotic, and they weren't the only people cradling the injured. "Fuck, Leo." Her voice broke.

"Please," Campbell whispered, tears streaming down his cheeks.

Merriam swallowed past the lump in her throat, keeping pressure on her shirt that had already soaked through with blood. She knew basic field care, but this was *bad*. The kind of bad that was too advanced for even the magical properties of fae blood to fix. Leonidas was Bonded to Campbell, the rune tattooed on his sternum and flanked by antlers that spread across his pecs, but that gifted blood couldn't change the fact that Leonidas was only human.

"Save him, please save him," Campbell begged, his voice rising in a wail.

Merriam's chest tightened to the point she couldn't breathe. She knew the pain that laced Campbell's voice, the loss that didn't shatter a heart so much as rip it straight from the chest. She would give anything to keep Campbell from having to experience that.

The world seemed to pause around Merriam as something turned over in her mind. "He's only human," she whispered.

Campbell was curled around Leonidas' head, and Merriam reached out a hand to grasp his shoulder. "Cam, he's human. Let me get him to a hospital."

Campbell lifted his face, confusion and a deep, raw pain mingling in his eyes. "What?"

It was just a chance, and a wild one at that, but she had to take it. "Earth has doctors that can help him."

Campbell still didn't fully comprehend, but the hope in Merriam's voice was enough for him to latch on to. "Go," he said.

Merriam carefully slid into Campbell's spot, holding as much of Leo's head and shoulders in her lap as possible before taking a deep breath and sliding her rings against each other.

Her vision went blurry as she Traveled, the magic in her blood swirling happily even as her body threatened to shut down with the use of it. She was also only human, despite who shared her soul. Nausea rolled through her stomach, and she fell to the side, worried she might vomit on Leonidas. When the immediate urge passed, she pushed to her feet. "HELP!" she screamed, her voice breaking. "HELP ME PLEASE!"

They were on the outskirts of a park, the horizon barely showing the beginning signs of dawn. No one would be here. A frustrated scream tore from her chest, tears cutting tracks through the blood and grime on her cheeks. She turned, a light flickering on through the trees, and her hands slammed over her mouth at the sob of relief that surged up her throat.

A campground. There was a campground across the park. Merriam took a few shuddering breaths to regain her voice, running closer. "Help please! Call 911! We need a hospital!"

A few more lights flicked on, and she saw someone stumble from a fifth wheel with a phone raised to their ear. "Please help! Help!" Merriam cried again, stumbling back across the dew-damp grass to sink to the ground next to Leonidas. She brushed a hand across his face, his skin cold and clammy. "Just hold on a little bit longer, Leo. Please, just hold on."

A woman came running over. "My wife is on the phone with a dispatcher, they said—Jesus Christ." The woman put a hand over her mouth, stopping several feet away when she saw Leonidas' ravaged body.

Merriam pressed her shirt to his chest, feeling the faint rise and fall of his breathing. Time stretched into oblivion, but her eyes didn't leave him until she heard the wail of an ambulance. It stopped next to where she sat with Leonidas, and the back doors flew open as three people jumped out.

Two came up to Leonidas with a stretcher, and Merriam scrambled backward to get out of their way. They spoke to each other, listing his wounds as they checked his vitals and loaded him onto the stretcher.

The third, who looked even younger than Bellamy, draped a blanket over Merriam's shoulders, pulling her attention from Leonidas.

It hadn't even registered to her that she was shirtless aside from the band of fabric around her breasts, adrenaline staving off the chill in the air.

"What's your name?" the EMT asked gently, guiding her to the ambulance.

"Merriam," she answered.

"Last name? Do you have any identification on you?"

"No, we didn't bring any."

"What happened?"

"We were attacked in the woods. A bear," Merriam answered simply, her eyes returning to Leonidas as an IV was placed in his arm.

"Can you tell me who he is?" the EMT asked, stepping between her and the body.

Merriam almost laughed that this poor kid must think he needed to protect her from seeing any further trauma. "Leo, my ... my brother."

"Do you know if he has any allergies?"

Merriam shook her head.

"Sutherland, come on," a paramedic called from the back of the ambulance.

Merriam climbed in ahead of him, leaning forward to hold Leonidas' hand. An oxygen mask had been slipped over his face and an IV inserted into his arm, dripping pain meds or maybe antibiotics.

The paramedics mostly ignored her, trying to do what they could for Leonidas. Merriam's eyes stayed locked onto the shallow rise and fall of his chest, her hands gripping his fingers desperately. "Hold on, Leo, just hold on," she whispered the words so quietly they weren't audible over the noise of the ambulance.

The EMT tried to get her attention at first, to ask her more questions, but she ignored him. Tears slipped slowly down her cheeks, dripping from her chin onto the crisp white sheets beneath Leonidas. She realized she must look like Hel, but she was too physically exhausted to care.

"We're doing everything we can for him," Sutherland assured her. "But you're wounded, too."

She finally looked at him, noticing the gauze and antiseptic he was holding, and nodded.

Merriam was ready for the cleansing sting against her wounds, almost craved the way she knew it would ground her and clear the fog of fear from her mind. The gauze was cold and wet when it brushed her skin, clearing the blood and grime from her face, but no pain came.

Sutherland frowned, intently searching the side of her face.

Concerned, Merriam lifted a hand to her temple. Her skin was unbroken.

She dropped her hand, looking at her fingers in shock, then reached to slip her fingers beneath the cloth tied around her arm. The gash was gone. Healed.

It shouldn't be.

She shivered, tightening the blanket around her shoulders and leaning forward to press her forehead to Leonidas' knuckles. That strange power vibrating in her veins made her incredibly uneasy, only adding to the other emotions that clouded her mind. "Don't you dare fucking die on me, Leonidas," she whispered.

Panic had started screaming the second Leonidas disappeared. He hopped around, dipping his head to where Leonidas' blood had soaked into the grass. Tufts of down floated around him as he flapped, finally tilting his head up to Campbell.

Campbell stared at the bird, his fingers digging into the dirt as he tried to wrap his brain around everything that was happening. One second his heart had been breaking as the man he loved lay bleeding in his arms. The next, Leonidas had been gone, whisked away to Merriam's homeland for reasons he couldn't quite comprehend. Indigo eyes raised to look around at his surroundings, the battlefield even more chaotic now than it had been during the fighting.

He rose on shaky legs, glancing back down at Panic. "Let's go try to find everyone else," he said. Panic blinked at him, scratching at the ground when Leonidas had been. "I know. We just have to trust that Mer knows what she's talking about."

Across the clearing, Rovin ran from the woods, a gray wolf with bright green eyes leading the charge ahead of him. The Ranger spied Kodi,

Aleah dumping water over his face to wash it of black blood as a medic tied a bandage around his arm.

"Kodi!" Rovin called.

Kodi blinked the water from his eyes, a grin breaking out over his face.

Aleah held her hand up as Rovin approached, her palm slamming into his chest. "He's got an assload of broken ribs and a concussion."

"*Minor* concussion." Kodi gingerly kicked her out of the way, holding his hand out to Rovin, agony making the smile on his lips waiver. "Absolutely worth it to be a dragonslayer, if you ask me."

Rovin clasped it. "Glad you made it out in one piece, brother."

"Barely!" Aleah exclaimed, folding her arms across her chest. "He's lucky I don't—Ryddan!" she dropped to her knees, throwing her arms around the wolf's neck.

Ryddan tipped his head back, licking at Aleah's freckled face.

"Where's Mer? Have you seen her?" Rovin asked, anxiety bright in his eyes.

"She made it back." Bellamy limped over, and Ryddan shifted into a fae, throwing himself at Bellamy. The Ranger caught him with a slight grunt, steadying himself as he tucked the child against his chest and turned his eyes towards the crowd forming in the makeshift camp. It took him only a few moments of searching to realize he hadn't spotted any of the other mercenaries. "Is everyone else ...?"

The smile fell from Aleah's face, and Kodi squeezed her hand. "Jasper's with some medics in intensive care. They wouldn't let me stay. He ..." she broke off, eyes flicking to Ryddan. "He was in pretty rough shape. But he'll make it. He has to." Her brows knit together, but she shook herself from the negative thoughts. "I haven't seen any of the others yet."

"I can help you look," Bellamy offered. Ryddan's arms tightened around his neck.

"I'll go," Rovin said. He scanned the crowd, the knot in his stomach growing tighter and more tangled with each moment that passed as he waited for Merriam to show up. His gaze returned to the young Ranger and the prince in his arms. "Stay with your kid." A smile tugged at one corner of Rovin's mouth, and he reached out to run a hand over the back of Ryddan's head.

Ryddan pulled his face from Bellamy's chest, looking at Rovin with wide green eyes. "Where's Molli and Ria?"

"They're around here somewhere," Rovin answered, managing to keep the worry out of his voice.

Aleah spied Campbell stumbling through the camp and ran over to him with a squeak. She dipped underneath his shoulder, helping support him as she brought him over to sit next to Kodi. "We need a medic!" she called over her shoulder, examining him for injuries amidst the blood that covered him. "Where are Leo and Calysta? Were they with you?" she asked.

Campbell swallowed, tears filling his indigo eyes as he looked at her. Panic flew in before he could speak, landing on a pile of crates across from Campbell and shaking out his feathers, head turning and bobbing as he surveyed the tent.

Aleah's mouth went dry. "No. Nonono."

"Mer took him off world," Campbell choked out. "She thought maybe … maybe the human medics there could help him. But it was so bad." He broke down again, Aleah darting forward to hug him close.

"It'll be okay. If Mer took him, he'll be okay." She couldn't consider any alternative.

Campbell drew in a shuddering breath, wiping his palms across his cheeks and smearing blood—both black and red—across his face. Aleah smoothed his hair back before grabbing a damp cloth to wipe his face. But Campbell's gaze locked on Bellamy, and his throat bobbed as he swallowed, choking on the words. "Ev—" He stopped, jaw trembling as his eyes went blank, the sound of her neck snapping replaying in his mind. "They killed Evangeline," he whispered.

Bellamy felt it like a punch to the gut, and he clutched Ryddan tighter. He wanted to ask questions, but the child in his arms grounded him before his mind could even start to spiral. There would be time later, when Ryddan wouldn't have to hear it all.

"I'm sorry," Campbell choked, his gaze refocusing on the Ranger. "I couldn't—couldn't—"

"It's not your fault," Bellamy interrupted quietly, his chest tight. He sank down to Campbell's other side, physical and emotional exhaustion sapping the last of his strength. "We all knew the risks."

Campbell leaned into him for a moment before sitting up straighter. "What about Calysta? Is she here?"

"She wasn't with you?" Aleah asked.

"I left her with a water nymph. He didn't bring her here?"

Aleah frowned, glancing around agitatedly. "It's been chaos. Maybe I missed her? If she was badly hurt she could be in intensive care with Jaz."

"I'll look for her," Rovin interjected, spying Dio in one of the other open tents. "If she's still in the field, we'll find her."

Aleah nodded, throwing her arms around Rovin's waist and squeezing tight.

The vise around Rovin's chest had loosened when he heard Merriam was okay, but only marginally. She was wounded and had been on the verge of complete exhaustion when he'd last seen her. There was no way to know that she and Leonidas would be safe over there, no way to know if Merriam would even be able to find help.

But Mollian could make sure they were okay.

Rovin let out a slow breath. Action always made him feel better. Movement kept his mind clear. So he mapped out a plan in his head as he walked towards the captain: have someone track down Mollian so he could help Merriam and Leonidas, then find Calysta and help any of the other injured get to medical care.

"Captain." Rovin saluted.

"Rovin." Dio's eyes were tired, his face haggard. "I'm glad you're here. We need to search the battlefield … take inventory of the dead and find those who were too wounded to move themselves. We also need to send a group, probably two or three, to follow the demons that fled and figure out where they're going. Have you seen the demonslayer?"

Rovin stepped further into the tent, looking from his captain to the commanders that also stood around the table. "She's not here."

Dio's head snapped up at that.

"Have you seen King Mollian since the fighting started?"

"He was there when the dragon fell, but he ran off shortly after. I think he was looking for Merriam."

Rovin blinked, worry tightening in his gut. "Let's hope he found her."

He ended up taking a team to walk through the battlefield and separate the living from the dead. The dead also needed to be sorted. Demons were tossed into piles for disposal, probably burning. The fallen Guard were taken to a tented area to be identified so their families could be notified and their remains handled with the proper respect. The nymphs were brought to the opposite side of the clearing, just inside the treeline. Not to separate them, but to keep their bodies from direct exposure to the rising sun while honoring the nymphs' traditions of resting under the open sky.

Rovin started with a quick sweep of the field to check for any survivors and spotted a water nymph with his back against a blighted tree. "Do you need help?" he called, jogging over.

The nymph shook his head, lifting black eyes to Rovin. "Not me," he said. "I need to find her friends."

Rovin slid to a halt in the dead leaves, his gaze dropping to the body the nymph held as time seemed to stop. "Calysta." He sank to his knees, blood rushing in his ears as he brushed a lock of pale pink hair away from her face, pressing his fingers to the ashen green skin of her neck to search for a pulse he knew he wouldn't find.

Merriam woke in a panic surrounded by bright, sterile white light and uniform furniture. Her mouth was dry and fuzzy, and her entire body felt pressurized.

Her memory came back to her in a rush, Leonidas being wheeled into surgery, the massive amounts of internal injuries he'd sustained. She'd fallen asleep in a waiting room, her body having given all it had to offer.

But something had woken her, a familiar presence stirring in her chest.

She stood with a groan, her legs protesting. Her fingers were freezing, and she shoved her hands into the pockets of the sweatshirt she'd taken from the gift shop in an attempt to blend in and draw less attention to herself. She walked over to the nurses' station, clearing her throat. "My brother came in this morning for a bear attack. Leonidas?"

The nurse's brow creased in a thoughtful frown, and she typed something into her computer.

Merriam bit her lip, her nerves completely frayed and apprehension tight in her belly. That *otherly* magic still poured through her blood, setting her teeth on edge. But other than a little soreness that could probably be equated to how she'd slept, all of her injuries had healed. Merriam swallowed, lifting a shaky hand to her left temple and applying pressure, gently at first, then more firmly.

No pain radiated from her skull, from bone that should still need a couple more weeks to finish knitting itself back together. She pulled her hand away, staring at her fingers as anxiety crept through her blood.

"Ah, yes, it looks like he's still in surgery." The nurse interrupted her thoughts. "That's not to worry, though. His injuries were extensive, so he's bound to be under for a while. Meanwhile, I've got some paperwork I'll need you to fill out. Just routine information, insurance, that sort of thing."

Merriam nodded, taking the clipboard and pen that the nurse slid over the desk.

She ducked back into the waiting room, setting it down on a chair before walking back out into the hall.

She needed fresh air. Her head swam with fear and uncertainty. Merriam knew that nothing on Nethyl would have saved Leonidas, but how much had she risked in bringing him here? People on Earth asked so many damn questions and tracked every little thing. And what about when Leonidas woke up? The language of Nethyl's humans was similar to English, but he only rarely, if ever, used it. How would the nurses react when he woke up speaking gibberish? Not to mention the way that her blood swam with—

"Ria."

Merriam gasped, lifting her gaze from her feet and squinting against the sunlight that backlit Mollian as she ran to him. "Molli, what are you doing here?" she said against his chest, the new magic in her blood surging to life in his presence, making her lightheaded.

"You were gone. I felt you, and then I didn't."

Merriam stepped back, her hands on either side of his face. His hair was still crusted in black blood, streaks of his own on his cheeks, and she glanced around, worried about the people coming in and out of the hospital.

"It's fine, I'm glamored," he assured her. "And haven't gone into the hospital for the same reason. I know not to mess with whatever technology is in there."

"How did you find me?" Merriam asked.

Mollian looked her over, pale green eyes scanning every inch of her. "I followed your trail, asked people questions. Are you okay?"

Merriam nodded, leading him to a bench outside and sinking into it. "I'm fine. Leo got clawed pretty badly. He needed surgeons, modern medicine like they don't have on Nethyl. Because he's human, because he can't wield magic, they could work on him. I didn't think any further than that."

Mollian ran his thumb over the back of her hand, a small smile playing on his lips. "I know. I asked a nurse coming off shift. I could feel you inside, but didn't want to risk disturbing anything, so I tracked down the medical crew who found you, too. They won't be asking any questions. Did you find Rydd? Did everyone make it back?"

She briefly recounted the rescue, then paused. "Oren saved me. When you took your magic back ... I still had his." She worried at her bottom lip, tears lining her eyes. "I forget sometimes that I have that part of him. That I always will." A tear slipped free, but the sorrow she felt was equally laced with a warm comfort. She looked up at Mollian. "Do you ever feel him in me? Can your magic sense the presence of his?"

"In the stillest moments, yes." He squeezed her hand, but his brows pulled together. "I didn't mean to leave you without any of my magic, though. I didn't even notice I'd pulled it all back. I put you in danger, and I'm sorry."

Merriam shook her head, her throat tight. "Molli, what happened? I felt you take it and then ... and then it came back, but ... it feels different."

"I separated Tymecht from the Gate."

"What?"

"When that cord snapped, all of the magic—all of the life and energy the Gate was feeding into Tymecht—poured free. I just ... sucked it up. It needed somewhere to go, so I pushed it to you." Mollian said it like it was all so simple, but Merriam knew him well enough to catch the shift in his body language.

She searched his face, but his gaze stayed focused on the sidewalk. "This magic isn't yours."

Mollian smiled, but it lacked any warmth. "I could have taken apart that dragon piece by piece, Ria. And that was without effort. If I *tried*, I could change the entire fabric of a world." He swallowed, finally meeting her eyes. "It's terrifying. How strong it is. How much I want to keep it."

Merriam lifted a hand to his face, tears lining her eyes as anxiety churned through her.

"Nothing would ever be able to touch you again. Not you or Ryddan or Sekha." He leaned his cheek into her palm.

"Molli," Merriam whispered, feeling the strength of that strange magic flowing through her, the otherness of it.

"I want to keep it. I want to keep it and protect you and everything else I love. I want to be untouchable." Mollian balled his hands in his lap, pressing his lips together as it roiled underneath his skin, pushing him for action.

"You can give it back," Merriam said. "I'm fine. Ryddan is safe. And nobody can question your ability to protect your country, Molli. You saved us all *without* that magic. You don't need it. You're a king in your own right and have earned your crown ten times over."

Her faith in him had always been overpowering. But whatever energy flowed through him, that was overpowering, too.

"We can take anything the universe has to throw at us. I promise. Don't take the extra weight of this." Merriam took one of his hands, holding it to her chest as she rested her head against his shoulder.

He didn't say anything, just leaned against her. He'd never lied to her, and he wasn't going to start now. *It wants things from me, Ria.* He wanted to Cast it, but didn't. *It's not mine. It's not mine, and it knows it. But I don't know if I care.*

They sat like that for a while, each using the other to settle themselves after so much had happened. As they sat together, the magic cycled through them. With great effort, Mollian pulled all of that other magic back into himself until Merriam was left with only what was his own. She felt it leave her, and even though knowing he took the full weight of it on his own worried her, she said nothing.

"I don't want to leave you here," Mollian eventually said.

She sighed. "You have a country to run, Lord King. One that was just under attack, at that." Merriam sat up, meeting his gaze evenly. "I'll be fine here. As soon as Leo is stable enough to move, I'll come back."

"You're a four days' ride away from Umbra. I can leave Rovin with some of the other Guard to stay behind with supplies and horses."

"I used to make my living through treachery, remember?" Merriam cracked a smile. "I'll steal a car and drive most of the distance on this side of things. Let everyone go home. I'll meet you there. We'll *both* meet you there."

He ran a hand fondly over her hair. "You'll be okay until then? You'll stay safe?"

"I promise."

They stood, Mollian raising his hand so Merriam could press her palm to it. Then he stepped back, Casting her a final *I love you* before Traveling back to Nethyl.

Donova raised a hand to her throat, claws playing across her skin as she thought. The shaking that accompanied the portal's disappearance worried her. Only a heavy disruption of magic would have caused a reaction like that, which meant whoever had closed the portal had done so forcefully.

She turned abruptly, dropping her hand and strutting to her desk. She clicked her tongue in annoyance when she saw Ryddan's blood spilled on the floor. It would have been nice to have that kind of magic in her stores, but if Dronin did somehow manage to make it back, not having the djuhlin's blood would absolve her of any blame for not opening a new portal.

For now, she brushed past the mess that had been made of her supplies, searching only for the things she needed to dreamwalk. She drew the spell together quickly, drawing a circle on the floor, lighting her candles, and finally digging the point of one claw down the opposite forearm. Her lips moved with a silent incantation as she raised her arm over her head, tilting her head back to let black blood drip over her face. Then she sank to her knees in the circle, closing her eyes to dream.

Donova's heart thudded in her chest. Calm. Steady.

But she stayed rooted in her own mind.

Never before had the warlock been unable to conjure a dream when she'd called for it.

A tremor ran through her, and she cast her mind instead to her home along the barren cliffs of the sulfur sea. But even as she whispered the words, she could feel the power within her running slow and sluggish, dissipating from her very being.

Her eyes blinked open, tracks of black blood still dripping down her face, and she rose to her feet, stumbling over to the window. "This is not possible." The words fell from her lips as her fingers curled into the ledge. Along with the steady loss of her own power, she watched the realm outside also leach of energy.

The byrds still flying around where the portal had closed began to drop from the sky, landing lifelessly on the rocky terrain below. The strikes of lightning in the sky grew steadily less frequent.

And as Donova watched, her chest tightened, unable to draw in adequate air to breathe.

The energy of her world was leaching, and soon there would be nothing left.

Traveling from the hospital left Mollian roughly an hour's walk from where the battle had been fought, but he wanted the time to clear his head. So he walked, feeling that unfamiliar magic roll underneath his skin in uncomfortable waves. He opened one of his hands at his side, letting it loose to brush across the trees, pulling the dead leaves free and ripping them into tiny pieces with only half a thought.

"You're going to have to learn to listen to me," he whispered, feeling it reach further and further away, searching for an outlet. He sighed, cutting a trail of minor obliteration as he walked.

The air seemed to vibrate around Mollian, alerting him to the ley line beneath his feet. The battlefield was close. He could hear the general clamor of a large group of people just over the hill. And now it was time to be a king.

Mollian headed for the tents on one side of the battlefield, eyes scanning how much of the carnage had already been cleaned up. Fires dotted the clearing, burning piles of dead demons, and though many of the fallen Royal Guard and nymphs had been collected, there were still some lying in the blood-soaked dirt, waiting. A pang of sorrow speared him when he saw the death toll. So many had died. So many that he was charged with ruling, with protecting. He'd closed the portal, yes, but so many had been lost before he'd been able to rip Tymecht free. Mollian would live with that for the rest of his life.

The magic inside of him flared with his erratic emotions, and he bit the inside of his cheek to keep the tears from his eyes as he made his way toward the camp and the people who'd put their lives on the line at his command. What was he even supposed to say to them? What words could possibly be enough to let them know how much he admired them or how thankful he was for their bravery?

Part of him wanted to disappear, to run back to Merriam and avoid facing the aftermath of everything. But a guardsman looked up, calling out when he spotted him. "It's the king!"

Mollian winced, a wave of guilt crashing over him that they'd noticed his absence. *Legends, they might think I left them.* But cries from the camp interrupted his thoughts, and he was completely and utterly unprepared for the words that reached his ears.

"All hail King Mollian!"

"The Protector of Nethyl!"

"Long live the king!"

As Mollian walked by, people knelt.

"It was an honor to fight alongside you, Your Majesty," one Ranger told him as he passed, and others voiced the same sentiment.

Tears of a different nature lined Mollian's eyes at the deference. And when Dio walked through the crowd and dropped to one knee at his feet, they fell down his cheeks.

"Glad to have you back, Your Majesty," he said after rising.

Mollian clasped him on the shoulder, the cheers from the Guard still ringing around them. "What is this, Dio?" he asked. "I don't—" he broke off, his voice threatening to crack. *I don't deserve this.*

"It's respect, Mollian, and well-fucking earned. You risked your life fighting alongside these people. They won't soon forget that." Dio put his own hand on Mollian's shoulder, meeting his gaze evenly. "You are their king, not just in name, but in here"—he tapped Mollian's chest with his free hand—"where it counts."

More tears cut down Mollian's cheeks, and he brushed them away with a watery laugh. "That's incredibly melodramatic, Captain."

"Maybe, but doesn't make it any less true." Dio smiled before dropping his hands. "Did you find the demonslayer? Rovin and the mercs have been looking for her."

Mollian nodded, and they started walking toward one of the command tents. "She's off world with one of the mercenaries, but she's safe."

"Glad to hear it," Dio said, then moved straight into business. "Let's head to central camp, where you can address the Guard. It'll do them all good to hear the words of victory from your mouth. Then visit the med tents after that, if you're up for it. We've already got a couple groups of Rangers tracking the demons who fled, and the rest of the Guard is either getting medical attention or clearing the dead. The plan so far is to—"

The captain was cut off as a small form came sprinting through the camp. "Molli!"

Mollian dropped to his knees, opening his arms as Ryddan slammed into his chest. He cupped the back of Ryddan's head, holding him close as his emotions threatened to overwhelm him.

But he knew, kneeling there in the dirt with his arms around that child that never should have been—a child like him—he knew that he would figure out how to work through everything.

They only took the rest of that day to recuperate from the fight, packing everything up to head back to Umbra the following morning.

Mollian met with a few representatives from the nymphs, thanking them for their aid and promising them that he would do his best to ensure they never again endured the kind of persecution they'd been subjected to in the past.

Jasper, Campbell, and Aleah were staying behind an extra day to lay Calysta to rest. "Take care of Kodi," Aleah told Mollian and Rovin, arms folded across her chest.

"I'm a dragonslayer, little merc, I can handle a few days of travel," Kodi interjected from where he sat on the back of a cart.

"I wasn't talking to you." She kept her eyes on both of them. "Don't let him do anything stupid."

"We'll get him back in one piece," Rovin promised, and Aleah squeezed him and Mollian goodbye because she couldn't squeeze Kodi.

Mollian found Ryddan with Shiloh, helping them make final preparations for the wounded. "Can I steal the prince for a moment?"

Shiloh smiled down at Ryddan. "I'll miss the help, but we'll make do."

"Where are we going?" Ryddan asked, following Mollian through the broken-down camp.

"You'll see," he answered casually.

They found Bellamy, Mollian motioning him over, away from the throngs of people. When Bellamy reached them, Mollian lowered to a knee to better meet Ryddan's eyes. "I love you, kid. You're my favorite nephew, and I wouldn't trade you for this world or any other."

"I'm your only nephew," Ryddan pointed out, glancing curiously from Mollian to Bellamy.

"True, but you're still the coolest kid in all of Sekha." Mollian smiled, flicking his gaze up to Bellamy. "You belong in Umbra, Rydd. I know your father wasn't from this realm, but you're a Stonebane through and through. Never question that, okay?"

"I know," Ryddan said.

Mollian searched his face, watching the emotion in his bright green cat's eyes. "Good. I need you to know that, because I need you to know that you *are* my family, and nothing will *ever* change that. But I was wondering ..." he fought back a smile, trying to keep his serious disposition. "How would you feel about also being Bell's family?"

Ryddan blinked, looking up at Bellamy before cutting his eyes back to Mollian. "Like ... like he could be my dad?"

Mollian nodded. "If you want."

Ryddan turned to Bellamy, raising his arms as he nodded furiously. Bellamy scooped him up, tears lining his eyes as Ryddan's arms went around his neck. He met Mollian's gaze over Ryddan's shoulder and mouthed a thank-you.

Mollian shrugged, wiping tears from his own eyes. "We'll find you proper quarters in the castle when we get back to Umbra."

"Will Lydia have to live with us?" Ryddan asked.

Mollian held back a laugh, and Bellamy shook his head. "No, buddy. She'll still be around to help and take you to classes, but she won't live with us," the Ranger said.

The king bit his lip, watching his friend and his nephew—two major pieces of his family—and he let himself fully register everything they'd accomplished on their own. He'd torn an entire realm free of the Gate with only the magic he'd been born with. Three of them had infiltrated a demon world to rescue Ryddan, Bellamy the only one born with magic. And here, here his Guard had fought a Legends-damned *dragon* along with a whole legion of demons, and they'd *won.*

"I'll be back in a bit, okay?" Mollian told Bellamy before slipping away, walking across the battle-scarred clearing.

He'd lain awake most of the night, both trying to corral the magic that ran through him, and contemplating what to do with it. Merriam had told him he didn't need it, that they would be fine without it, but it had been so hard to believe only heartbeats after everything that had happened.

She was right, though. They had made it through on their own.

Mollian held his hands out, letting the power in his veins roam free, slipping into the blighted trees and tearing chunks and pieces free. But it wanted more, confirming what he already knew before he pulled it back in.

The unfamiliar magic that swirled through him required an outlet, required more than he knew he would ever be able to give it without losing himself to it.

Mollian sank slowly to the ground, digging his fingers into the grass and the soil beneath. He closed his eyes and pushed the magic in him down into Nethyl. It burrowed, tapping into the ley line.

Once the two magics touched, they melded; the power running beneath Nethyl ripping the excess from Mollian so quickly the breath left his lungs. He pulled free, panting as he knelt on the ground. The pressure underneath his skin was gone, and Mollian was surprised by how light he felt. He would have been invincible if he'd kept it, but even acknowledging that fact, the pure relief knowing he was no longer responsible for it made him dizzy in its intensity.

Magic swirled through his veins, but eventually settled comfortably, still powerful, still thrumming in his blood, but *his.*

SIX DAYS WENT BY with Leonidas in the hospital.

The first was the most excruciating.

Even when he was out of surgery, the doctors told Merriam that Leonidas might not wake up. He'd lost a lot of blood, and infection had set in.

But Leonidas was a fighter, and his Bonded blood worked with the antibiotics they pumped into his system to stave off the infection. He woke up halfway through the second day.

"Leo," Merriam said softly, reaching out to squeeze his hand.

His fingers flexed against hers, his eyelids fluttering.

Merriam swallowed against the lump in her throat, tears springing to her eyes.

His body was heavy with sedative, but his heart raced as he looked around the unfamiliar space. He struggled to sit up, pulling at the tubing in his nose. Dull pain radiated from his abdomen as his muscles flexed, and he fell back with a groan. Fear and anger and confusion poured through him in a strange cocktail, and he growled, unable to get his mouth to work right.

"Leo, calm down, it's okay," Merriam soothed, standing over him. "You're on Earth, in a hosp—in a med house."

Leonidas turned his head to her, his brow furrowing. "Cam," he croaked.

Merriam sat back down, not wanting to add to his anxiousness by hovering. "He's okay."

Leonidas nodded, trying to swallow against the dryness in his mouth.

She grabbed him some water and helped him drink.

Leonidas closed his eyes, trying to clear the fog from his brain. "You saved my life, Mer."

Merriam squeezed his hand, her fingers cold. "You're not allowed to die on me and leave me alone with all the magical beings."

He huffed out a painful laugh. "I guess we should go home before they get into more trouble."

"You almost died, Leo. Your body needs time to begin healing. You had extensive internal injuries and need to stay in bed for a while, until they know that everything is working right." Merriam grabbed his hand. "I promise I'll get us home as soon as I know moving you isn't a death sentence."

She had put her old information on the insurance forms, using a fake name, and managed to hold off handing it over until the day before they were ready to leave. Her hope was that they wouldn't run anything until they were long gone.

Four days after he woke up, Leonidas was able to stand, and that was as much as either of them would wait for. It was ridiculously easy for Merriam to lift a set of keys from a patient, using the panic button to help her locate the car.

And then they were driving north, mere hours away from home.

Merriam took them back to Nethyl, as close to the merc house as she could get from the side of the road. Leonidas was still weak, and she took the brunt of his weight as they walked up the street. He leaned heavily against her, still in a hospital gown and grimacing with the effort of moving up the sloped street.

A loud scree cut through the air, a shadow dropping quickly from the sky.

Panic had been circling almost nonstop since Campbell had forced him back to Umbra with the others. He landed on the ground in front of them, stamping at the cobblestones as he screamed at Leonidas.

"I know. Be mad at me later, though," Leonidas told him with a grunt. "Go get Cam." He made a motion at the bird, signaling for him to go home and for help.

Panic glared at him, then took off.

It didn't take long after that for Campbell to come racing down the road, Jasper and Aleah close behind.

Campbell skidded to a stop in front of them, tears lining his indigo eyes as he took in Leonidas' pale appearance. "What in Legends' fuck are you wearing?" he asked, but threw his arms around him, taking the brunt of his weight from Merriam.

Leonidas grunted in pain, but refused to let Campbell pull away, burying his face in Campbell's curls and breathing him in. "I love you, buck."

Aleah came at Merriam so fast, she was almost knocked from her feet. "I'm so glad you're both okay."

Merriam hugged her tight before pulling away to meet Jasper. Tears slid down her cheeks as she wrapped her arms around him.

"No crying over me, Marshal. I made it out alive—that's what counts." One of his hands was wrapped, three fingers missing. A huge, thick scar ran the entire side of his face and neck, and he wore a patch over the eye he'd lost. One of his wings was tucked into an awkward sling, held immobile. "You brought back our falconer. I owe you for that." He pulled away from Merriam to greet Leonidas. "I'll need to get on your schedule for some rehab, brother," he said, gently clapping Leonidas on the back.

"Consider it cleared," Leonidas replied.

"Where's Calysta?" Merriam asked, looking around.

Campbell shook his head, squeezing her hand.

"I don't ... I don't understand." Merriam stepped back, her blood running cold.

"She's been given back to Nethyl," Aleah said quietly.

Merriam pressed the heel of her hand over her heart, the familiar ache of grief squeezing her lungs.

Jasper led them back to the merc house, and they took turns filling in the parts of the story that they knew.

"We should hold a wake," Merriam said, sucking in a breath and wiping tears from her cheeks.

"Once Leo has time to recover a bit, we'll plan one." Jasper smiled, his single silver eye shimmering with emotion. "Out in the forest where we used to hold bonfires. We'll honor her the way she deserves."

Merriam sat with them for a while longer before heading up to the castle with Aleah. "How is Kodi doing?" she asked as they walked, arms linked together.

"Too well for his own good," Aleah huffed. "He broke most of his ribs and popped his shoulder out of place when he fell off the dragon, the idiot. Now he's making everyone call him dragonslayer."

Merriam's head fell back with a laugh. "I'll make sure it catches in court."

The mercenary rolled her eyes. "Please refrain from inflating his ego until he's off bed rest. He already makes the worst fucking patient."

"No promises." Merriam briefly dropped her head to Aleah's, and her throat threatened to close with the emotion that washed over her. The threat to her home and her family was over, and the amount of relief, grief, and joy that fact filled her with was overwhelming. "I missed you," she said.

Aleah squeezed her arm. "I missed you, too."

They parted ways at the gates, Merriam telling Aleah she would meet up with her later to see Kodi. She reached out for Mollian, and just felt his returning brush against her mind when she heard a commotion from the side of the courtyard.

She rounded the corner, leaning a shoulder against the stone of the castle.

Rovin was leading a training session for a few Ranger hopefuls, but stopped his instruction when his eyes landed on her.

"No rest for the wicked, Lieutenant?" she called, lips quirked in a smile.

Without hesitation, Rovin ran to her, slid his hands into her hair, and kissed her.

Merriam's arms went around his neck, pulling herself closer to him as warmth and giddiness spread through her chest. For the first time in a long time, Merriam pushed every worry from her mind, threading her fingers into Rovin's hair as she kissed him back and let herself claim the happiness that wrapped itself around her heart.

Catcalls floated up from the young Guard, directed at Rovin more than at Merriam.

He pulled away, brushing a thumb across her cheek with a soft chuckle. "I should finish up with them."

She untangled her fingers from his hair and rested her hands against his chest with a soft smile. "Find me when you're done."

"Sir, yes, sir," he whispered, brushing another kiss against her lips. A rapturous grin lit his face, those impossibly deep brown eyes sparkling as he took a few steps backward before spinning around and jogging to the training ring with a call for everyone to settle down.

Merriam waved to the trainees, who were still watching her, then followed Mollian's pull to the war room. He was in the middle of a meeting with Captain Dio and the commanders, but immediately stood when she walked in.

We made it.

She almost laughed as his voice filled her head. *Fucking Hel.*

Then he walked to her, lifting her off her feet as he squeezed her and her arms went around him. The tethers between them twisted, strong and secure in each other's presence. Together, as they were always meant to be.

Mollian set her down, and she followed him to the table.

"Welcome back, Marshal," Dio greeted. "We were just discussing the best way to handle the demons who were left behind."

Merriam dropped into her customary seat, tossing her braid over her shoulder and folding her hands on the table in front of her. "What have we got?"

Five years after ...

Merriam drags her arm over her brow, wiping it free of sweat as she drops to the ground to stretch her legs, leaning forward and breathing through the burn in her muscles.

"Can I take your weapon, Marshal?" a trainee of the Royal Guard asks.

"Yes, thank you." Merriam smiles up at them, releasing her hold on the toe of her boots to hand over the wooden sword. "After you're done with cool-downs and have cleaned up after yourselves, go get breakfast and shower." She raises her voice so that all of the trainees in the courtyard hear. "You'll have no duties this morning. The ceremony will start at midday."

A disjointed chorus of– "Yes, Marshal" – follows. While finishing her stretches, her eyes wander across the courtyard to a separate ring where the Rangers are training. It's a light day, mostly calisthenics, and her gaze lands on Rovin.

He's holding onto a pull-up bar, the muscles in his arms rippling with each movement. When his arms fully extend, a strip of golden tan skin shows between his shirt and the waist of his pants, showing off the deep v of his lower abdomen. He drops to the ground, pulling up the hem of his shirt to wipe sweat from his face and giving her a full view of every defined, flexed muscle.

Merriam rolls her eyes, knowing he's seen her watching and is deliberately showing off. She hops up, heading back into the castle and up to her room to shower.

Rillak is at his usual post outside the door to the royal chambers. "Ya just missed His Majesty. Said he'd meet ya in the war room. Big day ahead an' all."

"Thanks, Rillak," Merriam replies as the guard opens the door. "Will you be getting relief before the ceremony?"

"I wouldn' miss it, Marsh," he assures her.

Merriam strips as she walks, dumping her clothes in a hamper by her bedroom door and walking into the bathroom. She turns on the tap to the shower, letting the water heat up as she shakes out her braid and twists her hair onto the top of her head.

The stream of near-scalding water feels marvelous against her skin, and she closes her eyes, lathering soap against a washcloth. Halfway through washing, she hears someone enter the bathroom, and moments later, arms wrap around her, pulling her against a chest that feels cold compared to the temperature of the water.

"I was almost clean," she complains halfheartedly, tilting her head to the side to give access as Rovin runs his lips over her shoulder and up her neck, his stubble scratching against her skin.

"I can help with that," he murmurs, biting her earlobe.

Merriam shivers, turning to face him and resting her arms over his shoulders. "It's a busy morning, and I haven't eaten yet."

"Me neither." Rovin grins, leaning in to kiss her and sliding a hand down to her hip, pressing her against the hardened length of him.

"As insinuating as it sounds, I really do have a tight schedule," she says against his lips.

"It's so fucking hot watching you run things, though." Rovin runs his hands down her body, calluses scraping against her skin. "Training sessions, war room briefs, my sanity up the wall ..."

Warmth completely separate from the water pouring over them spreads through Merriam, and she rises onto her toes to pull Rovin into another kiss, sliding her tongue into his mouth. Her nipples pebble, brushing against his chest and sending electric sensations directly to her clit. She hooks one leg over his hip and grinds against him. Her hands slide over his skin, tracing a familiar path across his body. "Fuck it, no breakfast and we can squeeze in a quickie."

Rovin grabs her thighs, hoisting her up so that her legs can wrap around his waist, and pushes her against the wall. "There are eggs and toast on your nightstand."

Merriam slides her hands into his hair, brushing a thumb over his cheek. "Legends, I love you."

"I know." Rovin smirks, running the tip of his cock along her entrance. He bites back a groan at how wet she already is and presses into her.

He knows her body well, and the hunger behind his touch draws filthy words from her mouth as he moves inside of her. Her hands thread into his hair, her head falling back as his lips find her neck. When her breaths become shorter and her legs tighten around him, he drags a hand up her side and pinches her nipple. "Let it out, pet." His hand drops back down to her hip, and he grinds her against him. The friction against her clit sends her over the edge, and she cries out as pleasure explodes through her, her legs holding him deep inside of her as she convulses around him.

Rovin kisses her, swallowing her cries and quickly following her over the edge with a groan. Merriam releases her hold on his hair and runs her fingers through the wet strands as she breaks the kiss, resting her head against his neck as she catches her breath.

Rovin steps back from the wall, and she drops her legs to stand. He holds her against him for a moment, running a hand down her back and pressing a kiss to her temple before reaching behind her for shampoo.

Merriam finishes washing up, watching him with a stupidly enamored gleam in her eyes. She wrinkles her nose at her continued infatuation as she dries off before moving to the bed to eat. Rovin soon comes from the bathroom, a towel wrapped around his waist. He grins at her when he sees her happily sitting on the edge of the bed, slightly bent over a plate. He walks over, gripping her chin and brushing a few crumbs from the corner of her mouth with a thumb. "I adore you."

Warmth floods Merriam's chest, and she smiles up at him. "I know."

Rovin pulls a uniform from the armoire, and after a final glance in the mirror to make sure everything is in place, gives her a parting kiss before heading out.

Merriam quickly dresses and braids her hair, grabbing her weapons belt before heading down to the war room, where a small committee is gathered to run over the last details of the ceremony. She slips into her seat next to Mollian, who gives her a knowing look at her slight tardiness, but doesn't comment.

Bellamy joins them with Ryddan right before they're ready to head down into Umbra. The young prince is dressed in a deep green that matches his eyes, his straight white hair grown out past his shoulders now. The front pieces are pulled back, giving a clear view of the aspen branches tattooed on his temples. He's tall and lanky, his head up to Merriam's chest.

"Ria!" He runs up to her excitedly. "I'm camping with Captain Dio's daughters tonight, and Mordecai even said we won't have classes to-morrow!"

Merriam looks from Bellamy to Mollian, knowing they all have plans for that night. "You two have been in cahoots, I guess."

Mollian scoffs in mock offense, a hand pressed to his chest. "You think that as King of Sekha, I've had time to waste on nonsense?"

Merriam elbows him in the side. "Yes, yes, I do."

The party makes their way down into the city, where Merriam and Ryddan follow Mollian and Master Graigory onto a raised platform.

A large crowd is gathered, close to every citizen of Umbra and several from nearby cities. Vendors line the streets, selling all sorts of foods, some with games set up for the children.

Graigory beats a large gong, the sound echoing off the mountains and drawing the attention of the gathered crowd. He gestures to Mollian, excitement shining in his eyes.

"Welcome," Mollian greets. "For the past five years, I have been work-ing closely with the roadsguild to change the course of not just Sekha, but all of Nethyl. They have worked tirelessly to take this dream and make it a reality."

Merriam watches Mollian as he continues talking, pride blooming in her chest. Her *mehhen* has grown in the five years since he ripped Tymecht from the Gate. He'd created multiple task forces to monitor the demons left behind. The demons are good at staying hidden, but as far as anyone can tell, their reproduction rates are slow. They tend to stay away from larger populations, and they move quickly, so tracking them is an intensive process, but attacks and casualties had diminished exponentially even in just the first year.

Nymphs were now employed to help with agriculture and port traffic on rivers and in bays. Fair folk and humans have been elected as guild-masters and overseers based on their qualifications, regardless of their inability to use magic. Change takes time, but this is the beginning of a safer, happier Sekha.

And then there's this—the railroad. Five years of construction, set-backs, and workarounds, but there is now a line of track that connects Umbra to the major port of Do Lech that can be used to move goods and passengers from one to the other in a day and a half.

Other tracks have also started construction, and even some of the most remote cities of Sekha will soon be connected.

And Mollian had done this. Mollian, who had been an energetic trou-blemaker of a child who always knew too much and decorated weapons in his spare time, now every bit a king. Not only is he fair and just, but he pushes Sekha forward, changing the course of the nation for the better in every way.

You're staring again, Mollian Casts as Graigory steps forward to deliver his speech.

The whole world is staring, Lord King, Merriam points out, reaching down to squeeze his hand as her throat tightens with emotion. *I'm so proud of you, Molli. Oren would be so fucking proud of you, too.*

Oren, in all of his Legendom, would tell me I'm an idiot for having volunteered to spend so much of my time working so closely with Master Graigory. Mollian snorts softly. *Thank you. I couldn't have done this without you.*

I'd argue that point, but there's still nowhere else I'd rather be.

When Graigory finishes his speech, Mollian gives the signal, and several swaths of fabric are pulled from the hulking frame behind them, revealing a dark, shiny steam engine with a few cars behind it. The crew climbs aboard amidst frenetic cheers from the gathered citizens, fire up the engine, and chug off with an almost deafening blare of its horn. The *choo-choo* echoes off the mountains as the train takes its first load of cargo down to the coast.

When they climb down from the platform, Ryddan runs off to join the other children, and Merriam walks with Mollian through the crowd as he greets his people with warmth, joining a few of them in carnival games.

As the sun sinks below the mountains, the two slip away from the festivities, grabbing a couple of horses and heading into the forest. Noises filter through the trees as they crest a ridge, shouts followed by laughter.

Merriam and Mollian dismount, tying their horses next to several others before joining the party.

The mercenaries have built a fire on the bank of a hot spring. Leonidas has his arms around Jasper, pinning his wings and dragging him toward the water despite the threats being flung at him, and throws himself and Jasper into the spring.

Jasper breaks the surface, adjusting his eye patch with his two-fingered hand as he moves to the shallows to shake out his wings, showering Leonidas with warm droplets in the process.

Leonidas laughs, holding his hands up in an attempt to block them. Long scars cross his chest and stomach, but his tattoo, the Bonding symbol bordered by antlers, is mostly intact, a few lines cutting through the antlers where his injuries had cut too deep.

Campbell jumps onto Leonidas' back, pulling him down into the water while Jasper distracts him.

"Unfair!" Leonidas protests before his head goes under, tattooed arms flailing dramatically.

"Demonslayer!" Kodi calls from the top of a cliff. He stands on the edge with Aleah and Rovin, all three of them dripping. "You and His Majesty have some catching up to do!"

Then all three of them leap, tucking their bodies in an almost synchronized flip before straightening out to hit the water. They break through the surface and swim to the edge.

Merriam strips down to her underclothes, running to jump in and meet them.

Rovin scoops her close against him, tipping her head back to kiss her.

"You taste like wine, Lieutenant. Is it wise to be throwing yourself off a cliff while inebriated?" she teases.

Rovin tosses hair from his face, releasing her to move to the edge and pick up a bottle, taking a deep swig before passing it off. "I don't think you have a leg to stand on here, and it's a party."

"No wise decisions allowed!" Aleah calls, tossing her a fresh bottle.

The cork has been mostly loosened, and Merriam pulls it free with her teeth and tips it back, chugging while the others cheer her on.

"Atta girl." Rovin takes the bottle from her when she finally lowers it.

They swim together for a while, Jasper sitting on the shore while the others stay mostly in the water. Panic monitors it all from the trees.

The moons climb into the sky, and two more figures appear up the mountain.

"You're late, Bell!" Kodi calls.

Bellamy and Shiloh walk through the trees, each holding a basket. "Someone had to bring the food," he replies.

Shiloh had put on a few performances in Umbra that day, the large crowds too good to pass up, and Bellamy had been at every one, still just as enamored with their showmanship as he was on day one. Shiloh now splits their time between Do Lech and Umbra. Do Lech is better for business, but Umbra holds people who have become family over the years.

Though Shiloh is still not a fighter, the mercenaries accepted them into their circle without hesitation, and Kodi loves Shiloh if only for the fact that their presence gives him something to tease Bellamy about.

They all climb from the water, drying off by the fire as they eat.

"I've got a pretty big job I'll be heading out for in a few days if you'd like to join, Mer," Kodi says. "Some of the scouts think they've found a whole nest of demons out in North Audha." Though a few commanders had pushed back against Kodi's promotion, Captain Dio had granted him the rank of lieutenant. The Ranger is still shit at following direct orders, but the demon hunting team under his command is the most successful by far.

Merriam, who'd been mostly doing work around Umbra for the past couple of months due to everything with the train, immediately perks up. "You speak my language, dragonslayer. Have someone send the details to my office in the morning. I'll work my schedule around it."

Once everyone has eaten their fill, Mollian brushes his hands against his legs. "Well, should we get this party started, then?"

Aleah and Kodi smile at each other, moving to sit in front of him.

He pulls out a tattoo kit, setting everything up as Aleah shifts excitedly.

"Aleah, do you Bond yourself freely to this fae?" Mollian asks.

Aleah nods, holding out her arm. There's a pink aster tattooed on the side of her wrist. Each of the mercenaries and Merriam have a matching one in memory of Calysta.

Mollian looks at Kodi. "And you freely Bond yourself to her, giving her your blood and the magic in it?"

Kodi nods, taking the knife Mollian offers him and cutting a line down his forearm. Mollian holds a small cup to the wound, collecting the blood that drips from it.

Aleah takes Kodi's arm with her free hand as Mollian mixes Kodi's blood into ink and starts pressing it into Aleah's skin. She licks the excess blood from the cut, holding eye contact with him. "I'm yours, Kodi. And you are mine."

He squeezes her hand, an uncharacteristic openness in his expression. Devotion shines in his bi-colored eyes, reflecting the flickering fire as she is marked with the Bonding rune: a tall, skinny loop cornered with two curved lines and two dots on opposite sides. "Until the day I die, little merc, I am wholly yours."

Mollian finishes the tattoo on the inside of Aleah's forearm, all of Kodi and Aleah's closest friends bearing witness as they are Bonded. They have a formal marriage ceremony planned for later in the summer, which will be a much more extravagant, wild affair, but they wanted to do this part among family.

Merriam glances at Rovin, biting her cheek. She had Bonded herself to Mollian when she was seventeen, and, though it was completely unheard of, again to Oren after his death. She wonders if it sometimes pains him that she will never be able to Bond herself to him.

Rovin pulls her against his side, running his thumb over the dip beside her hip bone and pressing his lips to her temple. "Technically speaking, you've got more magic in your blood than I do, pet. And I would Bond myself to you in a heartbeat."

Merriam tips her face up to graze her lips over the stubble on his jaw. "Maybe one day, if you're lucky," she whispers, knowing full well that that's not the way it works. She couldn't regift blood that had been gifted to her.

When he's done with the tattoo, Mollian smoothes a layer of protective paste over the fresh ink. Aleah and Kodi climb up the cliff, raising their clasped hands together as the others cheer before jumping into the water below.

Merriam runs with her friends back towards the hot spring, Panic swooping low overhead. There are still demons roaming Sekha, tracks being built to connect the country, Royal Guard to train, and laws and legislation to be written. But she pushes all of that to the back of her mind. Because outside of helping Mollian run a country, there are these people that she loves, and there is nothing but time for everything else.

Acknowledgements

To you, the reader. Thank you for being here and trusting that I had a plan after everything that happened in *Leaves*. I hope you enjoyed the adventure! And for every one of you who reached out to me to let me know how much you enjoyed *Leaves* and *Mountains*, thank you. Your kindness, enthusiasm, and love for my characters made such a huge difference on the days when this book was fighting me and kept me from second guessing everything I was doing.

Josh, you've remained my constant support. Thanks for selling everyone on my axe murderer books and being the best cheerleader. You're incredible, and I love you so freaking much.

Murs, it would've been so much harder writing a book about tethers without you. All the car travel, sober-drunk convos, and non-personing. That's it, that's the sentence. (also I love you)

The hive—Cass, Murs, Sarah, and Tay—it goes without saying that this book wouldn't be what it is without you guys. From all the way back in the days of faeries and scaries, you've helped me shape this duology into everything it needed to be. Every comment, opinion, and brainstorm about this story made it so that this thing is now out in the world. You're all the best aunts. Our specific brand of chaos literally fuels me, and I would be lost without the four of you. I love you all to pieces. Thanks for being the sisters I never had. Also I'm freaking proud of all of you and slipping easter eggs for your stories into mine will forever be a favorite thing.

Kelsey, Rachael, Sarah, and Shelby, having y'all's eyes and minds in this manuscript was, once again, the absolute best time. Your insight and opinions were absolutely essential to the polish of this story. Please know I never take any of you for granted, and I hope you stick around forever.

To my family, your support continues to mean the absolute world.

There's so much I can say, but just know I love you and am so thankful to have you in my corner!

Dad, you get a special shout out for being my go-to guy for all things roads. It might not be in the Jedi Order, but I'm honored to have been able to grant you Master-by-proxy regardless.

That's a wrap, y'all! See you in the next world. <3

About the Author

Carissa Hardcastle is a lifelong adventurer and bookworm who will never turn down fast food, still listens to 2000s pop punk, and always greets wildlife that crosses her path. Though fiction has been her passion since she was young, she also spent seven years as an air traffic controller in the Air Force, where she cultivated a love for all things aviation. Carissa grew up exploring the Sierra Nevadas of California, but now lives in Colorado with her husband. Mountains are her happy place, and much of her writing pulls inspiration from the grandeur and magic of the Rockies. When not writing or out finding adventure, she enjoys consuming horror and fantasy in any medium available.